MOMENT OF TERROR

The crowd pressed forward. Molly tried to hold her ground, but felt herself being inexorably pushed toward the barrier. Panic rose, instantly making her frantic.

Holding tight to Petey's hand, she began to inch sideways. The crowd shifted, someone shoved, and for a second Molly teetered, falling forward. But then she regained her footing and started to inch her way again, only . . .

Petey was no longer holding her hand.

She turned and looked, her heart pounding.

He was gone.

**NOWHERE TO RUN ... NOWHERE TO HIDE ...
ZEBRA'S SUSPENSE WILL *GET* YOU —
AND WILL MAKE YOU BEG FOR MORE!**

NOWHERE TO HIDE (4035, $4.50)
by Joan Hall Hovey

After Ellen Morgan's younger sister has been brutally murdered, the highly respected psychologist appears on the evening news and dares the killer to come after her. After a flood of leads that go nowhere, it happens. A note slipped under her windshield states, "YOU'RE IT." Ellen has woken the hunter from its lair ... and she is his prey!

SHADOW VENGEANCE (4097, $4.50)
by Wendy Haley

Recently widowed Maris learns that she was adopted. Desperate to find her birth parents, she places "personals" in all the Texas newspapers. She receives a horrible response: "You weren't wanted then, and you aren't wanted now." Not to be daunted, her search for her birth mother — and her only chance to save her dangerously ill child — brings her closer and closer to the truth ... and to death!

RUN FOR YOUR LIFE (4193, $4.50)
by Ann Brahms

Annik Miller is being stalked by Gibson Spencer, a man she once loved. When Annik inherits a wilderness cabin in Maine, she finally feels free from his constant threats. But then, a note under her windshield wiper, and shadowy form, and a horrific nighttime attack tell Annik that she is still the object of this lovesick madman's obsession ...

EDGE OF TERROR (4224, $4.50)
by Michael Hammonds

Jessie thought that moving to the peaceful Blue Ridge Mountains would help her recover from her bitter divorce. But instead of providing the tranquility she desires, they cast a shadow of terror. There is a madman out there — and he knows where Jessie lives — and what she has seen ...

NOWHERE TO RUN (4132, $4.50)
by Pat Warren

Socialite Carly Weston leads a charmed life. Then her father, a celebrated prosecutor, is murdered at the hands of a vengeance-seeking killer. Now he is after Carly ... watching and waiting and planning. And Carly is running for her life from a crazed murderer who's become judge, jury — and executioner!

Available wherever paperbacks are sold, or order direct from the Publisher. Send cover price plus 50¢ per copy for mailing and handling to Penguin USA, P.O. Box 999, c/o Dept. 17109, Bergenfield, NJ 07621. Residents of New York and Tennessee must include sales tax. DO NOT SEND CASH.

WHERE'S MY BABY?

Elizabeth Ergas

**ZEBRA BOOKS
KENSINGTON PUBLISHING CORP.**

ZEBRA BOOKS are published by

Kensington Publishing Corp.
850 Third Avenue
New York, NY 10022

Copyright © 1994 by Elizabeth L. Ergas

All rights reserved. No part of this book may be reproduced in any form or by any means without the prior written consent of the Publisher, excepting brief quotes used in reviews.

If you purchased this book without a cover you should be aware that this book is stolen property. It was reported as "unsold and destroyed" to the Publisher and neither the Author nor the Publisher has received any payment for this "stripped book."

Zebra and the Z logo Reg. U.S. Pat. & TM Off.

First Printing: October, 1994

Printed in the United States of America

To Len, for taking the bitter with the batter.

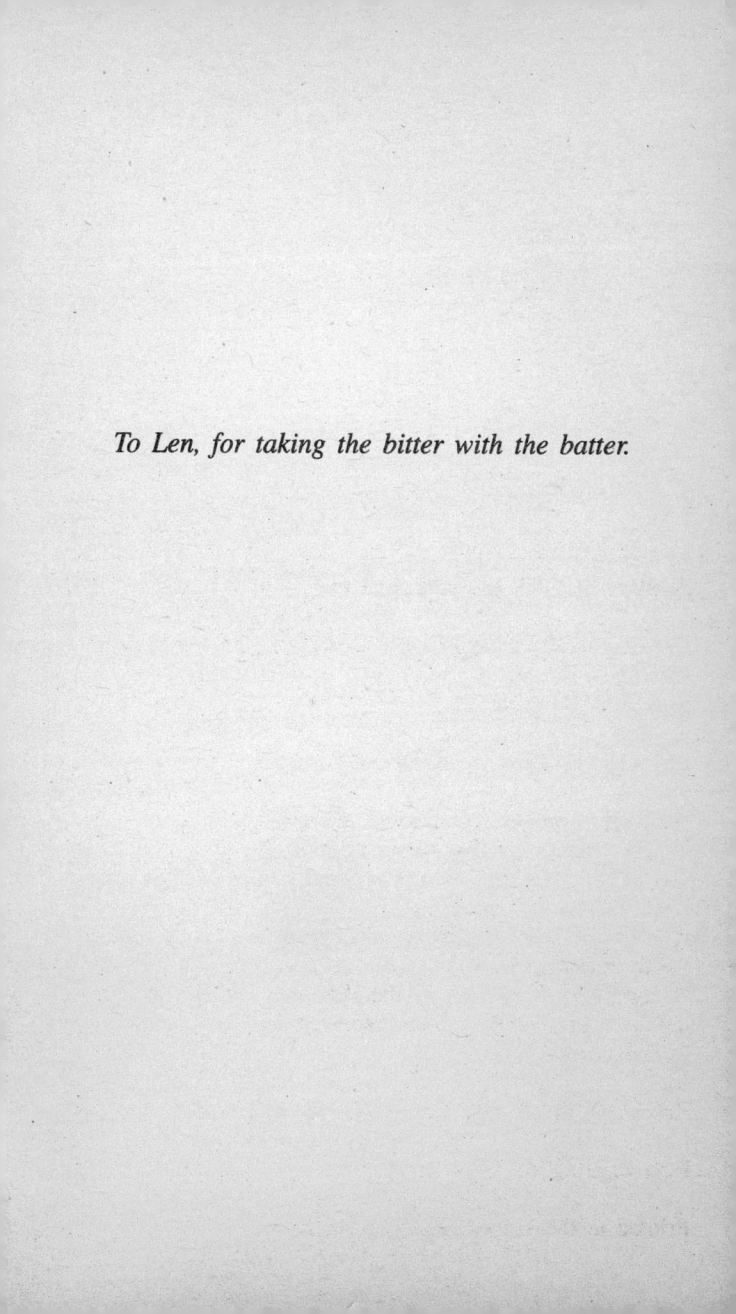

One

February
Rock Ridge, Connecticut

Buried with due pomp in Pilgrim's Hill Cemetery earlier in the day, Delia Clewett nonetheless called her daughter Irene at seven o'clock, as she did every evening.

Shortly before, Irene had excused herself to go into the kitchen where she could take comfort in privacy from Mr. Jack Daniel, her good friend and ever-more-frequent companion the past six years. The February world was stark beyond the wide kitchen window with its cheery blue café curtains. Irene leaned over the sink, staring out to the yard, past the naked limb of the oak Douglas kept swearing to cut down to let in more light. Nothing out there but hard earth under a thin crusting of leftover ice and snow from a surprise storm over the weekend. It would be cold, lying in a silk dress under six feet of frozen earth.

A gust of wind rattled the oak, scraping the branches against the side of the house. Irene abruptly retreated and immediately the dark-backed window reflected her image. A younger Delia; an older Karen. Three generations of natural blondes with delicate features. Only one generation left. *Easier to be dead,* she thought, shivering, and hurriedly closed the curtains with such force they continued to swing on the brightly shining brass rod.

Working on automatic, her trembling fingers dropped ice cubes into a glass and sloshed a generous three fingers of her dear friend Jack over them from the bottle she kept hidden behind the corn flakes. It took an awful lot of Jack's special comfort to numb the edges, but she didn't care. She couldn't have made it without him after Karen's death. Not without his smoothing of the pain, his blurring of reality.

"I suppose you're going to use mother's death as an excuse to fall into the bottle again?"

Irene stiffened. Her painfully thin body instantly locked into aching rigidity, then slowly swiveled. "And if I am?" Nancy, at forty-two—six years older, but looking a good couple of years younger, elegant in a black silk suit and pearls—shrugged and made a helpless little gesture that suddenly had Irene furious. "Is that it, the breadth of your concern? No sisterly advice? No answers? No *involvement?* No wonder you can't control your children." Nancy blanched, the sudden pallor accentuating her prominent cheekbones and the dark wings of her eyebrows, and Irene discovered to her dismay she was still sober enough to feel shame. "I'm sorry. That was a low blow."

"It's okay."

It wasn't okay and they both knew it, but the evening of their mother's funeral was not the time to delve into festering family wounds, no matter how good it would feel to get into a down-and-dirty fight. Nothing like it to vent the emotions. Irene had learned all about venting emotions from her other good friend, Dr. Virginia Powell, the psychiatrist who had saved her sanity after the death of her only child. *For what?* she often wondered, but kept it to herself. Easier to play the game, the life-goes-on survival one where the principal players were zombies and everyone else pretended they weren't.

"It really is okay, Irene. You feel like taking a chunk out of someone, and who better than someone you know will forgive you?"

"Will you?"

"We're family. She was my mother, too, you know."

"That's no answer."

The distant sound of young male voices raised in argument suddenly erupted and as quickly died when an older male voice barked an impatient order. Nancy rested her hip against the counter and cocked her head. Remembered amusement sparkled in her eyes. "They remind me of us. Always bickering, one wanting what the other has, simply for the wanting, nothing more."

"Is that the way you remember us?" Irene took a healthy swallow, then raised the cool glass to her temple, where the first throbs of a headache pulsed. She closed her eyes, welcoming the pain, focusing on it, hoping it would distract her.

"That's the way it was."

Mr. Daniel was helping Irene to a clear understanding. She opened her eyes, glared at Nancy. "Mama always liked you better."

"God, Irene, you're not going to bring that up again, are you?"

"It's true! She always said you never gave her a day's trouble. Perfect Miss Nancy, with her perfect marriage and her perfect children and her perfect life and—what was perfect was the way you managed to keep everything from her." Hot, heavy, stinging tears brimmed, dripped down her cheeks. She scrubbed at them, forgetting she held the glass, sloshing liquid over her face. "Shit!" She slammed it down onto the counter and turned her face aside. "I keep on thinking it would have been easier if she had cancer or a heart attack or something, not . . ."

"Not an accident."

Not like Karen.

Both sisters heard the silent words as clearly as if they had been shouted. Both chose to ignore them. Nancy pushed the glass away with one hand, fleetingly touched her sister's arm with the other, bit her lip when she felt the thinness of the flesh, the hard bone beneath. "Did you talk to Keith today?"

"Mama's hairdresser? Why?" Her eyes narrowed; belligerence pouted her lips. Sibling rivalry had obviously outlived Delia.

"He says they were on the phone when . . . when the van smacked into her car. He thought they were cut off, or she hung up on him, more likely. It wasn't until after, when he heard about the crash—"

"Mama was on the phone with him? Why?"

A smile tugged upward the corners of Nancy's lips, those thin yet sensual lips she got from her father's genes along with her dark coloring. "She was giving him hell. She didn't like the color, not in daylight. Had too much pink in it. She also didn't like the cut. Too short in back. It showed too much of her neck."

"Sounds like Mama," Irene agreed, remembering Delia's penchant for complaining. It was a family joke that her address book listed the number for every consumer complaint department in the tristate area. Amusement momentarily lightened her face, in that instant making her the younger sister in appearance as well as fact. "She was on the phone. For Mama, that's kind of like dying in the saddle."

At that precise moment the phone rang. Irene gave a nervous little jump, automatically reached for the wall unit, not even thinking it was seven, the time her mother always called. And because she and Nancy had just been talking about Delia, she didn't think it strange at first when a familiar-sounding voice said, "Irene. Listen!"

"Mama? Mama?" she said again, thinking Delia's voice sounded flat, far away, as if she were . . . *Dead! She's dead!* a voice in Irene's head screamed, while Nancy tugged at the receiver shouting, "Who is it? Who is it?" Irene shoved at her, but for all her seeming fragility, Nancy hung on like a pit bull. "I'm here. I'm listening. What is it, Mama?" She was screaming, she couldn't help it.

Delia's voice whispered into her ear, thin, urgent, mesmerizing. A low moan escaped Irene. Delia ignored it, went on whispering.

Nancy finally succeeded in wrenching the receiver away. The force of it caused Irene to stagger backward, her eyes huge, the blue of her irises so dark they looked like black agate marbles, dominating her suddenly chalk-white face. She began to tremble; her hand went to her chest and flattened over the spot where her heart pounded a fast, frighteningly arrhythmic beat.

Nancy pressed the receiver to her ear. "Mama, it's Nancy. Mama?"

The sound of heavy footsteps pounded down the hall, and Douglas, Irene's husband, burst into the kitchen, Nancy's Andrew right behind him. Their two boys, Robert and Frank, crowded in on their father's heels. Douglas quickly surveyed the room, taking in his wife's shell-shocked appearance, the half-full glass of bourbon near her hand, his usually calm sister-in-law calling "Mama?" over and over again into the telephone. "What the hell's going on here?" His narrowed gaze focused on Nancy, his eyes boring into her like twin blue laser beams.

Nancy held out the receiver. "It's Mama, but she won't talk to me."

Douglas ripped it out of her hand. "Hello? *Hello!*" he hollered, but the only answer was the humming of the wires. He slammed the receiver onto its cradle, frowned at Irene. "Who was it?"

"Mama. It was Mama."

"Delia?" Douglas Hall snorted in amusement and shook his head. "Not likely," he said, and offered a silent prayer Delia Clewett would not be the one to pioneer communication between the quick and the dead.

"A crank," Andrew Larson said. "Nuts come out of the woodwork at times like this. They read the notices in the paper. Forget about it."

Nancy glared at him, all at once unaccountably furious with his stoicism, his imperturbability, his conviction that he always knew what was what. "It *was* Mama!"

"Did you talk to her?"

Resentment flashed in Nancy's eyes. "Irene answered the phone."

A peculiar silence gripped them as all eyes focused on Irene. She knew what they were thinking, what they were too polite to say. Even the boys, fourteen-year-old Bobby, Frank nearly twelve, had the knowledge of what she was in their eyes. She had never felt more like a drink, had never *needed* one so desperately, but using every ounce of willpower, managed to suppress the urge. She had that much pride left.

"Irene?"

She hated the way Douglas spoke to her, the wary note in his voice, the care he took not to upset her. She was past needing that, thanks to her mother. If anyone had told her this morning, the day of her mother's funeral, she would have cause for joy this night, she would have thought him or her crazy. But now ...

"Baby?"

God, she hated it when he called her that. Karen was her baby. Her baby was dead. But not anymore.

Her eyes flicked to her glass, saw the ice was melting, then jerked away, back to Douglas's face. "Karen," she said, and had the satisfaction of seeing the quickly concealed pain behind his eyes. He wasn't better than her, just different. He didn't like to speak of Karen. It was his way of coping. But that, too, would have to change, now that Delia had told her. . . . She sucked in a breath, let it out slowly. She had their attention; indeed, they were all staring at her. "Mama said Karen is back! She's been reincarnated!" She felt it burst from her, heard the elation, the joy, the relief in her voice. Saying it made it real, somehow.

Everyone stilled, a black-garbed curiosity; real-life Tussaud. The refrigerator hummed breathily; skeletal oaken fingers scraped the window; an ice cube shifted, clinked noisily against glass, slid into bourbon oblivion.

Frank poked his brother in the ribs, rolled his eyes upward. Bobby snickered, slapped his hand over his mouth. Muffled snorts filled the silence. Inelegant as it was, it seemed to say it all.

Two

Manhasset, New York

Organization, Molly Deere thought, as she searched for Petey's left sneaker under the empty fish tank she kept meaning to turn into a terrarium. That was the word they were going to live by from now on. She'd make a chart, do it right. Just as soon as she had the time. Yeah.

Time. She glanced at her watch, groaned, and admitted defeat. The sneaker was not lurking under the fish tank or in the cabinets or under the sofa or in any of the other places she had previously found it. This morning, this gray and drizzly morning, when she was running later than usual, the famous lurking sneaker had found a new place.

"Petey," she hollered, hoping he would recognize the firmness in her tone, "you're going to have to wear another pair of sneakers. Mommy's late."

Silence. Molly didn't like the sound of it. Not at all. "Petey? Did you hear me?" With more effort than she liked, she levered herself off her knees and got up. God, she remembered the days when she would have leaped up without a thought for stiff back muscles and protesting knees. It was probably true, what they said about hitting thirty, that things started to go. *Go where?* she wondered, acutely aware she had passed thirty two years ago.

A depressing thought. Still no sound from Petey, upstairs, ostensibly searching for the shy sneaker. She headed for the stairs when simultaneously she heard the toilet flush and the shrill of the phone.

"Damn!" she said under her breath, lest Petey's four-and-a-half-year-old ears be tainted. A call this early couldn't bring good news. *Please, God, don't let Mrs. Parr be sick,* she prayed, then snapped an apprehensive, "Yes?" into the phone. Nervously she tucked strands of her dark shoulder-length hair behind her right ear, reviewing her schedule, looking for ways to juggle time if the ten-time grandmother couldn't pick up Petey after school.

"You sound frazzled. It's too early for it," said the sardonic voice of Kent Durwood, station manager of WAND and her immediate boss.

Molly thanked God it wasn't the babysitter as she thought of many and varied retorts. Prudently, she held her tongue. Kent, a swinging bachelor even in the AIDS-cautious nineties, wouldn't understand. Didn't want to understand. So she said, "Yeah, right," and then, "what's up?"

He became all business. "A small plane went down in a schoolyard. It's in your neck of the woods, or I'd give it to Mel. You can get there quicker. I need you live ASAP."

"Terrific," Molly mumbled, and wrote down the particulars. She hated any story that had to do with little kids, and from the sound of it, this was a bad one.

"Oh, forget about court," Kent went on. "What's his name—"

"Gonzalez."

"Right. His sentencing in Queens has been postponed. He's got a date in Nassau first. Give ADA Riley a buzz."

Molly grunted and Kent took it as good-bye. She stood for several seconds, steeling herself against the coming ordeal, then went to check the tote in which she kept the paraphernalia of her job to make sure her tape recorder was where she had left it and she still had some blank cartridges.

"Mommy."

She whirled about and there was Petey—Petey, her pride and joy, standing in the doorway looking as if the world had come to an end. Ruthlessly she pushed aside Kent Durwood's exhortation to hustle her butt. Motherhood took precedence. "What is it, honey?"

"Sneaker," he said, and ran out of the room.

Molly followed him upstairs, into the bathroom, and looked past his pointing finger.

"Dead," he said. "Drownded in the water."

Molly frowned, then carefully forced herself to smooth her face. Petey was having a problem with water, and it needed to be addressed. Another item for her organization chart. She'd put it right up there at the top. Petey came first—always had; always would.

Quashing her worry, she adopted a playful attitude. "Oho, the elusive sneaker," she said, and plucked it from the cold water of the commode. Behind her Petey sniffled, shifted from shod foot to sock-clad one. She gave him a quick smile and dropped the sopping sneaker into the sink. "Any idea how this happened?" Big brown eyes, misted with emotion, met her own hazel ones. "No? Well, we'll get to the bottom of this mystery some other time. Right now Mommy's in a rush, so put on your other sneakers." She turned him about, gave him a gentle pat on the behind, and ordered him to march, forestalling his plea for her to "fix it quick." Petey, much like his father, had little patience for delay, wanting what he wanted when he wanted it. In a child the trait was tolerable; in an adult it had been insupportable.

She dropped Petey at nursery school, then studied a map. She had to get to the South Shore and traffic was heavy, slowed by a freezing rain that slicked the roads. Muttering imprecations against Manhattanites in general and Kent Durwood in particular, who thought Long Island was one cozy neighborhood, she concentrated on her driving and listened to WAND—"990 on the AM dial, the magic WAND, with news of your neighborhood night and day"—without paying particular attention. If anything big broke, they would use the special three-note attention grabber. Her exit came, and once off the parkway, she had no trouble finding the disaster area. Following the trail of flashing ambulance and police lights to the Brenton School, she cruised slowly until she found a place to park. Automatically, she rechecked her tote. Then, resigned, she waded through the churned mud that once had been a neatly manicured playing field toward a scene that surely had been conceived in hell.

New York City

Day dawned in New York with all the appeal of lumpy, ice-cold oatmeal. Zachary Slater, drinking coffee from his special "Best Father in the World" mug, watched the night slip away with as much enthusiasm as a condemned man. The birth of a new day was the start of an adventure, and he had long ceased to think in hopeful terms. He went through the motions, he owed that and more to Lauren, but there was no more joy in his life, no more music in his soul.

He hunched his shoulders, trying to keep the promise he had made to himself, not to dwell on his loss. He had to accept it, enfold it, make it part of the fabric of his life and continue in whatever direction he chose. That was, after all, what he counseled others: life goes on. *Yeah, it sure does,* he mused, thinking whoever first said it should have been shot.

Ah, physician, heal thyself, he silently mocked, wishing there were shortcuts to the slow, laborious process. He had emerged from his personal tragedy in a transformed state. Gone was his optimism, his fundamental belief there wasn't anything that couldn't be worked out. Gone. Vanished in the blink of an eye, the tenets that had been the cornerstone of his professional life. Life, the one with a capital L, had proved him wrong, proved it with a vengeance that came to haunt him in every waking hour, sometimes even following him down into sleep. Those were the worst times of all, those nighttime hours when phantoms stalked his dreams.

Life goes on. His certainly had, although he had altered it drastically, knowing instinctively he had to change if he were to survive. He took a sip of coffee, placed the mug on his desk, careful of the stack of file folders threatening to teeter over at the slightest provocation. They were a silent reminder of his new life, the strange turn his interest had taken.

Maybe not so strange after all. Wasn't this curiosity about past lives directly related to his loss? He asked himself this question in the deepest part of the night, and in moments like these, when the earth hovered between dark and light and anything was possible.

With a muttered oath he rose and stood with his back to the room. It felt as if every muscle in his large body was clenched tight with tension. Slowly he forced himself to relax until his tall frame took on a more casual stance: wide shoulders sloped more naturally; thick muscles in neck, arms, and thighs eased. Now only his eyes gave him away. Dark gray, bleak as a winter ocean, they held the remembrance of pain.

Faced with choices, he had taken those which promised the chance for the best survival. He didn't regret giving up his practice, not once the decision was made. Patience, also, had fled, and he couldn't in good conscience treat the tortured souls who had placed their well-being in his hands.

Without the grind of a daily schedule and a heavy patient load, he was free to follow other interests. His investigation into past-life regressions was only one, and a minor one at that. A whimsy, perhaps, compared to his work in the field of trauma. His future lay there, he suspected, reflecting on how much he enjoyed teaching, giving students the benefit of his years of practicing psychiatry as applied to the new techniques of caring for survivors of catastrophic events. But the hours he spent in the classroom were bought with agonizing hours in the field. The old Zachary Slater would have been twisted out of shape by the horror, the suffering, the inhuman trials forced upon innocent souls. The new Zachary Slater had been seasoned by his own tragedy, his spirit forged by a trial by fire. He had been there; he knew.

Heavy thinking for a dawning day. Gray light defined the world as he stared at the small patch of earth that passed as a garden in the midst of the concrete city. He opened the window, ignoring the chill, anxious to feel the life humming around him. Happily, it was everywhere, in the sudden blast of a radio alarm set to a heavy-metal station, the shrill of a phone, the slam of a door.

Behind him, his own household was slowly waking. The sound of Mrs. Sadecki's voice drifted down from the second floor of the town house, loudly admonishing Lauren to get out of bed. Zachary smiled. His gem of a housekeeper fought this battle almost every morning. His daughter was never eager to leave the warm nest of her covers. *Slugabed,* Janine used to tease her, *you'll sleep your life away.*

Janine . . .

No! He'd think of Lauren, only of her. Janine lived in memory now; best if he remembered that.

Nothing of his early-morning depression showed on his face by the time Lauren, washed and dressed in a pair of clean denims and a bright red sweater, bounced into the kitchen. Her hair, the color of ripe wheat, was caught by two jaunty red barrettes at the sides of her head, then flowed down her back in shimmering waves. An intelligent child, she was curious about the world. If shadows sometimes haunted her large gray eyes—well, it was only natural. In time she would heal.

"Five more days," she said, breathless from dashing down the stairs.

"Sit," Mrs. Sadecki ordered, hands planted on her ample hips, "the cereal is ready. Today, farina." Lauren made a face which the housekeeper ignored. On a cold morning a growing child needed a bowl of hot cereal. It was one of the precepts on which to raise healthy children. Having done so six times already, with four strapping sons and two daughters successfully launched into the world, Anna Sadecki saw no reason to change.

Zachary winked at Lauren as she came to kiss his cheek. "Five days to what?"

Lauren looked exasperated, even more so when a full bowl of cereal was placed before her. "To *Valentine's* Day, of course."

Of course. Zachary sighed inwardly. Wasn't five—no, five and a half—too young for romance? Then he looked at his daughter, really looked, trying for objectivity, and saw the innate femininity, the core of the lovely woman to come. He sighed again, this time aloud. "And who do you expect a valentine from?"

"It's that Ryan," Mrs. Sadecki interjected, refilling his mug from the fresh pot she had made. "All day long it's Ryan this and Ryan that. I'll bet Ryan eats his cereal."

Lauren giggled and dutifully dug into hers. Zachary was impressed. Teasing, he asked Lauren if she would point out the young man when he dropped her off at school.

"You eat, Dr. Slater, I'll go," Mrs. Sadecki said, when the phone rang. She placed a plate of toast before him with the air of one who would not be gainsaid. She was only slightly less strict with him than with his daughter. When she came back, Zachary immediately saw by the look on her face that something terrible had happened.

He took the call in his office. He didn't want Lauren to overhear. The voice on the other end of the line spoke of death falling out of the sky. An obscenity, made all the worse because it had been visited upon children. "Hurry," the voice said.

Zachary made the necessary calls to set his team in motion before leaving his office. Formerly a den, he had converted it into a comfortable room filled with books and file cabinets and leather furniture in which he had expected to spend the day transcribing notes on his latest case history on past-life regression. A fascinating study. The subject, a terminally ill elderly woman, wanted some sort of reassurance, however ephemeral, of continuing life. In their last session, she had gone back to a former life in which she had been a virgin sacrifice in a pagan ritual. He hoped she would be able with a little prodding and a lot of luck to pinpoint the culture and the time. It was good material for the book he planned.

It would have to wait. He had his jacket on and his car keys in his hand when he bent to place a kiss on Lauren's shining head. "Something's come up. Mrs. Sadecki will take you to school, pussycat."

Lauren looked disappointed but resigned. "Will you be back when I get home?" Zachary shrugged, knowing he couldn't make any promises. "Will you be back when I go to bed?" An anxious note had crept into her voice. Zachary told himself she was only reacting to his tension, but he knew it wasn't so. She feared he would go away. Like Janine.

"If I'm not, I'll call, pussycat. I promise."

"Promise" was the magic word. Since Janine's death, he had never made Lauren a promise he knew he couldn't keep.

The ride out to Cedarhurst didn't take long. Running against the morning rush hour, he broke the speed laws with impunity. At the accident scene he identified him-

WHERE'S MY BABY? 23

self as the head of the trauma team to the officer in charge, Police Chief Thomas O'Brien. "What've we got?"

The policeman plunged right into grim reality. "Six dead so far, plus nobody from the plane walked away. We don't know what's under it yet."

Zachary nodded brusquely. "Keep me posted. Try to detain the relatives until a member of my team sees them."

"Sure, Doc," O'Brien said. They both knew grieving family members seldom listened to anyone.

The morning wore on. The death toll mounted. The most seriously injured had been dispatched to area hospitals. The walking wounded remained, and Zachary concentrated on them, ignoring the local police, the county teams, and the boys from the FAA. A member of his team, grim-faced but controlled, thrust a cardboard container into his hands. "Coffee tastes like shit, but at least it's hot."

Zachary drank, not tasting, just absorbing the warmth. Half a field away he saw Chief O'Brien talking to an attractive young woman. He sipped and watched her, grateful for the respite. Of average height, no more than five-seven, he estimated, with a slender build, she was dwarfed by the burly chief, yet even at a distance he recognized a core of strength that enabled her to hold her own. Definitely not a relative of one of the victims. Too calm. She said something to O'Brien and they both turned in his direction. Then she nodded to the chief and walked toward him.

Zachary's cup was empty, he should get back to work; but he stood, watching the young woman make her way through the churned mud. She was bundled up against the cold, and even her bulky down jacket couldn't conceal the elegant lines of her body, the fluid grace with which she moved. Her dark hair was being buffeted by the wind. Impatiently, she tucked the flyaway strands behind her ears. It was then he saw the microphone and knew she was with the press.

"Molly Deere," she said, "with WAND, Dr. Slater." She stuck out her hand and Zachary automatically took it. A firm no-nonsense grip. His eye had been true, she was about five feet seven inches, a good seven inches shorter than his six feet two. Greenish eyes rimmed by brown and flecked with gold regarded him directly, with no subterfuge. "Chief O'Brien said you're in charge of the trauma team. I'd like an interview." Perhaps she read the refusal in his eyes; perhaps she only anticipated it. "Just a few words. Please?"

Beyond her shoulder he caught sight of a little girl with hair the color of corn who reminded him of Lauren. Only Lauren's hair wasn't sticky with blood and her eyes weren't staring inward, caught up in the memory of hell. "Sorry, not now," he said, more brusquely than he intended, yet he was slow to move. For an instant their eyes met. Something sparked between them, surprising him. He ignored it. The little girl needed him.

Three

Harry Kemp didn't hear about the disaster at the Brenton School until he was almost at work. The blond bimbo's fault, but Harry wasn't complaining. Not after last night. No sirree. The blonde—Sheila? Stella?—had taken him places he'd never been before, and for a man of Harry's appetites and experience, that was no mean feat. Sated, Harry had slept deeply, another surprise.

Demanding payment, the bimbo woke him. She had a job interview at a Fannie Mae company down on Wall Street and didn't want to be late. Given the state of the economy, competition for jobs was fierce. She asked for an extra fifty. For lunch. A girl had to eat, she complained, and the Koreans who owned the popular salad bars charged an arm and a leg.

Harry gave her the fifty, figuring a girl with her energy level in bed had to keep up her strength. Besides, he didn't care; he was all for free enterprise.

He forgot about her almost before the door closed on her aerobically trimmed derrière. A man with money could get all the Sheilas and Stellas he wanted.

And Harry had money. Pots of it, as his mother would have said, the whining bitch.

Harry didn't like thinking about her, so he didn't. He simply switched his thoughts, cleansed his mind, and the bad memories disappeared. Like magic. Magic he had practiced for over thirty years.

Showered and shaved, he dressed in an eight-hundred-dollar suit, one of many, that even with excellent tailoring couldn't quite cover a burgeoning paunch. Finally, he slipped into a cashmere overcoat and took the elevator down to the basement garage of his luxurious high-rise co-op. He didn't remember to turn on the radio until he was through the Midtown Tunnel in Queens, where his business, Encore, Inc., was housed in a warehouse in Maspeth. Tuned to 990 AM, one of New York's twenty-four-hour all-news stations, because he wanted to know what was happening all the time, he heard the three-note flourish they used for special bulletins. He raised the volume, honked at a van trying to sneak ahead of him into the exact change toll lane. *". . . We go live to Molly Deere, on the scene at the Brenton School in Cedarhurst, Long Island, where a small plane has crashed into a field. Molly?"*

Harry swore as a taxi made a suicidal bid to cut him off. He maneuvered the Cadillac as if he were in a demolition derby, having the satisfaction of seeing the taxi veer off, the cabbie shouting profanities through his partially lowered window.

Grinning in victory, Harry paid the toll and sped onto the LIE. The radio crackled, Molly Deere's pleasant voice filled the car. *" . . . No telling at this time if any bodies are under the plane. It crashed onto an athletic field near where school buses let off arriving students. Debris is scattered everywhere, some of it still smoldering. The scene is chaotic as police cars, rescue vehicles, fire department equipment, and ambulances respond to*

WHERE'S MY BABY? 27

the emergency. It will get worse as parents, who are being notified of the tragedy now, come to the school to learn the fate of their children." The station anchorman broke in with a question. Harry lowered the volume. He had heard enough.

Fate. It had to be. An opportunity like this was too good to be true.

Or was it?

Only one way to tell.

His hand reached for the cellular phone as he speeded past his exit. "Angela, it's Mr. Kemp," he said, overriding her nasal greeting.

"Oh, hi," she replied breezily, "we was jist wondering if you're okay. I mean, it's not like you to be late an' all, an'—"

"I'm fine, babe. Something's come up, though, and I might not be in at all."

"A private auction," Angela guessed, relieving Harry of the need to come up with a convincing lie.

"Smart girl," he said, then paused. If he were successful he might need a couple of days. "I may have a lead to that blanket chest the broad in Connecticut wants." To Harry women were babes, bimbos, or broads. "They're rare, especially if they've been carved and painted, so I need to chase every lead. This could mean a bundle."

"Yeah," Angela said.

Harry could hear her gum crack through the static stuttering through the line. He said a curt good-bye and concentrated on driving. He kept the radio tuned to WAND, but they only mentioned the disaster in the headline capsulization of the news.

No matter. Fate had already stepped in.

As he neared the school, Harry left the main road and

turned onto a quiet street with large houses set far back behind fences and walls, pulling the Cadillac well up on the shoulder in front of a screening bank of trees. He sat in the car for several minutes. No traffic came down the street.

Cold drizzle bathed his feverish face as he casually walked to the back of the car. A fortuitous patch of muddy ground lay under the rear bumper. It only took a matter of minutes to smear mud over both front and rear license plates. Satisfied, he rummaged through a small suitcase he always kept in the trunk. Quickly he switched his dove-gray muffler for a loud plaid and donned a pair of glasses with heavy black frames. Tinted yellow, the nonprescription lenses almost obscured his light brown eyes and took attention away from a slightly crooked nose and fleshy lower lip. Thinning mousy-brown hair receded from his forehead. He slicked it down and combed it straight back.

The Brenton School was less than a mile away. The scene was chaotic; the smell of aviation gasoline, burnt rubber, and other, better left unidentified odors tainted the air. The athletic field was choked with rescue vehicles, fire apparatus, and police cars. Harry drove slowly past, noting that a major cable network's TV van had just arrived and the crew was hurriedly setting up.

If he was going to act he would have to do so quickly. His palms, sweaty with excitement, slipped on the wheel. He speeded up, and once out of sight executed a U-turn and stopped, engine idling, on the verge.

Should he?

It was risky.

It was also too sweet an opportunity to resist.

"What the hell," Harry said, wiped his palms on his expensive cashmere overcoat, and set the car in motion.

He found a spot under a goal post, then took a deep breath, fixed a worried frown on his forehead, and headed into the confusion.

A policeman touched his arm. Harry fought not to flinch. "Stay back," the young officer said. "You can't go any nearer."

"My child," Harry choked out, the mixture of fear and excitement churning within lending him verisimilitude. Method acting at its finest.

The officer immediately looked sympathetic. "Over there." He waved to an area a good distance from the wreckage of the plane.

Harry nodded and walked in the indicated direction. People were milling about, civilians like himself, many teachers and the first-arriving parents, in addition to the children. Most of the kids looked shell-shocked. Harry thought they had nothing to complain about. Not when a goodly number of their peers were across the field, growing stiff in black body bags in the makeshift morgue.

It was immediately apparent there was no formal organization. Harry had no doubt that would change, but right now chaos reigned. Swiftly he scanned the area, noted several clusters of children, huddling close to each other, like litters of newborn kittens. No good.

The adults were doing nothing to help. Stark terror made a mask of a middle-aged woman's face. Her body wracked by deep shudders, she kept mumbling to herself. Behind her a young man stood, coatless in the chill drizzle, eyes blank. Perhaps it was warm where he was.

Harry took it all in at a glance, noting especially the way arriving parents quickly separated their chicks from the group and hurried them away. No one questioned them.

"Joanne!" The voice was high and strident, verging on hysteria. "Joanne! Mama's here, baby! Joanne! Where are you?"

Everyone turned to look—everyone but Harry. He kept his eyes on the children.

"Joanne! Baby!"

Harry watched three little girls edge closer to the middle-aged woman, saw the terror in her eyes change to horror. Apparently tapping a hidden reserve, she squared her shoulders and started to walk toward Joanne's mother. It didn't take a rocket scientist to figure out Joanne's mother was looking in the wrong place. She would have to take that long trek to the other side of the field.

Realization brought hysteria to the woman. Her screams cut through the air, sharp, gull-like, penetrating. Children started to cry; some threw their arms around each other, hugging for all they were worth. Others just stood and stared, too numbed by tragedy to react.

Except for one little boy. He simply turned and walked away.

Nobody followed him; nobody even seemed to notice he had left.

Fate.

Harry didn't hesitate. He went after the boy as fast as he dared, scooped him into his arms, and had him across the field and into his car before Joanne's mother had stopped screaming.

Four

For Molly Deere, it had been one of the worst days of her life, and it was only midafternoon. The body count, estimated at first to be six, rose slowly to eight and then to nine as the critically injured, most taken to area hospitals, died. All four people in the small plane had died, burned beyond recognition. Names of victims were being withheld pending identification and notification of relatives. Standard stuff.

Seven children and two teachers had been taken by helicopter to sophisticated burn units on Long Island and in Queens. Five of the children and one teacher were in critical condition. Molly made frequent calls to the hospitals; she took it as a positive sign that no one's condition had worsened. She said as much to Kent Durwood during a periodic check-in.

"It'll change," he said flatly. "The TV people have been breaking into programs with special updates. The pictures are pretty gruesome."

"Tell me about it," Molly mumbled.

"Oh, yeah." That was apparently the extent of Kent's sensitivity. He didn't miss a beat. "I need interviews. Try for one of the parents with a dead kid or one of the

FAA boys, and keep after the head honcho from the trauma team, that Dr. Slater. See if you can get a good quote."

Molly felt bile rise in her throat. "Do you want an 'Act-of-God' one or a 'Let's-blame-the-politicians' one?"

Two beats of silence and then Kent's voice came, showing more than a bit of annoyance. "Tell me if it's too much for you, Molly. Mel or one of the others would love to get a chance at a juicy story like this."

The threat was real. Much as she'd have liked to tell Kent Durwood where to go, Molly knew she couldn't afford to. She was Petey's sole source of support; she wouldn't do anything to jeopardize his well-being. She swallowed the bile and part of her pride as well and informed Kent in as clipped a voice as she could manage that she would do quite nicely, thank you.

"Never doubted it, cookie," he said, and hung up.

"Bastard!" That said, Molly zipped up her down jacket and went outside. The first person she saw was Police Chief Thomas O'Brien. He was big and rugged looking, and the corners of his eyes were creased by deep-set lines. Although he had been outside for hours, his face whipped by wind and sleet, his skin looked gray. Molly clicked on her tape recorder and shoved the microphone under his nose. "Anything new, Chief?"

He didn't look happy to see her. "We're going to clear the wreckage. The heavy equipment should be here any moment."

"I thought you weren't going to do that until tomorrow. There's no danger of fire, is there?"

O'Brien sighed, remembered Molly was radio, and said, "No. The Fire Department has sprayed enough foam to ensure there's no hazard from fire."

WHERE'S MY BABY?

Instinct warned Molly the chief was holding back. "So why are you moving the plane today?"

O'Brien sighed again. "There's a child still missing."

East Stroudsburg, Pennsylvania

". . . According to Police Chief Thomas O'Brien. The missing child, six-year-old Timothy Newell, may have wandered off in a daze. At least, that is what officials hope. Meanwhile, rescue workers comb the wreckage. This is Molly Deere, 990 WAND, live from the Brenton School on Long Island."

Harry Kemp fiddled with the Chevy Blazer's radio. It wasn't as good as the one in the Cadillac, left behind in a storage place in Jersey. He was losing the New York station to a combination of distance and lousy weather. It didn't matter; he had the information he wanted. They still didn't know if the kid was missing or dead, which meant they'd keep the search local.

Snow came hurtling against the windshield out of the dusk. Harry let the radio scan, searching for a weather report. He needed to know how hard it was snowing in the Poconos. He didn't have far to search. The local stations were all issuing weather bulletins. They expected a minimum of five inches.

Harry decided he had another hour, maybe two, before he'd be forced to find a motel. He needed food and rest.

And a telephone.

Molly dragged her hand through her dark shoulder-length hair and stared down glumly at the remains of an onion-and-mushroom pizza. "Timmy Newell is missing, not dead."

"How d'you know?" Denise Heywood refilled her glass with wine and looked inquiringly at Molly over her bright red half-glasses, which had slid down her nose.

Molly held her hand over her glass. "No thanks. No more. I'd fall on my face."

"Be good for you," Denise said in her pragmatic way. She nudged Molly's hand so she could pour. "I listened to your report. You said they're still combing the wreckage for bodies. That means they think Timmy could have been under the plane."

Molly shuddered and took a healthy swallow of wine. The last thing she had wanted to do tonight was rehash the tragedy. But when Denise called and said she was bringing a pizza—"Don't say no because I'm not listening and you'll be doing me the favor because Harold has to work late again tonight and Sandy's studying at a friend's and James is going to a basketball game"— Molly had discovered she didn't want to be alone after all. Now she took another swallow and shook her head.

"What does that mean?"

"He's not under the plane."

Denise, who had been eyeing the pizza, lifted her gaze. "You sound very sure."

"One of the little girls said she saw him after the plane crashed."

"No kidding."

"She was hysterical, so she's a poor witness."

"Tough."

"Yeah. It is. But O'Brien got a 'maybe' from one of the teachers, and ... I don't know. Something's not right. Call it my reporter's nose."

WHERE'S MY BABY?   35

"Which will be in your wineglass if you don't go to bed. Go on," Denise urged, taking off her glasses and stowing them in her oversized purse. "I'll clean up."

Molly gave her a tired smile. "I can do it."

"Yeah. I know. Wonder Woman and Brenda Starr all rolled into one."

Molly's smile grew wider. "You got that right."

When Denise's short, stout body was all bundled up in coat, muffler, and mittens for the dash to her house next door, she paused and cocked her head. "It's so quiet. Not a peep out of him all night. Petey have a hard day?"

A frown creased Molly's forehead, then disappeared. But she couldn't erase the faint trace of worry that lingered in her eyes.

"What?" Denise crossed her arms over her chest. "Tell me. I raised two kids, you know. Three, counting their father."

Molly laughed, as she was supposed to. "It's nothing." Denise didn't budge. "Nothing except . . . he gave me a hard time with his bath again. Whatever it is, this fear of water, it's getting worse."

"He oughta see a doctor. I told you."

"His pediatrician says he's fine."

"Well, it sounds to me as if Petey is remembering the trauma of a past death. I've told you before. He could be reacting to something he remembers." She ignored the way Molly stiffened. "I've got the name of a doctor who helps you find out about your past lives. I bet he'd be interested in Petey."

"Terrific." Molly opened the door, letting in a gust of chilly damp air.

Denise laughed. "I can take a hint."

Molly touched her on the sleeve. "Thank you for tonight. I needed to talk."

"No problem. I was rattling around in that big house all by myself." She stepped outside, then turned back. "I'll get the name of that doctor to you tomorrow."

Molly shut the door. Hard.

"Trauma of a past death, my Aunt Minnie," she muttered as she walked through the house, turning off lights, making sure the windows and doors were locked, a nightly routine that had been Roy's, during the brief seven-month tenure of their marriage.

Roy. He had left her the day she'd told him she was pregnant.

Immature jerk, Molly thought, as she always did when her thoughts happened to stray to him. The all-American boy with a slightly skewed moral code.

Feckless.

The perfect word to describe the man who was the biggest mistake of her youth, yet she could never be sorry for it because he had given her Petey. She certainly hoped he was happy, somewhere in Texas, with a new wife who had brought two children to the marriage.

He had never even seen Petey.

Maybe it was his own flesh and blood he didn't want.

Molly rattled the kitchen door, harder than necessary. Never seen his son. If she lived to be a hundred she would never understand a man who could cavalierly ignore his own child. Especially not when the child was as wonderful as Petey.

But Roy didn't know how wonderful Petey was.

"Immature jerk," Molly said out loud, and stomped up the stairs. The old house was quiet. Raised in Brooklyn, Molly had found it necessary to adjust to the quiet of the suburbs when they bought the house. It still unnerved her a bit, especially at night, but she could handle it.

She could handle anything. Hadn't she proved it? Wasn't she doing it, every minute of every hour of every day? Wonder Woman. "That's me," she murmured, and looked in on her sleeping son.

A small lump in the middle of the bed, Petey was covered to the chin in his beloved baseball-motif comforter. He lay on his stomach, one hand clutching a toy truck she had bought him for his last birthday. A snazzy red model racing car lay on the pillow near his head.

Molly tiptoed into the room, stubbed her toe on a dinosaur robot. She swallowed an oath, bent, and picked up the garishly painted toy. She would have to do something about Petey's slovenly ways before they became habit. Another item for the organization chart.

He was sleeping the sleep of the innocent. Molly's heart gave a funny bump as it always did when she realized he was hers. She removed the car and the truck, tugging to get it free of his possessive grasp, gently moved a lock of dark brown hair off his forehead, and placed a kiss on his smooth cheek. He stirred but didn't waken, and after watching him for several minutes, just enjoying the sight of him, Molly left the room as quietly as she had entered.

She was so tired she took off her clothes in record time. In a faded flannel nightgown and fuzzy pink slippers, relics of her college days, she went into the bathroom, removed her makeup, and slapped moisturizer on her skin. "Teeth," she reminded herself, and dutifully brushed them.

"Good-night," she said to her hollow-eyed image in the mirror, and turned off the light.

Plink. Plink-plonk. Plink-plink-plonnnnnk . . .

Molly turned on the light. Water dribbled out of the faucet. She stared at it, suddenly thinking of Petey, of Denise, of . . .

"What a load of bull." Viciously, she twisted the faucet all the way closed.

When Douglas wasn't home by seven, Irene Hall developed a severe case of self-pity. Three fingers of her buddy Jack assuaged the feeling of abandonment somewhat, but did nothing for the rage which built as the antique tall-case clock in the foyer chimed eight.

Douglas must have a new chippy.

God, the humiliation of it.

Irene didn't have to take it. At least, not sober.

She marched into the kitchen, freed Mr. Daniel from his current hiding place behind the vacuum cleaner in the utility room, poured a generous shot, then defiantly left the bottle on the counter.

Fuck Douglas.

No, that was wrong. That was what *he* was doing. To somebody else.

She didn't care; hadn't she told herself that the last time and the time before that? She didn't care, but she'd be damned if she would feed him. Thirty seconds later the roasted chicken was in the garbage can, platter included, a gift from Douglas's Aunt Margaret, a dried-up old prune with baroque taste. Irene had never cared for the plate. Aunt Margaret, either. Dumping it made her feel better, but only marginally. Throwing out the potatoes and salad helped. For good measure she added the silverware, and was reaching for the crystal when the phone rang.

WHERE'S MY BABY?

"Hello," she said, expecting a contrite-sounding Douglas.

It wasn't him.

"Hello, Irene. Listen carefully," Delia said, sounding even flatter, even *deader* than she had a week before. Delia didn't talk long, not nearly long enough to satisfy Irene. She wanted details, *craved* them. Where was Karen? *Who* was Karen? When could she see her, have her back?

Delia had no answers. Yet. She hinted, promising more.

Irene couldn't wait, hated feeling helpless. Her baby was out there, lost to her somewhere in the world. She wanted her. Now.

A creaking sound made her wince. So many noises in a house, especially at night. And when you were alone the noises were unfriendly and somewhat menacing and it didn't matter that you were well past the age when things like that should bother you. She was thirty-six years old, for crying out loud. Thirty-six. God, was that all she was? When she looked in the mirror she saw a woman older than time.

Thirty-six and alone.

But she wasn't really alone, not with Jack, that old smoothie, to keep her company. Why couldn't Douglas be as faithful as Jack? Stupid question. Marriage was a disappointment, like everything else in her life.

Except Karen. Karen, her beautiful blond angel who had gone to heaven.

And was now back. Delia said so.

Douglas didn't believe her mother had called, didn't believe in reincarnation—and, bottom line, didn't believe in *her*. His own wife.

Irene picked up Douglas's favorite crystal ashtray and

threw it in the garbage can. While she was in the kitchen she freshened her drink.

Karen was back. She *was*. She *had* to be.

The house had never been empty with her in it. Never. Not even when she was a baby and Douglas was just starting his own ad agency. He had always been late then, too. But she hadn't minded it then.

Not with Karen in the house.

Without making a conscious decision, Irene went upstairs. Karen's room, pink and white, with a canopied bed and ruffled curtains and shelves crammed with stuffed animals, seashells, and pretty china figurines, waited. If possessions, *things,* could hold the stamp of a soul, then Karen still lived in the pretty preadolescent room. It was exactly the way she had left it six years ago.

Irene flipped a switch and soft light spilled from a white ginger-jar lamp with a pink ruffled shade onto the bed. It illuminated Mr. Bear-Face. Faithful, much loved companion, the stuffed bear lay against dainty white silk pillows trimmed in the finest Mechlin lace. Irene had insisted he be returned when Karen . . . when Karen hadn't come home. She scooped him up, held his well-worn body in a fierce hug. "You miss her, too, don't you?" Solemn black button eyes stared. "Come, we'll go see Karen."

Back in the den, a fresh drink at her elbow, the bottle within easy reach, Irene played the scenes of her daughter's life. Preserved on tape, it was all there, a moving record of a too-short existence. Karen, a blond angel, went from cherub with fat cheeks to toddler to little girl, always with Mr. Bear-Face somewhere in view. "See," Irene said to him now, "there you are, looking spiffy, I might add."

She changed the tape. An older Karen frolicked across the screen. Birthday parties. Picnics. School outings. Dance recitals. Piano recitals. Karen, tightly squeezing Mr. Bear-Face, waving, hanging out the window of the bus taking her to camp.

Camp.

Irene hadn't wanted her to go, but Douglas had insisted. He had been a camper, had wanted his daughter to experience it. Irene had hated the separation, hated the camp. So far from home. A symbol of Karen's growing independence. Finally, she had hated it because it was the place where Karen had . . .

Drowned.

Irene flung the bear away, reached for the bottle. Karen swam like an otter, was as at home in the water as one of Neptune's own sweet nymphs.

It hadn't mattered.

Karen was gone.

Suddenly Irene felt cold; goose bumps pebbled her skin. Briskly she rubbed her arms, but to no avail. The cold deepened, penetrating skin and muscle and bone; pierced the marrow.

Karen was gone.

Drowned.

Until . . .

. . . *The sea shall give up her dead.*

Five

"... *And help and support will be continued, for the parents as well as the children, either in a group or on an individual basis, for as long as it is needed.*"

Molly lowered the microphone. "Anything else you want to say?"

Zachary thought a moment, staring at the childish pictures depicting President's Day lining the corridor walls, then signaled no.

Molly raised the mike. "*That was Dr. Zachary Slater, head of the trauma team. In a related story, the search for six-year-old Timmy Newell continues. Police officials won't release details, but it is believed they have witnesses who saw the boy after the crash. This is Molly Deere, WAND, from the Brenton School on Long Island.*"

"That's that," she said. "Thanks. I appreciate it. I know how busy you are." She stuck out her hand. "Well, I'd better get to a phone with this. Thanks again."

Her small hand was dwarfed by his. Zachary held it a couple of seconds past politeness, then quickly released it when he saw a glint of speculation in her eyes.

Nice eyes. Hazel. More brown than green at the moment. "I, uh, hope it's what you wanted. I mean, I hope it's okay."

Molly patted her oversized tote, which had swallowed the tape recorder and mike. "It's just fine." Suddenly she felt strangely gauche, was relieved when an insistent beeping started.

Zachary cleared his throat. "That's yours, I think."

"Oh! Yes." She pulled the beeper from her pocket, frowned as she studied the readout. "I've got to call my office."

"Ah—" It was Zachary's turn to feel awkward.

Molly waited, but he didn't continue. "Well," she said, "good-bye."

"Good-bye." Considering his schedule, Zachary stood too long watching her as she walked away.

Kent was his usual sweet self when Molly got through. "The Newell kid's parents have called a press conference. Word is they're going to kick butt."

"Okay." She couldn't generate much enthusiasm; the story gave her the willies.

Obviously she wasn't very adept at hiding her feelings. "This is the top of the news. I'm pushing the state's budget woes out of the lead for it. Tell me if you're bored." Although he sounded stuffed up and nasal, his voice still had enough bite to make a rattlesnake happy.

Molly ignored his sly provocation, reminding herself she had a mortgage to pay and a son to educate. Hadn't she heard that by the time Petey was ready for college it would cost in excess of a hundred thousand dollars for four years? Petey, bright as he was, would most probably go on to graduate school.

Kent sneezed twice in rapid succession and loudly blew his nose. Molly bit back an automatic "God bless." He would get professionalism, nothing more. "Do you want the Slater interview now?"

Kent responded in kind. "Sure. Ready when you are." When the tape ended, a pregnant silence ensued. Molly waited him out, knowing he wouldn't disappoint her. "Real exciting. The shrink sounds like a lot of fun."

She bit her lip. "Dr. Slater didn't seek us out. Perhaps the Newells will be more to your liking."

"They'd better be. Okay, cookie, move it on over there. We wouldn't want to miss it."

A prince of a person. During the short drive Molly wondered if Kent's personality improved any in his private life. She arrived at the Newell house one second behind the Consolidated Broadcast News van and pulled her Taurus into the driveway on their tail. Grabbing her tote, she scrambled from the car.

"Hey," the driver shouted, "don't block us."

"I won't. I'll be long gone before you guys have unhitched your cables," she hollered right back.

The van's rear doors opened and a lithe man jumped out. "Well, if it isn't Molly–Uh-Oh. How're you doin'?"

"Just fine, Charlie. You?" Molly raised her cheek for the friendly peck Charlie Lee, CBN's most talented remote cameraman, automatically offered.

"Can't complain."

"Why not?" Molly countered.

They both laughed. It was an old routine.

Her laughter stopped abruptly when she caught sight of the large maple on the Newells' front lawn. Festooned with yellow ribbons. A blast of cold air buffeted the tree and the yellow ribbons fluttered.

"Bummer," Charlie said, and zipped his down vest closed. In the most frigid weather Molly had never seen him wear a jacket with sleeves. "What's cooking here? The beautiful talking head is acting *verrrrry* mysterious."

"That's because he doesn't know." They watched as Lloyd C. Cranshaw, CBN's on-the-spot reporter, checked his makeup in the van's side mirror. "Kent said the Newells aren't happy. That was the extent of the info." She saw the front door open. "It shouldn't be long."

Charlie grinned as he backed away. "Later. A beer?"

"Maybe soon. You covering Gonzalez?"

"Yep."

"Catch you there."

The front door of the Newells' large colonial closed, without anyone emerging. Molly took the opportunity to interview the neighbors. She asked standard questions and got standard answers. The Newells were the nicest people. A perfect family. Timmy was the sweetest little boy. The next-door neighbor, Phyllis Bronck, had put up the yellow ribbons, the ones near the ground, she confessed. Her son, fifteen-year-old Scott, had done the upper branches. She pulled on a tall youth's sleeve. "This is Scott."

Molly said hello, held up the microphone, asked a question out of politeness.

Scott blinked at her. "Where's the camera?"

Molly pushed the stop button. If she had a nickel for every time . . .

"Oh, look. Isn't that something?" Phyllis Bronck said.

It was something, all right. Although the temperature hovered in the low thirties, the Newell family had come out of the house coatless; each wore a bright yellow T-shirt with Timmy's picture on it. He was a beautiful boy with a face full of freckles surrounding a short pug nose. A grin revealed the dark spot of a missing front tooth.

Sadly, Molly wondered if Timmy would ever grin that way again as she made her way back to the driveway through the growing crowd. Most local TV channels had sent remote crews, and some units were recording for pools. Molly stepped over the thick cables, maneuvered until she was satisfied she was well within audio range.

Timothy, Sr., his face the prototype for Timmy, Jr., began at once, his tone truculent, bordering on belligerent. Almost two days had passed. Timmy was still missing. He stopped just short of accusing the police of incompetence. He wanted the FBI.

Reporters screamed questions. Timothy, Sr., put his arm around his wife. Timmy was alive, they both knew it. Either he was lost or. . . . They were offering a reward. Ten thousand dollars. No questions asked. Just send Timmy home.

Susan Newell, slender body shivering, answered several questions, teary voiced. Molly admired her for being able to speak at all.

The interview came to an abrupt end when Timmy's father held up his hand. He indicated the grim-faced men standing to one side. "My family and I are going to join the searchers now."

Reporters surged forward, churning up the lawn, trying for one-on-one interviews. Molly had gotten a number of good quotes from the Newells the day before. She dictated her report, then made her way back to her car to call it in. She passed Charlie. "What did you think?"

He gave her one of his party-time inscrutable stares. "Yellow isn't my color."

Molly fervently hoped it would never be hers, either.

Kent reminded her he was using the Newell spot for the top of the news. Go bother O'Brien, he ordered. See how the police like being called incompetent.

Molly could almost hear him licking his chops. She found Police Chief O'Brien in the field, watching a team of frogmen dive into the frigid water of a small lake not too far from the grounds of the Brenton School. He was red-faced to the point of apoplexy, and it wasn't because of the biting wind.

With her tape recorder off, she asked if he thought Timmy was in the lake.

"Got any kids?" O'Brien asked.

"A boy. Four-and-a-half."

"I've got two girls. Fifteen and eighteen." He gazed over the water, gunmetal gray under the totally overcast sky. "You leave no stone unturned."

Molly stared at the waves chopping the pebbly shore. Unease prickled the nape of her neck. Petey. So afraid of water. Was Timmy afraid of it? According to Dr. Spock, it wasn't unusual in children their age.

Petey.

Timmy . . .

There but for the grace of God . . .

O'Brien shouted to one of his men, his voice jerking Molly back to reality. Petey was fine, was probably wheedling Mrs. Parr out of another oatmeal-raisin cookie right about now.

The chief turned his back to the lake. "For the record?"

Molly faithfully recorded O'Brien's views, then thanked him for the interview.

"I don't want any thanks," he said in a gruff voice. "All I want is the kid, safe and sound and back where he belongs."

Irene met Nancy for lunch in a small restaurant in midtown. They had tickets for a matinee performance of the latest British import. Neither sister had thought their mother would mind them going, so soon after her death. The tickets had been costly; the show was a major hit of the season and had been sold out for a year. Delia had been nothing if not practical.

Nancy got there exactly on time and was annoyed when ten minutes passed with no sign of her sister. When Irene finally breezed in the door, slightly out of breath, her face flushed and an air of suppressed excitement crackling the air around her, Nancy had to grab for the remnants of her patience. "We don't have much time. I ordered Cobb salad for both of us."

"Fine." Irene slid smoothly onto the chair the waiter held out. "Jack Daniel's, on the rocks." She accepted a linen napkin from him and frowned at Nancy when he left. "I don't want to hear it."

Nancy fiddled with the pearls in her three-strand choker. "I didn't say anything."

Irene just smiled, not speaking until after her drink arrived and she had taken a healthy swallow. "You don't have to say anything. I can hear you thinking."

Nancy primly sipped mineral water. "Drinking is no way to solve your problems." She almost said "drowning yourself in drink," but remembered in time.

"Really?"

"Don't be snide. You know it isn't. We've been over this before."

Nancy was now nervously playing with her knife. In a completely unpremeditated gesture, Irene reached out, stilling her hand. "I know, Nancy, I know." She tapped the rim of her glass with one of her brightly painted crimson nails. "I don't need to drink, at least, not the way I did before."

"Oh?"

"Nancy." Irene gripped Nancy's hand and squeezed, hard. Bright excitement flamed in her eyes.

"What is it? What's happened?"

"Don't look so suspicious. It's nothing bad, I assure you."

If this had been meant to reassure, it failed miserably. "It's not that business with Mama, is it?" The arrival of their salads forced her to wait until they were served and the small ceremony of choosing a dressing attended to before she could continue. "I hope it isn't that nonsense again, Irene. You *do* know the dead don't make phone calls?"

"You believed it when it was happening." Irene had the satisfaction of seeing Nancy look guilty, but only for a moment. She held up a hand. "I know ... don't tell me. Andrew says it can't possibly be so, and you believe him." Her voice became higher in pitch, louder in volume. "What does he know? What do any of you know? Mama says Karen is back, and I believe her."

"Shh. People are looking."

"Let them," Irene said belligerently. Nevertheless, she

moderated her tone. "Why are you all acting this way? What does Mama have to gain by saying Karen has returned? Tell me that."

"Mama is dead. Someone is playing a cruel hoax."

"That's Andrew talking."

"What if it is? Oh, Irene, I don't want you to get hurt. Can't you understand that? None of us do—me, Andrew, Douglas most of all." Irene's lips pursed stubbornly. Nancy sighed. "Don't jump at me, Irene, but I think you need help. Have you been seeing Dr. Powell?"

Irene's air of excitement intensified. "Yes! Yes, I have. As a matter of fact, that's where I was this morning."

"Have you told her you think Mama called you from the Great Beyond?"

"I certainly did." Surreptitiously she crossed her fingers. The psychiatrist—and everyone else—knew about the first call, nothing more. Delia wanted it that way.

"Good." Nancy speared a piece of chicken breast. "She helped you when Karen died. She'll help you get over Mama's death, too."

"Actually, she's referred me to another doctor. Well, he's not really practicing, not anymore."

Nancy slowly lowered her fork. "Just what is he doing?"

"Research."

"Research." Nancy made it sound like a dirty word.

"He's interested in trauma and its aftereffects. He's writing a book."

"On trauma?"

"In a way."

"In what way, Irene?"

"Oh, Nancy, it's the most wonderful thing! He's interested in past-life regression. He hypnotizes you, takes you back into former lives to see if what's bothering you now, in this life, has its roots there."

"Irene, your problem has nothing to do with—"

"There's a school of thought that believes certain souls have an affinity for one another, that they travel the same paths in every life. They—"

"Irene! Are you listening to yourself? Really listening?"

"Which means Karen has lived before, and so have I. Don't you understand? I'm going to be able to see her, be with her—"

"Don't *you* understand? This is your grief talking. I can't believe a reputable doctor would encourage . . ." She narrowed her eyes. "Just who is he?"

"His name is Slater, Dr. Zachary Slater."

"Irene, this is nonsense! I can't believe Virginia Powell condones this . . . this hocus-pocus. Why, I can't believe I'm sitting here, hearing this. It's as ridiculous as if you said you were going to consult a fortune teller."

Irene smiled, a trifle sadly. "I did, Nancy, last week. It was nothing but bunk. She was convinced Karen is still dead. This is different. This is real. Dr. Slater's a psychiatrist. He'll help me go back into my past lives, and if I'm lucky I'll see Karen there! Don't *you* see? It will prove Mama right."

"Mama's dead, Irene. *Dead.* The dead don't make telephone calls. There's no proving them right or wrong."

Irene shook her head. "Reincarnation is real, and I'm going to investigate it with Dr. Slater's help."

Nancy's mouth was open but no sound came out.

Irene placed her drink in her hand. "Here. You need it more than I do."

Fort Wayne, Indiana

The motel on the outskirts of town was old and gone to seed. Harry thought the word "seedy" more than appropriate in the place where John Chapman died. "Seedy. Johnny Appleseed. Don'tcha get it, kid?" he asked.

But he didn't expect an answer, not really. Not when he kept the kid doped to the gills. "That's all right, kid, you sleep. You ain't missing much."

He tuned the television to CBN and was rewarded with a picture of Lloyd C. Cranshaw whispering solemnly into his mike, the Newell family lined up behind him, looking grim and determined. Ten thousand dollars was a big deal.

The camera zoomed in for a close-up of one of the Newells' T-shirts. Timmy's face filled the screen, freckles the size of dimes, then abruptly it was gone, replaced by the picture of a burning building. Harry clicked to another channel, got the local news.

Fort Wayne. He had expected to be farther west by now. "Friggin' snow," he said, and checked the sleeping boy once again before going out to get food and a newspaper.

The damn motel didn't have a phone in the room. A cold wind sliced through him the instant he stepped outside. A phone booth stood in front of the donut place across the highway. It didn't have a door. As the wind hurried him along, Harry determined to make only those calls that were absolutely essential.

Six

The sky grew overcast in a matter of minutes as huge gray clouds scudded like frightened sheep, covering the bright blue. A wind, too, arose suddenly, blowing sand, teasing blankets and clothing, intensifying the sharp, briny smell of salt-laden air.

A runaway beach ball hit Molly's hip, skimmed over her abdomen. The high sounds of excited children's voices roused her from a somnolent state as they chased the ball down the beach. She felt a scratchy woolen blanket beneath her. Levering herself onto her elbows, she slitted open her eyes, saw the light had dimmed, and that people were scooping up their belongings, running away.

Wind showered sand against her exposed flesh, whipped her hair, stinging it across her face, into her eyes. They watered, closed, and when she opened them again she was alone on the beach. Panic curled in her stomach. The people were standing on top of the dunes, far above and behind her, gathered in a tight group. They pointed and yelled, backed by the lightning-streaked dark-gray sky.

Molly couldn't hear. The panic uncurled, spread

throughout her body. Her limbs felt heavy, numb. She knew. She knew, but she was powerless to move.

And then she could move, could turn, could see. An angrily churning sea, high waves, dark green and cobalt blue, tipped with rabid-looking yellowish-gray foam, combed unendingly in, hungrily devouring the beach. Far better not to see, not to know the approach of doom.

Run!

Molly heard the warning in her head, tried to move.

Run! Run! Run run run . . .

She was at the foot of the dunes, trying to climb; scrabbling, searching for footholds, trying with desperate sweat-slippery hands to use tough beach grass to haul herself up. Sand slipped; precious inches were lost with every lunge.

Higher!

Dread invaded her heart; she didn't need to look up, to see the people's faces, to read the horror there, to know how little time was left.

Water lapped at her feet.

They extended their arms. She stretched, straining upward, but the gap widened, became unbridgeable. Safety retreated. Her heart pounded heavily; her throat clogged, she couldn't breathe. *I don't want to turn. I don't want to see how close it is.*

She turned, as she had to, and there it was, coming closer with each beat of her heart. Huge. An unstoppable juggernaut.

Tidal wave.

Tsunami.

Death.

She screamed a silent scream into the roaring maelstrom that towered over her, sucking the last atoms of oxygen from the air.

WHERE'S MY BABY? 55

Drowning ... dying ... dead ...

Molly bolted upright, shocked out of sleep. Trembling and soaked in sweat, she felt her flannel nightgown cling to her body like an unwanted second skin.

A dream.

She crossed her arms, hugged herself tight.

Not a dream; the dream.

Again.

Still shaking, she looked at the clock, saw she had only half an hour till the alarm went off. Raking her sweat-soaked hair off her neck, she rolled to her side, fumbled the alarm button to the off position, trying but failing to keep her eyes from the empty side of the bed. It would be luxury indeed to be able to turn to someone, to be held, petted, fussed over, to share the nighttime terror. Zachary Slater's image teased her mind, was promptly banished. An interesting man, not exactly hard to look at, but he hadn't been bowled over by her charms.

God, she was adding depression to terror. She could still feel it lurking in the corners of her mind. Her nightgown was clammy, draining body heat. Best to get up, shower away the cold. At least she could take care of her creature comforts.

She made the water as hot as she could bear, standing under the stream with her face turned up, sighing as it banished the residual dream chill. When she was warm again she soaped her body, suddenly aware of its curves and valleys, the silky-soft texture of her skin. With chagrin she realized her nipples were hard; she was semiaroused. Something else to blame on the nightmare. Without it she wouldn't have thought of a hard male body in her bed.

How long had it been? She leaned her forehead on

the tile, closed her eyes, and chased the memories of her love life. It had been meager at best since Roy had left. Pregnancy, motherhood and old-fashioned survival had taken precedence. Dates were infrequent. Only Glen Rowley, a detective she had met while covering a lurid homicide, had managed to get past her reserve. They had dated several times, but when it had looked as if he wanted more, she had backed off. *Why?* "Answer that and you get the Kewpie doll," she muttered.

By the time she was dressed and had put on her makeup, she was back to normal, ready to tackle a sleepy Petey, who wanted to snuggle into the warm cocoon of his covers rather than face the chilly February morning. She won the tussle, as usual, because she was the mother and he was the child, she explained when he complained, and was just pouring milk onto his cereal when there was a knock on the kitchen door. She waited a moment to make sure Petey picked up his spoon, then twitched the red-and-white gingham curtains aside. Denise stood on the back step, looking squat and ungainly as usual, bundled against the winter chill.

Cold air accompanied her into the warm room. Molly shivered, closed the door with her hip. "It's cold out there."

"Sure is. I saw your car." Denise waved at Petey. "Hi ya."

" 'Lo," he replied, his mouth full.

"Swallow, then talk," Molly admonished. Petey gave her an angelic smile and dug his spoon into his cereal.

Denise laughed. "It sinks in after a while, believe me." She touched Molly's arm. "It's late. Everything okay with you two?"

"We're fine. I don't have to be in court until ten. Coffee?"

WHERE'S MY BABY?

"Mmm, no thanks. I can't stay. Sandy needs a lift to school. I've got her science project in the back seat. I just came by to give you the name of—" She lowered her voice to a stage whisper. "You know, the doctor."

Molly stiffened. Nothing was wrong with Petey. Nothing. He was going through a stage. *The huge wave towered over her, broke....* Nonsense. Nothing to fear. Everyone dreamed. She blinked; Denise waited expectantly. Molly didn't know if she approved of someone meddling into Petey's past lives, assuming the whole thing wasn't a hoax. "Look, I—"

"Here. Take it. It can't hurt to have the doctor's name." Molly reluctantly accepted the folded piece of paper. Denise glanced at the clock. "Uh-oh, gotta run. See ya, hon."

Another blast of cold air whirled into the warm kitchen. Molly automatically locked the door, staring distastefully at the piece of paper. The whole idea was nonsense. She didn't have to keep it, didn't even have to look at the name. Her mind made up, she crumpled it, was about to toss it in the garbage when behind her Petey gave a yell.

"Petey? What ... ?" Alarm turned to instant resignation. Petey had managed to overturn the milk and a river of white was sluicing over the edge of the table. Her own fault; she should have put it away at once.

Petey's face screwed up, began to turn red. Molly righted the container with one hand, and grabbing a dish towel, stemmed the flow of milk with the other. "It's all right, Petey, no harm done. Finish your breakfast."

"Through," he said, and slid off his chair.

"Wash your hands and face," Molly yelled to his retreating back. She listened, didn't hear the sound of running water. "Petey! I mean it!"

* * *

She wrestled with the problem as she sat in the first spectator row in a courtroom on the third floor of the Queens Criminal Court building. She couldn't ignore it, not in good conscience, but she wasn't about to subject Petey to poking and prodding and probing and God knows what else without the assurance that it was sanctioned by the AMA. No witch doctor was going to get his hands on her child.

A door opened in the front of the courtroom and a bailiff came in. Molly checked her watch, spread her hands in a "What's happening?" gesture.

The bailiff had no difficulty reading it. "The prisoner isn't here yet." Confidingly, he leaned over the wooden divider. "If you ask me, we're waiting for more than the prisoner."

"Oh?"

"Yeah. This Gonzalez sentencing is hot. Judge Dexter W. Buchanan never misses a photo opportunity. We're waiting for Frieda Gilchrist to finish in Supreme. You know her, she's Cable Vision's artist. Always makes the judge look good." He grinned. "If you want coffee or something, you've got time."

"Thanks." She watched him settle at his desk with a copy of the *Daily News*. Coffee sounded good. She hefted her tote, was reaching for her coat when someone tapped her on the shoulder.

"Thought you'd be here." Grinning, Glen Rowley leaned down and gave her a quick kiss.

Molly felt a bit witchy as his lips brushed hers. Had she conjured him? He was as presentable—and twice as good-looking—as she had remembered.

He straightened, brushed a lock of wavy brown hair off his forehead, and looked around. "No action, huh?"

Molly inhaled the scent of his aftershave, was powerless to prevent her cheeks growing pink as she remembered the direction of her early-morning thoughts. To cover her embarrassment, she scooped her coat off the railing and stood. " 'They also serve who stand and wait.' "

"Beautiful and smart. I love Kipling."

"Shakespeare, I thought." He took her hand, smiled warmly. Molly tried to quick start her hormones, but they remained quiescent.

"Actually, it's Milton, and the correct quote is 'They also serve who *only* stand and wait,' " an amused voice drawled. Charlie Lee sauntered over, winked at Molly, shook hands with Glen. "So how's one of New York's Finest? Caught any bad guys lately?"

Glen laughed good-naturedly. "Sure have. In fact, I'm testifying next door. The Ridley case. Lewis Ridley, slime who likes to sell drugs to little kids. The son of a bitch got greedy and whacked his partner. You covering him?"

"Afraid not. We're here for Gonzalez. It's one of our favorite stories. Another rapist-robber off the streets. Justice triumphs, after six rapes and over seventy armed robberies. Not to mention the assorted minor charges." He turned to Molly. "What's doing? Lloyd's afraid his makeup will run. It's hot as Hades out in the hall."

"We're waiting on the lead players. Shouldn't be long."

Charlie hesitated, looked sideways at Glen, then back to Molly. "Lunch?"

"Sure."

Glen checked his watch. "I'd better get back." They

left Charlie in the hall with a worried Lloyd C. Cranshaw, who stood puffing furiously on a cigarette, directly under a No Smoking sign. Glen had Molly's elbow, steered her away. "I don't know how Charlie can stand that guy."

Molly thought of Kent, how she'd like nothing better than to never have anything to do with him again. "It's a living, I guess."

They stopped in front of one of the courtrooms. Glen glanced through the window in the door. "Looks like they're returning from chambers." He grazed Molly's cheek with the backs of his fingers. A hint of unsureness briefly inhabited his thick-lashed brown eyes. "Would three be a crowd at lunch?"

Molly said no, then spent the next hour wondering why a terrific guy like Glen Rowley didn't turn her on. Bright, interesting, and good company, he was obviously still attracted. And best of all, he liked Petey. *A relationship doesn't just happen. You have to work at it.* Oft-repeated words of wisdom from Margaret Shay. Molly quickly slammed a mental door. The last thing she wanted was to share head room with her mother.

The bailiff shouted "All rise" as the judge finally entered the courtroom and the sentencing of Hernando Gonzalez got under way. The artists, some seated in the jury box, others in the first row of the spectator section, worked busily, viewing the participants through binoculars to get details. Barbara Riley, an assistant district attorney, had anticipated the press's interest and had dressed accordingly in a stylish red suit with an ivory silk blouse. She maintained a cool smile of satisfaction as the charges and the accompanying penalties were read. Hernando Gonzalez was going away for a very long time.

The judge called a lunch break when it became apparent the proceedings would carry over into the afternoon. Molly grabbed a burger with Charlie in a restaurant across the street. Glen came in as they were leaving, grumbling he was late because the prosecutor hadn't wanted to interrupt the complicated technical testimony of a forensic pathologist.

"Glen's a nice guy," Charlie said, as they waited to go through the metal detectors in the lobby of the courthouse. "You oughta give him a chance."

"I like you better when you're inscrutable," Molly retorted.

"Ouch!" Charlie shook his hand as if he had just touched fire.

Court was not quite ready to reconvene. Molly buttonholed several of the victims, who had come to court for the personal satisfaction of seeing Gonzalez sentenced. She got her best interview from Cecilia De Santis, who said the experience of being held up at gunpoint had changed her entire outlook on life. "It's not the material things he took from me that are important. Jewelry, money—those things can be replaced. It's the other things he stole I'll never forgive him for. I can't go into a building or get on an elevator or simply walk down a street without looking over my shoulder. He even follows me into my dreams. He took my peace of mind. He changed my way of life."

The proceedings recommenced with the clerk reading the litany of charges and the judge imposing the penalties. Molly let her thoughts wander, but came to attention when a silence settled over the court. The judge steepled his fingers and pinned Gonzalez with a hard stare, then gave him the opportunity to speak before final sentence was passed. He was going to do fifteen to thirty years.

Gonzalez shifted in his chair, turned his head from side to side, half-rose, mumbled something, and then subsided. His lawyer leaned toward him, whispered in his ear. Gonzalez shook his head, rubbed the back of his neck, twisted his upper body to face the spectators. His eyes, so dark a brown there was almost no definition of the pupil, searched the rows.

The bailiffs, standing to the sides and rear of the prisoner, straightened their stances, suddenly on alert. A rustling noise emanated from the gallery as people shifted in their seats and began to whisper. Frieda Gilchrist swung her binoculars from Gonzalez to the spectators, focusing her magnified gaze on Gonzalez's common-law wife. She selected a pastel from the tray on her lap and within seconds had sketched in the outline of the young woman's face.

The judge banged his gavel. The defense attorney hastily arose to make an application to the court for waiving of costs and fees. The judge listened, barely restraining his glee. It gave him the opening he wanted and Judge Dexter W. Buchanan was not about to miss this golden opportunity with the media so well represented in his court. Making a show, he picked up the papers, aligned them precisely, and returned them to a file folder which he then carefully closed. He stared down at it for long moments, then leaned forward, clasped his hands, and placed his forearms on the file. Each movement was deliberate and calculated; Hernando Gonzalez was about to have the weight of the judicial system land on his deserving shoulders. "We are here today, Mr. Gonzalez," the judge began in a ponderous tone, "solely because of your love of money. Other peoples' money," he said, and paused, to ensure the reporters, busy scribbling, got it right, "and because of that fact, I . . ."

He got no further in what would no doubt be an eminently quotable denial of the defense's motion when Molly's beeper went off. She fumbled it from her pocket, expecting it to be Kent, impatient for the story. Instead, the readout was the number of Mrs. Parr, the baby-sitter who picked up Petey at his nursery school every day. Mrs. Parr never called. Never. Unless something was wrong.

Molly stared at the red digits, almost paralyzed with fear, until they began to blur together. Petey! She had to get to a phone! Strength came surging back. Rudely she shoved past people on her way to the aisle.

The telephones were opposite the elevators. One was free, and thankfully it worked. She fumbled the money, finally got it right, and at the dial tone punched in the number with a finger that shook so badly she had trouble depressing the buttons. No answer until the third ring. "Is Petey all right?" Molly screamed. She thought she would die until she heard the reply. *Accident. Flu. High fever. Measles. Polio.* Polio? Firmly she slammed the door on her rabid imagination.

"Yes. He's fine."

Molly's head dropped forward; she took several deep breaths to calm herself. After a few seconds her heart stopped tripping in her ears and her supersensitivity where Petey was concerned kicked in. Mrs. Parr sounded serene, but hadn't *now* been unspoken in the last sentence? "Did something happen?" A pause, long enough for Molly's heart to start a triple-time beat again. *Chicken pox. Whooping cough. Broken leg. Yellow fever. Smallpox . . .*

"I didn't want to call," Mrs. Parr said, "and then I thought about it, and, well—"

A lump. Petey has a lump somewhere and the kindly

grandmother doesn't know how to break the news. "Just tell me, Mrs. Parr. What's the problem?" Amazing, how steady her voice was when she was operating on nerve alone.

The problem turned out to be water. Again. Petey had had a run-in with a drinking fountain in nursery school. "You know how it is, how the water can all of a sudden spurt up and get in your nose and you can't breathe?" Molly did know, and knew that Petey wouldn't laugh it off the way most children would. "He was still crying when I picked him up," Mrs. Parr explained, justifying the call to herself as much as to Molly.

"I understand." And she did. She just wished there had been no need for it. "What's he doing now?"

There was a thump and then a wait as Mrs. Parr let the receiver drop and went to see what Petey was doing. "He's coloring. He looks okay now."

Molly spent several minutes reassuring the elderly babysitter that she had done the right thing in calling. She trusted Mrs. Parr, who besides Petey watched two of her grandchildren and a little girl of three. After hanging up she stared into space, then called Kent. The conversation was as brief as she could make it.

Charlie was waiting a respectable distance away. "Need any help, Molly—Uh-Oh? A lift home? A shoulder to cry on? A beer? No service too big or too small."

"Thank you, no. I'm fine."

"Coulda fooled me."

"Really. I think I'll call it a day."

The wind swirled dead leaves about her feet as she hurried through the early dusk to the municipal parking lot behind Queens Borough Hall. She'd parked her Taurus on the upper level, under a light, as she was always careful to do. She slid onto the seat, threw her tote into the back. She had to get home, find the slip of paper Denise had given her—was it only that morning?—and call the doctor.

Petey needed help.

"Oh God," she moaned. What was she going to do?

Drive home, for starters. The trip to Manhasset didn't take very long, yet Molly thought it forever before she rushed inside her empty house. She blinked as the fluorescent light in the kitchen came on. Where had she left the paper? She searched, even looking in the refrigerator, on the off chance she had shoved it in there with the milk.

Nothing.

Molly closed her eyes, concentrated, tried to relive the morning's events. At last a smile curved her lips. She put her hand in the pocket of her slacks, found the folded piece of paper. "Gotcha!" she said, and unfolded it. When she read the name printed there in Denise's large, childlike block letters, she started to laugh. The laughter, born of nerves stretched beyond the breaking point, soon turned to tears. When she was able, Molly walked into the living room and sat in the dark until it was time to pick up Petey.

Seven

Irene stood on the curb for long minutes after she got out of the taxi, staring at the town house, oblivious to the biting wind. The house was typical of Murray Hill, a three-story narrow brownstone with tall old-fashioned multipaned windows. Decorative black wrought-iron railings lined the short flight of steps leading up to the front door; the same pattern was repeated in protective bars across the windows of the basement and first floor and in the fence topped by sharp spikes. The motif was repeated even on the low fences bordering the squares of earth at curbside, guarding winter-bare trees which cast thin shadows in the pale sunshine. Window boxes with trailing ivy graced the wide window ledges. The house was well cared for, the windows sparkling in the weak sunlight, the sidewalk in front of the property clean swept, with none of the breaks, cracks, or buckled concrete usual in city pavement.

The house was little different from its neighbors, yet Irene gazed at it with a rising excitement that did more to put color in her cheeks than the insistent wind. A man walking a black Scottish terrier passed her, turned back to give her a second look. Irene realized he had walked by before. Nervously she touched her gold earrings, then anchored her leather clutch purse firmly under her arm and climbed the short flight. A discreet brass nameplate to the left of the carved wooden door simply read SLATER. Irene licked her suddenly dry lips and quickly pushed the button underneath.

The door opened only as wide as a chain would permit. A face lined with a network of fine wrinkles appeared in the aperture. "Yes?"

"I'm . . ." Irene cleared her throat, started again. "I'm Mrs. Hall. Irene Hall. I have an appointment with Dr. Slater."

The face moved. Up, then down. "Eleven o'clock."

"Yes," Irene said, then stared, dumbfounded, when the door abruptly closed. Automatically she checked her watch. Eight minutes to the hour. Did she have to wait out in the cold?

The door opened again as suddenly as it had closed, this time unfettered by the chain. "Come in. Come in. Is too cold to stand out there."

Feeling somewhat foolish, Irene stepped into a warm foyer redolent with the smell of lemon polish. Her eyes adjusted to the dimmer light while the woman closed and locked the door. The small entranceway was simply but elegantly furnished. An antique mahogany drop-leaf table fit snug against one wall, a tall vase with an arrangement of fresh flowers sat on a chased silver tray atop it, beneath a gilt-framed mirror that reflected a brass-and-crystal carriage-lamp chandelier. A straight-backed chair stood to one side of the table. The walls were covered with a textured wallpaper in a shade between cream and ivory. A small watercolor hung above the chair.

Irene assessed the furnishings with a knowledgeable

eye. Whoever had furnished the foyer had taste and the money to indulge it.

The face with the myriad wrinkled lines turned out to belong to the housekeeper. She divested Irene of coat, gloves, and scarf and deftly steered her down a short hallway toward the back of the house. When they reached a closed door she knocked, then opened it and announced Irene.

"You go on in, missus," she said. "Doctor's waiting."

Irene quelled the impulse to smooth the skirt of her dress. The woman made her feel as if she were a young girl on her way to see the principal. But then the man inside the room came forward and took her hand and Irene forgot the housekeeper as she looked into his eyes. This man had known suffering. Somehow, knowing he was a kindred spirit made her feel comfortable, even though he wasn't what she had expected. Although his dark hair was shot with silver and deep lines grooved the corners of his eyes and mouth, he couldn't be more than forty. Probably not even that.

"You're young," she blurted, the thought instantly translating into words.

Some days, when the past rode his shoulders like an albatross, Zachary felt at least a hundred, first cousin to Methuselah. Now, though, he merely smiled. Her surprise amused him. "Is that a problem?"

"No. Not if you can help me."

"Good." His smile deepened. "That's what we're going to find out." He indicated the room, inviting her to find her own seat, subtly telling her she was under no pressure. She chose the leather couch. Zachary picked up a manila folder and a lined yellow pad and pen, and instead of going to the chair behind his desk, sat in an armchair adjacent to the couch. He quickly ran through her vital statistics and medical history.

When he had everything he required, he put the pad into the folder and tossed it onto the low coffee table. Irene watched him apprehensively. Her hands moved constantly, smoothing imaginary wrinkles, touching her hair, her earrings, fiddling with the clasp on her purse.

Zachary settled more deeply into the chair. "Now, Mrs. Hall, I'd like you to tell me why you've come to me."

Irene stiffened, leaned forward. "Didn't Dr. Powell tell you?"

"I'd like to hear it from you."

Her palms were clammy; she rubbed them on the skirt of her wool dress. It was so hard to talk about it. Couldn't he just hypnotize her and let her be with Karen again?

"Mrs. Hall?"

"I . . . my daughter died. Karen. I . . ." Her lips were dry again. She licked them.

"Would you like something to drink? Coffee? Tea? There's water in the carafe on my desk, if you'd prefer."

She'd like bourbon, straight, but knew by now that wasn't the way to see Karen again. "No. Thank you. I'm fine. It's just so hard. To talk about it."

"I know. I understand. Take your time."

Irene looked into his eyes and saw that he did understand. It made it easier. She leaned back and told him about her daughter and how much she wanted to see if they had lived together before.

Zachary listened, not interrupting, only nodding when

he felt it appropriate. When she finished, he smiled at her. "We need a break. Coffee, or tea?"

"Tea," Irene replied, thinking of her laundry room at home and the bottle of Jack Daniel's hidden behind the bleach. "Tea is fine."

He spoke into the intercom and minutes later, as if only waiting for her cue, the housekeeper came bustling in with a tray. She was introduced as Mrs. Sadecki, without whom Dr. Slater professed to be unable to cope.

While they drank tea and ate slices of coffee cake warm from the oven, Zachary briefly sketched the divergent theories about past-life regression. Irene, who listened with bright-eyed attention, looked alarmed when he explained that a prevalent theory supported the view that regressions were expressions of unfulfilled personality traits. "If someone is meek and submissive, let's say, the person might regress into a life where he or she took risks, and was a pioneer or someone frequently in high jeopardy. This view explains regressions without the need for any discussion of reincarnation. It's logical in that it says everything comes from within ourselves, our psyches. The regression isn't into a past life at all, it's merely another manifestation of the personality."

"But . . . what about reincarnation? That would explain the regressions." Irene's thin body was rigid, and her eyes burned with passion. "Reincarnation is possible, isn't it?"

"That's one theory, certainly," Zachary said in a mild tone. "Why don't we see how we do? Time enough to look for explanations when and if we find something to interpret."

"Yes." For the first time since she'd entered the

house, Irene relaxed. This was what she'd come for. She had no doubt she'd succeed. After six long years, she was about to see her beloved Karen again.

Des Moines, Iowa

Harry scratched his three-day growth of beard as he filled the Blazer's tank at a self-serve no-name gas station on the outskirts of town. The place was run-down and neglected looking and suited him just fine.

Impatiently he gave the hose a jiggle, hoping to speed up the rate of flow a bit. No such luck.

The station was deserted, save for a lone attendant who slouched in the doorway of the small office, well out of the gusting wind, watching Harry with dull mud-brown eyes.

Harry scratched his abdomen. He badly needed a shower. He was worse than ripe, but the luxury of hot water and soap would have to wait. Body odor was part of his disguise. It kept people at a distance.

"Passin' through?"

Apparently not everyone was finicky enough. The attendant had left the office's dubious comfort to appear disturbingly close to the Blazer. Harry moved to block his view of the interior.

"Um."

"Helluva day for travelin'."

Harry shrugged, gave the hose a good tug, angling himself and the suddenly sociable attendant to one side.

"Gonna have us some good snow afore long. You'll wanna stay off the road. Get you an' your kid safe. He sick?"

Shit, Harry thought, *why couldn't the dumb-ass fuck*

have stayed where he belonged? He pulled the nozzle from the Blazer's tank and used it as a lever to move the attendant farther away.

"Flu."

"Lot of it goin' around."

"Yeah. Guess so. Got sick at his grandma's funeral. Very contagious. Got things running out of both ends."

"No shit."

Precisely, Harry thought, pleased to see the dumb-ass retreat. "Gotta get him home to his momma. She's for sure gonna blame me."

The dumb-ass nodded understanding. Man to man. "You kin pay inside," he said, as he disappeared into the dim interior.

Harry followed moments later, money already in his hand. The sooner he was on his way, the better. Much to his chagrin, the dumb-ass was still inclined to talk.

"Headin' west?" he asked.

Nosy bastard.

"South. Topeka."

How had that slipped out? That's where she *lived, the bitch. Mother. God, he hated being even this close to her.*

Harry pocketed his change, gave the dumb-ass a good-buddy two-fingered salute, and hurried outside. The dumb-ass had got it right. Snow was beginning to fall.

Winter in the heartland. He remembered it well.

Several minutes later he found Interstate 35, which he took north. When the snow was swirling so hard and fast he veered across the lane marker, he pulled into the first big cheap chain motel he saw. He roused the kid enough to get some soup down him, then put him out for the night. The room was streamlined for economy, but it had a phone. Harry dialed from memory.

One more day.

Molly poked and pried as delicately as she could, but Petey showed no effects of his earlier trauma. He wolfed down his favorite dinner, hamburger and french fries, then conned her into letting him watch a Disney movie on television.

Still too keyed up to settle, too upset to eat her own dinner, Molly called Denise and asked if she wanted company. Denise was delighted; Harold was watching the Knicks. "Want Sandy to sit?"

Molly wanted Sandy. "The refrigerator's stocked," she said five minutes later when Sandy bounced through the back door. "Help yourself. Petey can have fruit if he's hungry."

"No problemo." Sandy fluffed her honey-colored bangs and winked at Petey. They both knew they'd be into the ice cream before Molly got next door.

Denise was waiting. "Coffee? I've got new decaffeinated beans. They've got a touch of hazelnut and—screw the coffee. You look like you could use a brandy." When she discovered they didn't have any brandy, she made them each a screwdriver. "Healthier," she said. "Cheers."

Molly took a sip and raised an eyebrow. "Did you run out of orange juice?"

"Drink. It's what the doctor ordered."

"Speaking of doctors—" Molly said.

"I *thought* that's what brought you over, but why are you so tense?" She tilted back her head and peered up at the much taller Molly through her red half-glasses.

"It's Petey, isn't it?" Bright-eyed with interest, she didn't wait for Molly to answer. "You're going to call that Dr. Slater, aren't you?"

"Where did you get his name?"

Denise settled herself more comfortably in her chair. "You're not going to believe this," she said, and started a long, involved story which featured the first cousin of a neighbor of the mother-in-law of one of her colorist's customers. When she finished, both their glasses were empty. "Want another?"

Molly pushed herself out of her chair. "No, thanks. I'd better be going."

"But what do you think?"

"I don't know *what* I think. I don't know what *to* think."

Despite what she told Denise, she sat up very late. Thinking. Recommendations through the beauty parlor were not to be trusted. But she had met Zachary Slater, had liked him. Enough to trust him with the well-being of her son?

Her gut instinct approved. She told herself to go with it. She'd call him in the morning.

Then she looked in on Petey, sleeping like the innocent soul he was. There was nothing wrong with her Petey. Not one damn thing.

After dinner, Mrs. Sadecki cleared the table with alacrity, almost snatching Zachary's plate before he finished the last bite. He winked at Lauren. "Someone's got a hot date!"

Lauren giggled, a sound that never failed to tug at his heart.

"I heard that!" Mrs. Sadecki called over the noise of running water.

Zachary went over and turned off the taps. "Leave them. Lauren and I will finish up tonight. You don't want to be late."

The housekeeper paused, torn. One night a week she traveled to the Polish church in her old Brooklyn neighborhood. It was a long way and subway service was unpredictable at best.

"Go."

"I'll just put up coffee. You'll want it fresh later."

Working side by side with Lauren had a good feel to it. Zachary was sorry when the few dishes were rinsed and set in the dishwasher. She was growing up so fast; he wanted to experience every moment to the fullest. "What's on schedule for tonight?"

"I have to finish my valentines. There's only two days left!"

"Want help?" Lauren nodded, and Zachary soon found himself assigned the task of cutting out heart shapes from red cellophane paper. She was giving a card to everyone in her kindergarten class. "Don't forget one for Mrs. Sadecki," he warned. Lauren gave him a long-suffering look more suited to a teenager.

They worked companionably, Lauren chattering away. Zachary marveled. His daughter seemed to have an interest in anything and everything that came within her ken. But even her bright curiosity flagged when tiredness drooped her eyelids.

"Bed," Zachary ordered, watching her yawn. He supervised her nightly rituals, then read to her until she fell asleep, sitting on the antique rocker he and Janine, then three months pregnant, had found at an estate sale in Connecticut.

Memories. Bittersweet. But precious nonetheless.

Restless, he went downstairs to his office. Work was the antidote for the creeping depression he couldn't seem to shake. Thank God he had something interesting to keep him occupied.

Going immediately to the cabinet where he kept the tapes, he picked out the one marked "Hall, Irene—1—2/11," and inserted it into his tape recorder. He pressed a button and Irene Hall's voice, clearly showing her nervousness, filled the quiet.

"Do you use drugs?"
"No. Nothing like that."
"Then how will you hypnotize me? What if it doesn't work? Will you use drugs then?"
"Don't worry. Just listen to my voice. Relax. Listen to the sound of my voice. Listen."

Zachary stopped the tape, pressed fast forward several times, until he had the place he wanted.

"You are five years old today, Irene. This is your birthday. What are you doing?"
"I'm getting ready for my party."

Lisping, slightly petulant, the voice of a five-year-old.

"A party! How nice. Who is coming to your party?"
"Nancy's coming. Mama says she's gotta. I don't want her. She's too old."
"Who is Nancy?"
"My *sister*. Everybody knows that."

"I see. Now just relax. We're going to travel again. We're going to go farther back. Relax, Irene. Go back. Go back. You feel light. Like a feather. Go back. Back."
"I'm cold."

The hair on the nape of Zachary's neck stood up. Irene's voice, yet it wasn't Irene's. No matter how many times he heard the change, it always affected him this way. Like a solid blow to the gut.

"Why are you cold?"
"We are very poor. There's little to keep us warm." A hint of impatience tinged the voice.
"Where are you?"
"In our hut. In the forest."
"Tell me about your life."

The girl who was Irene yet wasn't Irene continued to speak. From time to time Zachary made a note, but for the most part he just listened, as fascinated as he had been the first time he'd regressed a patient. This other Irene was describing a hard life, a life of deprivation and want.

"We don't have enough to eat. We are always hungry. It's all right for me, and for the others, but the baby ... the baby cries all the time. When she isn't crying, she's coughing. It's terrible. I can't stand it when she coughs! If only we had some meat, I could make a broth. It would nourish her. She grows so weak."

She paused, and Zachary heard his own recorded voice asking why they didn't have food. Was there no game in the forest?

" 'Tis the king's game, sir! 'Tis death to hunt it!" A sly note insinuated itself. "There be ways, though, and my pa is clever-like, but . . ."

Another pause, this one rather long, and then there was a scream.

"What is it? What's happened? Tell me!"
"The baby! The baby's dead! Ohhhhhhh . . ."

Sounds of weeping, heartbroken sobs, filled the room. Zachary pressed the stop button. He had brought her out of it then, brought her up through the years until he had Irene Hall back again.

"Do you remember what happened?"
"Yes. Yes. I remember."
"How do you feel?"
"I feel. . . . Oh! It was Karen! I know it was Karen!"
"Who was Karen?"
"The baby. The baby was Karen."

Sounds of weeping, followed by Irene blowing her nose.

"She's dead! My baby is dead! My Karen is dead!"

WHERE'S MY BABY?

Zachary stopped the tape, pushed the recorder away. He couldn't take it again. Not tonight. He poured himself a Grand Marnier, drank it in two large gulps. A hell of a way to treat a fine liqueur.

The session hadn't ended on a sour note. He'd think of that, think of the shining light in Irene Hall's eyes as she walked out the door. "I'll be back," she'd said. "I can't wait to see Karen again."

Torture, and for what? Was it real? Or was it a delusion, an elaborate charade put on by a mind so hurt it would do anything to heal itself?

That's for you to find out, doctor, he told himself, and poured another shot. He turned on the radio and clicked off the lamp.

"It's twenty-nine degrees at eleven forty-seven in New York, and this is the latest news from WAND, 990 on your radio dial. On Long Island today, the parents of six-year-old Timothy Newell said they have had no reliable response to their offer of a ten-thousand-dollar reward for his safe return. In the Bronx an off-duty cop was stabbed while coming to the aid of a robbery victim in the subway. In Queens convicted rapist and armed robber Hernando Gonzalez was sentenced to fifteen to thirty years. The President is set to meet with top advisers next week on the . . ."

Zachary sat in the dark, sipping and listening. He knew that before too long he would hear Molly's voice. He wondered if there was enough Grand Marnier in the world to give him the courage to call her.

Eight

Mitchell, South Dakota

From a distance, it looked like any other town along the straight ribbon of Interstate 90. To Harry, though, in a poetic mood most probably brought on by a combination of highway hypnosis and the imminent profitable end to his journey, it seemed to rise out of the flatlands like a humpback whale skimming a tranquil sea.

"Hey, kid, we're almost there. Yes sirree. Anytime now." The boy stared groggily out the window, ignoring Harry and the elbow he playfully poked into his thin ribs.

Harry was undaunted, suddenly wanting to talk. "You're gonna like it where you're going. Good air. Open spaces." *Not a cramped little house on a mean street on the wrong side of town where nobody was happy, least of all* her, *and because she wasn't, you couldn't be, she saw to that, and . . .* Christ! Where had that come from, those thoughts he never allowed to leak into his brain? Too close . . . he was too damn close to her. It did funny things to him.

An eighteen-wheeler thundered past; the Blazer shook in its backwash. Harry forcibly returned himself to the present. "Yes sirree, kid. Someday you're gonna thank me. Just see if you don't." Boy, was that ever the truth. The kid had had a lucky escape, and he had old Harry to thank for it. Must've been born under a lucky star. "Yeah, kid, it was your lucky day when I came along. Someone to take care of you when you needed it the most." Where was the kid's mother when he needed her? Bitches, all of them. Why, even the dead kid's mother had made it there faster than the kid's. What was her name? Joanne. Right. He should remember that. Gotta take care of future business.

He took the exit for the downtown area and expertly wended his way through the streets. He had been here before. Neat houses with small, well-kept lawns; a goodly percentage sporting For Sale signs, staked out front right alongside the mailbox. A slice of real-life America.

The houses slowly gave way to commercial enterprises. Harry turned onto Main Street, cruised by the heart of downtown, noting many of the stores had For Rent signs in their windows. Everywhere you went, the economy sucked. He thanked his lucky stars he had a hedge against it. *You'll never be any good, never amount to anything, you mark my words, Harry, are you listening?*

Harry was listening, all right, and he didn't want to. Not to a voice he hadn't heard in over thirty years. He slowed the Blazer when the light on the corner ahead turned to red. Breathing deeply, he forced her out of his mind. By the time the light changed, he was back on track ... focused.

Up ahead on the right he could see the Corn Palace. It never failed to amuse him, a big building decorated on every flat surface with murals made from multicolored ears of corn and seeds, topped by fanciful onion domes, spires, and minarets, rising out of the flat South Dakota earth, looking for all the world like the Taj Mahal would if it were stuck on the moon. No, that was the wrong image. The Taj Mahal had style and grace and, above all, elegance. The Corn Palace was hokey; pure kitsch—Americana with a vengeance.

Nobody ever accused Americans of having taste, and the Corn Palace seemed to exemplify that view. Harry couldn't have cared less. His only interest was its drawing power; at any given time tourists flocked to it, awed by the audacity of spirit that could envision, much less produce, such an attraction. An ever-changing work of art.

He drove slowly by, appearing to anyone who would give a damn to be looking for a parking space. Just another tourist. *Come on kids, get out. Ethel, you got the camera? Stand over there. C'mon. I wanna get a picture of you under the eagle. Jeez! Lookit them feathers. Who'd'a thought corn'd come in all them colors?*

Today was no different from any other, he was happy to see, although it was the middle of February and the frigid temperature and biting wind were more conducive to pursuing indoor activities. Parking spaces were at a premium, most spots filled by vehicles with out-of-state plates. Harry slowed even more, seemingly serious about finding a spot. Minnesota. North Dakota. Nebraska. Iowa. A Winnebago from Washington, taking up two spots.

A lot of kids about, on vacation for the Presidents Day holiday school break, bundled up against the unfriendly elements. Good. He had lucked out. Again.

Fate. It had guided him, right from the beginning.

Wisconsin. New York. New York. Florida. Harry

made a right turn, went down two blocks, passed parking lots, full for this time of year, made another right, came slowly up on Main. The street spaces were all taken. Minnesota. Texas. New York. Connecticut. Another New York. Hard to get away from the bastards. Nevada.

Harry sucked in his breath, his hands tightened on the wheel. North Dakota. Nebraska. South Dakota. South Dakota. New Jersey.

Around the blocks again. Harry paid as much attention to the view from the rear as he did to the road ahead.

New York. Connecticut. New York. Dirty tan van with Nevada plates. A man leaning against the driver's door.

Harry slowed, tapped the brakes until he coasted to a stop right next to him, leaned across the kid and lowered the passenger window. "Hey, fella! You going out?" The man stared at the kid, couldn't take his eyes off him. "Mister?" The man slowly transferred the stare to Harry. "You leaving?"

"No."

A woman slid over into the driver's seat of the van. The door opened a crack, the man pushed it closed without taking his eyes from Harry. "Major?"

Harry, self-styled major, although he had never risen above the rank of private in the land of napalm and Agent Orange, nodded. "Edward Robinson?"

"Yes."

"Wife?"

"Clara."

"Children?"

The man sucked in a breath, jerked his body back. "My ... son. Billy. He's dead. Eight years now."

"Tough," Harry said. "How's the potato business?"

The man's eyes narrowed, spearing furrows across his brow. He looked like he wanted nothing more than to take a poke at Harry. Instead, he straightened and answered in an even tone. "Cantaloupes. Hearts of Gold."

"Right," Harry said. "Cantaloupes. That's what Winnemucca's famous for, after all."

"Fallon."

"Yeah, right. Fallon. Who could forget?"

The man licked his lips, flicked his eyes to the kid. "That him?"

Business first. Harry looked fondly at his latest hedge against recession, wiped a trail of drool from the left side of his mouth with the edge of his sleeve. "You got it?"

For answer the man rapped on the window. It lowered a few inches. The woman held up a navy blue duffel bag.

"Unzip it."

The man rapped again. The woman unzipped the bag enough for Harry to see inside.

The broad sure was on the ball. Harry found himself looking at his favorite sight. "Move it around. Let's see what's under the top layer." The broad widened the aperture, showed Harry what he wanted to see.

"That him?" the man asked again.

"Yeah," Harry answered. "Stay put." He pulled away, making sure Edward Robinson, cantaloupe farmer from Fallon, Nevada, purchaser of a stolen child, got a good, long look at the Blazer's Iowa plate.

It was easy after that. Harry found a parking space a little over a block away, not too far for the kid to walk, since he was none too steady on his pins. Harry liked to think of himself as a considerate kind of guy. Why go out of your way to do something mean when a kindness would serve just as well?

Not that the kid appreciated it. Harry wound up having to carry him the last half a block. Shock followed by days in a drugged stupor tended to take the starch out of you, especially if you were a kid. Harry understood.

Clara Robinson stood next to her husband, a tall woman with a plain face framed by an abundance of coarse brown hair that waved in wild disarray to below her shoulders. Her eyes were fixed hungrily on Harry's burden. When they neared, she took a step forward, reached out, then quickly withdrew her hand when her husband spoke softly into her ear. She licked her lips, looked ready to spring, like a lioness on the alert.

Harry kept his eyes on the duffel.

Edward Robinson spoke. "Twenty thousand. It's all there." Harry wanted to count it. Edward was agreeable. Clara still looked like she wanted to pounce.

"Inside," Harry said. "The broad stays out here."

He got no argument. The deal was made. Harry emerged from the van carrying the duffel bag. Clara was inside and they were pulling away from the curb before Harry got to the end of the block.

The Blazer seemed strangely empty without the kid. Harry got back on 90, heading east. No telling what the Robinsons would do, although they were now as guilty as he was. Foolish to take chances, though. Edward had been cool enough to try and find out where the kid had come from. Harry had told him not to take any vacations in the East for a while, as much to protect himself as the Robinsons.

Scratch my back and I'll scratch yours.

Which reminded him. He needed a bath and a shave. A truck stop on the outskirts of Sioux Falls was the answer. Harry showered, shaved, and put on a clean pair of jeans and a flannel shirt, then went out and put back on the Blazer's original New York plates. Iowa got flipped into a convenient Dumpster along with the jeans and shirt he'd been wearing for the last four days. Beardless, with his down jacket reversed so the tan side was out, navy in, he bore little outward resemblance to the scrofulous major.

After grabbing a quick bite, he got back on the interstate, this time heading west. It wasn't the most elaborate plan, but who would figure him to double back? Certainly not the cantaloupe farmer.

About three hundred and fifty miles to Rapid City, all of it easy, straight down the interstate, as flat and boring as the land it traversed. The only diversions were the signs advertising Wall Drug. Harry made good time, doing well over twenty miles above the speed limit, going with the flow, the Blazer eating up the miles.

On the eastern outskirts of Rapid City he found a used car dealer and sold him the Blazer, telling him he was tired of driving and was going to fly the rest of the way to California. The dealer yawned, showing several holes where molars had once resided, said, "Yeah," and completed the paperwork in record time. He even let Harry call for a cab on his phone, all magnanimity. It was an excellent deal.

Harry took the navy blue duffel, a briefcase, and a plastic carry-on suit bag out of the Blazer. He told the cabbie to take him to the biggest motel or hotel near the airport. One with a lounge.

"Lookin' fer action?" the cabbie asked.

Harry scratched his face, was momentarily surprised to find the itchy beard gone. "Yeah."

"Got just the place," the cabbie replied.

Harry couldn't complain, tipped him generously when fifteen minutes later they pulled up in front of an aging structure. While not the height of luxury, the hotel would do him fine. The lounge advertised live entertainment, a new group every week. Hot stuff.

Another shower, this one hot and steamy, took the kinks out. Dressed in slacks, sport shirt, and sport jacket, no tie, he discovered he was ravenous. In more ways than one. A successful business venture always increased his appetites.

First things first, though. A call to the front desk gave him the airline information he needed. Another call got him a reserved seat on a flight to New York leaving early the next afternoon. That done, he was free. Nothing stood between him and his pleasures.

He was anticipating a long night, and food was his first imperative. He ordered a Coors—"Keep 'em coming"—and as always when he was west of Kansas City, steak. A big, thick New York cut, rare. He wanted to see blood ooze. The waitress pursed her lips and batted her heavily black-mascaraed eyelashes, but Harry ignored her. She wasn't his type, and besides, he wasn't going to wait for her to get off work. He had an agenda, and waiting had no part of it.

In due course, Harry consumed a Caesar salad—for two, since the management wouldn't make an exception—devoured his steak and a big baked potato with extra butter and sour cream, and ate a huge slab of cherry pie, warmed, with a double scoop of vanilla ice cream. He was burping genteelly into his linen napkin when the waitress returned.

"Anything else?" She made it more than obvious his options were still open.

"The check." She waited, he smiled politely. She finally took the hint and after presenting his bill with a cute little dip, sashayed back to the kitchen. Harry forgot her before he rose to leave.

The lounge was a lure he couldn't resist, found by ear more than sight, a dark cave from which spewed loud music with a thumping beat. Standing on the threshold, waiting for his eyes to adjust, Harry felt the rhythm in his chest, responded to it with a growing eagerness.

Yes! This was his kind of place. Inhaling deeply, he sucked the smoky air into his lungs. Beer. Cologne. Sweat. A heady mix.

A long bar was to the left of the entrance, perpendicular to a small raised stage and an even smaller dance floor. Well stocked both with liquor and people. More people were crowded onto the postage-stamp dance floor, gyrating grindingly to the beat of the trio producing amplified music and buckets of sweat. The bandstand was bathed in multicolored lights; the rest of the place was murky at best, lit by candles in red glass holders set on small round tables crammed close together.

Harry took his time looking the place over. No surprises. Most of the men were in denims and plaid shirts; a few were dressed as he was, but they were in the minority. The women also were dressed casually, most opting for the western look as well.

Except for one woman sitting alone at the bar. She wore skin-tight black pants with a sequined top that captured the reflected light from the bandstand, kept part of it, and threw the rest off.

Directly into Harry's eyes. He made straight for her,

noticing details as he neared: high heels, topped by rhinestone-studded bows; carefully manicured nails, a two-color job; hair that looked sun-streaked, but which had probably cost her a small fortune and considerable time in a beauty parlor. She looked sleek and hot and ready.

Her name was Gloria.

Glorious Gloria, he said, and she laughed. She was drinking vodka, thank you, straight. Absolut, on the rocks.

A purist, he said, and she laughed again. Her breasts rose and fell against the sequined top. Harry stared, appreciating their contours, and almost forgot to order. But the bartender wouldn't allow that, and before he knew it he was sucking another Coors and she was bestowing upon another glass the crimson imprint of her lips.

There was no dearth of conversation. It was practiced flattery and she was very good at it. Harry didn't give a damn. He liked his women brash and savvy, and Glorious Gloria certainly seemed to fill the bill. They talked, they laughed, they both didn't see any reason to dance; it wasn't *their* kind of music. That gave them something in common. Her hand casually brushed down his arm, landed briefly, lightly, on his thigh. He hardened instantly, like a horny thirteen-year-old.

He immediately called for another round. The night was young. No reason to rush. Besides, he liked this part of the game. They drank, laughed, gauged each other.

The band took a break. Gloria slid from the barstool, teetered for a moment on her high heels. He put a steadying hand on her arm; she put a meaningful hand on his knee. Gave a little squeeze. She was going to the little girls' room. She'd be right back. Don't go away.

Harry had no intention of leaving. At least, not without her.

From the other end of the bar the bartender watched her weave her way through the tightly packed tables, came sliding his bar rag with a seeming aimlessness until he stopped in front of Harry. "You staying here?" Harry took a fistful of peanuts, popped them into his mouth one by one. The bartender took it as a positive response. "You want a bottle for your room? I got Absolut in the back."

Gloria sure seemed fond of it, and Harry was flush. Why not? He pushed money across the bar, gave the bartender his room number, and went to wait for Gloria in front of the rest rooms. When she finally emerged, he told her it had been worth the wait. She had on a new coat of lipstick, her hair was even more artfully tousled than before, and she positively reeked of a heavy perfume. The primping was wasted on Harry; he was going to have her no matter what.

He took her elbow, guided her gently toward the elevators, bent down, and whispered in her ear, "Obsession?"

"I don't have any," she replied, seeing where they were going and making no demur.

Harry momentarily tightened his grip. "Your perfume, I meant. Is it Obsession?" One of the few names he knew.

"No. No, it's not. It's Shalimar. I'm an old-fashioned girl."

And he had a bridge in Brooklyn he could sell her.

She had taken so long in the bathroom that the waiter was outside his room with the vodka. "Oh, how thoughtful," Gloria trilled, and sashayed inside. She threw her leather clutch purse on top of the bureau and reached to take off her earrings. She stopped, looked uncertain, and asked Harry if he minded.

"What?" He had opened the vodka and was busy trying to free two glasses from plastic-wrap prison.

"The earrings. Do you want me to leave them on? They're so long they tangle in my hair when ... *you* know."

Harry did know, and the thought was enough to harden him again. "I don't mind. Take them off. Take everything off."

She took him at his word. Naked, she certainly was glorious. His body further stiffened to attention. When she put her hands under her high rounded breasts and lifted, offering them to him, and then slid one hand down her slightly rounded belly to slip crimson-tipped nails into the luxuriant growth of dark-brown hair between her thighs, he knew he would never make it to naked himself. Not this first time.

He took her standing up, pushed back against the wall, her legs drawn up to circle his waist. He banged into her, bereft of finesse, straining and grunting to find his release. It was hard and fast and rough and explosive. At that moment he could have been fucking a llama, for all the difference it made. The body he was using had no meaning.

But Glorious Gloria had feelings, which she expressed, loudly. Harry apologized, not at all sorry. He poured her a stiff shot, assured her he would soon be in the same condition. She giggled, somewhat spoiling her sophisticated veneer.

It didn't take long for him to make good on his promise. This time they were both naked and in the bed with the coverlet and sheets pushed onto the floor. They were athletic and inventive, she more than he. This time he satisfied her.

He got up to use the bathroom, and when he came back, she had poured herself another drink. Her gaze raked him, focused on the one area of interest to her. "Again?"

"Again. Only this time, I'd like to do something a little different." He could see the fear leap into her eyes, intensify when she realized he held several towels.

"No. Nothing kinky. I don't do kinky." Her eyes left him, darted around the room, obviously looking for her clothes.

"Nothing so bad. I'll take care of you."

"I've got to get home. I've got a kid. The sitter can't stay all that late."

Bimbo bitch.

"It won't take long."

She put down the drink, started to back away. "No. Really. I don't want to."

Harry walked to where he had dropped his clothes, picked up his jacket, extracted his wallet. Taking out several bills, he dropped them one by one on the bed. One century. Two. Another. "For cab fare home," he said.

Her eyes burned, tore away from the cash, flicked apprehensively to the towels. "What?"

"Just your hands. It won't hurt. I promise." She didn't say anything. Harry picked up the three hundred, made a small roll, walked to the bureau, and stuffed it into her purse. It closed with a small click.

"What do you want me to do?"

The bimbo was truly bought and paid for. He had her lie down, tied her hands to the spokes in the headboard with the towels. "Comfortable?" She nodded. "Good."

WHERE'S MY BABY?

"What are you going to do?"

He sat down on the edge of the bed, put his hand on her soft belly, slid it up to cover a breast. Then he pinched her nipple. Hard. Her body bucked with the shock of it. Fear leaped naked back into her eyes. Dumb broad. He wanted the fear, needed it, fed on it. He was in control; powerful. There wasn't a bitch on earth who was his match. Not one.

When he was finished, he got up and handed her another two hundred. "For your kid," he said. "Why don't you stay home with him tomorrow for a change?" She grabbed the money, dressed in record time, and left, slamming the door.

Exhausted, Harry fell into bed. His last thought before he succumbed to sleep was of the kid. Maybe the cantaloupe farmer's wife would be good for him, but he doubted it. They were all alike.

Bitches.

Nine

After a morning spent covering the police press conference of yet another gang drive-by shooting, this one in Queens, and the afternoon at Kennedy, where a jumbo jet had slid off the runway on its belly while attempting take-off, Molly was ready to call it a day. There had been two dead in the early-morning shooting with the possibility of a third, who was currently holding on by the grace of God and the latest in intensive-care life-support equipment at Elmhurst General. The plane hadn't produced any fatalities, but there were enough casualties to keep even Kent happy.

"Good work," he said, when she called in her report. "I think I'll lead in with the dame who said she's going to sue the airline, the airport, and the city."

"Um," Molly replied, knowing Kent valued input from his reporters and it was to her advantage to keep him happy. A happy Kent was marginally better than an unhappy Kent.

"Did she mention the crew?"

She had lost the trend. "Who?"

"The litigious dame. Is she going after the pilot?"

Trust Kent. Molly used her driest tone. "She didn't

mention him. And since the majority of passengers are heralding him as a cross between Charles Lindbergh and Jesus Christ, I wouldn't hold out much hope."

"Too bad. The public loves pilot error, but only when they're killed in the crash."

"So instead of a dead scapegoat you've got a live hero. Six of one, half a dozen of another."

"I guess," Kent said, his voice taking on the tone that meant he was thinking. Before he could come up with someplace else to send her, she told him she was checking out. "Half a day, cookie?"

"Charge it to personal leave," she snapped, forgetting to keep her cool.

"Ah! Got your period."

"Clarence Thomas," she spat out, totally abandoning subtlety.

She got even angrier at herself when Kent laughed, telling her he'd welcome a suit for sexual harassment, claiming it would relieve the boredom of his day-to-day life. When she refused to play anymore, he reminded her she was due in Federal Court in Brooklyn in the morning. The long-awaited trial of a *capo* with operatic tendencies was scheduled to get under way.

Just what she needed, another long session in court sitting on her fanny, feeding the public periodic reports about a truly great and noble example of *homo sapiens* testifying against his former goodfellas. She steered her Taurus off the airport's loop road and onto the Van Wyck, which was more than usually congested. Out of habit she turned on the radio, just in time for one of WAND's frequent traffic reports. "*... Van Wyck. The problem is an overturned tractor-trailer in the eastbound lanes in the vicinity of Kennedy Airport. Rubbernecking is tying up westbound traffic. Avoid the area if* *at all possible. There is a reported tie-up on the LIE just east of the Clearview. Use alternate—"*

Feeling not one iota of remorse or guilt, she turned to an easy-listening station. If she had to be stuck in traffic, she could at least choose her own entertainment. The Taurus inched forward, Molly refusing to yield to a beat-up van with Jersey plates which was trying to cut across from the middle lane. The man behind her was more obliging, and in seconds the van zipped by her, using the narrow shoulder as an express lane.

Molly inched her way slowly to the nearest exit, then took the streets, heading in an easterly direction. She didn't realize where she was going, not consciously, until she was one block from the Manhasset community center, then she admitted to herself it had been her destination all along. She pulled into a parking lot at the side of the building and stared at the banner stretched across the upper story.

CAMP ABNAKI
DAY CAMP HEADQUARTERS
SIGN UP YOUR CHILD NOW!

Before she could change her mind, she headed around to the front of the building. A receptionist stopped pounding a typewriter long enough to tell her she wanted Ms. Zinzendorf, straight down the corridor, turn left, third door on the right.

Molly had no trouble finding the office, but hesitated outside the door. Perhaps this wasn't the best idea. Petey was still very young. What if he wasn't ready? What if she was pushing him into it? What if he hated it? What about his problem with water?

What if? What if? What if? You could what-if yourself to death. "What if you just go home and forget about this?" she muttered, trying to ignore the little voice in her head chanting, *Coward, coward, coward. Afraid to let your baby go? Going to tie him to your apron strings? Make him into a mama's boy?*

Telling herself to shut up, she rapped on the frosted-glass upper portion of the door, turned the doorknob, and pushed. A woman in her mid-sixties looked up from behind a cluttered desk. "Ms. Zinzendorf?"

The woman smiled, creating a cascade of wrinkles across her face, and waved her inside. "You must have met Connie. She insists on that *Ms.* business. Personally, it makes me a trifle uncomfortable. It's for you younger girls." Molly hovered in the doorway. Another vigorous wave. "Come in. Come in." She rose and held out her hand. "Gertrude Zinzendorf. *Mrs.* Actually, I'm a widow. Six years now since Felix is gone."

"I'm sorry," Molly said, a bit overwhelmed.

"Don't be. It was a blessing. The poor man had suffered so."

Molly could find nothing to say to that. Apparently Mrs. Zinzendorf agreed, for after pumping Molly's hand strongly, she invited her to remove her coat.

"I, uh, this won't take long," Molly hedged.

"First-time jitters," Mrs. Zinzendorf said. "Don't worry. Happens to the best of 'em, ah ... ?"

"Molly. Molly Deere."

The woman frowned. "Were you here before?" Molly assured her she hadn't been, wondering how long it would take her to place her name or to recognize her voice. "No matter." She seated herself behind her desk again and waved Molly to a chair. "What can I do for you?"

"I'm interested in the day camp for my son."

"How old is he?"

"Petey's four and a half now. He'll be five at the end of August."

Mrs. Zinzendorf clicked her tongue. "It must be very uncomfortable to be pregnant over the summer. My two were born in the spring."

Uncomfortable? It had been sheer hell. Alone, scared—no, terrified—of failing the life she carried as she had somehow failed its father ...

The woman pulled out a pad from under a pile of folders and opened the desk's middle top drawer. After rummaging for a few moments, she came up with a ballpoint pen. "I'd better write down the details before I forget them."

"Oh, no! I mean, I'm not sure if this is right for Petey. I only want information, Mrs. Zinzendorf."

"I understand. And please call me Gertrude. I have brochures floating around somewhere. Let me see if I can find one. They give a pretty good idea of what Camp Abnaki looks like and the activities offered. Is Petey athletic?"

"He loves anything to do with baseball."

"That's a start," Gertrude said approvingly. "So many children nowadays sit on their duffs in front of televisions. Using the remote control is their only athletic endeavor." She smiled apologetically. "Sorry. My personal bugbear. I'm sure you're more interested in hearing about the staff."

She talked about camper-to-counselor ratios, wholesome balanced meals, rainy-day activities. Molly smiled and tried to take it all in, was afraid she didn't have the proper questions. Not yet. As in everything, she would do her research before she committed to anything. Especially where Petey was concerned.

"And that about covers it. Now where . . . ? Here they are. I knew I had them." She handed Molly a full-color brochure. "This will give you a good idea, as I said. The camp is right here in Nassau County. You're welcome to drive out and have a look. The buildings are closed, of course, at this time of year, but you'll see the general layout and our main attraction, the lake."

Molly squirmed. Gertrude, perceptive for all her loquacity, immediately hunched forward. "Is there a problem with the lake? I assure you the campers are very well supervised, especially when engaging in water activities. That covers all water sports and any ceremonies conducted lakeside."

"I . . . no—" She took a deep breath. "Petey, ah, seems to be going through some sort of phase. Nothing serious, but . . . well, truth be told, he's somewhat afraid of water."

Gertrude sat back. "Not that it matters as regards Camp Abnaki, but how 'somewhat'? Does he refuse to bathe?"

"It's not his favorite activity, but I've managed so far."

The older woman shook her head understandingly. She hadn't missed the singular pronoun. "Last year," she said, "we had a first-time camper, also a little boy, who came to us with a fear of water. Wouldn't so much as put a toe in. We made sure he was always assigned his own counselor, one-on-one, anytime he was even near the lake. That included swimming instruction periods and canoeing and rowing, not that he would participate. Even when we had sing-alongs lakeside, we made sure he was covered individually. It took us until August to get him into a rowboat, but we managed."

Molly was impressed. "Did he enjoy it?"

"Heavens, no." Gertrude laughed. "We weren't even able to untie it, much less leave the dock. That's one stubborn little boy. But he'll be back next year," she said with satisfaction. "He's already signed up, so we must be doing something right. In any event, there's much to do at Camp Abnaki that doesn't involve the lake. I'm sure Petey would have an exciting, productive summer with us." She shrugged, turned one hand palm up. "As for his fear of water, well, we can hope he will learn to overcome it."

Hope. Was it really enough? Or was she fooling herself and harming her son in the process? Why had she been able to tell Gertrude Zinzendorf about Petey's fear when she couldn't pick up the phone and call Zachary Slater? Was it *her* fear blocking her? Was she afraid of losing control of her son?

Nonsense.

Did the fact she found Zachary attractive stop her?

Stupid. For all she knew, he could have a wife and twelve kids. And a mistress. And when had she admitted she found him attractive?

It didn't matter. The first and foremost concern of her life was her son. Petey came first.

Then what was the problem? Could it be the interview she'd conducted a few years ago with a female psychiatrist, who'd told her that save for a very few, all psychiatrists were crazy? But she would bet Zachary Slater was normal. While she was betting, she would also bet he was unattached.

She trusted her instincts.

Just like you trusted Roy? that annoying voice in her head asked.

Molly told herself to shut up. She had enough on her mind without dredging up old wounds. She thanked

WHERE'S MY BABY?

Gertrude Zinzendorf for her time, and surrendered her phone number at the older woman's gentle urging. Then she left, the brochure for Camp Abnaki held tightly in her hand.

Zachary was sweating, even though the temperature of the air in his office was comfortable. About ten minutes into the session and Irene was slipping easily backward. They had visited briefly at her fifth birthday party, more to orient him than for information, then gradually gone back in time, until Irene now reclined against the sofa, making wet-sounding baby noises. He was nervous, as he always was, poised on the brink of the unknown. Irene cooed, a sweet sound which elicited a smile from him, drawing forth as it did memories of the baby Lauren. If only he had known to grab those days, to hold on and never let go. If only ...

"Two AM? Already? Yes, I am coming. I shan't be late for matins."
"Irene?"

Snapped out of his reverie, Zachary sat forward, shoved the tape recorder closer to her.

"I know no one by that name."
"Who are you? What are you doing?"
"I am the prioress, and I have no time for idle talk ..."

Intrigued, Zachary waited, hopeful since she had already broken her silence. He wondered how she perceived him. Was he the voice of her conscience? He made a note to remind himself to ask Irene later.

"However ... you are not of us, so I see no harm in satisfying your curiosity. I must be about our nightly prayer. We have two new boarders this month, Isabella, daughter of our mighty baron, and Claire, wife to Sir Giles. Every effort must be extended toward them. 'Twould not do for me to be tardy."
"Why is that?"
" 'Tis obvious, I should think."
" 'Tis, I mean, it isn't obvious, at least not to me, my lady."
"I am the Prioress, or Abbess, if you will."
"And your given name?"

Zachary held his breath during a long pause. This woman was advanced in years, if her voice was an accurate gauge, and was in an obvious position of power. She wouldn't take kindly to impertinent questions. He thought he had lost her when she finally spoke again.

"Agnes. I am called Agnes of—"
"What? Agnes of what?"

No answer. Irene's eyelids flickered; her breathing was deep, slow, even. Zachary picked up her wrist, checked her pulse. It was steady. He waited, watching the seconds tick by on the clock he had placed for convenience sake on the coffee table. The seconds stretched to a minute, then two. When nothing had happened by the third minute, Zachary decided he had to intervene.

WHERE'S MY BABY? 103

"Irene, I want you to listen to me. I want you to travel, Irene. Come forward. Slowly. Slowly ..."

"My excuses. 'Tis pitch dark and we dare not burn more than a single candle. I could not locate where the chambress had situated my wimple. I am indeed going to be late. I am only thankful the bishop is not now gracing us with a visit."

"Agnes?"

"Of course."

Again the tart tone. Zachary bit back a smile. Agnes sounded like a tough cookie.

"I must hurry. This nunnery runs by my example, and the excuse of my illness will not be tolerated, least of all by me."

So she was ill. Perhaps that accounted for the hint of impatience in her voice. Surely a woman dedicated to the religious life would ordinarily be calm and accepting. Unfortunately, all he knew about that life he had gleaned from *The Song of Bernadette* and *The Nun's Story*, neither of which had told him very much. He asked whether her sisters would mind if she gave herself time to heal.

"There will be no healing."

"I am sorry you are so ill."

"I am dying. 'Tis most inconvenient."

Inconvenient? Zachary had dealt with death, the fear of it, the aftermath of it, even the anticipation of it, but never had he heard it described as "inconvenient." "Why is it so?"

Agnes continued almost absentmindedly.

"There is much to do to diminish our debt. I like it not to leave my sisters in such dire straits. It is true we have made a beginning with our school, but students come from the nobility, and great houses are scarce in these parts. Besides, boarders are hard to attract, and . . ."

"And . . . ?"

Nothing. He had lost her. He checked Irene's pulse again, was reassured. A glance at the clock told him she had been under for almost forty minutes now. Time to get her to come home.

"Irene, listen to me. You are going to travel again. Forward. Come forward—"

"Aiyeeeeeeeeeeee! Not now! 'Tis not the time!"

"Agnes?"

"I'm dying."

"I know. I'm sorry. Very sorry, Agnes, but you must let us go now."

"If only I had more time. Who will there be to protect her now?" Her voice faded, then came back stronger. " 'Tis said Rome is much more interesting a place than Jerusalem. She must go if she is summoned. Would that I were able to travel there, but of course, it is only for the chosen few. 'Tis one of my regrets . . . the other . . ."

"Perhaps you will get better and go there one day."

"Fool! Today is the date of my death."

Zachary couldn't resist trying to pinpoint Agnes's place in time.

"And what is that?"
"Are you so ignorant, or do you seek to distract me? Fie! It signifies not. I shall humor you. Why, we are at the midway mark of the century. Already we look forward, toward the fourteenth. But sadly, change comes creeping. It will not arrive in time."

Her voice faded. Zachary leaned close to Irene, saw her lips move, had to strain to hear.

"Who is there? Ah, here comes my sweet Claire. I shall give her my blessing. Perhaps it shall serve to cloak her for a time. Oh! She needs must hurry. It grows dark."

Silence. Zachary waited, one eye on the clock, hoping to get some clarification from Agnes, but knowing he should bring Irene back very soon. Still nothing. He decided to probe. "Agnes?"

Nothing. *It grows dark.* Chilling words.

With the trepidation he could never shake, despite the skill perfected during many sessions, he brought Irene slowly up out of the Middle Ages. He didn't permit muscles strained by tension to relax until she opened her eyes and he saw Irene Hall looking at him. "How do you feel?"

"I'm just fine." It was Irene's voice, yet he could hear an eerie echo of Agnes. She stretched, easing the muscles of her back, then tensed as memory rushed in. "It happened again, didn't it?"

"What do you remember?"

"I was Agnes," she said, "and I was dying." She coughed, leaned forward, clasping her hands together. "I'm very dry. Could I have something to drink?"

Zachary rang for Mrs. Sadecki and asked for a pot of coffee. Then he pulled over the pad on which he had taken notes. "Now, before you listen to the tape," he said, following a procedure he had instituted when he'd first begun investigating past lives, "tell me everything you remember."

It was a high all its own, traveling back in time, but it still wasn't enough. She needed Jack. Especially since it was 8:30 and dark as death outside and Douglas was late, as usual.

Where the hell was he?

She had traveled from the middle of the thirteenth century to the late twentieth in a little under an hour, and he couldn't make it from Manhattan to Rock Ridge in time for dinner.

Telling herself she didn't care, she went into the mud room and liberated Jack from the bottom of the strawberry jar in which she faithfully planted begonias every spring. Pink. White. Red. Beautiful.

So was the feeling Jack gave her.

She wandered into the kitchen, looked wistfully at the phone. Delia hadn't called again. She took a long, healing swallow, staring at the phone, *willing* it to ring. She wanted to tell her mother she had found Karen again.

Are you a religious person? Dr. Slater had asked. Irene had seen where he was headed, had disabused him of his false interpretation of the regression. The prioress—Agnes, what a graceless name—was not a repressed facet of her personality. He couldn't pin that one on her, and she had told him so in no uncertain words. She had been Agnes the Prioress in a previous life, and Karen . . .

Karen had been Claire. Poor wounded bird, seeking refuge in the nunnery while her husband Sir Giles followed some powerful baron or prince to the Holy Land on one of the popular Crusades. They had figured that out from the time frame and from Agnes's regret at not having seen Rome or Jerusalem. It was Claire who was to go. Summoned by Sir Giles, another male who did what he wanted when he wanted, without a thought for anyone save his precious self.

9:15. Where the hell was Douglas? Late was late, but this was ridiculous.

In a righteous frenzy, she stormed to the refrigerator, took out the plate with his dinner on it, let it drop on the floor, right in front of the door to the garage, where he'd be sure to see it the second he came home.

Too bad she couldn't tell Douglas about her regression to medieval times. Especially since she was pretty sure he had been the bishop, and from what Dr. Slater had told her about the proclivities of the male clergy of that time, Douglas the Tomcat was running true to form.

Ten

The view from the tower suite in the Chrysler Building was breathtaking, but Douglas Hall was oblivious as he stared out the Art Deco windows. He had to do something, but what? Irene was getting worse, and he had his meddling mother-in-law to thank for it. "Oh boy," he groaned, and dropped his head into his hands. He was getting as bad as Irene.

Delia was dead—dead and buried. Period.

It had been some crank who'd called, getting his or her jollies by torturing grieving relatives. It had to have been. That's what the police had said—"Change your number."

He hadn't needed them to tell him that. He had expected—what? That they kept a file on ghouls? That they would put in a call to some ghostbusters?

And suppose they could? It wouldn't make Irene better. She wouldn't let him have their number changed. There was no reasoning with her. Irene didn't *want* to get rid of Delia—Delia, who had talked of Karen.

Karen. Douglas clenched his teeth so hard his jaw ached. She had been a rare, beautiful creature who had brought joy and love to his life, but she was gone. Six years already; half her life.

But Delia said Karen was back.

"No! The dead don't come back!" he yelled, surprising himself and apparently his secretary, who opened the door and poked her head inside.

"Mr. Hall?"

"Sorry, Lorraine. Just thinking out loud." She stared at him piercingly, seeing the deep worry lines marring his handsome features, then nodded abruptly and started to withdraw. "Wait! I want—"

He drummed his fingers on his desk, thinking thoughts no sane or sober man should think. His brother-in-law Andrew had said something he couldn't get out of his head. He had called almost a week ago now, sounding apologetic, but Nancy was driving him crazy, and the engine driving her was Irene. Irene who had talked to her dead mother. Nancy wanted Irene to continue seeing Dr. Powell. Hell, so did he. They would get no argument from him on that. He had been about to hang up when Andrew had uttered the words that were haunting him.

Haunting ... how appropriate. Andrew hadn't meant anything. Not pragmatic, self-confident Andrew.

You saw Delia's body, Douglas. You identified her.

Had he? Of course he had. They had warned him she wasn't a pretty sight. He had taken one swift look and seen the pink-blond hair and said yes, that's Delia Clewett.

Rest in peace.

God alone knew she hadn't given him any. Alive—and now, dead.

He squeezed his eyes shut. He didn't *ever* want to remember what the rest of her had looked like.

Yes, Andrew, I identified Delia's body. She's dead, if that's what you were asking. Believe me.

"Mr. Hall? Are you all right?"

He opened his eyes. "Lorraine." He had forgotten her. "Yes. Thank you. I'm fine. Fine. Just fine." She looked doubtful, particularly when she noticed the new puffiness under his eyes. He fumbled in his pocket, withdrew a piece of paper. "We're, uh, missing some things around the house. My housekeeper made a list. Would you see if you can get them replaced? Especially the last item. My Aunt Margaret gave us that plate."

Lorraine quickly scanned the list, knowing at once Irene Hall was destroying things again. "No problem, Mr. Hall. I'll call Encore, Inc. They've been helpful in the past." Douglas winced and Lorraine bit her lip, but knew enough not to apologize. "Anything else?"

Douglas suddenly made up his mind. "Yes. Cancel my 2:30 appointment. I'm leaving and I won't be back."

Lorraine Fowling immediately looked concerned. Douglas's 2:30 meeting was with one of the agency's best accounts. Gently she reminded him. "That's the Perfect Puppy people."

Douglas shrugged. "I know. I've got something to do that can't wait." Not if he wanted to keep his sanity. "Ask them to reschedule at their convenience. After all, every dog has its day."

Miss Fowling looked blank. Douglas sighed and waved her out, immediately forgetting her, the Perfect Puppy people and their new campaign to reach what they called "yuppie puppies." His mind was made up. He was going to consult an expert. An expert on the dead.

WHERE'S MY BABY? 111

* * *

The secretary was apologetic. The medical examiner was on the phone and since he didn't have an appointment . . .

Douglas said he'd wait, although the place itself made his skin crawl and the memory of the last time he was here wasn't helping any. It was just a business office; he would think of it that way. Instead of processing tuna or puppy chow, they processed people. Dead people.

He shifted in the uncomfortable chair, trying to accommodate his trim five-nine frame. Perhaps he had better think of something else.

Good idea. Except that his mind immediately went to the night before. Quite a surprise Irene had had waiting on the kitchen floor. Stuffed veal, not one of his favorites. At least, not the way Irene prepared it. But then, he hadn't exactly married Irene for her culinary skills.

This line of thought was getting him nowhere. Irene needed help, and before he could give it to her, he had to satisfy himself. One little detail needed clearing up.

When finally he was admitted to the ME's office, he had to steel himself against the impulse to blurt out his question and have done with it. He had an idea the ME would understand. The man had probably had far worse to deal with in his lifetime, given his chosen profession.

Bernie Lufton rose from behind a no-nonsense steel desk and extended his hand. "Mr. Hall, what can I do for you?" Deep voice. Smoker-rough.

Douglas shook hands, took a seat in a straight-backed visitor chair, told the medical examiner he didn't mind if he smoked, all the while wondering what he was doing there. He got no help from the stacks of file folders on every flat surface, nor from the diplomas and faded photographs on the walls. He was also getting no help from Dr. Lufton, who seemed content to just sit, puffing on a noxious-smelling cigarette, and wait him out. In his business he was probably used to dealing with people who didn't talk.

That thought caused Douglas to squirm uncomfortably. He shouldn't be so squeamish. Death was ...

The end.

He hoped. At least, in this case.

The thought of Delia Clewett free to phone from the netherworld gave mobility to his tongue. In as pithy a statement as he could make, given the circumstances and his nervousness, he recited the facts as he knew them. Bernie Lufton listened courteously, nodding on occasion but not interrupting. As far as Douglas could tell, he didn't even press a hidden button to summon whatever aides came to escort the loonies away.

Silence descended after Douglas finished. Through the open door he could hear the sounds of people talking, the ring of a telephone. Just when he was beginning to think he had put the ME to sleep, he roused himself and leaned forward, pressed the intercom button.

"Rose, please bring in the Clewett file. That's Delia Clewett, with a W, if I remember right." He lifted an eyebrow. Douglas nodded. "Okay, Mr. Hall, while we're waiting, I think you've got two questions, or three, depending on how you want to look at it."

Douglas didn't want to look at it any which way, but he had started this and he was going to see it through. He wished it wasn't so warm, though. His head was beginning to spin.

"First," the ME said, holding up a nicotine-stained finger, "you want to know if we made a mistake."

Startled, Douglas sat forward, an inappropriate movement. "I—" he managed to say, only to be interrupted.

"Let me finish."

Douglas gingerly eased back into the chair. He took a deep breath and felt marginally better. "Sorry."

Dr. Lufton inclined his head. "Second, if we *did* make a mistake, is it possible Delia Clewett is still with us, to put it in the vernacular, which leads us to—oh, thanks Rose, that was quick."

"No problem, boss." The secretary gave Douglas a long look as she edged past.

"Third," Bernie Lufton went on, "the phone call. If we did indeed make an error, identified the wrong person, then the only thing that would preclude your mother-in-law's making a telephone call is if she didn't pay her bill. Those phone people are tough, let me tell you." He opened the file and looked down, then back up. "But we don't make mistakes, Mr. Hall. Not of that magnitude."

"I didn't—"

"Of course you didn't, but you're wondering, and who can blame you? Now, let's see. Delia Clewett, well-nourished Caucasian female, sixty-seven years old, height five feet two inches, weight one hundred twelve pounds, eyes blue, hair—pink?"

"Pink."

"Appendix scar, mole on left elbow, no other distinguishing marks. Shall I go on?"

"I never got past the pink," Douglas said, feeling decidedly sick. In these surroundings it was all rushing back. The shock of the accident, the trauma of seeing Delia in the morgue, the hysteria of the phone call . . .

"Sip this." A glass was shoved under Douglas's nose. He sipped, choked, then let the fiery liquid slide down his throat. "Rose!" a voice bellowed near his ear, and the next thing Douglas knew, someone had put something cool on the back of his neck and pushed his head down.

"Better?"

"Yes." He took a deep breath, cautiously raised his head. The room remained stationary. "Much better. Thank you."

" 'S okay." Rose handed him a glass and patted his shoulder. "Drink."

"I'm sorry," he said to both of them.

"Don't be." Lufton waved Rose out of the room. "You're not used to dealing with death. We are. Now, I think we have established that our identification was indeed correct, and you, in turn, buried the right person."

Douglas stared into the bottom of his glass. It was empty. Was this how easy it was for Irene?

"So, given that, we are left with the phone call on the night of Mrs. Clewett's funeral." Douglas didn't say anything. The ME shook out another cigarette and lit it. "There are a lot of nuts out there, Mr. Hall."

Douglas roused himself. "Don't I know it. That's the first thing I told Irene, but she's, well, been emotional ever since the death of our daughter, and—"

"Suggestible."

"Yeah. That too. She *wants* to believe this baloney."

"Does she drink? Take drugs?"

Douglas didn't fault him for asking. In his place he'd have made the same assumption. "She's an alcoholic, but she's under a psychiatrist's care. Has been for six years. I thought it was helping."

He got up, carefully placed the glass on the desk. There was nothing for him here, not that he had expected anything. At least now he could look Andrew straight in the eye and tell him he had identified the right woman. That was a relief. Self-consciously he fingered his tie, then held out his hand when the ME got up. "Thanks for your time."

"No problem." He let Douglas get to the door before he cleared his throat. "You know, there have been people, respectable people, some famous ones, as a matter of fact, who have sworn a relative or loved one has communicated after death. Usually it involves finding some important paper or item needed to settle the estate. Some say the deceased appears in a dream. Others . . ."

Douglas waited, knowing he wasn't going to like what was coming.

"Others say they've gotten phone calls. Phone calls from the dead."

Douglas drove straight home. Irene was out. He found the bottle of Jack Daniel's in the tank of the toilet in the guest powder room. What was sauce for the goose had damn well better be sauce for the gander.

Eleven

Molly loved Saturdays, and so far this particular Saturday was humming along. They were seated in one of Petey's favorite booths—a window one with a good view of the traffic on Northern Boulevard—in a diner that tolerated the eating habits of small boys. Petey, after much consultation with the waitress, had ordered silver-dollar pancakes, one of his all-time favorites, and had promptly drowned them in syrup. Molly thought her jeans were a bit too tight in the waist and had ordered a bran muffin and coffee.

Petey plied his fork and managed to engineer a small piece of pancake toward his mouth. At the last moment something on the street distracted him, the fork twisted, and the piece of syrup-soaked pancake landed with a plop on his official Mets sweatshirt.

"Petey."

He swiveled, looked at her, then followed her pointing finger until he noticed he wore a piece of his breakfast. With the aplomb of the very young or the truly messy, he scraped it off and shoved it in his mouth.

"Petey!"

"Did you see that car? The red one? I wonder if it

was a Corvette? Paulie's father drives a 'vette, did you know that?"

Molly didn't know and she didn't much care. Not about Paulie's father, and certainly not about the car he drove. What she did care about was the wistful note she thought she detected in her son's voice. Was it the car or that Paulie had a father? Hard to tell; impossible, if you were too much of a coward to ask.

"Did you?"

"Did I what, honey?"

"See it! It's this super-special sports car that's super cool and costs zillions of dollars and—"

"Zillions? Drink your milk, Petey."

"Yeah, and—Wow! Did you see that one?"

"Another Corvette?"

Petey gave her a look patented by the male human at the dawn of civilization. "Not hardly."

Molly tried not to smile. "Okay. Finish up. I want to show *you* something special. Remember we talked about you going to day camp? Well, I'd like to take a look at it today. Sort of get a feel for the place."

Petey let his fork drop into a puddle of syrup and pushed himself as far back in the booth as he could get. "When do I gotta go?"

"You don't *have* to go, Petey, you know that, and camp starts in the summer. July. Today nobody will be there, but we'll get to look at all the buildings and the fields where they play volleyball and soccer . . . and softball."

"Do they gotta choose you, like in Little League?"

"Yep. They gotta choose you. Drink your milk and we'll go take a look, okay?"

Gertrude Zinzendorf had given her good directions, and the map on the back of the brochure was explicit, leaving Molly free to ponder her use of blackmail to pique Petey's interest. After wrestling with her conscience she finally decided that any weapons a mother used were fair.

She turned down a little-traveled county road and made a left turn and then a right onto a narrow unpaved road to reach Camp Abnaki. A sign warned about private property and the sins of trespassing, but she had Gertrude's permission. She parked in front of a small building with a sign that said OFFICE. The air was chilly and slightly damp; the sky was gray and low, giving the place an abandoned air. Petey, never one to be overly affected by atmosphere, sidled close. She held out her hand. "Come on, Scout, let's go explore."

And explore they did, Molly following the map to the archery field, the arts-and-crafts building, the tennis courts, the basketball courts and, of course, the softball field. "How about that?" she asked. "Pretty nice, huh?"

Petey was trying to dig the toe of his sneaker into the hard earth. "I s'pose."

"You s'pose right."

She consulted the map. "Want to see where they play volleyball? I think it's over to the left somewhere." Right on the way to the lake. Casually she held out her hand. Petey put his small one trustingly in it; she felt like a Judas goat.

The volleyball court was right where it was supposed to be, but the trees that in summer must screen the lake did nothing to hide it in the third week in February. Petey took one look and froze. His hand jerked at hers, trying frantically to pull her back; big brown eyes looked up accusingly.

"No!"

"Petey . . ."

"No! No water. No!" With a wrench he broke free, went running.

Not surprised, but disturbed just the same, Molly went running after him.

Petey didn't forgive her, not even when she bought him a hot dog for lunch and didn't scold when a big glob of mustard dropped within an inch of the syrup stain. He was enjoying his sulking, and Molly let him be. She didn't really know what to say to him.

They were back on the road when inspiration struck. "How about a movie?" Immediately, she was rewarded with one of Petey's patented smiles.

"Popcorn?" he asked, ever the opportunist.

"Popcorn."

"With butter?"

Molly thought of the grease and chemicals and gave him a parental "we'll see." He accepted it with good grace; he was back to being Petey.

She drove to the nearest movie complex and was happy to see special Saturday matinees. "Look, Petey, they're showing *Pinocchio*. You remember, you liked the story. Want to see it?"

"Sure. Pinoke is oke," Petey said, and grinned.

The picture had been restored to its original magnificence and soon wove its magic. Petey sat quietly, munching popcorn, unmindful of the occasional greasy clump that landed in his lap. *You are what you eat,* Molly thought, and helped herself to a handful.

On the screen the little puppet wended his way through trials and tribulations with the charm that is the hallmark of Disney characters. Petey watched round-eyed as the Blue Fairy enchanted, laughed at the self-important bluster of Jiminy Cricket, cringed at the evil doings of Stromboli, the puppet master. "Don't tell lies,

Pinoke," he whispered, as the little puppet's nose grew long. When Pinocchio fell into company with Honest John and Gideon, and was carted off to Pleasure Island along with the foolish boy, Lampwick, Petey tugged on her sleeve.

She leaned down, whispered, "What is it, honey?"

"It's different. I don't remember this part."

"Shh. Just watch." Molly was caught up in the spell; she hadn't seen the movie since her own childhood.

"This wasn't in the book." This time Petey did nothing to modulate his voice. Several people turned; a grandmotherly matron put her finger to her lips and shushed him. He squirmed toward Molly, spilling popcorn. On the screen Pinocchio grew donkey ears and a tail.

Of course! She had forgotten Petey only knew the simplified version. No wonder this was unfamiliar; the version he knew had been edited to eliminate the more lurid adventures of the hapless puppet.

Suddenly memory jolted Molly. Wasn't this the part where . . .

It was. Too late. Molly took Petey's hand, squeezed reassuringly, whispered, "It's all right, honey, don't worry." On the screen Pinocchio and Jiminy Cricket jumped off one of Pleasure Island's cliffs into the water in a desperate bid to escape.

Petey jerked, slamming himself back into the seat. He had a death grip on Molly's hand. "Noooooo!"

"It's okay, honey. Pinocchio will be fine. Watch, you'll see." The grandmotherly matron glared at her.

"Nooooooo!" Petey screamed.

"Take him out," the grandmother hissed. "We're trying to watch the picture. He's disturbing everybody."

Molly gave her back her glare and then some, and

then forgot all about her as she struggled to help her son. Lifting Petey to her lap, she snuggled him against her warmth. His sturdy body was rigid. Gently she stroked his arm, whispered in his ear. "Trust Mommy, honey. Trust me. Just watch."

On the screen, things went from bad to worse. Pinocchio discovered Geppetto missing, learned he was inside the whale Monstro at the bottom of the sea.

Dear God, let me do the right thing! Molly prayed, torn between her gut desire to hustle Petey out of the theater post haste, and her reason, which argued that if he left, he would never learn not to run away. Besides, he wouldn't know firsthand that everything turned out all right.

You can't run from your problems, her mother always said. "Thanks, Mom," she mumbled under her breath, holding the stiff body of her son and remembering the way his father had hotfooted it out of their lives. *You should have told that to Roy.* Molly abruptly pushed her mother out of her mind, cringed inwardly when Pinocchio lay face down in a puddle of water.

"Drownded," Petey said, his voice filled with despair.

He might as well have said "I told you so"; Molly had no difficulty hearing the unspoken censure. "Just watch, Petey. Trust Mommy. Okay?"

He didn't answer. Why should he? He wasn't going anywhere unless she let him. He knew it and she knew it, so why bust your chops? Fervently, she prayed for the Blue Fairy. She didn't appear, but her voice came, after what seemed like an eon, praising the brave little puppet, making him a real little boy.

The lights came on and people began shuffling toward the aisle. Molly sat with Petey on her lap, uncaring of the dirty looks thrown her way as people were forced to climb over them. "See, Petey? Everything turned out all right. Pinocchio is okay. He didn't drown." She shifted him so she could look at his face. "Honey?"

Petey squirmed off her lap, stood white-faced in the sickly glow of the theater's yellowish lights, big brown eyes dominating his small face. He was breaking Molly's heart.

"Petey? Honey? It's a story. It's only make-believe." She bit her lip, hating herself for saying that, but she was desperate, and desperate mothers resort to desperate measures.

Tears welled, spilled over, ran down to splotch the already grimy sweatshirt. Fiercely, Molly hugged him, wishing to take the hurt out of him and into her. But they had removed the umbilical cord four and a half years ago, and osmosis didn't seem to be a real possibility at the moment. Petey was hurting and there seemed nothing she could do. "It's all right," she crooned. "It's all right."

Petey pulled from her grasp, looked at her with something akin to hatred in his eyes. "It isn't all right! It isn't! Pinoke was drownded. He was! He was! I saw it!"

"But the Blue Fairy made him real, Petey. You saw that, too."

"That was the make-believe part," Petey said, with the unswerving logic of a four-and-a-half-year-old.

Molly had nothing more to say. Petey was no longer breaking her heart; he had broken it, shattered it into a million little pieces.

No question this time. First thing Monday morning, Molly picked up the phone and punched Zachary's number. It was a relief to be actually doing it; it had been a struggle not to call the second she got Petey home Saturday. Sunday didn't even bear thinking about.

"Dr. Slater."

Deep and calm, the voice was—to Molly's ears—immensely reassuring. Her port in the storm. Wrong analogy. Port. Storm. Water.

Water is the problem. The enemy. Petey's enemy.

Molly took a deep breath, gave her name.

"Why, hello." He sounded surprised—and pleased.

Molly was too keyed up to pay close attention to nuances, or to follow social niceties. She plunged right in. "I—" She swallowed, tried again. "I, ah, was wondering. . . . That is, a friend gave me your number and I, ah—"

"Molly. Take a deep breath and tell me what the problem is."

She could do that. She did.

He listened; he was good at it. Very good. But he didn't handle children. Hadn't her friend told her?

No.

He could recommend someone, someone he knew personally, someone who was marvelous with children.

No. She trusted him.

He picked up his appointment book. He had a class at eleven; Irene Hall at two. "I can't—"

"Please. Dr. Slater—Zachary—I need help."

"It's okay, Molly. I'm going to help you. Help Petey, that is. What I started to say is, I can't see him until later today. Would three be okay?"

It would be perfect. Molly felt better already. She wasn't quite so alone anymore.

* * *

"No needles."

Zachary looked deep into Petey's solemn brown eyes and held up his hand scout-fashion. "No needles."

"No needles never."

"Petey," Molly chided softly, "Dr. Slater can't be expected to promise that. I thought we discussed this."

Petey didn't so much as flick his eyes in her direction. His gaze remained glued to Zachary. "No needles never," he repeated stubbornly.

Zachary hunkered down. "Never is a very long time, Petey. Perhaps we could compromise." Petey looked uncertain for an instant, long enough for Zachary to seize the slight advantage. "Do you know what compromise means?"

Petey shook his head, and using both his heels for purchase, hiked his body deeper into the cushions of the leather sofa.

"Careful," Molly cautioned. She threw Zachary an apologetic look.

"Don't worry, it's only a couch." He spared a few seconds to smile reassuringly at her, sensing she was as nervous as her son, if not more so.

Petey's right leg began restlessly drumming, driving his shoe into the leather with each stroke. Molly reached over and gently stilled the leg. "I'm sorry," she said to Zachary. "He seems to have forgotten proper behavior."

Petey angled his chin obstinately and glared at Zachary. "What's this 'compromise'?" he demanded belligerently, his tone making it very clear he wasn't going to like it.

"Petey! Have you forgotten all your manners?"

"It's all right. This is a special situation," Zachary said, without taking his eyes from Petey. He liked what he saw: Peter Deere, only four and a half, and scared, looked him straight in the eye. Such courage was rare and deserved nothing but honesty. "Okay, Petey, here's what compromise means," he began, and spoke frankly to the little boy.

Molly retreated as far as she could without actually moving away, sensing how important it was Zachary establish rapport with her son. Zachary might protest he didn't work with children, but he had a relaxed approach that seemed to be just what Petey needed. After some give and take—with Petey upholding his end of the bargaining—Zachary rose and held out his hand. Petey put his much smaller one trustingly into it. They were going for a walk, Zachary told Molly—males only. They had some points to iron out. Molly made no protest, smiled when she heard her son say, "Okay, if never's too long, then how about—" as the door closed. Petey, for all his tender years, could drive a hard bargain.

An hour and a half later, Petey was in the kitchen, making Mrs. Sadecki's acquaintance and sampling her just-baked brownies. In the office, Molly sipped hot tea as Zachary told her there was nothing fundamentally wrong with her son, at least that he could tell. If Molly agreed, Petey would be desensitized and in time his fear of water would fade.

"Will it work?"

"I can't promise he'll be another Mark Spitz or Greg Louganis," Zachary joked, "but he'll face the water without a qualm." He saw how apprehensive she still was, and he instantly explained. "Desensitization is the treatment of choice. There's no reason to believe it won't work. I can refer you to a child psychiatrist. He's tops in his field."

"No, Zachary, if you're willing, I want you."

"But . . . ?"

"There is no but."

"Tell me another one."

Molly laughed, a bit nervously, then admitted her neighbor believed Petey's fear of water was caused by a calamity in a past life. Zachary didn't laugh. Molly tensed. "Do you think he should be regressed?"

"He wouldn't have far to go." She looked stricken; he immediately sobered. "No, Molly, I don't think Petey's aversion to water is anything more than a normal phase of childhood. It would probably pass without any interference, but since you're so worried, we'll give desensitization a shot. Want me to call my friend?"

"No. Petey likes you. He doesn't trust everyone, but from what I could see, you two hit it off."

"He's a great guy."

"Then it's settled. When do you want to see us again?"

Zachary had to stifle the urge to ask her what they were doing for dinner. As he would with Petey, he would go slowly with his mother.

Twelve

April

"Everywhere I look there's nothing but mud. Mud and empty buildings. Twenty-five saloons we had, not so long ago. Now, well, you can see. Eight left, and I hear three're packin' up. I don't see no way for me to stay. Much as this here place's been good to me, it's time to leave."

The low voice sounded grumpy but resigned. Zachary moved the tape recorder closer to Irene.

"Where will you go?"
"I got no choice if I wanna live. I'll jist load the Cyprian Sisters—"
"Cyprian Sisters?"
"My girls."
"Your daughters?"
"Hell, no! They ain't no kin o' mine. Daughters! Now ain't that rich! They be whores, is what they be. I was jist bein' polite."
"Thank you, Miss . . . ?"

"Madame Sophia. Known throughout the territory. You won't find a harder workin' soul this side o' the River Jordan. Now, I been telling you as how I'm gonna put my girls into wagons again and follow them miners to the next hellhole, and when the mines thereabout play out, I'll go to the next. This ain't the best way to make a livin', but it's what I got. Although . . ." A smug smile spread over her face.

"Although?" Zachary prompted.

"I ain't tellin'."

"I won't tell anyone."

"Mightn't come true if I tell."

"Okay, don't tell me." Zachary grinned when she rushed into speech.

"A certain gentleman has shown an interest. He ain't made no commitment, now, mind you, but he's been hintin'. Says he don't care none what I done to survive. A body's got to do what it takes to keep flesh on the bone, he says. He be more interested in what he calls my 'business savvy.' I don't mind tellin' you, I won't be sorry to be shut of this life. He's talkin' about openin' a big hotel, build it of brick, so's it don't burn easy. He says my skills in runnin' a house'll come in right handy. He don't even mind if Sally comes along, long as she don't entertain men no more."

Zachary pulled a notepad forward and wrote:

Sally = Karen?

Madame Sophia went on talking; she was a loquacious lady.

WHERE'S MY BABY? 129

When Irene was awake they went over the session as they always did. She fidgeted, pulled at the pleats on the skirt of her pale yellow linen suit, and finally paced the room. At the point in the tape when she first mentioned the girl Sally, Zachary pushed the stop button and asked if Sally was Karen.

Irene was outraged: Karen would never—ever—be a whore. Not ever. Not Karen.

She was so agitated, Zachary couldn't calm her, could only stand by helpless as she stormed out.

The sound of the front door slamming brought Mrs. Sadecki out of the kitchen. Zachary was standing in the hall, a troubled expression on his face. Hand on cheek, Mrs. Sadecki wagged her head. "That poor missus. You ask me, something big is bothering her."

Zachary couldn't agree more. He only wished he knew what it was.

By the time Molly finally found the address on Eastern Parkway—she always got lost in Brooklyn—a large crowd swelled over the sidewalk into the street in front of a six-story red-brick apartment building. She double-parked half a block away, blocking a police car parked in front of a hydrant.

The crowd was mostly white males—dressed in black, as was the custom of the Hasidim—and it didn't take a genius to know its mood was very angry. A young woman had been yanked from her car at gunpoint in broad daylight. Carjackers, despite tough new federal laws, were becoming ever more brazen.

Molly skirted the edge of the crowd to reach the press area. Just in time. Flashbulbs popped and cameras whirred as the mayor, flanked by high-ranking police brass, moved to a bank of microphones. Once there, the policemen shifted to stand behind the mayor. He was on his own.

The symbolism wasn't lost on the crowd. A low-voiced muttering rippled outward, gaining in volume as it reached the fringes. Someone shouted for action; the streets were not safe. The crowd roared.

The mayor held up his hands, waited for them to settle, then gave a speech calculated to calm. It failed. The Chief of Detectives fared no better. What consolation was "doing everything possible" when a loved one was at risk every time she got behind the wheel? Angry mutterings at officialdom's attempts at palliation led to a call for civilian patrols.

"How about racial tension?" Kent asked, when Molly called in the story.

"There is none. The carjacker wore a mask."

"What? No racial tension in Crown Heights? What do you think the mayor and the big brass from the PD came hotfooting it to the boonies for? Come on, cookie, do your job. There's gotta be something. Dig a little."

When she burst out of Zachary's town house, Irene half-walked, half-ran, unaware of her surroundings, until a stitch in her left side forced her to stop. Panting, holding her hand pressed tightly against her ribs beneath her wildly beating heart, she leaned against a building and took stock. Madison Avenue, three blocks from 42nd Street.

Douglas's office was in the Chrysler Building, on Lexington. She could go there, let him take her to lunch.

No way. Douglas would see she was upset and guess it had something to do with Karen, and nothing turned

WHERE'S MY BABY? 131

him off faster. He didn't believe. He'd be sorry. Once she had Karen again, she'd ... Irene moaned softly, catching the attention of an elderly woman who stopped and asked if she was all right.

All right? God, that was a laugh. How could she be all right when her mother hadn't called with news of Karen in weeks? Everything was hopeless. The sun shone out of a clear sky, yet everywhere she looked she saw only gray.

"There's a coffee shop near here. You could sit down, get some water."

Water. Another laugh. She needed Mr. Daniel, that's what she needed. She needed him sliding down her throat, swimming into her bloodstream, clouding her mind.

"I'll help you there if you want." The elderly passerby was still standing there, an anxious expression on her face.

Irene pushed away from the building, stood up straight. Her side no longer pinched. "Uh, no thanks. I'm fine."

And she was. She had suddenly remembered the bar on the upper level of Grand Central Station. She didn't have to wait until she was home in Connecticut to commune with Mr. Daniel.

Zachary took one look at Molly's strained face and asked Petey if he would like a snack before they started. Petey was only too happy to race down the hall to the kitchen, well aware Mrs. Sadecki could be counted on for something delicious.

Molly sank down into the comfortable cushions of the couch.

"Hard day?" Zachary asked.

Molly shrugged, couldn't stifle the sigh that forced its way out of her. "Aren't they all?"

"As bad as that, hey?" Zachary sat on the couch, but far enough from Molly so they weren't touching. "Tell me."

"It's nothing. Nothing that doesn't go with the territory." She combed her fingers through her hair, laughed shakily. "There's never any *good* news."

"Never? Remember what I told Petey? Never's a very long time."

"Yeah. You're right. Never say never, but ... sometimes I worry I'll get so used to the bad things—the truly terrible things people do—that I'll become *inured* to them, lose my humanity." Like Kent. Kent, whose sensitivity index hovered in the minus range.

She looked so concerned that Zachary started to reach for her, ready to tell her that anyone who worried the way she did was a long way from losing touch with her humanity, when the phone rang. He recognized the caller immediately; sadness overcame him when he realized she was drunk.

Liquor had loosened Irene's inhibitions. She reiterated that Karen—*her* Karen, a soul so pure she had been an angel on earth—could *never,* never *ever* have been what he had suggested.

There's that word never *again,* Zachary thought. He knew any attempt to reason with her in her condition would be futile. "Are you alone?"

"Of course I'm alone. I'm always fucking alone. That's the whole fucking problem."

"Let me call someone. Your husband—"

"No! Don't you dare interfere. You don't understand. No one does. I never want to see you again. Never! I won't listen to anyone who believes Karen was a ... was a whore." She started to sob and slammed down the phone.

Zachary stared at the receiver for long moments, feeling Irene's pain. Apparently she had failed to find whatever solace she had sought with him.

A hand touched his arm. He turned to find Molly looking at him with concern in her eyes. "A problem?"

"It goes with the territory," he replied, and they both laughed. It felt good to share with someone again.

Shouts of childish laughter came from the kitchen. A beautiful sound. Impulsively he blurted an idea he had been hopefully entertaining. "I've got a house on Fire Island," he said, watched with dismay as Molly's hand fell from his sleeve and her eyes lost their warmth, took on an impersonal glaze. "No. It's not what you're thinking. I take Lauren out for weekends, starting in May, if it's warm enough. I thought ... that is, maybe ... you and Petey would like it. How about Memorial Day weekend? Mrs. Sadecki will be there, if you're wondering ..."

Molly was, he could see it written on her face. "It would be a good test for Petey, the ferry ride and being near the ocean. And ..." Honesty compelled him to say everything on his mind. "I'd like the children to get to know each other better. What do you think? You don't have to give me an answer right now. Please, won't you think about it?"

Molly said she would.

Harry finished making a backup of his personal files and locked the floppy disks into the bottom drawer of his desk. That done, he pushed his chair back, put his feet up on top of the desk, crossed his hands over his middle, and stared off into space.

The warehouse hulked silent and dark around him. The lamp on his desk isolated him in a pool of yellow incandescent light, an island surrounded by a near-complete blackness since there were no windows to admit light, even if the streetlight outside had been working. Two skylights begrimed with years of soot were positioned over the warehouse proper, where row upon row of pallets held his inventory. So effectively did they filter sunlight and moonlight, the overhead fluorescents were kept on all day.

His thoughts were as gloomy as his surroundings. Business had fallen off. He had to do something. Harry Kemp was a survivor. No soft economy was going to best *him.*

You'll never amount to anything, Harry, you mark my words, Harry, you're a good-for-nothing, Harry, just see if I'm not right, Harry.

Harry's feet came off the desk and hit the floor so hard his soles tingled from the blow. He swiveled his chair until he faced the computer, hit the keys, invoking his password, the sound loud, chirpy like a chicken, in the stillness. He scrolled the file, stopped briefly at two entries. One was surefire; the other was best left alone. He closed the file, opened another, studied the neat rows of numbers.

He needed the money.

Harry picked up the phone. The conversation was short and sweet. He stared off into the darkness, knew it wasn't enough. He would have to pull more than one job.

The jobs would be too close together.

The risk was too high.

His index finger tapped the screen. Something wasn't kosher. He could feel it.

He needed the money.

You'll always be a bum, Harry, it's plain to see, Harry, don't come asking me for money someday, Harry.

Sweat beaded his forehead. Damn bitch. When would he ever be rid of her?

One more call.

The slurred voice answered in the middle of the fourth ring. "Whaaa?"

Harry crinkled the plastic bag he used for an otherworldly effect, whispered eerily.

A gasp, then a strangled "Mama!"

"Listen," Harry crooned. "Listen."

Thirteen

Move!
Now!
Run! Faster! Faster!

She wasn't going to make it. She *knew* she wasn't going to make it. Doggedly she slogged through the sand.

Faster!

She couldn't breathe, couldn't suck enough oxygen into her starved lungs. Mustn't stop. Mustn't.

Climb. Desperately she grabbed at the sparse vegetation, pulled herself up inch by slow inch. The sand gave no purchase, fought her for space. A mighty roaring, rushing sound filled the air, freezing the blood in her veins, weakening her with fear. *Climb!*

Too late. She wasn't going to make it, was going to die. It was almost upon her, it was . . .

Towering over her, an immense wall of greenish-black water. She screamed, loud and hard, the sound mingling with the elemental screaming of the sea.

Molly abruptly awoke, heart racing, skin clammy with fear.

The dream had come and gone. Again.

* * *

"Maybe you died on Krakatoa." Denise pushed her glasses up and reached for another piece of cinnamon-raisin toast. "You know. In the tidal wave. Thousands of people drowned."

"How lovely." Molly sipped coffee as she peered out of the window over the sink. Petey was happily kicking his soccer ball around the yard.

"You should ask your doctor friend."

"Mmm."

"He could regress you, find out why you keep having that awful dream."

"One patient per family is enough."

Molly couldn't have given Denise a better opening. "So who said you have to be his patient? You're seeing him, aren't you?" Molly didn't answer, so Denise did it for her. "Of course you are. You've got a date tonight."

"It's hardly a date."

"Is Petey going?" Denise licked butter off her fingertips. "Of course not. This is different. He wants to see you without the children."

Molly couldn't argue. Zachary had said much the same when he'd suggested they go out for the evening. After spending several Saturday and Sunday afternoons at zoos and museums—and just lately, the aquarium, a test for Petey—Zachary had asked to see her alone.

"Tell him about the dream. He'll be fascinated."

"Who wants to talk shop on a date?" A mistake, Molly knew, turning to see the sudden gleam in Denise's eyes. "Forget it."

"Tell him when you're at Fire Island. Surely you can find the right time then."

"Who said we're going?"

"You're going," Denise said, just as the phone rang. "That's probably him. Go on, tell him."

"You're impossible," Molly said, and picked up the phone. The voice of a mature female asked for Molly Deere. "Speaking."

"I thought it was you," Gertrude Zinzendorf replied, after identifying herself. "It bothered me for weeks, and then one day I was listening to the radio and I knew."

"Tell him," Denise whispered.

Molly pleaded guilty to being on the radio and excused herself, covered the phone, and hissed at her friend, "It's not him."

"Too bad." She collected her oversized tote and got up. "I've got to run. What time do you want Sandy?"

"Seven-thirty."

Denise took off her glasses and pointed them at Molly. "Good. Better to tell him in person. Do it tonight."

The door closed with a sharp click. Molly sighed loudly and went back to the phone. "Sorry."

"No problem," Gertrude replied. "I just wanted to touch base with you. I want you to understand, I'm not pressuring you. I didn't want our enrollment to close without warning you. I feel Petey would benefit from a summer at Camp Abnaki."

Molly did, too, but she didn't feel she could make the commitment. Petey was making progress with Zachary, but he hadn't been severely tested yet.

Fire Island would present the perfect opportunity. Molly told Gertrude she would get back to her.

With one eye on the clock, Molly pawed through the drawer where she kept her lingerie, searching for a pair of white pantyhose. More particularly, a pair without a run. She needed to straighten the drawer and replenish her stock. She'd put it on her organization chart, just as soon as she got around to making it.

"Aha!" She pounced on an unopened package, and quickly but carefully wriggled into the pantyhose. She was late, but so was Zachary, and for one moment she wondered if he was going to stand her up. It wouldn't matter, this wasn't really a date. That's what she had told Denise and she believed it . . . but she got a queer sinking sensation in her stomach when she thought of him not showing.

"So don't think," she admonished herself, and slipped into a flared skirt and a cotton sweater in a bold geometric design.

A rap sounded on her partially closed door. "Molly?"

"Come on in, Sandy."

The teenager opened the door wide and promptly slouched against it. She looked at Molly admiringly. "Hey, neat. What're you going to wear with it?"

Molly held up two different earrings. "Which?"

Sandy tilted her head, eyes narrowed. This was her area of expertise, if Denise was to be believed. She once told Molly that Sandy could spend hours deciding on the appropriate accessories.

Molly jiggled the earrings. "I'm late."

"So's he. Maybe he's had an accident," she said, with the callowness that seemed to come naturally to the young. Mortality only applied to those over thirty.

Molly again experienced that queer sinking sensation in her stomach. This time it had more bite. She didn't like to think of Zachary hurt. "I'm sure he's just caught in traffic." That ought to propitiate the gods of chance and highways both.

"Um," Sandy said. "Haven't you got bigger ones? Like the kind that dangle from hoops?"

"This is it. Choose."

Sandy recognized the tone. She chose, although her expression clearly stated what she thought of the choices. Molly hurriedly put them on, then started rummaging in the bottom of her closet, looking for her favorite pair of low-heeled pumps. She really ought to clean the closet.

"Whaddidya say?"

Molly hadn't realized she'd said it aloud. "Nothing important. Did you want something, Sandy?"

"Oh, yeah. Petey wants to watch a movie. Okay?"

"Sure. Just as long as you don't keep him up too late."

"Yo," Sandy said, and disappeared.

Molly found the shoes and then had to search for her small leather purse. A glance at the clock had her frowning. Zachary was almost half an hour late. More out of habit than real worry, she switched on the radio she kept on her bedside table. Only a minute to the traffic report, and . . .

WAND's three-note signal for a breaking story blared out. *"We now have a live report from WAND reporter Eleanor Perez, on the scene where a three-year-old child has disappeared from a street fair in the Bronx."* Molly sat down on the edge of her bed. *"Although unwilling to label it a kidnapping yet, police here have called the disappearance of three-year-old Mary Ann Szell suspicious. It was several hours ago when the little girl's mother, Helen, noticed her missing."*

The static of an open line stuttered from the radio. Molly, who didn't envy Eleanor the story the least little bit, knew she had grabbed one of the principal players

WHERE'S MY BABY? 141

for an interview, probably the mother. *"I just turned around to pay for the food. She was right by my side. I swear I wasn't turned around for more than a few seconds and she was gone. Just like that. Gone."* Helen Szell's anguish came through loud and clear. She was living every mother's nightmare.

"Molly! Doorbell," Sandy called from downstairs. "Want me to get it?"

Molly turned off the radio, scooped up her jacket and purse, and headed for the stairs. "Thanks, I'll—" she started to say when Petey screamed. In the four-and-a-half years since his birth, Molly had heard all the sounds her son could make. Or thought she had. This wasn't the funny-sounding whoop he made just before he threw up, nor the agonized wail that signaled some bodily injury, nor the other thousand or so sounds she was familiar with. This was something new, something that froze the blood in her veins, something she could have happily lived her life without hearing. It was, in the vernacular, a scream from hell.

She must have flown down the stairs, for suddenly she was at the bottom, barely missing a collision with Sandy, who stood there, eyes wide, her upper body swaying, as if her feet were nailed to the floor.

The doorbell was ringing constantly and someone—presumably Zachary—was banging on the front door.

"Open it," Molly shrieked, as she rushed past Sandy. Only a couple of steps to the living room, but she thought it took an eternity to get there. The television was on—a familiar-sounding movie theme was escalating in volume—and Petey . . .

Petey was pressed back into the couch, sturdy body rigid, thick-lashed brown eyes wide and glassy with shock.

"Petey, honey," she whispered, and started to move toward him.

Someone put a hand on her shoulder, gently staying her. "Let me."

Molly jerked her eyes from her son to Zachary's face. He looked calm and capable. But she had never before abdicated her responsibility. She didn't know if she was capable of doing it now.

Zachary seemingly had no trouble reading her mind. "Trust me," he said, and when she swallowed, then nodded once, tightly, started to move toward the petrified little boy. "You," he said to Sandy, who had come into the room with him, "turn that thing off."

Only then did Molly identify the movie. "Good grief," she whispered.

Jaws.

Rolla, Missouri

After two days of hard driving, Harry knew he had to take a break or go crazy. The baby had wailed nonstop for most of the first day, and now lay limply, hiccuping her distress. She was noisy and messy and a whole lot of trouble. Harry couldn't figure out why anyone would want so much trouble, but want it they did, to the tune of twenty thousand dollars.

A lot of money, but he was earning it. The hard way.

As much as it was, it wasn't enough. There was a certain life style to which he was addicted, and he couldn't exactly invest his money and watch it grow. Not the way the IRS examined cash deposits in excess of ten thousand. Not that interest rates were exactly high. But low as they were, they still were a whole lot better than nothing.

You're a bum, Harry, you'll never be anybody, Harry, you'll wind up with nothing, Harry, mark my words, Harry.

"Shut up, bitch!" The words exploded from him, startling him as much as the baby, who started to wail again. "Shut up," Harry yelled. "Shut up, God damn it!"

The baby opened her mouth wider, showing a lot of pink gum and pretty white baby teeth, and began to wail even louder. He jiggled her arm. "Shush, baby. Shush."

To his surprise, she stopped. He patted her round little tummy. She burped. "Good girl. Very good girl." She closed her eyes and fell asleep, with the suddenness common to exhausted infants. Pleased, Harry drove until he saw a low-end chain motel. He needed food and sleep, and he needed to make some calls.

An hour later he sat staring at the telephone. The room was blessedly quiet, save for the hiss of the air-conditioner and the occasional baby snore that came from the other bed. Harry had cared for her as he would for any valuable investment. He had bathed her, fed her, watched her drop back to sleep.

Now he had to attend to business. Future business.

But the broad in Connecticut gave him an antsy feeling. No matter she was his best bet for another score.

He didn't like it. No way. No how. No sirree.

But . . .

These things took time. You didn't just pick up the phone and tell someone their dead kid was back, available for a fee. No way. He invested time and patience in every deal. You had to prepare the field, plant the idea, nurture it, chivvy them along when they appeared to balk.

It wasn't easy. He had been calling the broad since her old lady bit the dust, back in February. He had let her stew and worry and get so anxious she was almost foaming at the mouth. He could hear it in her voice.

But . . .

She was trouble.

He had also heard that, if he cared to listen.

"Shit," Harry said, and picked up the phone. He started talking the minute he heard her voice. "Hello, Irene. This is the major. Delia contacted me, and . . ."

At last! Walking quietly—because for once Douglas was home, watching a baseball game in the den—Irene went to where Mr. Daniel waited in the umbrella stand by the front door. With her buddy pressed tightly to her thin bosom, she hurried into the kitchen, got a glass and ice, and after the first deep swallow, turned on the small transistor radio she kept on the windowsill above the sink.

The major had said to listen to the news. She'd find something of interest, something that proved he could deliver. Fumbling a bit, she managed to tune to WAND, then stood, eyes closed, drinking and listening.

"Still no word on the whereabouts of Mary Ann Szell, the three-year-old girl kidnapped Saturday afternoon from a street fair in the Bronx. Police are investigating . . ."

Irene knew instantly. The major had taken that little girl. Taken her to return her to her rightful parents.

Irene's pulse accelerated. *Karen's next,* he had said.

Irene raised the glass, hesitated when she felt the familiar smoothness touch her lips.

Slowly she lowered it.
Karen was coming home.
Irene poured good old Jack down the drain.

Fourteen

May

The corridor of the Brooklyn courthouse was packed with members of the press. On alert for hours, anticipating word from the grand jury, they felt their patience wearing thin. Molly didn't imagine that the five men whose fates hung in the balance would sympathize, but then they weren't getting much sympathy from the press. They had been charged with being members of a ring operating in Queens and Brooklyn, and indictments for the carjacking incident in Crown Heights in April, among others, were expected.

"Come on," Molly muttered under her breath. Sometimes it seemed as if she spent the better part of her life waiting in places like this. The corridor was dim; every other light fixture was out. Either the city was saving on electricity again or they didn't have the money for light bulbs. Flip a coin.

"God, it's hot in here," she complained, waving her hand in front of her face in a futile attempt to stir the air.

"It's the humidity," Charlie Lee said, his broad face glistening with sweat.

"I don't care what it is. I want out of here." She glanced at her watch. "That can't be the time. What on earth is taking so long?"

"Come on, Molly–Uh-Oh. You know how these grand juries are, and this case is hot. They want to make sure they get it right."

"Come on, yourself, Charlie. You know if the DA wants a ham sandwich indicted, he'll get a ham sandwich indicted."

"My, my, when did we get so cynical?" When they both glared at him, Lloyd C. Cranshaw held up his hands in mock horror. "Sorry, children."

"Go check your makeup," Charlie growled. "It looks like it's running."

Molly watched Lloyd head for the nearest reflective surface at a fast clip. "That wasn't nice."

"It was effective and that's all that counts. That man gets on my nerves. He'd bother you, too, if you had to be around him all day."

"I've got Kent," Molly reminded him.

"Yeah." Charlie knew it was no contest between Lloyd and Kent. "But you don't have to look at him." Molly rolled her eyes and laughed. "That's better. I thought you forgot how."

"Just a bad patch, is all."

"Petey?"

Molly shrugged. Zachary had tried to reassure her Petey hadn't backslid too far. His argument that great white sharks scared many people—and the movie monster was designed to do just that—certainly had merit. But Petey hadn't been scared ... he had been terrified, had been as close to catatonic as she ever wanted to see him. If Zachary hadn't been there she didn't know if she'd have been able to deal with it, and *that* scared her.

"Molly?"

"Zachary's invited us to Fire Island for the Memorial Day weekend. He thinks it'll be a good test for Petey."

"He's the doc." Charlie squinted at Molly as a slow grin curved his lips. "Do I detect a blush? Can it be this problem goes beyond Petey?"

"It's hot in here."

"Not that hot. Why don't you face up to it, Molly–Uh-Oh? The good doctor turns you on. You're human after all. Go away with him. It'll do you and Petey some good."

A stir in the crowd saved Molly from a reply. The doors to the Grand Jury room opened and the DA emerged, a smile creasing his face. Reporters surged forward, waved microphones in his face. The temperature in the corridor went up a few degrees under the hot TV lights. Molly got what she needed and quickly ran outside to get reaction from the crowd that had been steadily building during the morning. People were angry, which always made for a good spot.

Predictably, Kent was happy with the most outrageous interview. "We'll have to bleep the expletives, which is a pain in the ass, ha ha, but all in all you did good, cookie." Molly made a noncommittal sound. "Real good."

"Where to now, Kent?" The next high-profile trial, a dentist accused of sexually molesting six of his patients, was scheduled for the end of the week.

"Midtown, cookie. One of our state senators is holding a press conference in an hour." He gave her the address.

"What's the word on it?"

"His problem's gotten out of hand. He's probably going to sign himself into a detox center."

Molly shuddered at the gleeful note in Kent's voice. The man was like a vulture, feeding on the misery of others. If you challenged him, he would say it was all for the job, but she wondered. He didn't have to enjoy it so much.

Her Taurus was a haven of cool air after the closeness of the courthouse. Traffic was the usual mess. Halfway across the Manhattan Bridge, Molly made a decision. She called Gertrude Zinzendorf on her cellular phone and enrolled Petey in Camp Abnaki. A positive step; it made her feel good. She trusted Zachary; if he said Petey was making progress—great white sharks notwithstanding—then she would believe him. After all, he was ...

She was heading north on the FDR Drive before she admitted to herself just what Zachary was, and before she could change her mind or lose her nerve, she reached for the phone again. This time she punched Zachary's number, and when he answered, she told him they would be happy to spend the Memorial Day weekend at Fire Island.

"I'm glad," he said. "Very glad."

Deep and warm, his voice made Molly shiver.

Irene arrived home exhausted, but it was a good exhaustion because she had accomplished a lot, visiting the bank and the lawyer handling her mother's estate. After talking with the major, she had known what she had to do, and all of it had to be done alone, because Douglas didn't believe and therefore couldn't be told.

He would have to be left behind.

Irene took a long cooling shower and thought about life without Douglas. She would miss him, she supposed, but it didn't give her a wrenching sense of loss in her gut.

Not like the one she had had when she'd lost Karen. She couldn't wait; she missed Karen so. Even those sessions with Dr. Slater had been better than nothing. They had given her hope while she was waiting, and now ... maybe she should go back to him? The major had said it could take a while for Karen to return, and she was so lonely.

She mulled over the idea while she blew her hair dry. Why not? She would tell him, though, that she wouldn't countenance another session like the last. Her Karen would never have been a ... she wouldn't even think the word.

Yes, it was a good idea. She'd call Dr. Slater first thing tomorrow.

Suddenly hungry, a glance at the clock told her Douglas was late again. Big surprise. Probably humping his latest conquest. She was welcome to him, whoever she was.

The kitchen was too quiet. Irene put on the radio, listened to an update on the disappearance of Mary Ann Szell. She hoped the little girl was back with her rightful parents by now.

How did the major know who they were? The question plagued her, and no matter how often she told herself not to worry, he knew what he was doing, she found herself coming back to it. What if he got her the wrong child? She'd know at once, of course. She'd know Karen in any form or guise. Hadn't she picked her out immediately in every past life?

God, she couldn't do this alone. She needed her buddy. Jack always soothed, made things clear. Just one drink. One little.... She reached for the phone almost absentmindedly, then stiffened when she heard her mother's voice. *"Karen's with the doctor. He's got her now. Look for her there."*

Delia had answered her prayers. She should have known her mother wouldn't let her down.

Amarillo, Texas

Harry pulled his Dodge Diplomat into the parking lot of a convenience store on the outskirts of Amarillo and staggered out of the driver's seat. Sore and stiff from driving, he was pushing it because he couldn't wait to get rid of the little girl.

Her fretful wailing followed him out into the Panhandle night, an unnecessary reminder of his desire to be quit of her. The air was cooling from the day's heat; the sky was a dark velvety blue, with sparkling star-gems sweeping into infinity. Breathtakingly beautiful, had he cared to look. Closer, the garish neon lights of the all-night store reflected dully in the oil smears dotting the asphalt. A smell of rotting garbage came from the Dumpster on the side of the building.

Harry slammed and locked his door—it wouldn't do to have some opportunistic kidnapper snatch the kid—and went inside the store. He had to use the john.

The store was busy, filled with travelers off Interstate 40, and also with locals picking up a six-pack or renting a video for the night from the meager collection under lock and key behind glass at the counter. Harry grabbed a package of chocolate-covered donuts and filled the largest container he could find with steaming black coffee. It smelled like tar and reminded him of the unholy wait he had had ten miles east of El Reno, back in Oklahoma, where a gang of the slowest roadworkers he had ever had the misfortune to run across held up traffic for the better part of an hour while they filled what looked like a miniscule pothole. By New York standards it wouldn't even have made the fix-it list.

He had to wait on line for the cashier, a dopey-looking kid with a sallow complexion and a sparse sprinkling of light brown downy fuzz on his upper lip. "That it?" he asked, and impulsively Harry shook his head no, grabbed a box of kiddie cookies in the shape of animals from a stack in the aisle behind him. Just because he was a nice guy.

The kid asked if he wanted a bag. Harry didn't, not because he was ecologically conscious, but because the kid did everything at the pace of molasses dripping from a keg. He picked up the donuts and cookies with one hand, took the coffee in the other, and backed out of the store, using his butt to open the glass door. Back at the Dodge, he bent to look in the window, could see the little girl was asleep, thank God. He put the coffee on the roof and was jiggling in his pocket for the keys when a voice spoke from behind his left ear.

"This your car?"

His answer was a growled, "Who wants to know?" He swiveled his hips, angling his shoulders around, and when he saw who wanted to know, his bowels clenched and his stomach took a nosedive about as far down as his knees.

The cop was born to intimidate, built like a bull, with a big round head sitting almost on his shoulders, looking like a snowman constructed by an inept five-year-old. But instead of snow, this behemoth was made of muscle and sinew; Harry doubted there was an ounce of fat on him. A slab of a lantern jaw jutted belligerently, but his most distinctive feature, besides two little eyes staring suspiciously, was a mashed-in remnant of a nose. To Harry the most intimidating things about him were the big silver badge on his wide chest and the flashlight, held in a meaty paw, which he was playing about the interior of the car, while the other hovered protectively over his service revolver.

"This yours?" He said it in the patient, pseudo-polite tone they all use before they pull the bricks down on your head.

"Anything wrong, Officer?"

The cop didn't answer; they never did. Part of the game. Let the jerk sweat. The flashlight did a thorough sweep, back and front, including the floor area.

Harry started to sweat, began to raise his arm to wipe his forehead, then thought better of it. Never let the fuckers see you were nervous.

"Let me see your registration and license, please."

The fucker wasn't going to let it go. Harry indicated he had to reach into his pocket; the cop moved his big round head forward a fraction of an inch.

Harry took it as an okay. He was sweating in earnest now, thinking fast. The papers were legit, but the plate number and state didn't match, not for the last fifty or so miles, since he had helped himself to a Texas tag at a rest stop. His own Jersey tag was in the trunk.

Buying time while he thought, he put the donuts and the stupid kid's cookies on the roof next to the coffee. If he wasn't such a nice guy, if he hadn't stopped to buy the goddamned animal crackers, he'd have been gone before Smokey rolled in. The cop had pulled up at an angle behind him, partially blocking the Dodge. If by some miracle he could get his keys out and get into the car without getting his ass blown off, he would have to ram the fucker's car to get away.

Shit.

The cop was getting antsy. Harry could tell by the way he shifted his weight, a subtle thing, but it told him the fucker was getting ready.

Getting ready to end it all, the sweetest little set-up he'd ever had. Not to mention his freedom.

Nothing lasts forever, Harry thought philosophically, his hand on his wallet, ready to make the cop's day rather than have his hide punctured by lead, when the stupid fucker made a mistake. He swept the inside of the car one time more, nothing he hadn't done at least a half dozen times already, only this time the little girl woke up. As the light beam hit her eyes, she did what she did best: she opened her mouth and started to scream.

The cop flinched, mumbled "Jeez," under his breath.

Harry whipped out his keys and made sure the cop saw them before unlocking the door. He leaned inside, making soothing calm-the-baby noises. The brat wailed louder. Harry could have kissed her.

"What's the matter with her?"

Harry could tell from his voice he didn't know shit about kids. Surreptitiously he gave her a pinch. Obligingly her screams went up in pitch and volume.

"Jeez," the cop said again, "can't you do something?"

"Dunno. Only one can calm her when she gets like this is her momma."

The cop switched off the flashlight, motioned with it for Harry to get in the car.

Harry needed no urging. He threw the donuts and cookies in the rear, and on an impulse, handed the cop the container of coffee. "Here, you might as well take this." He jerked his head toward the red-faced brat. "I'm in kinda a hurry."

"Listen, you shouldn't leave a kid alone. It isn't safe. Not these days."

"Yeah," Harry agreed.

"I'll move the car," the cop said, and raised the container in a salute. "Thanks."

Fifteen

It was spring and the grass was green and the dogwood trees were weeping pale pink blossoms over the lawn of the Brenton School. A far cry from the day last February when death fell out of the sky, but to Molly this day in May was in some ways a sadder one.

It had been billed as a rally, in support of the Newell family, to show the world that hope still shone brightly for Timmy's safe return. But the atmosphere was strained, for the people were powerless. In the three months since Timmy's disappearance, law-enforcement officials had not come up with a single clue to his fate.

Of course, there was another purpose to the rally—a very practical one. They—none more so than the police—wanted to put Timmy's case back on the news. Police Chief Thomas O'Brien didn't mince words in his speech. "Unlike the parents of the other victims of that tragic day, the Newells cannot bury their dead and get on with the process of living. Not knowing if their son is alive or dead is the greatest heartache. Someone somewhere knows what happened to Timmy. We need the widest audience possible to find that person. We must never give up until we do."

After he finished filming, Charlie Lee made his way through the large crowd in the gymnasium to Molly. "A real class-A bummer."

"You get no argument from me." She nodded in the direction of Susan Newell, Timmy's mother. "I don't know how she's managing. I'd be in a room with nice thick foam walls by now."

Charlie shrugged. "You do what you gotta do. Looks to me as if she's gone on with her life."

Molly narrowed her eyes. "What do you mean? She looks awful."

"She's pregnant."

"Really? How do you know?"

Charlie shrugged again. "Can't say. All I know is I'm outta here, thank God. If I never see another yellow balloon it'll be too soon."

Molly watched Susan Newell closely after Charlie left, trying to see what he saw. She couldn't, but she'd take his word for it; Charlie often had a sixth sense about such things. In her early thirties, Susan looked about ten years older than she had in February. Drawn tight, the skin of her face hugged the bones, emphasizing new lines at her wide-set brown eyes and around her mouth. She must have been pretty . . .

Before.

How do you get through the days after your child disappears? How do you keep from losing your mind? How do you keep on living? Molly certainly had no answers. She wondered if Susan Newell did. She should interview her, ask all the harsh, insensitive questions the situation engendered. Kent would want it; no, Kent would *demand* it. Susan was the most pathetic figure in the room, dressed in her now-faded yellow T-shirt with Timmy's picture on it, her expression barely concealing thinly disguised despair. Women like her were meat and potatoes to Kent.

"Molly." Zachary's voice murmured close behind her ear. She shivered, a purely visceral reaction. He put his hand on her shoulder, turned her.

"I didn't realize you'd be here."

"I'm still counseling some of the children." He studied her face, saw the bleakness deep in her hazel eyes. "What's wrong?"

Molly sighed, got a firmer grip on the microphone in her sweaty hand. "Nothing. Nothing's wrong. Nothing that a miracle wouldn't cure."

Zachary saw the direction of her gaze. "Go interview her. That's the way you can help."

"You're right. Thanks for reminding me." He removed his hand; Molly felt cold where it had rested.

"And . . . Molly?" Suddenly he looked unsure, not like the cool, calm Dr. Zachary Slater who was always in command. "Don't run away after you're through. All right?"

It was more than all right. All at once Molly didn't feel so downcast anymore.

Zachary followed Molly to Mrs. Parr's house. The first thing he asked after they got out of their respective cars was if she could get a sitter for the evening.

"I guess Sandy could sit."

A smile tugged Zachary's lips. "The *Jaws* lover?"

Molly chuckled, something she could do now that Petey wasn't almost catatonic with fear. "It wasn't really her fault, you know. Petey told her he was all better."

"I know. We had a long talk about that. Actually, it's

WHERE'S MY BABY?

a very good sign. He's recognized his problem and he's working on it. Now, if he only had a little more patience..."

"Forget it. Patience isn't his long suit." *Like his father,* she added mentally.

"Zach'ry!" The subject of their discussion came running out of the baby sitter's house. "Zach'ry! Look what I made!"

Zachary bent down and obediently examined Petey's latest attempt at art. Molly's heart gave a queer little lurch. This was the first time in his young life Petey hadn't run right to her.

She was being a goose. A jealous goose. But still ... something about the way they looked together, the big, well-muscled man and the sturdy little boy. Regret joined jealousy. As much as she loved Petey and tried to be everything to him, by rights he should have two parents. Damn that immature jerk she'd married. Not that she missed him.

"Mommy?"

Molly surfaced to find Petey looking at her quizzically. "What, honey?"

"Don'tcha wanna look?"

"Of course I do." She studied the streaks of paint, trying to get a glimmering of what they represented, very aware of Zachary standing close, of Petey eyeing them both anxiously. To a casual observer they would look like a family.

"From the artist's early period, I would say. Definitely modernistic. A fine rendering of a bucolic scene."

Petey eyed Zachary suspiciously. "What's this 'colic'?"

"*Bu*colic. It means pastoral, having to do with the country."

"You mean cows?"

Zachary smiled. "Something like that."

"It's very nice, honey. Very . . . imaginative."

If Petey heard his mother, he didn't let on. His eyes were fixed on Zachary, every line of his body radiating hurt. "It's s'posed to be your garden, Zach'ry. Look . . ." He plucked the picture from Molly's hands. "See? This is the tree you like so much," a finger poked two vertical black lines with a streak of brown inside, "and here is the bench we sit on sometimes when we talk." Two short vertical lines with a horizontal bar of black paint striped across it.

"Ah, yes. Very nice." Petey didn't look convinced. "Very, very nice," Zachary hastily amended.

Petey smiled sunnily. "You kin have it."

Zachary hesitated, glanced at Molly, and in that brief contact she could have sworn he knew what was in her heart, could sense the fear she had of competing for Petey's attention. Warmth suffused her, a rush of feeling for this sensitive man, but a feeling of shame quickly followed. Was she so insecure? Had she no faith in her son?

Of course she did. She ruffled Petey's hair, loving the fine, silky feel of it. He ducked out from under her hand, as he had been doing lately—such signs of affection were for little kids, which he most definitely was not, he had announced. She smiled at Zachary and received a grin in return.

"Thank you, Petey. I shall treasure it."

"Are you gonna put it up?"

"You bet."

"Where?"

"Petey!" Molly grabbed his hand and urged him toward her car. "Where are your manners? Once you give something to someone, it no longer is a concern of yours."

"That's stupid. It's *my* picture."

"No. It's Zachary's picture now. You gave it to him."

"So why can't he tell me where it's gonna be?" Petey asked with a child's straightforward logic.

"Petey!" Molly rolled her eyes heavenward. Her son was like a pit bull; once he got hold of something he was loath to let it go.

Hiding his amusement, Zachary gravely employed diplomacy. "I think I have just the spot for it, Petey. It would look good on the refrigerator, don't you think?"

Petey thought it would, which put an end to the discussion. Molly got him belted into the Taurus and went around to the driver's side. Zachary held her door open. "Do you want to follow me? The streets can be tricky around here."

"Don't worry. You're not going to get away from me."

That remark occupied her fully during the short ride.

They went to a small French restaurant known for its cuisine and romantic ambiance. Several times during dinner Molly wanted to ask Zachary what he had meant, but her courage failed her. That, or maybe she knew what he meant, knew it in her heart and soul, and just didn't want to admit it. She had been out of things for so long—too long—she felt awkward and unsure.

Suddenly he leaned forward, one arm extended palm up across the table. Molly automatically put her hand in his, looked questioningly deep into his eyes, the color of smoke in the flickering candlelight. His thumb began to make lazy circles on the back of her hand. The rush of sensation it caused sent shock waves deep into her body. Feelings that had long been numb were all at once janglingly awake and ... aware.

"Zachary ... ?" Her voice sounded strange and unsure to her ears. Her world had just turned on its axis; her stomach flip-flopped with the suddenness of it; her insides tingled, as if a ballet troupe of butterflies danced "The Waltz of the Flowers." He said something—she saw his lips move—but she couldn't hear him above the rush of blood roaring through her system. She thought it had something to do with dessert, but that couldn't be right, and then he was standing up and pulling her with him with one hand and signaling the waiter with the other, and she finally understood.

They weren't going to make it through dessert.

He pulled her into his arms the instant they were outside. He was big and strong and he was holding her in a crushing grip, but Molly reveled in it. Being in his arms felt right. A groan tore from his lips and then they came down hard onto hers and his tongue plunged deep inside her mouth, and with it all thoughts flew from her head. The kiss was so intense she sagged against his body; he secured her by tightening his arms and dragging her closer, molding her soft curves against his hardness; making her instantly aware of the state of his arousal. Instead of frightening her it caused her to feel an overwhelming joy.

He pulled his head back to look at her. Her eyes were closed; the rising moon cast the shadow of her lashes across her cheeks. He kissed the shadow and then each eye, slowly savoring her before moving his lips hungrily to her temple and down her face until he reached the ultrasensitive place behind her ear. She shuddered in his

WHERE'S MY BABY? 163

arms; his body tightened as he brought his lips back to hers.

Light flashed over them and shortly after, footsteps crunched on gravel. Neither noticed. It took the clearing of a throat and a softly spoken, "Excuse me," for them to spring apart.

Zachary put his arm around Molly, swung her behind him so his body protected hers. A purely instinctive gesture, no doubt the product of some ancestor's warrior genes. A couple walked past into the restaurant. The woman kept her eyes averted, the man gave Zachary a grin. When they were alone again Zachary faced Molly. "Sorry." His voice was still not back to normal.

Molly tilted up her head and frowned. Zachary knew he would never forget how lovely she looked, her skin made pearly by the moon's light, a hint of it gleaming in her eyes. "For what?"

She wasn't making it easy. His eyes fell to her lips—now he knew their texture and taste—then moved lower, touching on her breasts. Her nipples were pebbled, pushing against the thin material of her dress. He groaned, barely restraining himself from dragging her down into the bushes like a conqueror plundering his prey.

She licked her lips, leaving them glossy.

If he thought she had done it consciously, he would ... with no inconsiderable effort Zachary got hold of himself. He would take her home at once. He wouldn't even kiss her goodnight. He didn't dare. And then she said something that banished his good intentions to the hell they deserved.

"There's a motel near here."

He stared at her so intently Molly feared she had made a terrible mistake. But then he laughed, more a gust of relief, and crushed her to his chest. He kissed her once, hard, and set her back. Eyes made black by night studied her face.

"You're sure."

"I'm sure."

They had to stop at a drugstore first. He sensed her nervousness when he returned to the car. He took her hands in his. "All you have to do is say no, Molly. I'll understand."

"No. I mean, it's okay. I want . . . I want you."

Zachary took care of the formalities at the motel. Finally, alone in their room, Molly put her hand on his arm, staying him from turning on the light. She felt better about saying what she had to in the dark. "Zachary . . . I want you to know. I've never done anything like this. Never gone to a motel. I . . ."

Gently, he brushed a lock of hair off her forehead, tangled his fingers in the silky strands. "It's all right, sweet Molly. It's all right."

She grabbed his wrist. "I . . . I haven't been with anyone since . . . since before Petey was born." The darkness hummed; Molly wished she could see Zachary's face more clearly, then was glad she couldn't.

When he spoke, his voice was husky, sending shivers through her. "You make me proud, sweetheart." His hand stroked the nape of her neck. She sensed him bending toward her, and then his lips took hers again, and after that, nothing seemed to matter. She went up like flames in his arms, becoming a creature of needs and desires, wanting to give and to take. And when finally they were both naked and he lowered her down onto the cool sheets, she was almost mindless with her passion. He slid over her, and although his unclothed

WHERE'S MY BABY? 165

body was big and hard with well-developed muscles, she welcomed his weight.

All of a sudden Molly felt his muscles clench. He drew in a harsh breath, and in the next moment left her. He was back almost immediately, a small foil packet in his hand. "Almost forgot. Help me, Molly. Help me."

It took only a few moments, and then he took her in his arms again and she opened for him and he surged deep into her. A shudder wracked him; he stilled, dropped his forehead onto hers, took a deep breath. "You feel so good, Molly. So incredibly good. You couldn't possibly know how good you feel." Her eyes opened and tried to focus; a smile of triumph curved her lips. "Witch!" His mouth slanted down and across hers; his tongue plunged in and out.

After that they were lost, caught in a world where sensation ruled, a dizzying spiral, up, up, higher and faster, escalating into something almost akin to pain. Everything was raw, immediate, an insatiable hunger that fed on need and desire and finally peaked in a burst of white-hot pleasure.

A long time after, Zachary carefully disengaged from Molly and rolled to his side. He put one arm around her and dragged her close. There were a million things he wanted to say, but they would have to wait. He knew now was not the time.

She stirred and tried to rise. He pulled her back against him. "Don't."

"I've got to go."

"Not yet."

She tried again, but his arm tightened, settling her more firmly against his body. Her hand came up between them, flattened on his chest, her fingers tangling in the dense black hair there. His body tightened.

"Zachary?"

Gently he pushed her onto her back. His hand swept over her breasts, down over her waist and thighs, came back up to rest on her belly. Her skin was silky smooth, damp from exertion.

"You're beautiful, Molly. Beautiful."

Capturing her hand, he guided it down his body, let her feel his hardness. Her hand tightened around him; he groaned with the sensation. Once she knew his need, her own roared to life again.

"We'll go slower this time. Slower, Molly."

Zachary's intentions were good, but passion overwhelmed him and his last conscious thought was that there was always next time.

Sixteen

Grand Canyon National Park, Arizona

It was about twelve hours, give or take, from Amarillo to Flagstaff, and about another hour and a half to the south rim of the Grand Canyon. Harry had figured a comfortable fifteen, giving himself an edge for safety. But after the run-in with the cop from hell—the fucker had sure turned out to be a dumb-ass, just like about everybody else except Harry—he no longer had the luxury of a cushion.

No, the cop had seen to that. Because of him, Harry had had to go flat-out for Arizona, passing through New Mexico in a blur, after losing time early the morning after his narrow escape trading the Dodge for a Ford pickup that had seen better days. It could have been an entry in an ugly-truck contest, with its rust spots and dents, but the thief in used-car-salesman's clothes who had sold it to him swore it still had plenty under the hood.

He hadn't lied. It had gotten Harry to his rendezvous in good time. Him and the brat.

God, he couldn't wait to unload her. Almost time. He patted her tummy. "Baby going bye-bye." She wailed.

Harry cringed. Try and be nice, see where it gets you. It was a no-nevermind. The brat would be just another entry on his private spreadsheet soon.

Time for business. He concentrated on driving, joined the line of traffic inching along the canyon's perimeter road. Jane and Chester Johnson of Grant's Pass, Oregon, were right where they were supposed to be. Harry spotted them the instant he drove into the scenic turn-out. He passed them by and parked at the far end, the nose of the pickup edging the road. Ready for a quick getaway. Always.

Camera slung over his shoulder for camouflage, he sauntered along the path, seemingly awed by the view, but in reality never taking his eyes off the couple. They stood in front of their vehicle, a dusty blue Ford, nervously eyeing every car. Jane was extremely petite, the top of her head just reaching her husband's shoulder, and from a distance Chester appeared to be of no more than average height. That was okay; the brat's people hadn't exactly been giants.

Harry walked slowly past them, ostensibly looking for a good spot to take a picture. The Grand Canyon lay spread before him in all its purple, pink, and gold grandeur, but he could only think of green. This trip he had certainly earned his money.

Click. Click. Click. Tourists oohed and aahed, worked on cramming four-and-a-half billion years' worth of history into a single picture frame. World by Kodak. Amen.

"Walter! Get over here by your mother and sister. Turn around, damn it. Smile!"

Walter was a little shit who looked like he would like nothing better than to push Sis over the railing. His mother grabbed him, managed to hold him still long

WHERE'S MY BABY?

enough for dear old Dad to snap a few shots. Then Walter squirmed out of her grasp and rushed to the railing, leaned so far over he very nearly tipped the odds in gravity's favor.

Harry used the to-do this caused to approach the Johnsons. Up close they looked more like brother and sister than husband and wife. His hair was a dirtier blond color, but they both had pale blue eyes and short, almost pug, noses. Her left eye had a slight tendency to wander.

Harry introduced himself as the major. Jane clasped her hands together and began to rhythmically thump her chest. Her right eye never left his face. Chester displayed his nervousness by shifting his weight from foot to foot. He spoke first, the words coming fast and jerky. "You've got her? Rachel?"

"Yes."

"I want to see her." This from Jane. A breathless, squeaky little voice.

Harry hoped she wouldn't keel over from the excitement. "Later. The money first."

"Rachel first. Jane wants to see her."

"No."

"Look here, major, my wife wants to see the baby. We have a right to ... ah, see what we're paying for." Chester the Bold.

"No," Harry said, and started to leave. Behind him he could hear Jane and Chester buzzing away. He walked slowly.

"Major! Wait!"

Harry grinned. He would have bet it would be the broad. The grin was gone when he faced them again. "Yes?"

"We'll show you the money and then you'll let us see the baby. All right?"

"Done." Harry was nothing if not reasonable.

The money looked like twenty thousand always did. Beautiful. A tan duffel this time. Harry had quite a collection.

Chester kept a good grip on it. "Now, take us to Rachel."

The brat was quiet for once. Jane cooed at her through the pickup's dirty window. "Isn't she sweet?"

Harry could think of other, more eminently suitable, words. He kept his counsel, however. The Johnsons would find out soon enough. "Well, there she is. Now hand over the money and she's all yours."

Magic words. Jane started to glow. Chester didn't make a move. "How do we know she's Rachel?"

Harry stifled a sigh. Chester was fast becoming a pain in the ass. Luckily, Jane intervened before he could say something ill advised.

"Nana told us the major would bring our Rachel back to us, Chester. She wouldn't lie."

The fact that dear truth-telling Nana had made this statement after her death apparently did not signify. Harry never ceased to be amazed at the gullibility of the pigeons.

"I don't know, Jane . . . this whole thing is—"

Jane clutched his arm. "Oh, look. She's smiling at me! She knows her mommy, don't you, precious?"

Chester was smart enough to know when he'd lost. Thirty seconds later Harry had the money and they had the brat.

* * *

WHERE'S MY BABY?

The ugly old pickup lasted as far as Peoria, six miles north of Phoenix. Harry sold it at a service station to an ancient leathery-skinned coot who wanted it for the money scrapping it would bring. That done, Harry walked to the edge of the road and stuck out his thumb. The sun was mellowing from gold to red as it slowly sank toward the western horizon, but it was still hot; he started to sweat immediately, was soon soaked. Cars passed by; no one appeared to have charity in his soul.

Harry's temper was on the boil when an eighteen-wheeler finally ground to a halt. A man with the bushiest, blackest beard he had ever seen stuck his head out of the right-side window. "How do I know you ain't one of them escaped convicts? There're signs all along 17 warning not to pick up anyone."

Harry lifted his overnight case so the trucker could see it. He kept the duffel at his side, partially concealed by his body. "Would a convict have luggage?"

This seemed to satisfy the trucker. He withdrew his head, opened the door, and barely waited for Harry to scramble aboard. He didn't say another word.

His taciturn nature suited Harry just fine. He wasn't in the best of moods and would just as soon not have to hold up his end of a conversation. The truck's cab wasn't air-conditioned; he was still sweating like a pig and was beginning to smell like a goat. His silent companion had an offensive body odor and expelled garlic fumes into the close confines with every breath.

Harry indicated he wanted out as soon as they reached the downtown area. He left the trucker with a salute and received a thumbs-up in reply. No stranger to Phoenix, he soon oriented himself. Only a short walk to a well-known hotel. The sun was down and the air was beginning to cool with the suddenness so startling in the desert. He didn't mind the walk, although carrying so much money always made him nervous.

He made it to the hotel without incident. A line of taxicabs waited. He had to tip the doorman, who hovered over them like a hen over chicks. With the caution that was now habit, Harry waited until they were pulling away from the curb before telling the cabbie to take him to a hotel near the airport. The cabbie wasn't the garrulous sort—Harry wondered if it was the effect of his body odor—and they made the trip in silence.

The hotel was the kind of place that catered to traveling salesmen. Pleased, he paid off the cabbie and surrendered his overnight case to the bellboy, a man well into his forties if he didn't miss his guess, who made the mistake of reaching for the tan duffel. Harry snapped at him. "I'll keep that."

"Sorry, sir."

"It's okay," Harry said, but it wasn't. Stupid to call attention just because he had had a hard day. Hard day, hell. He had had nothing but hard *days*, ferrying the brat across the country—and whenever he thought about the cop in Amarillo. . . . He told himself not to think. Time for fun.

The hotel had a room and Harry filled in the form. The bellboy took his overnighter up to the room, the two of them alone in the elevator. Harry studied the back of the bellboy's head for a time, then made a decision. "Uh, maybe you can help me?"

"Sir?" Knowledge lurked in the eyes he flicked to Harry. What he was about to hear he had heard at least a thousand times before.

Harry recognized the awareness and immediately cut to the chase. Money changed hands. The bellboy would send someone to Harry's room in about an hour. Harry called room service, and much to his surprise, his meal was waiting when he stepped out of the shower.

The woman who knocked on his door sometime later was a bit older than he liked. A tall brunette with a lush figure verging on plumpness. It didn't bother him; he liked women with something to grab. He gave her a long look. She stood still, unfazed, walked regally past him into the room when he motioned with his head.

They got down to business at once. Delilah—she acted like he was supposed to believe it was her name—fancied herself experienced. What Harry wanted, though—what he *needed,* to work off the stress of the brat, the cop, the difficult Johnsons, and the smelly truck driver—was something new. But everything had a price, as he well knew, and he soon found Delilah's. She lay naked, bound hand and foot, legs spread wide, within minutes of Harry's hard-earned money—a fat roll of it—disappearing into her purse.

If what she saw in his eyes frightened her when he was naked and looming over her, she didn't show it. "You will be gentle, won't you?"

Humor from a whore; just what he needed.

"Shut up, bitch!" Harry balled his fist. Delilah ceased being amused within a very short time.

Seventeen

Zachary turned off the tape recorder and watched Irene slowly orient herself, wondering how she would react. This session, the second after what he thought of as "the break," had been the strangest by far. He wasn't so sure resuming the sessions was wise. She had been close to hysteria the day she had run out, and from the subsequent phone call, she had run right into a bottle of booze.

She blinked rapidly several times; her blue-shadowed eyelids were almost the exact shade of the irises beneath.

"How do you feel?"

"I'm not sure."

"Do you remember?"

She made a funny little hitching sound—half-gasp, half-laugh—as if she didn't know whether to be amazed or embarrassed. "I think so."

"Good. Tell me."

With a swish of mint-green silk over nylon, she arose and began wandering about the room, touching various objects as she went. Her posture was stiff; she appeared agitated.

"Irene?"

"What? Oh! You want to know. I was him—Thomas—wasn't I?"

Zachary made a note. "You tell me."

"All right! I was Thomas! He was . . ." She shuddered, crossed her arms over her chest, and rubbed her upper arms vigorously.

"Are you cold?"

Irene shook her head no. "Where were we?"

"Thomas."

"Ah, yes. Thomas. He—I—was a leper. Is that possible? Can I have been a *man?*"

"This is all uncharted territory. There are no positive answers. Remember our first session? I said past-life regression is open to many different interpretations, and one of the prevailing theories is that there is no such thing as regression. Everything takes place in the mind. All these people you've 'remembered,' these vastly different personae, female *and* male, could be coming from inside your head." He could tell she didn't like that particular explanation.

"But if it is the other—truly a regression—is it possible? Could I have been a man?"

"Why not?" Irene nodded thoughtfully. "Was Karen with you in this life?"

Amazing how the mere mention of her daughter's name had the power to transform her. Her face fairly radiated happiness. "Yes, she was. She was my mother, Margery, the woman who came into the men's lazarhouse and kissed me. Imagine! It took such courage, but then she loved me so. She—"

Zachary made an exasperated sound and snatched the phone off the hook. Irene began to wander again. Zachary watched her as he listened, wondering anew at her unusual restlessness.

The conversation was short. After it ended, he stared out the window for several moments. His little patch of garden brimmed with burgeoning life. The magnolia tree that gave him such pleasure had reached its peak a few days ago. Under the gentle urging of the springtime winds, the blossoms were already beginning to fall, covering the area with a delicate carpet of the palest pink, a timely reminder of the cycle of death and rebirth. "Something's come up and I have to leave." The something was the violent gunshot death of a Brooklyn high school teacher. The student body was traumatized; the school wanted Zachary's team to help with the mop-up. That had been the exact word used, "mop-up." The kinder, gentler world was still in the future.

"That's okay."

Her eyes were very bright. "Are you sure you're feeling all right?" He wouldn't leave if he felt she needed him.

"I'm fine. Truly. Go ahead. I wouldn't want to detain you."

"I'll send Mrs. Sadecki in with a tray. I expect you could use some coffee."

"Thank you."

He left, although something about her still bothered him. He dismissed it, already thinking ahead to what he would find in Brooklyn. Wondering if he would see Molly there.

Irene couldn't believe her good fortune. She waited tensely for Mrs. Sadecki, who came after what seemed an eternity, cluck-clucking about the way poor Dr. Slater

WHERE'S MY BABY? 177

had to rush out. "They call, night and day, these people. Always it's rush, rush, rush." She plunked the tray onto the coffee table. "They call and he runs. Always."

"Thank you." Irene wondered if her mother hadn't placed this particular fortuitous call.

"You're welcome." Mrs. Sadecki beamed at Irene. "Is good cake. Still warm. You eat. You too thin."

Although she was so nervous her hands were shaking, Irene dutifully took a bite of the rich coffee cake. "Um, delicious." Irene nibbled another small bite. Would the old lady never leave?

Mrs. Sadecki made her slow way to the door, clicking her tongue disapprovingly when she glanced at the mess on Zachary's desk. "He won't let me touch, you know?"

Irene understood. "Men are like that."

They shared a smile. At the door, Mrs. Sadecki remembered she had a message. "Oh, missus. Doctor say take your time. You stay as long as you like."

Irene counted five heartbeats after the door closed and then sprang to her feet. There were dozens of files; she would have to go through all of them to make sure she had the right one. She didn't mind. Karen was close; Irene could feel it in her bones.

Zachary listened to WAND as he drove, hoping to hear Molly. He couldn't seem to get enough of her. Just thinking about her was making him hard. A terrific way for the head of the trauma team to arrive on the scene.

He had dominion over his hormones by the time he got to the school. A good thing, for he saw Molly immediately after double-parking his six-year-old Regency in front of the building. She was talking to Charlie Lee, but left him and came to Zachary at once. "Hello."

He was inordinately pleased by it. He wanted to sweep her into his arms and greet her properly, but he contained the urge. Barely. "Hello, yourself." She waved to the CBN van as it went past. "Are you through here?"

"Yup. I wrapped it up about five minutes ago. I'm supposed to be on my way downtown. The McVey jury will be coming in anytime now." She was so close he couldn't breathe, much less think. He looked at her blankly. "Racketeering. Labor union. Front-page headlines in all the tabloids for the past week. Where have you been?"

Zachary could have told her that practically all he'd thought about for the past week was her—how she looked, how she felt, how she tasted—but neither one of them was ready to hear it. For at least the fiftieth time he told himself to go slow. "Uh, what about later? How about dinner?" Molly remembered their last dinner; he could see it in her eyes. "I promise to feed you."

"You'd better. I need my strength around you."

She left then, and Zachary was grateful. Much more, and his thoughts would incinerate him.

Eighteen

From his vantage point behind a large monument in Pilgrim's Hill Cemetery, Harry watched Irene as she waited at her mother's grave. Waited for him; for the major, rather.

What in hell's name was he doing here? The broad was poison. He *never* let the pigeons see him until the last, and then he kept it as brief as humanly possible. Most of them were so excited at that point the risk seemed minimal. They could deal with Boris Karloff dressed as Frankenstein's monster and wouldn't notice. Perhaps it was their own daring, or the prospect of getting their dead kid back. The only thing that mattered was that afterward they couldn't point a finger in his face. Damn straight.

So what was he doing here? Especially after that near-fiasco in Amarillo. Hadn't that overdeveloped musclebound cop taught him anything?

Obviously not. She was poison; all he had to do was look at her to know. A skinny broad. He didn't like skinny broads; they were usually all mouth.

You'll see, Harry, someday you'll see, Harry, someday the whole world will see, Harry, they'll know what a useless failure you are, Harry, Harry, Harrrrrrrrrrr-rrrryyyyy . . .

Shit. He'd be outta here if. . . . It all came down to money. There never seemed to be enough. The skinny broad had it and he needed it.

She was pacing now, careful not to step on the grass over the grave. Mama's dead, sweetheart, he wanted to tell her. Dead and buried and rotting away.

She was poison; he knew it. But she was going to win this silent tug of wills.

For that he'd make her wait a while longer.

The voice came from the hill above and behind her, and although she had been expecting it—had been fervently praying for it—it still made her jump. A bad way to start; she didn't want him to know how nervous she was.

It came again. "You have the money?"

"Major?"

No, it's fucking General Motors, he wanted to shout. Who the fuck did she think it was? How many people did she think were returning dead kids? Did she think just anyone could do it? Did she think he was so successful he sold franchises? This broad was poison all the way through. He decided to ignore her question, keep her off balance right from the start.

She was getting braver, starting to turn around. Mustn't have that. "Don't move!"

"I need to talk to you."

"So talk."

She didn't like it, that was plain, but if she wanted the kid . . .

"All right. I . . . I won't look at you."

She wanted the kid. Harry could have bet his—her?—money on it. Poison. Good thing he always planned. Nothing much, but a detail here and there, and even his best friend wouldn't know him. Thanks to the heels on his scuffed cowboy boots, he was three inches taller than his five-ten. The Stetson had also added to his height, besides casting his upper face in shadow. Dressed simply, in jeans and plaid shirt, the shirt was open enough to show a deep V and the thicket of false dark-brown hair tufting over it. It itched. He couldn't wait to get it off.

"I have the money. The . . . the half we agreed on, up front. You'll get the rest when I have Karen back."

He didn't like her tone, didn't like her whole attitude, thinking she could dictate to *him*. But . . . the broad wanted a special order. She was really off a wall, telling him mama had told her who the kid was. Even if he got so drunk his brain was fermented he would never do such a thing. Never.

But she had been so sure dear mama had called from the Great Beyond he had checked his telephone bill. No calls to Rock Ridge he couldn't account for.

Poison. Poison with a big balance. If he kept reminding himself of that fact, he wouldn't think of all the thousand and one things that could go wrong. On top of everything else, this skinny broad was a juicer. Her appearance confirmed what he had known from the first time he'd heard her slurred voice. Which probably accounted for the call from mama. Booze could make you believe fucking Cleopatra was on the line.

"Major?"

"Leave the money by the grave and walk away. Don't look back. I'll contact you when I have the kid and tell you where to meet me."

"When? When will I have Karen back?"

"When I call and tell you I've got her, that's when."

She didn't like it, but that was just too fucking bad. She couldn't dictate everything. No way. He knew her type. Rich bitch. Could get anything she wanted. All she had to do was flash the green.

"How will I recognize you?"

"I'll do all the recognizing that's necessary."

"Okay."

Of course it was okay. It *had* to be okay. Harry had taken as much interference as he was going to take. Only one little detail to tidy away; for forty thousand he could humor her. "So, Irene, who did mama say Karen is now and where do I find her?"

She told him. He felt a flicker of surprise. Go figure a broad. Then she did as ordered, left the duffel and walked away.

Sure as shit she looked back.

By the time he got home, even the hefty feel of the twenty thousand wasn't enough to assuage his growing anger. He should take the twenty thousand and forget the whole thing. The broad was bad news. She was also a gullible fool giving someone like him so much money on trust. She'd deserve what she got. It would be a helluva lesson.

That's what he'd do. He'd forget all about her.

He scratched his chest. Damn itch wouldn't go away. He looked at it under the bathroom light. Little red welts were rising on his skin. Great. Now he had fucking hives.

And all because of the broad.

Poison.

He stripped and got under the shower, letting warm water soothe the irritated skin. The nerve of the broad, telling him who to snatch. He made the phone calls, he decided who to grab, and he damn well decided *when* to do it, too! It was his scam ... *his*. *He* was in control all the way. Those were the rules. Everybody had to play by them. Everybody. Including the broad.

He shut off the water, patted himself dry. The little red fuckers were now a bright cherry color and were driving him crazy. Water hadn't been such a good idea. Powder. He needed powder. A search of the entire apartment turned up nothing. He didn't want to get dressed and go out. Not for fucking powder.

Kahlil. The damn doorman had yet to work off his Christmas tip. He got Kahlil on the intercom and told him to run to the drugstore and buy powder.

"I can't leave the door right now, Mr. Kemp," came the whispered answer.

Harry whistled a few bars of "Jingle Bells" and disconnected. Everybody had their own agenda. Even Kahlil—a damn doorman, for God's sake—thought he could get away with shit.

He poured himself a generous vodka–and–cranberry juice at the wet bar. One of his special prides, almost an entire wall of glass and chrome, it could have serviced the snootiest establishment, but it was all his. His alone.

God, what money could do.

The broad offered another tax-free twenty thousand. No way. Harry hadn't worked and sweated for years for some poison-carrying broad to come along and tell him what to do.

But how the hell did she come up with the name of this particular kid? Maybe she had it in for one of the parents, or she'd seen the kid and taken a fancy to it.

Maybe the hair color was the same. After years of working the scam, Harry wouldn't be surprised at anything people believed. As long as they *wanted* to believe. That was the key. But one thing he knew for sure: no one from the Great Beyond was making phone calls. Not without going through him.

God, he was beginning to believe his own shit.

Harry made himself another drink, doubling the vodka and leaving out the juice. His chest was on fire. Where the hell was Kahlil? By now he was so jittery and wound up he knew there was only one cure. He called a familiar number and was guaranteed service within the hour. "It's got to be Jillian." The syrupy voice on the other end of the phone assured him it would be Jillian.

One drink later—this one without the juice or the ice, either—Kahlil buzzed and said he had a visitor coming up.

"Where's the powder?"

"It's coming up, too," Kahlil said, adding that Harry could pay him later, no rush. He was good for it. Ha ha.

Ha ha, Harry thought, and yanked open the door. Jillian Raven, all six feet of her, was leaning against the doorframe. She took one look and grinned. "I hope I'm not overdressed for this party." Harry looked down, realized he was naked. Jillian held up a container of baby powder. "I can't wait to see how we're going to use this."

Harry wrenched it out of her grasp. "Very funny."

Jillian sauntered into the foyer, very much at home. "Where do you want me?"

Harry told her, watched her sashay down the hall and disappear into his bedroom. Quite an eyeful. Statuesque, with curves proportionate to her height, blessed with curly thick black hair and violet eyes. Harry knew for a fact everything was real. Everything but the violet eyes—contact lenses could do wonders these days.

He was about to follow her when the phone rang. Snatching it up, he snarled, "What?" His stomach clenched when he heard the voice of Carl Morgan, the business manager at Encore, Inc., his legitimate means of support. Morgan never called with good news.

"Mrs. Weimann died, Harry. I just learned about it today."

Clarice Weimann was one of Harry's best customers. Scratch that, *had* been one of his best customers. Something about the way Morgan emphasized the word "today" ...

"Harry? You know we special-ordered that crystal sculpture for her ..."

Harry began to see disaster looming. "So get on the horn. Cancel it."

"It came in today. Usual terms."

COD. Bile rose in Harry's throat. Fifty thousand dollars. He'd never unload it, would have to eat it. No sane person would pay that much money for a hunk of glass. An especially ugly hunk of glass. No one except Clarice Weimann. If the old broad weren't already dead Harry would kill her. He would ...

You'll never amount to anything, Harry, mark my words, Harry, you're a failure, Harry, you'll always be a failure, Harry, Harry, Harry, Harrrrrrrrrrrrrrrrryyyyyyyyyyyyyyyyy.

He fumbled the phone back on the hook and stared into space. If he had her before him right now, he'd ...

"Harry?"

Magnificently naked, Jillian gazed at him with her pansy-purple eyes.

Harry slowly balled his hands into fists.

Nineteen

"... *The temperature right now is eighty-four degrees going up to eighty-six. Stay tuned to WAND, 990 on your dial, for a complete Memorial Day holiday forecast coming up in eight minutes. Now for a traffic report we go to ...*"

Zachary stopped listening. Traffic was going to be a mess, especially since this was the first big weekend of the season; people would be pouring out of the hot city and heading for the beaches. Usually he dreaded it, but today he couldn't wait to get started. All that was holding him up was Petey's file. He couldn't find it.

"Mrs. Sadecki!"

She appeared in the doorway several minutes later, a smile on her face. "All ready, Doctor. We go?"

"In a minute. I can't seem to find a file."

Mrs. Sadecki bristled. "I no touch. You say never, never touch, I don't touch."

Zachary felt ashamed. "I wasn't accusing you ... well, hello, there it is. Misfiled." He plucked it from the drawer, frowned. He was meticulous about his files.

"Daddy? We're all ready. Are you going to get the car?"

WHERE'S MY BABY? 187

Zachary dropped Petey's file into his briefcase. "Sure am, pussycat."

Wincing, Molly watched Petey roll his clothes into a ball and shove it into one of their new pieces of matching canvas luggage. Petey packed the way his father had, with no regard for anything save speed. She wondered if it was in the genes. When he tried to stuff in his tyrannosaurus rex robot—he had already packed a stuffed dog, a dump truck, and two racing cars, plus two electronic games—she felt she had to intervene, although she had been told hands off, he was old enough to do it himself.

"We'll only be away for the weekend, Petey. You don't have to pack everything you own. Besides, I'm sure Lauren has plenty of toys at the house."

Petey stopped struggling with the gaudily painted toy and regarded her with innocent brown eyes. "Lauren's a girl."

Oho, Molly thought, *a touch of male chauvinism already.* "So she is, which doesn't mean she won't have toys or she won't share with you." She had to bite back a grin. Petey's expression clearly showed what he thought about girls' toys. From what Zachary hinted about his athletic daughter, Molly knew Petey was in for some surprises. She only hoped he could keep up. A year was a big difference at this age.

In went his baseball bat and glove. Molly glanced at the pile on his bed. "One more, mister. That's it." Dutifully, he sorted the pile, picking and then rejecting several items before choosing the soccer ball. "What about Lambie Pie? Aren't you going to take him?"

Petey added the soccer ball before he picked up his

all-time favorite stuffed toy, a mere whisper of its former glory. The yellow lamb had been a birth gift from her mother. "I'll carry him." Brown eyes defied her.

"Okay. Pack your bathing suit?"

Petey looked unsure, then nodded yes. Outside, a horn honked rhythmically. "They're here! They're here!"

Whooping, he raced from the room. Molly quickly pulled the ball of clothing out of the suitcase and tried to fold the clothes neatly. Most were already badly wrinkled.

"Mommy! Mommy! It's Zach'ry! Kin I open the door?" Petey shouted up the stairs.

"Wait, I'm coming." Molly rolled his clothes back into a ball and shoved them into the suitcase.

Despite the congested traffic, Harry had no trouble following Zachary's Regency. As a rule he tried to keep two or three cars between them, but it really didn't matter. Progress was so slow he had ample opportunity to react.

At first he thought they were headed for the Hamptons, a logical assumption, for he had seen the suitcases, but when they went south on the Sagtikos and exited at Bay Shore Road, he began to get a sinking feeling in his gut. Sure enough, instead of going east on Sunrise, they continued south into Bayshore.

Bad news. Harry would bet his next twenty thousand they were heading for the ferry.

No surprise. They left the Regency in a lot and made straight for the docks.

Fire Island. Just his lousy luck. How the hell could he

snatch a kid and make a clean getaway from a goddamned fucking island? A warning whistle sounded. He bought a ticket and at the last possible moment boarded the boat.

Molly couldn't remember when she had been so happy. For two and a half days they had done nothing but relax and play and eat. Zachary's house, a sprawling affair of cedar shingles and glass windows and walls, was screened by bushes and trees, giving them a sense of privacy. It had upper and lower decks, the upper wrapping around the sides. Tubs of flowers were spaced around them—petunias, geraniums, begonias, impatiens—brilliant points of color against the deliberately washed-out gray of the boards. The house had grace and charm.

Beyond it was the beach, pale sand sparkling cleanly under the hot, bright sun, and beyond the sand lay the ocean, dark green and blue, waves cresting whitely before ebbing into a rush of foam. Today only a few wisps of clouds, mare's tails, chased across the blue as sea birds caught the thermals, glided gracefully in a dipping, swaying dance. Beneath them people played on the beach, romped in the surf.

So far they had had no success with Petey. He would stay as far back on the sand away from the water as he could, and that was that. Not one step closer. Molly worried. Zachary told her not to. Hadn't he been right about the ferry? he had asked. Despite Petey's deep uneasiness, he had made the half-hour trip without a fuss. In stoic silence, pressed against Molly's side as far back in the enclosed passenger lounge as he could get, he had clutched Lambie Pie in a death grip and kept his eyes fixed on his feet. If he had looked a little green around the gills when they disembarked, so what? He had made the trip. So far, so good. Patience.

Trying to digest Mrs. Sadecki's idea of a light lunch, Molly lay on a chaise on the upper deck, listening to the high, excited squeals of Petey and Lauren playing salugi with Zachary. She closed her eyes. So peaceful. She could get used to it. Easily.

Zachary was spoiling her shamefully. He wouldn't let her do anything, including what she considered her fair share. In lieu of a house gift, she had wanted to take them to dinner. He wouldn't allow it, so she had bought Lauren a Victorian dollhouse. It had cost an arm and a leg, but the expression on her face had been worth it.

Dozing, she heard Petey yell, "Zach'ry! Zach'ry! You're too tall! I wanna be the monkey in the middle." Overlaying it was Lauren's sweet voice, as excited as Petey's. "Me! Me! I want to be the monkey. Please, Daddy, choose me!" Molly drifted, happy it was Zachary making the choice.

She awoke with a start, chilled and damp. A wind had whipped up, drawing the clouds down to meet the sea. Sand stung her body; briny spray doused her. The air was so thick she had trouble drawing oxygen into her lungs. Dread sat heavily on her chest.

Run!

She was alone on the beach. The people stood atop the dunes, pointing, yelling.

Run!

Her feet wouldn't move, she was stuck, she couldn't get away, she couldn't ...

The wave loomed ... huge ...

"Molly. Wake up, sweetheart, you're having a bad dream." She was shaking, was drenched with sweat.

Zachary eased down beside her, carefully took her into his arms. "I've got you. You're safe, sweet Molly. Safe."

"I'm sorry. I don't . . ."

"Hush." Zachary stroked her hair back from her brow and gently kissed her on the forehead.

Gradually her body ceased to tremble and she relaxed against him. His skin was hot and damp; he smelled of sand and sea and man. She had a strong urge to turn her face into him and lick the drops of moisture sparkling like diamonds in the mat of hair on his chest. She barely controlled herself. That was no way for a mother to act. Not when her chick could appear at any second.

Suddenly she realized how quiet it was. In the distance she could hear the incessant screaming of the gulls; closer, she could hear the breeze playing through the trees; closer yet, beneath her ear, the steady beat of Zachary's heart. No young voices.

"Where are the children?"

"I bribed Mrs. Sadecki to take them for ice cream." Molly struggled to sit up. Zachary gently pushed her back. "Relax. Mrs. Sadecki won't let them out of her sight. Trust me. They're as safe with her as they would be with us." He smiled into her eyes. "Now, tell me about the dream."

Molly shook her head. "No. It was nothing."

"You could'a fooled me."

"It's nothing."

Zachary outclassed her in stubbornness. He prodded until she finally broke down. She let a few beats of silence pass when she finished, then drew away, unconsciously signaling her inner turmoil. "Do you think I'm responsible for Petey's fear? Do you think it's genetic?"

"No and no."

"But . . ."

"You have a bad dream from time to time. Who knows why? The important thing is that it doesn't cripple you in your waking hours."

"No, but what if Petey senses my fear and—"

"Nonsense. How about some good news? Petey had a major breakthrough. He actually chased the ball into the water."

Molly put her hand on Zachary's chest. "He went in the water! That's wonderful!"

Her eyes shone with such excitement, he hated to punch a hole in it. She saw his expression; her fingers tugged on tufts of hair. "What? What happened?"

"A wave came up behind him and—er, uprooted him. He landed on his behind and came up screaming." Molly tried to squirm out of his embrace; Zachary tightened his grip. "It's all right, Molly. No harm was done. Petey's fine now. In fact, I would say he's better than fine. He recovered faster than I expected."

"But . . ."

"He's making progress. This was a big step."

"But why didn't you wake me? Petey needs me. I—" With exquisite gentleness Zachary bit her earlobe. A bolt of white-hot desire speared through her. "Petey . . ."

"Will soon be happily slurping his way through the biggest sundae money can buy. When I bribe, I do it right." His tongue delicately lapped at the tender hollow behind her ear while his hand stroked enticingly up and down her side. "Mmn. You taste good. A bit salty, but good."

"Salt isn't good for you."

"I know. I know." His hand came to rest beneath the fullness of her breast. Molly thought she would lose her mind with wanting him. She lightly raked her nails down his chest, was rewarded when he sucked in his breath. "So what can we do about it?"

"Want to take a shower?"

Molly purred. "I thought you'd never ask."

Harry couldn't believe his luck when the big guy went inside the house and the old broad left with the two kids. The big guy had seized his opportunity; he was going to get into the pretty lady's pants, if Harry didn't miss his guess. Well, the big guy's opportunity was also Harry's. Whistling tunelessly, he set out after the kids.

They had spent the better part of three days in close proximity, with no outlet for their passion, but now they were alone. They didn't make it to the shower. They didn't make it to the bed, either. They didn't even make it to the floor.

Zachary had hardly closed the sliding door when he had them both naked. He was fully, heavily aroused, and just looking at Molly almost made him explode. He put his hands around her neck and tilted up her chin with his thumbs. Then he lowered his head and opened his mouth over hers.

The force of the kiss caused Molly to sag against him. She slid her arms around his waist and tried to get as close as she could. His skin was burning. She made an inarticulate sound deep in her throat and tried to bring him even closer.

"Molly." Her name was a growl torn from deep in his chest. His hands moved to her breasts, cupped them. She pressed against him, making breathless sounds until his mouth found her and his hand trailed fire down her belly, dipped lower, testing her for readiness. Hot and slick, she started to convulse around his questing finger. His hands went immediately to her buttocks, lifted her. "Put your legs around my waist. That's it, Molly."

She reached between them and guided him, felt him thrust inside her with a power that took her breath away. Then she threw both her arms around his neck and hung on, for he took her on a ride that led her so high and so far she feared she might never return. But she trusted him to keep her safe, and that trust allowed her to fly, taking him with her.

After, she went limp in his arms. He groaned and tightened his hold. Her head lay on his shoulder. "I'm dead," she whispered.

He wrapped one arm tightly about her, while the other dropped to her buttocks. He squeezed. She made a startled little squeaking sound and moved against him. To her amazement, she felt him stir within her. "You're not human. You should have told me."

"I'm all too human. That's the problem." He lowered himself to his knees and carefully tilted her until her back touched the carpet. She smiled into his eyes as he secured her legs around his waist and started to move. "Again?"

"Oh, yes. Again."

"What's wrong with the bed?"

"Too far."

"I thought we were going to take a shower."

"Later."

She thought she heard him say—*if I live*—but couldn't be sure. She had her own survival to worry about; she was going up in flames again.

Twenty

Scarsdale, New York

The party Nancy and Andrew Larson held on the Sunday of the Memorial Day weekend was an annual event. An investment consultant with a prestigious firm, Andrew was expected to do his share of entertaining. Fortunately, Nancy loved doing it. They always hired the best caterer and the most popular band and spared no expense on decorations. This year Nancy had even commissioned two gigantic arches of red, white, and blue balloons to cross over the swimming pool.

Irene hadn't wanted to go, but couldn't come up with a good enough reason not to. After all, she couldn't tell Douglas she was afraid she would miss the major's call, so she dressed in a pale blue silk dress and went.

The party was in full swing when they got there. Expensive cars—including a Rolls and a Bentley—lined the Larson drive and were pulled up under the trees onto the front lawn. Douglas grumbled because they had to park some distance away. He didn't say it, but he blamed Irene for their being late. *So shoot me,* she thought, and left him as soon as they reached the back lawn. This promised to be one of the longest afternoons of her life.

Douglas headed straight for the bar. He knew many of the guests; he was even courting a few. His agency could always use a fat new account. Waiters saw he always had a full glass. He was beginning to relax, even to have a good time, when his sister-in-law caught up with him.

Nancy looked like a breath of spring in a flowered silk sundress, but her expression was as severe as deepest winter. "We've got to talk, Douglas. I'm very worried."

It was a beautiful day, if a bit warm and sticky, and he was feeling good, really good, after two—or was it three?—drinks. He didn't want to talk, at least not about anything of substance. He certainly didn't want to talk about his wife.

Nancy had other ideas and knew how to press them. Douglas had lived long enough with a Clewett female to recognize a no-win situation. They had wills of iron and never recognized personal defeat.

She led him to a spot far enough removed from the party to afford some privacy. He leaned against the trunk of an old walnut tree and took a long pull from his drink. His cold blue eyes regarded her dispassionately. "Okay, Nancy, you've got my undivided attention. What's so all-fired important it couldn't wait?" Annoyed, he didn't mind showing it.

Nancy ignored his tone, the none-too-subtle hint he wouldn't tolerate too much interference in his private affairs. There were things Douglas didn't know, and she was going to tell him. For Irene's good. She got right down to it. This was no time for hedging. Months of worry spilled out.

WHERE'S MY BABY?

Douglas was stunned. This was the first he had heard of a Dr. Slater and past-life regressions. He had thought Irene was still going to Dr. Powell. He had thought it a sign she was getting better when she stopped drinking. He had thought they could finally get on with their lives.

He had thought wrong.

Nancy made it very plain. As he listened, he sobered, and as he sobered, he grew angry. He didn't like being kept in the dark. He especially didn't like being put in this position.

"I had to tell you. Something's got to be done."

Something had to be done, all right, but Douglas doubted Nancy was going to like it.

Irene knew something momentous had happened the instant she saw Douglas's face. When he clamped his hand around her upper arm, yanked her to her feet, and announced to anyone within hearing distance that they were leaving, she was overjoyed. She didn't care that he was in a towering rage, nor wonder what had caused it. They were going home where she could be near the phone. That was all that mattered.

Douglas didn't say a word during the ride. He concentrated on driving, his eyes glued to the road, never once looking in her direction. It was fine with Irene. Once home, he stopped her from going upstairs. "Come into the den, please. I want to talk to you." Icily polite.

His control lasted only so long. "Is it true you've been seeing some quack named Slater?" He didn't so much ask the question as yell it. Everything Nancy had said had been tamped down, sealed within him like a pressure cooker, to simmer on the long drive. Now that they were alone, the lid was off.

By turns he was hurt, angry, mortified. Nancy had

said the quack was writing a book, thank you very much, Irene, that's just what his clients needed to see, his name prominent in some weirdo's account of an off-the-wall time-travel trip. How could she?

She could and she had, and he didn't give a damn about her, just about his name and his big-money accounts.

In an almost inarticulate rage, he said goddamn right that's what he cared about. That's all he had left. He certainly didn't have her and he didn't even know if he wanted her anymore. She would have to shape up or he was going to leave.

Divorce. For the first time the word was said. It vibrated in the air between them.

If Douglas expected a tearful scene, recriminations, perhaps a pledge to reform, he was doomed to disappointment.

"Divorce? Suit yourself," Irene said. As far as she was concerned, he was already a closed chapter.

"Janine never lived here. I bought the house after she died. The same with the town house. We lived in Connecticut . . . before. I sold everything. Everything."

Sitting on the lower deck, they were sipping iced teas, waiting for Mrs. Sadecki and the children. Fresh from a shower, her damp hair slicked back behind her ears, Molly didn't find Zachary's sudden confession at all strange. The questions had been between them, never more so than during the last couple of days. She shifted her position, took her eyes from the play of sunlight over water to focus on him. He was staring at the horizon. Even in profile she could see the starkness of his expression.

WHERE'S MY BABY?

"Lauren was a toddler, just a baby, really, when it happened. She doesn't remember her mother clearly."

Still Molly said nothing.

"She—Janine—had been unhappy." He swiveled his body so he faced Molly. "It was my fault. I had built up my practice, working day and night, doing whatever I had to do to succeed. It—I—was very successful." He leaned forward and set his glass on the broad railing. "Too successful. It took up time and energy, so much so, I needed a physical outlet. I've always been athletic, so I joined a health club and worked out as often as I could. Needless to say, I wasn't home enough."

A chill invaded Molly. She wasn't sure she wanted to hear any more. "Zachary . . ."

"I want you to know, Molly. After . . ." He shrugged, said simply, "You've got a right to know."

He was telling her she was important to him. When she didn't protest, he continued. "Ah, God, life can be rotten. I should have spent more time with her. I should have . . ." He got up so suddenly his chair tipped back. Molly put out a hand to keep it from falling.

Zachary strode to the far edge of the deck, stood with his back to her, facing the ocean. She didn't want to hear him recount his pain, knew she must, if their relationship was to deepen. It didn't take her long to make a decision. She went to stand next to him. He didn't look at her. "She died in an accident. A one-car accident on an empty road. The police were kind. They listed it as accidental. I was grateful, for Lauren's sake."

"That's a heavy burden you're carrying."

"I deserve it."

"Do you?" Molly asked, and would have said more, but just then Lauren and Petey came into sight. As soon as they saw the adults, they started to run.

"Daddy! Wait'll you see Mrs. Sadecki! She's all covered in goo and she couldn't wash because Petey got hysterical and it was all the rude man's fault and . . ."

"He did it on purpose. I saw him!"

Both adults looked at Mrs. Sadecki, who had followed the children at a slower pace. Her dress was smeared with streaks of what looked suspiciously like hot fudge.

Petey's favorite. Molly jumped to a logical conclusion. "Petey . . . ?"

Lauren recognized the tone and immediately rose to his defense. "It wasn't his fault, Molly, truly it wasn't. We were eating when a man stumbled against our table and knocked just about everything onto Mrs. Sadecki's lap."

"He was chust clumsy man. Is no big problem."

"He was mean. He did it on purpose."

Lauren shook her head, her big gray eyes, so like her father's, very serious. "I think Petey's right. I think he did do it on purpose."

"But, why . . . ?" Molly said.

"Who knows what motivates people?" Something in Zachary's voice made Molly aware he wasn't referring solely to this instance. Their eyes met and then he turned to the elderly housekeeper. "That dress is ruined. I'll see it's replaced."

"Dress is okay, Doctor. I wash it, it will be like new. You'll see."

Molly was eyeing the mess. "I don't know about that, Mrs. Sadecki. Those stains have probably set by now. You should have used cold water immediately."

"Is all right, missus. I fix." She carefully didn't look at Petey.

Molly had no such trouble. She crouched down so

they were eyeball to eyeball. "Well? Petey? I'm listening."

His face screwed up and started to get red, sure signs he was trying not to cry. "I'm a big boy! I don't gotta go in there!"

"Don't be angry with him," Lauren cried. "Mrs. Sadecki didn't want to leave us to wash up and Petey didn't want to go in the ladies' room. He shouldn't have to go if he doesn't want to. Right, Daddy?"

"Ah ..." Hastily Zachary swallowed a flip macho remark when he caught sight of Molly's expression. He lightly touched his daughter's shining blond hair. "It's not for us to say, pussycat."

Molly stood up. She didn't want to make this into a major deal. She eyed her son's none-too-clean T-shirt. "Mrs. Sadecki's not the only one who needs to change. We'll talk about this later, Petey."

He raced away, Lauren on his heels. The housekeeper started to follow, but Molly stopped her. "Thank you, Mrs. Sadecki, for taking such good care of him. I really appreciate it. You must be very uncomfortable."

"Is nothing, missus. He's a very nice little boy."

"He is," Zachary said, and the second they were alone again, drew Molly into his arms. "What?" he asked when he felt her tremble.

"Nothing. Everything."

"Things change." He dropped a kiss onto the crown of her head. "The worst problem you should ever have, sweet Molly, is Petey refusing to go into the ladies' room."

Molly tilted up her head, met his amused gaze. "Laugh all you want. This presents a real problem. What am I going to do?"

"Have you considered using the men's room?"

"Very funny."

"Or . . ." Suddenly he wasn't laughing anymore. Lightly, he brushed the backs of his fingers over her cheek. "Have you thought of introducing a male role model into his life?" A breeze lifted her hair, blew it into her face. Zachary carefully tucked the dark strands back behind her ears. Her eyes were more brown than green as she stared at him, as if seeing him for the first time. "Have you?"

"No."

"You should." He kissed her lightly on the lips and went inside.

Alone, Molly stared at the sea. She wasn't laughing, either.

Twenty-One

June

"Hi. I forgot to put this in the mail."

Gertrude Zinzendorf broke into a grin when she saw who was hovering in her doorway. "What a nice surprise. Come in and find a place to sit," the grin widened, "Molly Deere, WAND reporter." The grin shifted to rueful. "It took me long enough. I *knew* I knew you. Imagine, you're a celebrity."

Molly laughed. "Hardly." She started to put the check—final payment, no turning back now—on the desk, then hesitated.

Gertrude looked chagrined. "You'd better hand it over. Things have a way of disappearing around here." She opened an account book, ran her finger down a page, made a check mark. "Peter Deere. Good. I'm so glad he'll be with us this summer. We've got a good group. You won't be sorry you sent him to Camp Abnaki."

"Oh, I'm sure I won't. I—" Her buzzer went off. One glance told her it was Kent. "May I use your phone?" Gertrude located the instrument and pushed it toward her, sending papers flying. Kent was as excited as Molly had ever heard him. She scribbled a few notes, said, "Right away. No more than fifteen minutes. Tops." Then she hung up and sighed.

"Trouble?"

"There's always trouble. This time it's a hostage situation at the Queens unemployment office. Someone's benefits must have run out."

"It sounds dangerous. Be careful."

Gertrude's concern went a long way toward ameliorating Kent's "Hop to it, cookie, if you don't want to join the unemployment line yourself."

On the best of days Sutphin Boulevard was nothing to brag about, especially the blocks between Hillside and Jamaica, where the State and City of New York had seen fit to cram an assortment of official buildings. The biggest and most prestigious was the State Supreme Court, a dirt-encrusted marble edifice encompassing an entire city block, surrounded by a high iron fence, legacy of the fear of dynamite-loaded vehicles being driven up the stately steps. Neighboring buildings were much more humble in appearance, some unkind souls might even call them eyesores, but the people doing business at the Department of Real Estate, the Offices of the City Collector and all the other official bureaus and departments didn't give a damn. They wanted to get in and get out, as fast as possible.

Today, though, it seemed to Molly every man, woman, and child in the five boroughs had come to gawk. Some had even brought their pets. In her rush to get through the crowd, she had tripped over a poodle's leash and been harangued by its owner. Disheveled and hot—she had been forced to park three blocks away—

she finally arrived at the scene just as the police were establishing a line of sawhorses to contain the crowd. The press was likewise being penned. Molly didn't recognize any of the brass, so chose a likely-looking young cop. Cooperative, he gave her enough to call in a report.

Kent was pleased. He liked the idea of a roomful of hot, angry people without jobs being held at gunpoint by a man who only wanted to feed his wife and family.

"Swat team there yet?"

Molly looked at the roofs, saw figures moving. "They're setting up now. You want to record? I've got a witness who saw it happen. He was on his way out when the guy pulled the gun."

Kent wanted to record. "Great stuff," he said, when the short interview was over. "Call me with more."

The highest praise he had ever given her.

Five hours later it was over. The gunman surrendered to the police and the hostages, weary but eager to talk, filed out of the building to the applause of the crowd.

An hour after that, sweaty and tired, Molly was only too glad to call in her final report.

"No casualties?"

"No, Kent. No *Dog Day Afternoon*. Sorry."

"Cute, cookie. Got anything good?"

Molly gave him what she had, which included an interview with the chief negotiator, an experienced policeman with an impressive record. He had never lost a hostage.

Even Kent couldn't ask any more of her. Molly thought about a nice long bath all the way to Mrs. Parr's. No cooking tonight. They'd go the fast-food route, whichever Petey wanted.

Petey exploded out of the baby-sitter's front door the instant she stopped the car. She barely had time to notice his T-shirt had acquired some interesting new stains before he catapulted himself into her embrace, wound his arms around her neck, and gave her a smacking kiss. She returned it enthusiastically. "Had a good day?"

"Super!"

"That's my boy. Hungry?"

"You bet."

Silly question. Petey was always hungry. Molly let him slide to the ground. He was getting too heavy for her. "You pick a place for take-out, honey. Mommy's too tired to cook tonight."

Petey backed away a couple of steps. "We're gonna eat at the circus." The circus! She'd forgotten. Petey accurately read her expression. He backed up another step. "You promised."

So she had. But she was exhausted. "I know, honey, but I had a real tough day and I don't know if . . ." Petey was looking at her with his heart in his eyes. He wouldn't beg or cry or throw a tantrum like many kids his age. He wasn't that way. He'd swallow his disappointment, be unhappy for a time, then seemingly forget it.

But she wouldn't. And a promise was a promise. She knelt down so she could look directly into his eyes. "Look, here's what we'll do. We'll go home, get cleaned up, and I'll rest for a while. And then . . ." She touched her index finger to his nose. "And then we'll go to the circus." Petey let out a whoop and threw his arms around her neck again. His hug was fierce, and it made her feel like a heel.

By the time she had Petey bathed and had taken her own bath and had a glass of wine, she was feeling some of Petey's enthusiasm. Her feet still hurt from standing on the hot pavement during the long, tense vigil, but who but the wicked witch would let a small thing like that interfere in her son's pleasure? She slipped into a pair of jeans and was pulling a fuchsia T-shirt over her head when the phone rang. "I'll get it," she yelled, but her voice was muffled and she was too late anyway. Barefoot, she was halfway down the stairs when she heard Petey's excited voice. "Yeah! The circus! Wanna come?"

She tapped her son on the shoulder. "Is that for me?"

"I gotta go, Zach'ry," Petey said, and handed the phone over.

"Hi. I didn't know the circus was in town."

"Hi to you. There's one in Cunningham Park. It's not Ringling Brothers, but it's got elephants. That's the next-best thing to dinosaurs. I second Petey's invitation. Lauren would love it."

"No doubt, but I'm afraid not. I've got a follow-up counseling session with some students in Brooklyn."

"Oh, too bad. Look, I could take her. How about it?"

"Thanks, but no. You'd have to drive into Manhattan to pick her up. That's too much, especially after the day you've had. I've been listening. That was quite a situation in Jamaica."

"It ended okay. That's all that counts."

Petey came running back into the room, announced at the top of his lungs he was ready to go.

"Subtle, isn't he?"

Molly chuckled. "Are you sure about Lauren? It's no trouble. Really."

"I'm sure. Another time."

Petey looked up at her hopefully when she hung up. "Are you rested yet?"

"I'm rested."

"Yippeeeeee! Let's go!"

Wishing she could borrow just an iota of his energy, she laughed and asked if he could wait while she put on her sneakers. Petey allowed it was okay, but just barely.

There was quite a crowd at the park. Molly found a parking spot a fair distance from the entrance. The hot, humid day had turned into a hot, humid night. The only saving grace was a slight breeze that scarcely moved the limp leaves on the trees. Petey, of course, didn't let it slow him down. He shifted his weight from foot to foot. "C'mon. I kin smell the elephants!"

"Can. You *can* smell the elephants." *Everyone* could smell them. Molly wondered how the local residents felt about it. But soon the magic of a circus under the stars took over and she forgot the heat, the humidity, the smells of animals, food, and sweating human bodies. She even forgot her feet felt like lead.

Petey dragged her from tent to tent, prolonging his excitement by saving the elephants for last. They bought hot dogs and soft drinks and before too long Petey had mustard and cola on his T-shirt, and after he persuaded her to buy him french fries, he sported a big blob of ketchup, too. Molly dabbed at it with a paper napkin, but only made it worse. Petey looked like an advertisement for laundry detergent. Jackson Pollock would have loved him. "That's it. Nothing more will fit on this shirt."

The humor flew over his head. "Cotton candy. You promised."

Petey was the literal sort. "Cotton candy, but that's *it*." Even though it was spun sugar, Molly couldn't resist it, either. She took a bite and got it on her nose. Petey giggled. Pink strands were already all over his face. Too late, she remembered her camera. "Damn," she said under her breath, and pulled Petey close as the crowd surged around them. It was fully dark now and people were still arriving. More couples and fewer families.

"It's getting late, Petey. Time for the elephants?"

"Elephants." Petey beamed. Highlight time.

The huge beasts were the circus's drawing card. By far the most popular attraction, they were in an area off to one side, ringed by huge bales of hay. People stood packed deeply in front of them. Petey couldn't see, and Molly wasn't tall enough or strong enough to lift him, so she applied a skill she had perfected as a reporter. Ditching her cotton candy in the nearest receptacle—Petey refused to relinquish his—she took him firmly by the hand and used her free elbow to maneuver them past bodies and strollers until he had an unrestricted view. His delighted expression was well worth all the dirty looks and muttered oaths she'd engendered along the way.

"Tembo." Petey pointed with his cotton candy.

This close they were very big, and they made Molly nervous. She didn't like the way one of them was eyeing Petey, as if it was tired of being a vegetarian. Petey pulled excitedly on her hand. "Stay back. Keep close to me."

A trainer began to work with the elephants. Petey stared enraptured as they lumbered patiently through their paces. More and more people came to watch. Molly was jostled from the side and rear. She pulled Petey closer. She didn't like to be this near to the behemoths with the crowd hemming them in.

A baby elephant curled its trunk around its mother's tail. The crowd rumbled and pressed forward. Molly tried to hold her ground but felt herself being inexorably pushed toward the hay-bale barrier. Panic rose, instantly making her frantic. Whether it was a touch of claustrophobia or a healthy respect for the unpredictability of crowds, it didn't matter; she wanted out of there at once.

Holding tightly to Petey's hand, she began to inch sideways, saying, "Excuse me," "Coming through," "Let me out, please," and "Sorry," when she stepped on someone's foot. She wasn't even looking at the elephants anymore, all she wanted was to get some space. The crowd shifted, someone shoved, for a second Molly teetered, falling forward. But then she regained her footing and started to inch her way again, only . . .

Petey was no longer holding her hand.

She turned and looked.

He was gone.

Twenty-Two

He can't be gone. He was right here.

Clear thoughts, then Molly felt the dizzying sensation of her stomach dropping. Frozen except for her eyes, she took in everything in one encompassing glance. Faces. Bodies. Strangers, all. Petey had to be here. He *had* to be. Where could one small boy have gotten to so fast?

The crowd pressed. *Oh, God, he was being trampled underfoot.* Her eyes swept the ground. No Petey. Nothing. Nothing but ...

Pink.

Cotton candy. Lying abandoned.

Her vision began to blur. She was going to faint. *No. Mustn't. Petey. Petey needed her.*

"Petey!" she screamed, as loud as she could. People near her recoiled. "My little boy is gone. He was right here. Help me find him." They shrank from her; as if she had leprosy.

"Peteeeeeeeeeeeeeeey!"

No answer. She needed the police, and she needed them fast. Every second counted. First, security. Surely a circus this size had a security force?

She was thinking again.

A middle-aged man with a walkie-talkie approached. Heat had turned his face beet red; sweat beaded his high forehead. "Is there trouble? A woman said—"

"My little boy's gone. You've got to put people on every exit. You've got to do it now." Her voice was rising and even to her own ears she was beginning to sound hysterical. He wouldn't believe her, would waste precious seconds if she lost control. She had to convince him. Now. "Someone took him. Believe me."

"What's he wearing?"

Molly almost sagged with relief. Quickly she gave Petey's age and height and weight and described what he was wearing. The man spoke into the walkie-talkie. "Now call the police. Hurry." He searched her face for what seemed ages. Molly could only stand it so long. "Call them. Now."

Again he raised the walkie-talkie. Molly heard the crackle of static. His lips moved. For the first time she noticed he had a moustache. Drops of sweat ran off its ends. "Okay, lady, they're on the way."

Another man came running up. He gave Molly a quick once-over. "Whaddayagot?" Molly turned her body as Dripping Moustache repeated her story. She couldn't bear to hear it again.

Think. She had to think. She had to help find Petey.

"Miss?" Dripping Moustache had a grip on her elbow. "You want to come with me now? We'll just go on to the office and fill out a report."

Fill out a report? Petey wasn't a lost umbrella. She jerked her arm free. "No! I've got to stay here. Petey knows to come to the last place we were together, or . . ."

"To stand still and wait, or to go to someone in authority. Right?"

Molly blinked. Dripping Moustache reached for her arm again. "We all tell our kids the same thing. Now come with me. Petey isn't here."

He didn't want her making a big fuss. That much was obvious. Lost little boys were bad for business. *Business.* Suddenly her mind cleared. She needed a telephone.

Zachary was exhausted and emotionally wrung out by the time he left the school. The follow-up session had been tougher than usual because the kids in the economically deprived neighborhood were inured to violence. The brutal death of a teacher wasn't an isolated occurrence. They fully expected something like it to happen again, perhaps even to themselves. Most of them lived without hope of a better life.

Angry and disgusted, he felt impotent and frustrated by a society that didn't seem able to change such a situation. He would go home and have a nice cooling shower and relax in his comfortable house while these kids would—what? Go home and wait for a bullet to zing through a window or door?

He slammed his hand against the steering wheel hard enough to feel pain and then jammed the key into the ignition. The car roared to life and he immediately adjusted the air-conditioning controls to maximum. He drove with one ear tuned to the radio, hoping to hear Molly's voice, trying to remember if the repair work on the Brooklyn Bridge was finished or if they were doing it at night, in which case he would take the Manhattan or . . .

The three-note signal of a major breaking story interrupted his thoughts. At first he couldn't believe it, it was too preposterous to be true. He was tired, he was having an auditory hallucination, he was . . .

"... *When last seen Peter Deere was wearing dark-blue jeans and a red T-shirt with* ..."

Zachary applied the brakes so suddenly smoke rose as he skidded to a stop. Ignoring the honking and shouted curses from other drivers peppering the air, he made an illegal U-turn over the center divider and headed east as fast as he could go.

The house was dark when Douglas, late again, finally pulled into the garage. The apparent lack of welcome wasn't unexpected. He and Irene hadn't exactly been on the best of terms since Nancy's party.

Cautiously he opened the door into the kitchen. No surprise waited on the floor. No meat loaf or mashed potatoes or smashed glass. Good. He was too tired to clean up one of Irene's messes tonight.

The house was very quiet. He started to tiptoe, then thought better of it. This was *his* house. He'd go upstairs, take a shower, then have a nightcap in the den while he watched the news. With any luck, Irene wouldn't awaken. He'd had enough confrontation at work. The Perfect Puppy people were less than sanguine about the new campaign, as finicky as the dogs they fed.

Upstairs, still darkness greeted him. He paused with his hand on the knob of the master bedroom door, wondering if he would find Irene passed out. If she was drinking again, there was no hope for them. He wouldn't put up with it anymore. He had made that quite clear. He would call his lawyer and start the divorce.

No Irene in the bedroom. From long habit he went looking, not that he wanted to, but because he always had. He fully expected to find her dead to the world, a bottle of bourbon clutched to her chest, but she wasn't in the house or anywhere on the property. The tall-case clock in the foyer chimed the hour as he let himself back inside. Eleven. Where the hell was she?

More irritated than alarmed, he headed straight for the wet bar in the den, turning on the television as he passed it. He filled a glass with ice and searched behind the books on the third shelf of the bookcase until he found a bottle of scotch. Not that Irene was partial to it, if she could get her hands on bourbon, but he kept it hidden to ensure he could have a drink when he wanted one. Or needed one, as he did now. Where had she gotten to? Her car was still in the garage. Her clothes.... He gulped a long swallow, slammed the glass down, and climbed the stairs again, taking them two at a time. Irene's closet was full; but then, she had so much clothing, he couldn't tell if any was missing.

Back downstairs he picked up his drink, slumped onto the couch. A picture of a little boy filled the television screen. Something about a circus. A number appeared on the screen. Douglas's eyes slid to the telephone. He took another deep swallow, feeling the liquor slide cool and smooth down his throat. He'd be damned if he'd start calling around, asking for his wife. If she wanted to play games, let her. He didn't care. Where Irene was concerned, he had stopped caring long ago.

He poured another drink, spent long moments staring into its amber depths. A slice of truth. Ever since

Karen's death. . . . He downed the drink and quickly poured another, angrily turned off the television, where they were still talking about the little boy, apparently missing. Douglas couldn't bring himself to care about it. He had enough troubles of his own.

Twenty-Three

Nightmare.

If only. But this nightmare was real, and as the minutes and hours ticked away, it just got worse. Police came and went, first in the security office at Cunningham Park, and later in her home. They went over and over the evening's events. Molly eagerly complied, hoping something, perhaps one piece of information, would help lead them to her son.

Alive. *Please, God, alive and well.* It wasn't too much to ask, for a little boy who is all sunshine and love, was it?

"No, of course not."

Molly turned toward the comfort of the familiar voice, unaware she had been speaking her thoughts. Zachary handed her a cup of tea. She shoved it back at him, ran into the small downstairs bathroom under the stairs and dry-heaved over the toilet. The spasms rocked her body, rasped her throat raw, and left her trembling, hands braced against the wall, too weak even to slide down to the floor.

Strong arms lifted her, held her. She heard the toilet seat slam down and then she was turned and lowered until she sat. The sound of running water came as if from far away. The world suddenly went gray, tangoed into black, studded with sparkling dots of red and gold. She began to sway, her head lolling back, her neck no longer able to support it. Her voice was a whisper buzzing eerily through her brain. "Dizzy."

"Okay. Hang on, Molly. Hang on."

Her head was pushed down between her knees; a cool damp cloth was placed on the nape of her neck.

"Oh, God, what happened?"

Denise, that was Denise's voice, dimly heard through the roaring in her ears.

"She's feeling faint. She'll feel better soon."

"Let's get her upstairs. She's got to rest."

"No!" Molly tried to look up, but Zachary firmly held down her head. She didn't fight; she felt better that way. What seemed like an eternity later, she said, "Okay, you can let me up now," and instantly she was free. Slowly she raised her head. Zachary was leaning against the doorjamb, Denise behind him. She got to her feet, wobbled a bit, had to grab the edge of the sink to steady herself.

Zachary stepped back, nodding encouragingly. "You're doing fine."

"She's got to lie down. She's going on nerves alone."

Molly touched the older woman's arm. "I'm fine. Don't worry. Go home, Denise. There's nothing you can do." She said to Zachary, "You, too. Go home to your daughter." Denise gave a ragged little cry that ended in a sob. Molly rounded on her. "Don't! I can't take that!"

The policeman—detective?—who was in charge approached, said they were leaving; they had done all they could tonight. *But Petey's still missing,* she wanted to scream. They would be back in the morning.

Without them, the house was deathly still. Denise's husband came to the kitchen door, wanting to know if he could help. Molly told him to take his wife home, and after much fussing, Denise finally consented to go. She'd be back first thing. Molly gave her a fierce hug. It conveyed everything she couldn't say.

Zachary bolted the door behind them. "I keep a medical bag in my car. Do you want something to help you relax?"

Nirvana. Tempting, but she turned it down. She had to be alert. Her eyes flicked to the phone, on the wall next to the refrigerator. Petey's latest artwork adorned it, held in place by bubble-gum-pink pig magnets. *Ring. Ring. Ring.* It could be Petey, needing her . . . it could be the creep who took him. . . . Her eyes were twin pits of despair when she finally looked at Zachary. "I can't sleep."

"It won't put you to sleep. It'll just take off the edge."

"No." She couldn't—wouldn't—ease her way when God alone knew what Petey was going through. As a reporter she knew . . . shudders wracked her body; she reached out for the back of a chair to keep herself from falling. Zachary gripped her shoulders, held her upright, until by sheer force of will she controlled her body. "I'm all right now. Go home. Lauren will be wondering what happened to you."

"Lauren's fine. I called her. Mrs. Sadecki is there."

"I want to be alone." God, she was screaming like a shrew. She wrapped her arms tightly across her chest, trying desperately to hold herself together. If there were words to describe how she was feeling, she had never heard them.

Zachary didn't get angry or say any of the expected

things, but then, he was trained for situations like this. He merely looked at her gravely, nodded, said, "Okay—pretend I'm not here," and simply walked away.

Molly stood in the kitchen for a long time, her eyes fastened on the phone. It wasn't going to ring; not tonight, anyway, because she so desperately wanted it to, and *he* knew it, wanted her to suffer, to.... Selfish. Thinking of herself when she should be thinking of Petey.

Petey.

She had to be strong. There was no one else.... Oh, God, her mother! A quick look at the big wall clock and she knew it was too late to call, even with the time difference between New York and Arizona. Time enough first thing in the morning. Let her mother get a good night's sleep.

Somehow, she had to fill those hours. The house was so quiet now she thought she really was alone. Had Zachary taken her at her word and left? Suddenly the thought was unbearable.

All the rooms were dark. She left on the kitchen light and went quickly down the short hallway, poked her head inside the living room. No one. He had left. She felt abandoned, more alone than before, which was ridiculous, because she had told him to go. Then she noticed eerie light bouncing off the glass of the empty terrarium, and turning, saw it was a reflection of the television, and when she looked the other way she made out Zachary's form in the gloom, watching the picture without sound. He had to know she was there, but he didn't even stir.

Pretend I'm not here.

She wanted to thank him, but she couldn't. If she so much as uttered a single word—assuming she could get it past the lump in her throat—she would dissolve into tears, and she knew once she started, she wouldn't be able to stop. So she rushed upstairs, ripped off her clothes, and stood under the shower until her skin got all pruny and the soap, which she had dropped and was clogging the drain, was a white, gloppy mess.

Dressed in soft sweats, she pulled her hair into a ponytail and prowled the house. Upstairs, downstairs, from room to room. Sometime during the night she went into Petey's room, stumbled as usual over toys on the floor—he really had to learn some discipline—and managed to find Lambie Pie in the dark. Then she resumed her silent patrol, the little yellow lamb clutched tightly to her breast.

Morning came with the abrupt pealing of the front doorbell. The sky was still delicately pink, the world gray with retreating night shadows when she opened the door. To her surprise, Kent Durwood stood on the doorstep. While she stood there like a ninny with her mouth hanging open, he brushed past her and walked inside.

A big hand closed on his shoulder. "Not so fast, buddy. Let's put it in reverse."

At least seven inches shorter and thirty pounds lighter than Zachary, Kent dug in his heels and raised his eyebrows. "Call off your goon, cookie. We've got work to do."

Zachary, who had spent an agonizing night listening to Molly roam the small house like a lost soul, wanted nothing more than to take out his frustrations. His grip tightened. "You know this character?"

"It's Kent. *Kent.* You know, my boss."

Zachary reluctantly let the smaller man go. Kent immediately held out his hand. "Kent Durwood."

For a moment Zachary was nonplussed. *This*—this

short man with sloping shoulders, thinning hair, and the beginnings of a middle-aged paunch who looked like anyone's description of Caspar Milquetoast—was the son of a bitch with the sensitivity of a cobra? Amused, he took his hand. "Zachary Slater."

"Slater?" Kent frowned, then snapped his fingers. "The trauma guy. Lousy interview."

Zachary bit back a grin. Caspar Milquetoast with fangs.

Kent turned to Molly. "Come on, cookie, we've got lots to do. I've called in every favor and made promises I've no way of keeping this side of hell." He winked solemnly. "But they have no way of knowing that. Go do something with your hair and your face. You're a mess, and we don't have much time. I've got commitments from ABC, NBC, and CBN. I expect to hear from CBS any time now. I gave them your number."

"What's he talking about?" Belatedly Zachary closed the door.

"You tell the big guy. I'll scout around for the best location."

A spark of hope flared in Molly's eyes. "Petey's picture will be on national television. America is going to hear about him over breakfast."

The police arrived as the last of the press were stowing their gear. When the unmarked car drove up, those who were left rushed to it like sharks gravitating to a kill. Two men got out—the driver, a tall man with skin the color of expensive mahogany, and a well-built, good-looking man with wavy dark-brown hair. Surprise, then alarm, gripped Molly when she recognized Glen Rowley. It didn't help that Charlie Lee, his dark eyes

WHERE'S MY BABY? 223

brimming with sadness and a reflection of her own fear, put a hand on her shoulder and squeezed when he too saw Glen. *They had found Petey. They had sent a friend to tell her he was dead.*

The detectives expertly waded through the clamoring newspeople, not even bothering with the familiar "no comment." Glen came up the stairs slowly, a bleak expression on his handsome face. Molly couldn't breathe, much less speak or move. Charlie's grip tightened, and it was he who asked if Petey had been found.

Too late Glen understood what his presence could mean. "No. There's no news at all." He bent and brushed his lips over Molly's pale cheek. "Sorry, Molly, I didn't realize what you'd think. I pulled every string in sight to get assigned to the case. I figured you could use a friend on the force."

Everything had become surreal. Glen introduced his partner; again for Zachary and Kent. Detective Sidney Salem wordlessly acknowledged them. His eyes were kind, his voice warm and sympathetic; he seemed to understand Molly's pain. Molly didn't want sympathy; she wanted action.

Charlie left with a promise to call, shortly followed by Kent. Zachary drew her aside, said he also had to leave, promised to return as soon as possible. Molly suddenly, irrationally, felt abandoned.

The detectives took seats in the living room. Molly sat down, immediately sprang up again. She couldn't keep still, not when demons of doubt plagued her. How had someone snatched Petey from her grasp? Had she let him go? Had she seen the person?

The same questions the detectives posed, over and over again, pushing her to remember—details, impressions—for anything and everything she could recall. Exhausting mental work, and during the entire time the phone kept ringing. Denise faithfully manned it, for which Molly was grateful. She made short work of each call, wanting to keep the line open. Any minute the phone company was supposed to install another line.

After what seemed an eternity, Glen closed his notebook. "That's about it for now, I think." Detective Salem, who for the most part had remained silently watchful, nodded in assent. He diplomatically left before Glen.

Molly rubbed her damp palms on her thighs. "I've covered cases like this, Glen. You've got to move fast."

"I know, Molly, and believe me, we are. We've got good men on it." He hugged her, lightly brushed his lips over hers. "I like Petey, you know. He's a real cute kid."

Bless Glen. It reassured her that someone who knew Petey was working on the case. The phone shrilled. It rang again, and then a third time. Molly got to it in the middle of the fourth ring. Her voice was breathless, filled with the hope she couldn't quash. Maybe *this* was the clue.

"Molly Deere?" A pause, a cough.

"Yes. Please. Who is this?"

"Never mind who I am."

Molly tightly gripped the phone, almost ground the receiver into her ear. Denise came out of the bathroom, saw the look on her face, whispered, "Who is it? Is it . . . is it *him*?"

Molly licked her lips. "Are you calling about Petey?"

Another cough, dry-sounding, then the voice boomed into her ear. "God told me to call. You don't deserve a child. Any mother who would—"

Denise took one look at Molly's expression and gently prized the phone away. She held it to her ear for a moment then banged the receiver down. "Another loony-toony heard from."

Molly began to shudder, her eyes filling with tears. "Maybe they're right. What kind of mother lets her child be taken? What ... what ... oh—"

Denise reached for her just as she began to sob. "There, there, lovey, cry. Cry it all out. You'll feel better."

Twenty-Four

Denise proved a poor prophet. As the days went by with no word, Molly cried, often and bitterly. It didn't make her feel one bit better. With each rising and setting of the sun, she grew more frantic. Time was the enemy; with every second that passed, the hope of finding Petey dimmed.

She forgot what "normal" meant. She ate and slept only enough to keep going. Every time the phone rang she desperately prayed that *this* call would be a ransom demand, a painful prelude to the return of her son. But the one call she eagerly anticipated was denied her, and as the hours ticked by with no new twist, no sensational discovery, Petey's abduction became stale news. Even the unwelcome phone calls, those from society's less stable citizens, were beginning to taper off.

Three days after Petey's abduction she was sitting at the kitchen table staring into a cup of cold tea when WAND blared its three-note attention-getter. She jumped up to turn up the volume so fast her hip collided with the corner of the table. She never felt the pain.

"This just in. A psychic working with Queens detectives to find four-and-a-half-year-old Peter Deere has found

no evidence the boy was ever at the circus from which his mother claims he was abducted. WAND reporter Eleanor Perez is en route ..."

Next they would say she had never had a son, that Petey was a figment of her imagination. Someone was making pathetic whuffling noises, sounding like a whipped puppy cowering before an upraised belt. No! No matter how beguiling madness became, it was not for her. It couldn't be, not when Petey needed her more than he ever had before. The phone jangled; she snatched it off the hook. "Deere."

Kent's gleeful voice vibrated in her ear. "Did you catch the bulletin, cookie?"

"The psychic?"

"Yeah." Kent was almost chortling. "The guy is a blessing in disguise. It's dynamite. We can put the story back at the top of the news."

Molly was getting to know Kent better. Something in his voice ... "Kent, did you have anything to do with it?"

A small pause, and when he spoke again, his tone was as cynical as ever. "Me? You know it would be unethical for someone in my position to try to influence the news." Another pause, also uncharacteristic, then a gruff, "Eleanor says the police are keeping the swami under wraps. She's interviewing the cops now. You're next. Play the outraged mother to the hilt, cookie. The public loves pathos."

"... Cannot find a single witness who saw four-and-a-half-year-old Peter Deere with his mother that night. Also, the psychic, who went over every inch of Cunningham Park in the company of Queens detectives,

could find no evidence the boy was ever there. His mother, WAND reporter Molly Deere, claims she took her son to the circus . . ."

"Claims!" Zachary hit the steering wheel with the heel of his palm. "*Claims* she took her son to the circus . . ."

From the kitchen window, Molly watched the policemen moving about her property. She knew what they were looking for. Soon enough they would conclude she was innocent and conduct their search elsewhere. This was a necessary part of any investigation, especially when an expert cast doubt upon a story, even if the so-called expert was a psychic. Just another dreadful incident to endure. She would endure anything if it got her Petey back. But it hurt.

Petey. She couldn't think of what he might be going through. She couldn't . . . but if she did, if her treacherous mind slipped to the inconceivable, she knew there was nothing she *wouldn't* endure to have him safely home. So she watched Detective Salem oversee the men in her yard, poking and prying, looking for evidence of disturbed earth. She shivered, wondered where Glen Rowley was. Did *he* think she had murdered her son and buried him beneath the petunias?

It didn't take long. She didn't have much property. Detective Salem came to her back door and politely knocked, as if he hadn't known she was monitoring every moment. His dark face glistened with sweat. Ordinarily, Molly would have invited him in for a cool drink, but she'd be damned if she would under these circumstances. He seemed to understand. "We're just about finished, ma'am."

WHERE'S MY BABY? 229

"Finished with what? What the hell is going on here?"

Molly had never seen Zachary in a rage, but she had no trouble recognizing cold fury.

The tall detective nodded mildly as Zachary furiously burst into the backyard. "Dr. Slater. I was just telling Mrs. Deere we're leaving."

"Whose idea was this?" Zachary's eyes swept the yard, missing nothing. "Where's Rowley? Isn't he in charge? What did he do, send you to do the dirty work?"

"It's just routine, Dr. Slater." The detective transferred his gaze to Molly. His eyes, beagle-sad, were not unkind. "We won't be bothering you again."

"Damn straight you won't."

Zachary followed the police out of the yard and stood glaring until they drove away. Under other circumstances, Molly might have been amused and most probably flattered by his protective attitude, but at this point she was incapable of feeling much. When he finally stormed inside, she was sitting at the kitchen table, where she had spent the better part of the past week, staring at the phone.

"Okay, Molly, pack a bag. You're coming home with me."

Apparently, Zachary's rage had not abated. She could hear it in his voice, see it in every line of his body.

"No. I can't leave here."

"You can and you will. Denise has got the leaflet distribution well organized. She doesn't need your help. If you're worried about the phone, we can have the phone company reroute your calls. There's nothing more you can do here. Come with me, Molly. I can't protect you here."

"No!" She shot up so fast she surprised him into jumping back. So tense she shook; her eyes blazed with emotion. "No. I'm not leaving. This is my home, mine and Petey's, and he's going to return to it and I'll be waiting, waiting right here." She backed away from him. "I'm not leaving. Do you hear me? You want me to leave. My mother wants me to leave. She thinks I should come visit her until this 'nastiness' is over. What does she think is going on? This is my life and my home and no one can make me do anything. No one. I can protect myself."

If he hadn't been so anguished—and so personally involved—Zachary never would have pursued it, but he was, and years of training deserted him, along with the restraint of common sense. "Can you? Have you listened to what they're saying? They're suspecting you of . . ." One look at her stricken face and he stopped. No way he could put the ugly thought into words. "Molly . . ." He reached for her only to have her shrink from him. She looked like a little wild animal, besieged from all sides. He let his hand drop. In her state, any more would be mental abuse. Although it hurt him, he did the only thing kindness would allow. "Okay, Molly. I'll leave you alone."

". . . Learned that while detectives continue to search for clues to the whereabouts of little Petey Deere close to home, others have flown to Texas to follow up a lead—"

Texas?

Molly switched her gaze from the blankness of the window overlooking her nighttime yard to the portable radio on the counter next to the sink. Her eyes bored into the dull gray plastic while her mind whirled in circles.

What lead in Texas? Kent hadn't called about this, as he had with everything else. Maybe it was just in, maybe.... The phone shrilled, making her jump. She had the receiver pressed to her ear before the first ring ended. "Kent—"

"Molly," a voice snarled in her ear.

Oh, God. Texas! In reaction, she staggered until she bumped against the wall, the phone cord wrapped around her, too weak to untangle herself and walk the few steps to the nearest chair. She had vowed if she ever heard from her husband—no, her ex-husband—she would have a few things to say to him. But now, with the sheer surprise and under these circumstances, she couldn't mobilize her thoughts, much less give voice to them. So many things she had wanted to say, so many feelings that could be expressed, giving her freedom, finally allowing her to put the past to rest and go on with her life.

So many things, and now the opportunity was lost, for all she could do was listen as Roy Deere ranted and raved, accusing her of every crime imaginable, including the overwhelming one of embarrassing him in his new life. After the first shock of hearing his voice wore off, she found she didn't care, he couldn't touch her with his vituperation. She also discovered she had nothing to say to him. The time had passed.

He was going on and on, apparently not needing her input. "... and I told Rowley to get the hell out of my face. And I'm telling you, Molly, you're certainly one hell of a disappointment. I'm going to sue for custody of my son, and I have no doubt I'll get it. You're an unfit mother, not fit to raise my son. Do you hear me? I said I'm going to sue for custody." He stopped the tirade, either running out of breath or finally realizing he had been conducting a monologue. "Molly? Are you there? I'm going to sue for custody of my son. What do you have to say to that, Molly?"

Molly hung up.

Douglas came home at his usual late hour to find lights blazing from the downstairs windows. So his errant wife had decided to come home. He pulled into the garage and sat for several moments after he turned off the ignition, unsure of how he felt. Life without Irene was certainly a lot calmer than life with her. But they had a lot of history together, he and Irene. He guessed he owed her; she damn well owed him.

Irene wasn't waiting in the living room. Nancy, her back ramrod straight, sat on a ladder-backed chair with a woven-rush seat. Every facial muscle was drawn tight; her lips were a disapproving crimson slash across pallid flesh. Her husband lounged in Douglas's favorite upholstered chair, a snifter of brandy close at hand.

Neither one spoke. The ploy amused Douglas, but he hid it well. He hadn't risen to the top in the advertising business without learning how to play games. Without false modesty, he was a master. He put his keys and briefcase on a side table, nodded coolly to his uninvited guests. "Nancy. Andrew. Am I late?"

Nancy leaned forward stiffly. "Don't be cute, Douglas. Where is my sister?"

Deciding he could use a drink, Douglas fixed himself a brandy. He took a long swallow before moving to stand in front of Nancy. The position forced her to crane her neck so she could look at his face. "I have no idea where my wife is." He took another long swallow, looked into the amber liquid as if he could find answers there. "I thought you might know."

Nancy had had enough of being dominated. She arose in one fluid motion. Furious, seeing no reason to hide it, her dark eyes pinned Douglas. "I haven't heard from Irene in days. I called this morning and your housekeeper told me she hasn't been home in all this time. I checked her closets. All her clothes are here. Where is Irene, Douglas? *What have you done with her?*"

"Is that an accusation?"

Andrew shot up. "No one's accusing anyone of anything. Nancy's concerned, Douglas. We all know Irene—er, hasn't been well."

Suddenly the fight went out of Douglas. He sank down into the nearest chair. "I don't know where she is. I don't have a clue." Nancy started to say something. He held up a hand. "It's the truth, Nancy, believe it or not. I thought she'd be tired of whatever game she's playing by now and would come on home."

"Did she leave a note? Have you heard from her?" Nancy rounded on Andrew, glared. He got the message.

"Look here, Douglas, you must admit it looks suspicious. I mean . . ."

They all knew what he meant. Douglas resented the hell out of it, but he didn't have the energy to summon up the anger it deserved. Instead of raging, he lifted an eyebrow. "Care to dig up the garden?"

"Why, you . . ." Nancy raised her hand.

Andrew grabbed her wrist. "You two are behaving like children. We've said what we came to say. We're going now, Douglas. We expect you to take steps to find Irene. If you don't, we will."

Nancy, defiant, snapped, "I'm going to the police."

Douglas felt like an old man. "No police. Not yet, Nancy. I've hired a private detective. He's supposed to be the best. He'll find Irene."

"He'd better."

Douglas and Nancy stared long and hard at each other.

Nancy's lips started to tremble, and all at once she lost her hard edge. "Do you think she's all right?"

Douglas dragged a breath from deep in his lungs. "God alone knows. I sure as hell don't."

Twenty-Five

On a beautiful spring day a week after Petey's disappearance, Glen Rowley rang Molly's bell in the early afternoon. She opened the door but didn't invite him in. She still hadn't forgiven him for Roy.

"Where's Detective Salem?"

"May I come in, Molly?"

She leaned against the door and regarded him stonily. "Is he out in my backyard with a shovel?"

Glen sighed and shoved his hand through his wavy brown hair. "I'm alone. Please, may I come in?"

"Is he on a plane bound for Texas, by any chance?"

"Give it a rest, Molly. You know we had to check it out. A high percentage of snatches are made by noncustodial parents."

"Roy isn't a parent. How could he be when he's never even seen Petey?"

"The department considers him a parent."

Sudden fury blazed in Molly's eyes. "He's a body that produced the sperm I used to conceive Petey, and that's all he is, and you will just have to get it through your head. You and your department. Roy never has and never will have a claim on Petey, and if he sues me for custody, as he threatened, that's exactly what I'll tell the judge."

Glen noticed a man who was walking a dog stop to look. He could be a reporter. Gently but firmly he crowded Molly so she was forced inside, quickly following. She didn't object, but neither did her attitude soften. "I'm sorry, Molly, I didn't know Roy threatened you. If it's any consolation, I don't think he has a leg to stand on."

She just shrugged and walked away. With a deep sigh, he trailed into the kitchen after her. Papers were strewn over the table. He went right to them.

"Feel free," Molly said dryly.

Glen's eyes bored into hers. "I'm not the enemy, Molly." For long seconds they held each other's gaze, then all at once the tenseness left her. She took a deep breath and nodded. He indicated the papers. "A new flyer?"

She handed him one. "Yes. WAND is offering a reward for any information that leads to Petey's recovery."

Glen read it carefully. "It's good. Give me a bunch. I'll see they get good distribution."

"Okay."

"We're trying, Molly, you've got to believe that. We—ah, look, don't take this the wrong way. The department has cleared you. We're listing Petey's disappearance as an abduction."

"The psychic?"

"Deep-sixed."

"All you did was waste time."

He couldn't blame her for her bitterness. He knew as a reporter she was aware of the many aspects of an investigation. But the reporter was taking second place to the mother. Restless, he paced, finally wheeling to face her. She hadn't moved, was watching him with her big, wounded-looking hazel eyes. He remembered taking her on a picnic one hot and sultry July day. Petey had been little more than a toddler then, an adorable little boy with chubby knees and a merry laugh and ...

"Shit!" He reached inside his jacket, took out a piece of paper. "Look ... ah, hell. The department is going full-out on this, Molly, trust me. There's nothing, nothing, we won't do to find Petey. And that includes suspecting you and using psychics and following up every lead, whether from an upstanding citizen or one of the nut jobs. We want Petey back, safe and sound, as much as you do." He caught her eye, held it. "It's true."

"But ... ?"

"No but. Here," he thrust the paper into her hand. "Unofficially—as a friend—I thought you might want to get some outside help. Pamela's an ex-cop, experienced in this field; she's got a good find record. I worked with her; she's one of the best. And she's as tenacious as a bulldog. Think about giving her a call."

Pamela Marryat ran her business out of her home in Jamaica Estates—technically, out of her garage. Metal file cabinets, which all looked as if they had come from secondhand warehouses, covered every inch of available wall space. A desk, also metal, sat in the middle, directly under a fluorescent light, surrounded by the latest in office technology. The space was cramped, every inch utilized, bringing to mind the image of a submarine's command space. Molly knew state-of-the-art equipment when she saw it; Pamela Marryat had certainly not stinted on anything.

"Come right in, Mrs. Deere." A thin elderly woman with kind eyes.

"Thank you for seeing me right away, Ms. Marryat. I . . ." she swallowed painfully, successfully managed to push down the lump in her throat for the umpteenth time that day.

"I'm Ellen. Ellen Fishbein, Pamela's dogsbody."

A deep, rich chuckle came from the area behind the door, and when it was closed, Molly saw there was just enough space for a table and chair. A telephone and a computer were crowded onto the table. A short woman, as broad as Ellen was thin, rose and came forward, her hand extended. "Sorry, we're kind of cramped for space here. I couldn't get out before my *dogsbody* reached the door."

Molly took her hand. Pamela Marryat had at least a decade on her, evidenced by encroaching lines around her eyes and mouth, and silver streaking her hair. Brown hair, brown eyes. Nothing remarkable; except for her presence, so strong it fairly sizzled the air. Still holding Molly's hand, she studied her face for long moments, apparently liked what she saw. "Come. Sit. We'll talk."

Molly fumbled in her purse, took out the new flyer and handed it to her. "My son, Petey . . ."

Pamela sat down behind the desk and gave the flyer a quick but thorough scrutiny. Ellen left the room, quietly closing the door. "You said earlier on the phone that Glen recommended me."

"Yes." Molly began to play with her purse strap. "He came by earlier today and suggested I call you. I want to thank you for seeing me right away," she said again.

"Time is precious." Pamela waved her hand. "Is this the first time you've been away from your house since your son's abduction?"

Abduction. Molly inhaled sharply, then slowly let out the breath. "Yes, it is, and thank you."

"Relax. You've taken the first, hardest step." She frowned. "What are you thanking me for this time?"

"For saying 'abduction' instead of 'disappearance.' For not using that awful word—"

Pamela held up a hand, much like a traffic cop. "Let me guess. Alleged?"

Alleged. Lately it was one of the ugliest words Molly had ever heard.

Pamela patted her skirt pockets, momentarily looked annoyed. "Sorry. I tend to forget I've given up smoking. I've got a bet with my son," she pushed a picture of a sturdily built male replica of herself across the desk, "he's in his third year at Yale, that I can go two years without a puff. If I win he buys me something that gleams, as in gold. If he wins I'm supposed to buy him a car. Of his choice, no less. The smart-ass thinks it's a sure thing. He's got Ellen as his watchdog." While she spoke she watched Molly's face as she studied the picture.

Molly carefully put the picture back on the desk. "He's a fine-looking boy. What's his name?"

"Brandon. He was conceived during a late-night rerun of *On the Waterfront*. If it had been colorized my husband would have reached for the popcorn instead of me."

Molly smiled, then chuckled. Pamela shook her head approvingly. "Attagirl. We'll get along." Then, in a stunning switch, she asked, "What did Glen say about me?"

"You're an expert at finding missing kids and you're as tenacious as a bulldog."

"Are you sure he didn't say I looked like a bulldog?"

She grinned. "Never mind. Some things I don't need to know. Glen, the handsome devil—ah, filled me in on the investigation."

From the way she hesitated and the delicate way she chose her words, Molly knew Glen had been extremely cooperative. Anxiously she leaned forward. "What do you think?"

Ellen appeared, carefully maneuvering a tray. Pamela cleared a space. "Oh, good. Lemonade." She nodded to the photo of Brandon. "I keep that there to remind me of what my work is all about. I give you my promise, Molly Deere. I'll do my damnedest to see that Petey comes home. Safe and sound."

Molly fought against the sudden onrush of hot, painful tears. "Thank you."

Pamela pointed a finger at Molly. "That is the last, I repeat, the last time you will say thank you to me. Until . . ." Absentmindedly she patted her pockets again, grimaced when she remembered her abstinence.

"Pamela . . ." Ellen mildly chided.

"Oh, yes. Molly—that's Ellen and I'm Pamela, if we're to work together—the next time you thank me will be when you have Petey back in your arms."

Molly sank back into the chair. Ellen gently squeezed her shoulder. "Lemonade?" she asked.

Douglas had ceased to expect to find Irene at home, yet each time he drove up to the silent, dark house, he felt a pang. With all her problems, Irene was his wife. That fact gave him surprisingly strong feelings of responsibility, even in this age of revolving-door marriages. They had been through a lot together; he had rich memories. But that was only a part of it. He found he missed her. Even the messy surprises on the kitchen floor.

The smell of disinfectant and lemon wax hit him the instant he stepped into the kitchen. The housekeeper had a heavy hand. Pent-up heat enveloped him, combined with the odors to make him feel a bit queasy. He had overindulged at dinner, both in rich foods and with too much wine, but then he wasn't inclined to deny himself anything lately, including his newest employee, a June grad with pillowy breasts and long legs.

The room sprang to life when he switched on the light. Squeaky clean. Sparkling. Empty. Suddenly he wanted noise—something, anything—to stave off a deep swell of loneliness threatening to overwhelm him. He hurried from room to room, turning on lights, leaving a path of brightness. When he reached the den he automatically put on the television, winced when too-loud canned laughter blared out. One of the brainless sitcoms. Two dopey-looking teens traded insults while their cohorts egged them on.

He loosened his tie, sank into his favorite chair, and clicked channels, stopping on commercials, letting the familiar structure soothe him. Beautiful people, loud music, catchy dialogue. Miniplays, with only seconds to hook the audience. It took genius to create a good one.

He was a genius, but had Irene cared? Had she even known? Had she known what a cutthroat business he was in, how he had to hustle to make the big bucks he needed to keep her in luxury? Had she cared?

Tired, he let his head drop back and closed his eyes. Had he been so busy pursuing his own goals he had lost sight of everything? He rubbed the heels of his hands over his eyes, pulling the puffy skin taut. He didn't want to think, didn't want to remember, didn't want to let his mind touch on Karen . . .

Hot tears welled behind his closed eyelids, stinging, shameful. Tough ad men didn't cry, they just. . . . What the hell were they supposed to do?

"Fuck," he said when the phone rang. He looked at his watch, saw how late it was, growled into the receiver. His sister-in-law's worried-sounding voice buzzed annoyingly into his ear. Nancy appearing for the prosecution; he for the defense. No, he hadn't heard anything. Yes, he was worried. No, he wasn't thinking of going to the police yet, his PI was working on it. No, he didn't have anything concrete yet. Yes, it was a good sign, she hadn't heard wrong.

"Just what do you mean by that?"

Sarcasm and suspicion; it made him want to return some of the pain she was inflicting. "I mean her body hasn't turned up in any hospital . . . or morgue." She gasped; he immediately felt like a heel. But not for long. Nancy proceeded to vent her anxiety, verbally pummeled him until he felt raw. When he finally hung up he was so tired he didn't think he'd make it up to the bedroom. And what did it matter? He could sleep in any room he chose, could take all his clothes off and sleep naked, right here in the den. Who was there to care?

Shit. He was getting maudlin.

Where before he wanted light, now he craved dark. He zapped off the TV and turned off the lights. Saw a blinking red light. Christ, he always forgot. He jabbed the message button. Irene's voice spilled into the room. His heart lurched, started to beat so loudly he couldn't hear. With trembling fingers he hit the save button, replayed it.

"Douglas? Are you there? Douglas? Where the fuck

are you?" A pause. *"Christ! It's late, but then I shouldn't have expected you to hurry home. You never did."* Clinking sounds. Unmistakable. She was drinking again. *"Douglas? I wanted you to know. I have what I want."* Another pause. *"I finally have what I want."*

Douglas played it through again, then a third time. After midnight now, but he didn't hesitate; he was paying top dollar for special service. Day or night. He called a special number and began to speak when he heard a gruff hello. "She left a message on the answering machine."

"Good. Any background noises?"

Douglas thought, couldn't be sure. "Want me to play it again?"

"No. I'll send someone out for it right away."

Douglas carefully sealed the tape in an envelope. Then he sat down to wait.

Twenty-Six

The air was thick and hot, typical of late June in New York. The heat and humidity frayed tempers, heightened anxiety levels. A brownout, the third day in a row, didn't help. By the end of the afternoon, Molly's air conditioner wheezed laboriously. She ignored everything, busy poring over her finally realized organization chart. Looking for a pattern. Kent had culled the name of every child missing under suspicious circumstances from WAND's log for the past year for her. Not very many happy endings. Where was Steven Spielberg when you needed him?

Pamela, dropping in for a few minutes to pick up a list of Molly's assignments over the last three months, eyed the chart and answered the question. Happy endings only happened to cute little aliens. The rest of us have to make do with real life. Molly, who legitimately felt she had every reason to feel cynical, was taken aback.

"I have a list, too, in a computer file," Pamela said. "Every kid called in missing. Most of them never get so much as a whisper from the media. They're poor unfortunates who slip through the cracks every day." She patted her pockets, vainly searching for cigarettes, sighed loudly when she came up empty. "Don't mind me. The heat always gets to me. By the end of the day I'll have prickly heat all over my whoosis. Just like a baby."

Molly offered baby powder and a cold drink. Pamela passed on the powder and asked for a can of diet anything. Stopping smoking and trying to keep weight off at the same time was murder. Molly gave her the last can of soda in the refrigerator. She would have to go shopping later. The thought panicked her. She hated to be away from the phone.

As if she could will it to ring.

Pamela could chug a soda with the best of them. She finished hers in a few long swallows and absentmindedly crushed the can. "Don't get me wrong, Molly. What you're doing is valuable. The media covers the spectacular cases. There may be a pattern. Go for it. Analyze everything, but don't forget instinct. It can be your biggest tool, and I'm certainly not too proud to admit I use it whenever I can." She tapped the list of Molly's assignments. "Then again, maybe we'll get lucky with these. Maybe you made an enemy."

"Do you think so?"

"No. It's a double-check on the police."

The house seemed very quiet after she left. Molly worked, diligently filling in blanks in the chart. Busy recording names of parents and their marital status, recalling her recent raw brush with Roy, she jumped when the phone rang. Automatically she turned down the volume on the radio, at the moment WAND was advertising a wake-up service for people who needed more than an alarm, and nudged closer the yellow lined pad she kept handy. A woman's brisk no-nonsense voice assailed her ear. "Mrs. Deere?"

"Yes." As always, her heart beat faster when she didn't immediately recognize the voice. She picked up the pen clipped to the pad. "Speaking."

"I'm calling from Dr. Marlene Sinckler's office. We want to confirm Petey's check-up tomorrow at eleven."

Pain crashed into Molly's gut. She sucked in her breath, reeling. Petey's physical for Camp Abnaki. Didn't these people read the papers? Listen to the news? Surely Dr. Sinckler had compassion?

"Mrs. Deere? We want to confirm—"

Molly banged down the phone and immediately engaged the answering machine. The phone rang again. Sounding annoyed, the woman left the message Molly should call. She was reciting the number when Molly ran out of the house.

"You didn't overreact. Stop worrying," Zachary said. "There is no right or wrong way to react in a situation like that. She took you by surprise." He expertly flipped the hamburgers on the grill and grinned at Lauren, carefully carrying a bowl of potato salad to the outdoor table.

Lauren started to fuss with the paper napkins. "You don't have to bother with that," Molly said.

Zachary and his daughter exchanged a knowing look. "Uh-huh, she does. Lauren's going to her Grannie Emma-Jane for a couple of weeks. She needs to practice."

Lauren giggled. "Grannie Emma-Jane is very strict. 'A young lady must learn how to set a proper table.' "

"Quote, unquote," Zachary said. "Where are the buns?"

When Lauren went back into the house for the pickles, Zachary momentarily deserted his post. "I'm glad it doesn't bother you to have Lauren here. She misses Petey very much. I don't want her to feel left out."

Molly, who had wondered how she would feel, had been pleased to discover she wasn't small-minded. She didn't have it in her to envy Zachary his child. She handed him a package of soft rolls. "Who is Grannie Emma-Jane?"

Zachary retreated to the grill. "Janine was her daughter, an only child. Emma-Jane and Hugh dote on Lauren. She's their only kin. They have a comfortable sprawling kind of place in New Hampshire. Lauren goes to them for two weeks every year, plus they know they're welcome to visit with us whenever."

"What about your parents?"

Zachary slapped a hamburger hard; juice gushed onto the coals, making them spit and sizzle. "My dad died six years ago. My mother hasn't shoved her chair away from the bridge table since. She's in Florida, happy as a clam."

"I see." They had more in common; neither mother offered much in the way of support.

Night fell as they ate. Often during the meal Molly would catch Lauren's eyes on her, sad, bewildered, fearful. It touched Molly to know how deeply she felt Petey's absence. She wanted to clasp the little girl, to hug her as tightly as she could, to reassure her, but it was impossible. There was no reassurance, not in the empty hours that seemed to rush by with frightening speed, nor in the sweep of stars across the vast blue-black above, nor, sadly, within herself. There was no guarantee Petey would be back.

When the table was cleared and Lauren was inside, watching *Beauty and the Beast*, Zachary's voice came out of the soft darkness. "I think you should consider joining a support group, Molly."

"No."

"You wouldn't feel so alone."

"No."

"You wouldn't be giving up hope."

"No."

He came up behind her, but stopped short of touching. She could feel his warmth, his solidness. His breath stirred the hair near her temple. "You need help, Molly. Don't deny yourself."

She whirled, took a couple of steps back, eyes wide, gleaming, a magnet that caught reflected starlight. "I don't matter. Nothing matters except Petey. The only thing that will ever help me is to have my son back in my arms."

"You can't help him if you make yourself sick. You're petrified to leave the house. You hardly eat enough to keep yourself going."

"The phone—"

"You have an answering machine." He reached out, let his hand drop. They both knew the time for a ransom was past. Petey wasn't coming home fast. He wondered if she'd throw him out again if he pushed too hard. "Think about it, Molly. That's all I ask."

She didn't say no. Zachary took it as a victory of sorts.

Twenty-Seven

A week later Kent pointed out the obvious. "You gotta get off your ass and get back to work, cookie."

Molly looked at the phone as if it had just transmuted into a serpent. "I can't. I can't leave here."

"You can't pay bills with promises."

"I have money."

"I'm sure you do, cookie, and you'll have even more once Petey's home." His voice turned sly. "You'll be a cinch for a TV movie. Need an agent? I'll see you get big bucks."

"Kent—"

"Meanwhile, I need a warm body in Queens Criminal 10 AM tomorrow. The first three citizens of that carjacking gang face their adoring public. You covered the grand jury indictment back in May."

"That was Brooklyn."

"Yeah. After a short but bloody jurisdiction battle, the Queens DA hoisted the flag of victory. It's his party. Be there."

"Kent—"

"No need to thank me, cookie."

* * *

Everything was the same. Sitting on a hard wooden bench in Judge Judith Detweiler's third-floor courtroom while the lawyers plodded through the voir dire, Molly had ample time to think. Everything was the same and it hurt like hell. Life was going on, *her* life was going on, even though there was an empty cavity in her chest where her heart had been.

Why Petey? Why him out of the millions of children in New York? There had to be an answer, from which would come a happy resolution; she wouldn't countenance anything else.

A buzz of voices came from the front of the room, the lawyers' calm, confident, the prospective jurors' more hurried, betraying a tenseness built into the process of impaneling. Molly closed her eyes, pictured her chart, mentally ran down the names. Tabitha Gerard. Suzanne Lind. Wilson Whitman. Timothy Newell.

Timothy Newell. Something was there, something bothering her.

Amy Derleth. Mary Ann Szell. Michael Robert Barclay. Seven children—no, eight—who had disappeared into thin air.

What was it about Timmy Newell's disappearance that bothered her so? He was luckier than many others on her chart—at least as far as she knew. He and the seven others still had "open" written in under "disposition of case." Unlike three-year-old Catherine "Kitty" Schwenker, who had had the misfortune to meet a monster in human form. Kitty had been found stuffed into a suitcase with a plastic bag around her neck. Her stepfather's trial was pending.

Child abuse. Child pornography. *Pedophilia.*

WHERE'S MY BABY? 251

She was going to throw up. Right here, right now, sitting in the front row of the very proper Judge Judith Detweiler's courtroom. She clapped her hand over her mouth and made a dash for the corridor. The ladies' room was near the elevators, and thankfully, it was empty. So was her stomach, which produced bile. When she was through she rinsed her mouth, trying to avoid her image in the cloudy mirror. The woman with rice-white skin and dark circles under her eyes couldn't be her, could it?

Charlie Lee was leaning on the wall outside the rest room. "I heard you were here. You look like hell."

Obviously the woman in the mirror had sneaked under her skin. Molly laughed. It sounded hysterical.

Charlie narrowed his eyes; they almost disappeared into his cheekbones. "I don't see anything funny here. Have you taken a good look at yourself lately, Molly–Uh-Oh? This isn't doing you or Petey any good. You don't want him to come home to a broken shell, do you?"

"I just want him to come home."

A whisper, but Charlie heard her loud and clear. He winced, but stood his ground. "You don't have to go it alone. You've got people behind you, willing to help."

"Thank you, but . . ." She was about to say there was nothing he could do, but . . . "Charlie, do you remember the Timmy Newell story? February. The kid who disappeared when the plane crashed into the school out on the Island?"

"Sure I do." Charlie hunched his shoulders, shoved his hands into his pockets, said the same thing he always said when there were no words to cover the enormity of a tragedy. "Bummer."

"Do you remember anything peculiar about it?"

"You mean other than the kid just up and disappeared?" He shook his head. "No. Why? What's up?"

"Nothing. Only, something's nagging at me." She bit her lip. "What does it matter? That was February, and the circumstances of Timmy's disappearance were nothing like Petey's . . ."

"Only you keep on thinking about it, huh?"

"I've got a chart, Charlie, a whole chart of names of kids who have disappeared. I think about all of them, hoping, *praying,* there's some common denominator, something that will lead to Petey."

"So follow it up."

"I've wracked my brain. It's no good."

"Get your boyfriend to hypnotize you. Isn't that what shrinks do?"

February again, the day cold and drizzly, the sights and smells of the disaster scene at the Brenton School as gut-wrenchingly awful as they had been the first time around. With patience and care Zachary led Molly through the day. It helped immensely that he had been there; his questions were pointed and insightful. When Molly awoke they sipped Mrs. Sadecki's lemonade and listened to the tape.

"Nothing?"

She shrugged. "I don't know what I'm looking for. I don't even know whether I'd know it if I found it."

"Don't be too sure. You know enough to look for something. That's a good beginning."

Too much on edge to sit quietly, Molly moved around the room. "Maybe I only *want* something to be there."

"I don't buy that. Instinct is a powerful force. You shouldn't dismiss it out of hand." He thought a moment.

"Perhaps we're looking at this the wrong way. Let's try coming at it from another angle. What do you think happened to Timmy Newell?"

Molly stopped in front of the window. Zachary's postage-stamp garden bloomed lushly. Sadly, she remembered Petey's attempt at capturing it in paint. Lauren sat reading a book on the bench beneath the tree, the tree and bench Petey had drawn with two slashes of black with a daub of brown between. He had given the picture to Zachary, and she, poor unknowing fool, had been jealous. Only for a moment, but what a wasted moment. She shivered, crossed her arms over her chest, hugged herself tight. "I think a dirty, disgusting pervert has him; an inhuman monster of a pedophile has ... and ... and ..."

Gentle hands drew her back. One arm came around her waist, holding her snugly against his warmth, while the other slowly smoothed the hair back from her face. "Ah, Molly. You don't know any such thing, sweetheart. Don't torture yourself."

She tore from his grasp. "I don't know it isn't so, either. I don't know anything, anything, and the not knowing is killing me."

"Yes, I would expect so. But you have no way to alter it. It's a fact, an unpalatable one, but it's there. An unmovable rock." She looked so stricken, he softened his tone. "You're strong, Molly, very strong. Especially when it comes to Petey. Am I right?"

She took a deep breath, then another, slowly gathering herself. "Yes. I will do anything for Petey."

Again Zachary modulated his tone. His voice became brisk, professional. "So, what do you think happened to Timmy? Did he walk away from the Brenton School under his own power or did someone snatch him? And if someone snatched him, right there in front of everyone, is there something you recognize subliminally as being the same or similar in Petey's case? Think about it, Molly, maybe your subconscious is giving you a nudge."

"Maybe. Pamela said she often follows hunches."

"Well, now, if the redoubtable Pamela does it, who are we to argue?"

"Redoubtable? What did she do to give you that impression?"

"Okay, say formidable. She dropped by for a little 'chat,' under the heading of 'leave no stone unturned.' I never met a more focused woman. Her intensity is frightening."

"I know. By the way, she liked you, too. She said you have neat pecs and tight buns."

Zachary laughed. "My kind of woman." Lauren must have caught his laughter. She looked up and waved. Zachary waved back. "She's excited about going to Emma-Jane and Hugh's place. I couldn't disappoint her. Or them, for that matter."

"Why ever should you?"

"I hate to leave you, Molly."

"Leave?" Her hand flew to her throat. "I thought only Lauren is going."

"I'm driving her up. It's too far to go round trip in one day. I'll be away at least overnight."

"Oh. That's fine. Don't worry about me. I'll be okay."

"I know you will, Molly, but I'd like you to think about doing something while I'm away. We've talked about it before. I'd like you to go to a support group. You don't have to stay and you don't have to go again if you find you don't like it, but I think you should try.

A group meets not far from where you live. What do you say?" Molly turned from him to look out the window. Lauren was watching a butterfly, a rapt expression on her face. Zachary lowered his voice. "I can't fully understand what you're feeling, Molly. No one can, no one—except perhaps someone who's gone through the same thing. These support groups work, believe me."

"But Petey's coming home."

"Of course he is. But while he's away, you can help yourself learn to cope with the waiting."

"I'll see. No promises."

He kissed the top of her head. No promises. She sounded just like Petey.

"There's a man on line two who won't give his name. Should I put him through?"

Douglas raised bleary eyes from the storyboard set up across one wall of his office. Something was missing from the sixty-second commercial for air freshener, some necessary element that would give the product zing and excitement, but he couldn't find it. He couldn't seem to do much of anything lately. "What?"

Lorraine Fowling repeated her question with the patience she had practiced during the past few weeks. Her boss didn't seem to bring his brain to work most days. "Do you want the call?"

"Call? Oh, yeah, put it through." Anything was better than looking at the static pictures. "Hall, here. Who's this?" The instantly recognizable voice of the man he had hired to find Irene flowed through the line. Douglas sat up straight. "What did you find?"

"I've put it into a report. Do you want me to mail it?"

"Read it."

"Is the line secure?"

Douglas looked at the phone. The intercom was unlit. "Go ahead." The voice took on a military style, reciting words with little inflection and much precision. When it fell silent, Douglas barked a short sentence. "That's it?"

"So far."

"All you've given me is a bunch of negatives. She didn't take her clothes, she didn't take her car, she didn't take the bus or the train or a plane or a fucking camel, for all you know."

"Now, Mr. Hall, these things take time if they're going to be done right, you know."

"I don't know any such thing. Christ, I'm paying you enough for time and accuracy."

"Your wife isn't leaving a paper trail. She's obviously got cash. We're following—"

"Of *course* she's got cash. I told you she did. The woman is fucking rich. She got even richer when her mother died. Why the fuck do you think I married her in the first place?"

Silence.

Douglas swiveled his chair around and stared out at New York's magnificent skyline. Power. Riches. You could see it, feel it, smell it, taste it. The air throbbed with it. Noisily he blew air out of his lungs. "Shit. Forget I said that. It isn't true, in any event."

Silence.

"I said forget it."

"Forget what, Mr. Hall?"

The intercom lit up, Lorraine's voice announced Nancy on line five. That's all he needed, another go-round with his sister-in-law. "Tell her to wait," he spat out, and went back to line two. "Find my wife, God damn it, and do it fast. That's what I'm paying you to do."

Viciously he stabbed the winking button under line five. "Nancy, I'm glad you called. I just got an encouraging report on Irene."

"Do you know where she is?"

"Not yet. It's only a matter of time." And money. And money could buy just about anything. Hadn't Irene told him often enough?

Twenty-Eight

It took four days to impanel a jury. Molly sat through the opening arguments staring at the defendants, wondering how people could be so morally skewed that cruelty and violence became as ordinary as buying a loaf of bread. Their faces fascinated her. She tried to see emotion, feeling, a hint of what it takes to enable a person to stick a gun in someone's face to get a car. For the most part the defendants' faces were impassive. Perhaps that was the key; perhaps there was no emotion, no feeling in them.

What did the face of Petey's kidnapper look like? Was it devoid of feeling, of emotion, of pity for a small boy alone and frightened, separated from all that was familiar, from all that he loved and held dear? She mustn't think of it, else she would go mad, and with every day that passed now, with no word and no hope, the seductiveness of madness grew more appealing.

Once home each day she went straight to the answering machine. Hoping, always hoping. Today, a message from Glen Rowley. Nothing new; just touching base. Her mother. Wouldn't she like to come visit? Get away for a while? Resentment flared hot. "Not until hell

WHERE'S MY BABY?

freezes over," she muttered. Feeling unutterably weary, she waited for the last message. "Hello, sweetheart. Sorry I missed you. I'll try again later."

Zachary was back. Eagerly she called, unwilling to wait. Mrs. Sadecki said, "Doctor no home yet—later, maybe." Perhaps he had called from the road. To keep busy, she sorted laundry, but the routine chore proved depressing. No grimy pants, no food-speckled T-shirts. When the front doorbell rang she flew to answer it. Zachary hadn't waited to call; he had come.

Gertrude Zinzendorf stood on the steps, looking distinctly ill at ease, even more so when she saw Molly's expression. "Oh dear, I knew this wasn't a good idea, but I felt I had to come. I should have done this before, of course, but I was hoping . . ."

Molly stepped back, struggling to mask disappointment. "Please. Come in."

"I should have called."

"It's all right. Really. How about a cold drink?"

"No, uh, that's okay."

"I was just going to make myself an iced tea. How does that sound?"

Gertrude finally broke down, admitted it sounded fine and insisted on following Molly into the kitchen. The chart instantly drew her. When Molly handed her a glass she took it without turning. "What an ugly world we live in. I hadn't realized how very lucky I am. For the most part I deal only with happiness, while you . . . this . . ."

"This represents only a small percentage of the children who are missing, and it covers only the past twelve months. The private investigator I'm using keeps a complete listing. She said the sheer statistics boggle the mind."

"Such misery." Gertrude drained her glass, refused a refill. After rummaging through her capacious shoulder bag, she produced an envelope. "As I said, I should have done this sooner, but I'm a coward, I'm afraid, and I postponed it as long as I could." She handed the envelope to Molly. "Camp starts next week. This is a refund in the full amount. In good conscience I couldn't hold on to it any longer. I was hoping . . ."

Molly put the envelope on the table without opening it. "Yes. Thank you."

Gertrude hesitated, then said, "We will be happy to take Petey whenever he returns. There will be a place for him at Camp Abnaki."

Gertrude meant well, but her visit triggered the despair Molly struggled to contain every waking moment. Because she had to be strong, had to keep herself sane, she flew into activity, grabbed rags and polish, and went to work. An hour later the downstairs was gleaming, the laundry done. She went upstairs, attacked the bedrooms. When she finished, the windows were dark squares. Night had fallen and she hadn't even noticed. Somewhat dazed, she stared at what she had accomplished. Petey's room was clean and neat, everything in its place.

Everything but Petey.

It reminded her of King Tut's tomb. All the boy king's possessions gathered for his pleasure, but the boy king lay dead. Dear God, no . . . a silent scream clawed at her insides, struggling to get out. She couldn't, mustn't let it loose. She'd go mad, would run blubbering into the night, would howl like a wild beast in pain. Oh God, it hurt, it hurt so bad.

By sheer force of will, she slowly pushed back the incipient panic. Victory. For this moment, at least.

By witchcraft or telepathy, Zachary chose now to call.

His voice sharpened with alarm as soon as he heard her voice. "Molly! What's wrong?"

"Nothing." She took a deep breath, held it, then slowly let it out. "I'm all right, now that you're home."

"Actually, that's why I'm calling. My car broke down. Yesterday, as a matter of fact. I thought they'd have it fixed by now but they tell me it needs a part. It should arrive by tomorrow."

He wasn't here. The invidious panic surged anew. "Tomorrow?"

"I'm afraid so. They keep reminding me this isn't New York. Take delight in it, is what I think. I—" He broke off, rapped, "Something's wrong. I can sense it."

"No! It's nothing. I'm tired, is all. I had a long hot day in court."

"You sure?"

"I'm sure." She tried to instill confidence in her voice; she didn't want Zachary to think she had no backbone. "How's Lauren?"

"Her grandparents are doting on her, she's got friends to play with and the little boy she was sweet on last year said he's happy to see her."

"I'm glad. She's a lovely little girl."

"Yes. Uh, Molly? Have you given any thought to what I suggested?"

"Don't worry, Zachary, I'm fine."

But she wasn't, and he knew it and she knew it, never more so than when she ran into Petey's room, pulled out clothes and toys and books, wildly strewed them about. When it was a mess, when she couldn't move without bumping into a stuffed animal or stubbing her toe on a robot dinosaur, she flopped down on the bed, hugged Lambie Pie to her chest, and cried her eyes out. Then she got up, blew her nose, and went to the phone.

* * *

The house was typical of the neighborhood, a large colonial with a two-car garage and a nicely landscaped front lawn. A basketball hoop reigned over the garage.

A boy lived in the house. Or did he? Was his disappearance or death the reason for the group meeting here? The McLoughlin house. William and Theresa McLoughlin. "You'll see all the cars parked out front. You can't miss it." He had a nice voice, Mr. McLoughlin. Kind. Understanding. He had recognized her at once, she could tell from his brief hesitation, but give him credit, he hadn't said more than that she was welcome, come on over.

So here she was, sitting in her car on a hot and humid night, staring at the McLoughlins' front door. The people meeting behind that front door had lost a child. All she had to do was ring the bell and she would get help, would be with people who understood.

She couldn't do it. She wasn't like them. Her child was coming home.

A twist of the key; the car's engine roared loudly in the quiet of the spring night. Her hands were slippery on the wheel. Suddenly the front door opened, a path of golden light fanned over hedges framing a flagstone walk. A man's figure appeared in the aperture, waved. He walked quickly toward the car. "Mrs. Deere?"

Politeness won over cowardliness. She opened the window. "Mr. McLoughlin?"

"Bill. Call me Bill. We've been watching for you." Fortyish, of average height, with a long thin face made longer by a receding hairline, he bent down and put his hand through the window. Good manners dictated she take it. Margaret Shay hadn't raised her daughter to be

WHERE'S MY BABY?

a boor. Bill McLoughlin held on. "Won't you come in? I'm afraid you've missed most of the meeting. We're just about winding up, and then we'll have coffee and cake. What do you say?"

She could say little beyond yes while he still possessed her hand. He gave it a gentle squeeze and let it go as soon as she agreed. He talked about the weather and the state of his lawn, which she couldn't see very well in the dark, as they went up the walk. Suddenly she had butterflies in her stomach, which was ridiculous, wasn't it?

Obviously Bill thought so. Taking a good look at her white face, revealed under a fine crystal chandelier in the spacious foyer, he said, "Don't be nervous. No one here will judge you, Mrs. Deere."

Earnest brown eyes. Kind eyes. Molly looked closer, saw compassion and the knowledge of pain. "Call me Molly," she said, and was rewarded with his smile.

A sudden babble of voices reached them. "Sounds like the meeting's over." He took her arm. "Come. I'll introduce you to a few people. The rest will take care of itself."

To Molly's surprise, Bill was right. The first person he introduced was his wife. Theresa wanted to be called Tess, and she was, contrary to most hostesses, delighted to have Molly's help in the kitchen. A polite fiction. Molly arranged slices of coffee cake on a platter while Tess, short and comfortably plump, bustled about, talking nonstop. It didn't take Tess long to tell Molly about her tragedy: their son Noel had run away when he was fourteen. He had been murdered a year later.

Molly pictured the basketball hoop; her mind segued

immediately to Lambie Pie. Words clogged in her throat. Tess patted her shoulder. Noel had been rebellious, had been deep into drugs, had resisted help. He had given them no reason to hope.

Hope. Molly clung to that word as, at Tess's urging, she mingled. George and Marilyn Baer had lost a ten-year-old girl, Jennifer. Leukemia. The Galessos, Tony and Myra, had also lost a daughter. Seventeen-year-old Gina had fried her brain on drugs. She would be institutionalized for the rest of her life. In very good health, she would live a long time.

Everyone had a story; two stories, really. The first was a tragedy; the second was how they had learned to cope. Joann Mulder, twenty-seven, divorced, gave Molly a fierce hug instead of a handshake. Jason, her seven-month-old son, had succumbed to sudden infant death syndrome. "The hell of it is, Molly, I was suspected of murdering him."

Molly knew about that. All she had to do was close her eyes and Detective Salem appeared, dark face shiny with sweat, brown eyes beagle-sad, directing a squad of policemen as they dug up her yard.

Young and pretty, Joann was very, very brittle. "My ex's family still thinks I murdered him. Every time there's a story on SIDS, my ex-mother-in-law calls to tell me I got away with it."

Tess put a plate with a generous slice of cake on it into Joann's hands. "Eat. There's such a thing as too thin, you know." To Molly, she said, "Joann's husband left her after the baby's death. She went back to school and will graduate this year." She beamed as if Joann were her daughter. "She'll make a new life."

Joann crumbled the cake with her fingers and then set down the plate. "Careful, Molly. You're young. Tess is

WHERE'S MY BABY? 265

a firm believer in making a new beginning. Loosely translated, you'll have more children."

Molly sucked in her breath. Petey was coming home.

"You don't even have to be that young." Myra Galesso unabashedly dug into Joanne's discarded plate. "I hear the Drummonds adopted. They've got to be pushing fifty."

Tess nodded agreement. "John is fifty-six. Carla can't be much younger. Maybe they adopted an older child?"

"They got a newborn." Myra lowered her voice. "They're loaded, you know. A lawyer arranged it, I hear."

Molly made a careful mental note. John and Carla Drummond. Rich people with a can-do lawyer. What else might he be up to?

"Whatever. The important point is they're going on." Tess helped herself to another slice of cake. "It's healthy, not like those poor Griffens."

"What did happen to them? I don't think anyone ever told me."

Molly was grateful to Joann. She also wanted to know what had happened to the poor Griffens.

"Lily's mother died. Cancer." Tess clicked her tongue. "Lily is waiting to hear from her."

"Her mother?" Joann raised her eyebrows. "I didn't think Lily was a flake."

Tess shrugged. Tragedy did strange things. "Barry said a cousin, somewhere out West, I think, knew a couple who were reunited with their reincarnated child. A relative who had passed over told them about it. Now poor Lily is running to psychics trying to find out where Stevie is."

Marilyn Baer laughed strangely. "You mean who he is."

Tess rounded on her. "If poor Lily and Barry take comfort from it, then who are we to criticize?"

No one wanted to.

Molly made another mental note.

Twenty-Nine

Molly called Pamela first thing the next morning. Scratchy-voiced, Pamela sounded as if she had had a hard night. Belatedly, Molly wondered about her marital status. "Uh, Pamela, if this isn't a good time, I'll call back. There's nothing urgent."

"Everything's urgent. And if you're wondering if I've got a man here, no such luck." She laughed throatily.

"It's none of my business."

"Sure it is. Don't you want to know if you've hired a PI who drinks like a fish and screws anything that moves?"

"I know that's not the case."

"Why, because Rowley recommended me?"

"Nope. Because Ellen wouldn't put up with it."

Pamela hooted. "In a nutshell, I'm divorced, six years now, and I drink only on social occasions. I leave it to you to define 'social occasions.' As for my ex, he had a midlife crisis and after counseling and therapy decided to restructure his life. I didn't figure in it. Sidney's remarried, an airhead with a thirty-eight-inch bust, and living in Florida. Last I heard, Dee Dee'd given him herpes. Couldn't have happened to a nicer guy. What've you got?"

Just listening to Pamela sometimes made Molly breathless. Redoubtable. Zachary's word for her. It fit. "I don't know if I've got anything."

"Give. I'll be the judge." Molly told her about the support group, about the fixer lawyer. "Get a name?"

"Drummond. John and Carla. No one mentioned the lawyer's name and I didn't want to push. I figured if he was into black-market babies, he might have a sideline into other things."

"Anything's possible." Pamela grunted. Molly could picture her, a hand blindly searching for a cigarette. "Good work. Actually, I'm covering some of the same ground. I keep an ear to the support groups as a general proposition. You never know what you'll come up with. Guys like the Drummonds' lawyer crawl out of the muck every once in a while. Anything else?"

Molly couldn't think of anything. Pamela said she'd be in touch.

The day started out typical New York HHH. Hot, humid, and hazy. Driving to the courthouse on the Grand Central, Molly was grateful for the Taurus's air conditioner. Even this early, a yellow haze floated just above the horizon. The radio blared a warning to the elderly and those with heart or lung problems. Air you can see and smell isn't good for you.

Molly felt sticky and uncomfortable. Her cotton blouse and skirt clung to her skin by the time she made the short walk from the municipal parking lot to the Korean-owned convenience store on Queens Boulevard across from the courthouse, where she bought a container of black coffee. The short, stocky man with a gold-rimmed front tooth who presided over the cash register was the owner's first cousin. Next year he

hoped to get the family money to start his own business.
"No bagel?"

"No bagel."

"You gotta eat," he said, shaking his head and ringing up the coffee at the same time. He sounded more like Bensonhurst than Seoul.

"Yeah," she said, thinking, *You ain't gotta do nothing.* Clutching the paper bag, she dashed across the boulevard in the middle of the block, deaf to the sudden blaring of horns. She had to watch it. That sneaky sly self-pity was creeping into her thoughts again. She didn't matter. Petey did. Only Petey.

She picked up all four New York dailies from the stand in the lobby before taking the elevator to the third floor. By the time she finished the coffee she had skimmed through them. She gave away the three tabloids and kept the *Times,* doing the crossword while waiting for the proceedings to get under way.

At a little after ten, the judge called for the jury and the prosecution resumed its case. The current witness was a big florid-faced man in his middle fifties. With a heavily muscled upper torso and a face whose features appeared mismatched, he looked like Hollywood's idea of a bouncer, but was in reality a medical-supply salesman who worked out. He had served with the Marines, where he had done some boxing, which probably accounted for his face. The defense lawyers, all three of them, had a hard time believing such a man would meekly give up a brand new Lexus. The witness said it had been easy. Once they stuck a gun in his face they could have whatever they wanted. That had included Whitney Houston's new CD, he pointed out in an aside. The jury laughed; the judge banged her gavel.

The trial proceeded at a snail's pace. With three defense lawyers, a lot of the same ground was being covered. Molly took notes; she would cull the most interesting tidbits and call in a report later. As if responding to a mental cue, her beeper went off. Kent. Molly wasn't sorry. She had lost weight and the bench was hard; her fanny was sore.

Since most of the rooms were in session, the hall was relatively empty. A few people leaned against the window wall. Some were reporters Molly knew; none gave her a second look. The telephones were free. The elevator stopped on the floor just as she dropped her quarter in the slot and punched in the familiar number. Two people got off—Glen Rowley and Pamela Marryat.

Molly's heart dropped into her stomach at the same time her knees turned to gelatin. Still clutching the phone, she fell back, her spine making painful contact with the metal shelf beneath the phone; she never noticed. A voice squawked from the receiver. It sounded like a demented chicken.

Glen took the phone. "Rowley. Who's this?" He listened, said, "Yeah. Okay. We've got it. Yeah. Yeah. 'Bye." The entire conversation took no more than ten, twelve seconds. A lifetime.

Molly fought for breath, silently pleaded for them not to speak. If they didn't say anything, everything would be all right. A voice in her head started to scream. *Peteeeeey!*

Pamela moved to stand in front of Molly, blocking her from view. Her face was unreadable. She glanced at Glen. They had been partners long enough to be able to speak to each other without words.

Glen won, or lost, depending on one's view. "We've found a body. A young boy."

Blackness descended with the swiftness of a diving

hawk. Glen grabbed her arms, held her limp body upright. Voices came dimly: Pamela, hissing, calling Glen an unfeeling jerk; reporters buzzing questions; Glen, harshly ordering them to get out of his face.

"Can you walk? The vultures are circling." Pamela, her voice tight, controlled.

Molly fought a short, vicious, internal battle, came up a winner. She pulled away from Glen, stood alone, if wobbly. Her eyes were wide, stricken; a beleaguered doe. "Petey . . . ?"

"Hey, Detective, what's going on?"

Glen snarled at the reporter, told him to take it elsewhere. A flashbulb went off. Another.

"Hey, Molly. What did he say? Have they found Petey?"

"Is he dead?" A new voice.

Dead. Dead. Dead dead dead dead . . . Peteeeeey . . .

Pamela vented her feelings in four-letter words. She got a good grip on Molly's arm, steered her toward the elevator. Miraculously, it came fast.

"Police," Glen said, and evicted the three people in the car, then he and Pamela rushed Molly inside. Glen put up his arm, barring the reporters from entering. It would give them a respite; the stairways were kept locked. As the doors closed, Molly could see a stringer for one of the wire services rush to the telephones.

The elevator smelled of stale perfume and sweat. No air. At least, Molly's lungs didn't seem to be working.

Glen took a deep breath. "I need the name of Petey's dentist."

Molly closed her eyes.

"They don't know anything for sure. This is just procedure." Pamela's voice.

Somewhere someone was screaming. Molly couldn't

think, couldn't ... the screaming was inside her head, wasn't loud enough to block out the world. If Petey was dead, she wanted to be with him.

"Molly ... Petey's dentist? I need the name."

"Stop pushing her. She's had a tremendous shock. She'll be okay in a few moments."

Molly felt Pamela squeeze her arm, knew she was wrong. She would never be all right again. Never.

The elevator stopped with a jolt; the doors slid open. Reporters milled in the lobby, made a rush toward them. Flashbulbs went off. Questions were shouted.

Dead dead dead dead dead ... Peteeeeey ...

"They must use drums," Glen said, half in disgust, half in grudging respect. Then he and Pamela repeated the performance, each grabbing one of Molly's arms and convoying her outside.

The day had turned dark. Black clouds scudded across the sky. As they hurried down the steps, a few drops fell. Big ones.

"Where's your car? I'll take you home." Pamela frowned at Glen when he started to speak.

Molly pointed toward the municipal lot. It took a lot of effort, mental and physical. They started walking, picked up the pace when the rain began in earnest. All of a sudden Molly stopped. "Tarloff."

Glen had his notebook out. "Double f?"

Molly nodded. "Sheldon. He's got pictures of clowns in his office."

"Where's his office?" Pamela and Glen.

The voice in Molly's brain didn't want to stop screaming and let her think. She forced it into the background. The sooner she answered, the sooner they'd let her go back to it. "Plainview. Old Country Road. I don't remember the number."

"Good enough." Glen returned the notebook to his pocket. "You'll be okay?" The question was for Pamela.

Molly never heard her reply. She was back with the voice.

Molly surfaced as Pamela pulled into her driveway. The rain was pelting down. "Do you want me to put it into the garage?"

What did it matter? Molly got out without answering; Pamela shrugged and followed. The house was damp and rain-dim. Molly stood in the foyer, as if she didn't know what to do now.

"Do you want hot tea?" Pamela, shaking herself like a dog, shut the front door and turned on the lights. Molly looked corpse-white in the sudden glare.

Molly made a little flipping gesture with her hand. Pamela interpreted it to her liking. She made tea in the microwave and added a generous slosh of vodka, the only thing alcoholic she could find. She put the mug directly into Molly's hand. "Drink. I don't know how it tastes, but you don't have a choice. It's this or the cooking sherry."

Molly drank, shuddered. Pamela sipped instant coffee, grunted when the phone rang. She edged Molly away, picked up the receiver, listened, said, "No comment," and hung up. "We'd better use your machine. We're going to get a lot of calls like that."

"It's on. It'll ring four times."

"Too long." Pamela adjusted the ring to two. "This gets rid of them faster. What does your message say?"

Molly took another swallow. "Leave a message."

"Succinct. I like it."

Molly moved to the back door, pushed the curtain aside and stared at the rain. "Pamela?"

The older woman knew what Molly was asking, knew she was unable to put her dread into words. "I don't know. A lot of little boys are missing."

Molly turned around. "When will I . . ." She licked her lips. "When will I hear?"

Pamela automatically checked her watch, shrugged. "It's getting late. It could be tomorrow."

Molly absorbed this new blow. "Tomorrow." A whisper of anguish. She went back to watching the rain.

A little past 3 AM Zachary pulled up in front of the house. A beat-up Chevy sat in the driveway next to Molly's Taurus. The house was dark; it had a shuttered look, as if it mourned. Of course it was dark, what the hell had he expected at this time of night? And as for the other, well, his imagination, nothing more.

He rubbed his hand over his face, grimacing when he felt the stubble of his nighttime beard. His eyes were grainy and his muscles ached from driving nonstop, but once he had heard, nothing could keep him from coming home. Not even the oh-so-cute mechanic who refused to guarantee the work if he took his car before he gave the okay. The guy wanted to test it. More like he wanted to squeeze a few more hours of his exorbitant labor charge out of him. "Fuck you," he had told him, surprising himself almost as much as the other man. He would bet the mechanic had him pegged as a New York highbrow who didn't even know the word.

The PI answered the door. Even in the middle of the night she looked like she could take on an army. Sylvester Stallone in drag. She gave him a sour look.

"About time you got here." *Well, hello to you, too.* "She's out in the backyard, went as soon as the rain stopped. I couldn't get her even to try to sleep."

They were inside now, and although the foyer was dim, reflected light from the living room showed the strain on Pamela's face. Gruffness to hide worry. He could understand that. He also knew she wouldn't take kindly to sympathy. "Go get some sleep, Ms. Marryat. I'll take over now."

She bristled, puffed out her chest. "The Marines have landed, huh?"

No sting. Pro forma all the way. Time to let down his own shield. "She may need your special strength tomorrow. You can't be there for her if you don't get any rest."

She studied him for a long moment. "I think I'll go on home, then. She's got a lousy couch. I'll be back first thing."

Zachary nodded. "How do you like your eggs?"

Pamela slapped her pockets, smiled ruefully. "Mentholated with a filter would be nice." She looked at him hopefully. "Say—"

He held up his hands. "Sorry."

"I didn't think so." She made a shooing motion. "Go on, I'll see myself out."

Zachary took her at her word. He walked through the dark house and let himself out the back door. He almost tripped over Molly, sitting on the top step, shoulders hunched, arms wrapped around her knees. A purely defensive position. She didn't say anything after a quick glance up, just tucked her head down again like a hedgehog caught in the open.

He tapped her on the shoulder. "Scoot down." She obligingly shifted to the bottom step. Zachary eased down behind her, carefully positioning his legs on either side of her so her back rested in the notch his body made. He slowly coaxed her backward until her head met his chest. Then he wrapped his arms around her, his hands clasping hers where they tightly clutched her knees, and pulled her body as close as he could get it.

They sat in silence. He thought she dozed, but he couldn't be sure; he knew he did because his head snapped back and he awoke with a jerk. He shifted, pulled her a bit closer. He couldn't have slept for long; the nighttime shadows hadn't traveled very far. Suddenly she spoke, startling him. "Tess called. From the support group. I went, you know. She wanted to come over, but I wouldn't let her. I wouldn't let Denise stay, either."

"Hmm."

"Ellen brought Pamela's car. She kicked her out. Said we didn't need a bunch of sparrows twittering around. Denise drove Ellen home."

Zachary said "hmm" again. Molly didn't seem to require more of him at the moment.

Gradually it lightened. From somewhere close by, a bird gave a sleepy peep, tried it again, then, apparently warmed up, gave it all he had. Zachary tried to stretch his cramping back muscles without disturbing Molly. When it was light enough to see details of form and color, she pulled away and stood. Still with her back to him, she turned her face toward the tree where another early bird trilled his song. "It's tomorrow now."

Zachary slowly got to his feet, careful of sore, stiff muscles. He didn't know what to say. So much for an expensive education and untold experience.

Molly was looking at him now. Her face was empty, ready to be filled by sorrow or relief. He checked his watch. It was later than he had thought. "How about some breakfast?"

She shook her head. The thought of food made her queasy. "I need a shower."

"Good idea. Don't use all the hot water." He thought she tried to smile, but it wasn't a very successful effort. While she was upstairs he busied himself in the kitchen, making coffee—extra strong—and rummaging through the refrigerator and pantry. The doorbell rang when he was counting eggs. He had just opened the door to find Pamela there—no big surprise—when the phone rang. They looked at each other and then made a dash for it. Because it was more Pamela's purview than his, he let her answer it.

"Marryat," she said, then "Glen."

Zachary stiffened. All his attention concentrated on Pamela; nevertheless, he felt Molly enter the room. She went to stand next to Pamela, her face as bleached out as the old much-washed terry-cloth robe she wore.

Pamela held up a hand, palm out. A warning? Zachary sucked in his breath, tried to prepare.

"You're sure?" Pamela asked, nodded her head, said, "Okay. Thanks." She faced Molly. "It's not Petey. Rowley says the ME's sure."

For an instant no one moved. Then Molly burst into tears. They let her cry; she needed it.

Thirty

July

Both Zachary and Kent objected when Molly switched with Eleanor Perez over the July Fourth holiday. Zachary wanted her to go to Fire Island and Kent didn't like his employees monkeying with his schedule—"fucking with it" were his exact words. Eleanor had a new boyfriend who was talking Virginia Beach, she was grateful; Molly shamelessly traded on it. She had Eleanor go over everything about the Mary Ann Szell kidnapping. Looking for a pattern. Always looking for a pattern, something to add to the chart. Mary Ann and Petey were both snatched from their mothers' hands; aside from that, there were no clues. Nothing. A big *nada*.

Molly hadn't expected much. Not really. She had the nagging feeling she had missed something, something in her own experience. If she, Petey's mother, couldn't put a finger on a clue, then how could she expect someone else to do it for her?

"That's bullshit," Zachary said, when Molly told him about it. "Bullshit, pure and simple. You're assuming guilt because it feels good."

"That's bullshit," she shot back, and when he grinned, said hotly, "it's nothing but psychiatric shit. I'm surprised at you, I didn't think you took that crap seriously."

"You can take the doctor away from Freud, but you can't take Freud away from the doctor. You're looking at one psychiatrist who can shovel it with the best of them. Now, what's on tap for today?" With Lauren in New Hampshire, Zachary spent almost all his free time with her. Today he had arrived at her house before eight, bearing a paper bag with hot, buttery croissants and two containers of coffee. He didn't trust Molly to have coffee in the house. She wasn't much on details lately.

Somewhat miffed because secretly she thought he might be right, she checked her tote for blank tapes, the action so familiar she could do it without concentrating.

Without being overt about it, Zachary studied her. She wore a sundress, a sop to the unbearable weather, and was thin, fast approaching gauntness; her collarbones stuck out and he could see the delineation of her upper ribs above the gentle swell of her breast—and there were hollows where shadows dwelt beneath her eyes. From day to day he could see them darken. Her agony ate at his heart. But short of crawling into her skin, there was nothing he could do, nothing more than what he was doing, making sure she had food to eat and at least tried to rest, if not to actually sleep. Big deal. Some hero. The feeling of powerlessness was an acid fueling his frustration.

Thinking of his frustrations and trying to imagine what hers were was a humbling experience. His voice gentle, he repeated the question. "What's your assignment?"

"A real toughie. Coney Island."

"You're kidding. Sunburns are big news?"

"You forget the annual hot dog–eating contest. Last year one of the contestants fainted."

"Kent must have been overjoyed."

"Yeah." She could never again think of Kent as a heartless son of a bitch. He had handed her the magic 3-D glasses and let her look at the depths of his soul. God, how she yearned for the good old days when she'd thought him Adolph Hitler, Vlad the Impaler, and Arnold Schwartzenegger in the *Terminator* all rolled into one.

"Penny?" Zachary said softly, but he didn't really need it. Frail and without defenses these days, she was easy to read. If—no, when—he got his hands on whoever had done this to her . . . shit. There was that feeling of powerlessness again. "Want company? I could put sunscreen on your back."

"How about I call you later? Maybe we'll get a bite or something?"

"Sounds good. I'm easy. If you don't mind, I think I'll hang around here." Two could study that damn chart until their eyes crossed.

She shoved a pair of dark glasses on her nose. "Why don't you go out to Fire Island?"

"Will you come out later if I do?" She shook her head no. He hadn't thought so. "Call."

The first thing Douglas did when he got home from his club where he had played the best eighteen holes of his life and qualified for the annual Master's Tournament was check the answering machine. Nothing. He didn't know whether to be sorry or not. Life without Irene was proving to be less complicated and more enjoyable. If it weren't for Nancy and her bloodhound tendencies, he might even be able to say he was content.

Since he had spent so long at the club's wood-paneled, tradition-drenched bar, recounting his amazing eagle on the eleventh hole to anyone who would listen, he had to hustle. He had to shower, shave, and pick up the June grad in good time so they could have a leisurely dinner at Le Cirque before going on to the theater. Whistling, he didn't want to answer the phone when it rang. He'd let the machine take it, but ... funny. He knew it was her. "Irene."

"Douglas."

Her voice was thick. Christ, she was loaded, and it wasn't even dark. At least, where he was. Remembering the investigator's instructions, he tried for subtlety and came up with bluntless. "Where the hell are you? You've got us all worried."

"I'll just bet I have."

"Nancy's very upset, Irene. She's your sister. If you don't care about me, you should care about her." Shit, for a man who made his living being clever with words he was certainly botching this. It sounded like a trite script from a B movie.

"Fuck Nancy. She doesn't give a shit about me. She just can't stand when she's not the center of attention. Tell her to stuff it."

"Why don't you tell her yourself? Call her, or better yet, give me your number, I'll have her call you."

"Hold it."

Muffled sounds of Irene talking to someone. For the first time, suspicion dawned. A man? Was that what this was all about? Had she let someone into her pants and gone off squandering money on him? "Who're you talking to?" he blurted, the instant she came back.

Her voice took on a crafty note. "No one. Anyway, what's it to you? You don't care about me. You haven't cared for a long time. You're more interested in your business and your girlfriends than you are in your wife who was miserable and unhappy and ..."

The same shit all over again. The same song she had been singing ever since Karen ...

Before too long her diatribe dwindled to incoherency and soon deteriorated into sobs. It was a relief when she slammed down the phone in the middle of a hiccup.

An explosion in a two-family house in Bushwick resulting in a two-alarm fire put an end to Molly's coverage of the hot dog–eating contest. The fire had gone to three alarms, threatening nearby buildings by the time she arrived, and rescue units were preparing to make a second search of the building. Neighbors reported two children unaccounted for; the rest of the occupants, six adults, two men, four women, had been taken out in body bags.

One of the first firemen on the scene gave Molly a terrific interview as he sat on the ledge of his engine, periodically gulping oxygen from the mask pressed to his sweat-streaked, smoke-blackened face. A loud crackling, a roaring and a shower of debris and hot live embers heralded the top floor's collapse, crushing everything beneath. Before the wreckage had settled, Molly was phoning in her report. When she got back to the roped-off area, the first thing she saw was the CBN van and the familiar face of Charlie Lee. "Hi. I didn't expect to see you today."

Charlie grunted, spared her a quick glance as he continued to set up equipment. "I traded. I need the bread." He grinned. Charlie always needed bread; he couldn't pass an electronics store without going in and emptying his wallet. "What's your story?"

"Eleanor had an opportunity to find out if Virginia really is for lovers, so I took her slot."

"Yeah, I read you." Charlie straightened, hefted his camera to his shoulder, slowly panned the scene. Motions he had gone through innumerable times before. He had an eye for detail, for finding the perfect shot, the one picture that told the story. A toddler's shoe lying on its side in a puddle after a devastating fire; an old woman's face, a single tear tracking through a web of wrinkles as she told of losing her life savings to a con artist; a young mother, mouth a dark "O" of anguish, wailing the loss of a child in a car accident; a gang member, dressed in black leather, face defiant as he was frisked by a cop after the brutal slaying of a rival gang member. He stopped filming, fiddled with the focus, made another slow sweep of the crowd. CBN liked crowd reaction.

A blonde wearing a gauzy two-piece dress and a disgruntled expression yelled to Charlie, "Ready? We've got to move it. We got here late."

Charlie grinned at Molly. "She's new. Rachel Godwin-VanHorn. Leading candidate for Dragon Lady of the Year. We've got a pool going on how long she lasts."

"She's prettier than Lloyd."

Charlie winked. "That's your opinion."

Half an hour later it was over. The two missing children had been found dead in a closet. A rescue worker had been rushed to the hospital with chest pains. Four firemen were treated on the spot for heat exhaustion.

Charlie found Molly staring after the ambulance taking the two little unfortunate children away. Its lights were flashing but there was no need for the siren. "Bummer," he said, as he always did when a tragedy touched him deeply. He tapped her on the shoulder. "It's quitting time, Molly–Uh-Oh. Want to grab a burger and a beer?"

For the first time, she noticed how late it was. "I can't. I promised Zachary . . ." Her eyes narrowed. "Charlie, you always pan the scene first, don't you?" He nodded. "How long do you keep the tapes?"

He shrugged. "A week, ten days, tops."

"What happens to them?"

"Generally they're degaussed and used again."

"Damn."

"Why're you asking? Talk to me."

"It was only an idea. It doesn't matter now." When he just stood there, looking stubborn, she sighed. "I'd hoped you still had the tape on the Newell story. Something about it still bugs me. I can't get away from it."

"Well, hell, why didn't you say so before? It just so happens I keep some of the field tapes on open stories. Makes the wrap-up nice and tidy if they solve it."

"The Newell tapes?"

"I should still have some. Give me a call. I'll set you up with a viewer and anything I've got."

Molly grabbed his arm. "How about right now. We can pick up a pizza. My treat."

"Double cheese?"

"Whatever you want."

WHERE'S MY BABY?

* * *

Zachary arrived at the CBN offices on Tenth Avenue with two pizzas and a six-pack of Coke an hour after Molly and Charlie. He had told them it would be easier if he picked it up; this way he could be sure Molly wouldn't order anchovies. Even the thought of anchovies made his skin crawl. He found Charlie and Molly in a darkened viewing room with their eyes glued to a monitor. He hit the lights, said, "Delivery," and plunked down the boxes on a vacant chair, the only available surface.

Charlie tilted back his head and sniffed like a wolf scenting prey. He got up, stretched, and reached over Molly's head to shake Zachary's hand. "How's it going?"

"You tell me."

Charlie shrugged. "It's going." He took a can of Coke, popped the top, chugged half in one thirsty swallow. "Time for the inner man. Which one's double cheese?"

"Both." Zachary rubbed a soot smudge from Molly's cheek and gave her a hello kiss on the nose. She smelled of smoke and the floral-scented shampoo she always used. "Tough day?"

"The worst."

"I can imagine. I heard your reports." Her eyes clouded and he backed off. She had enough to contend with. "What are we doing here?"

"Hey, you'd better get over here before I finish this by myself. You can tell him while we eat, otherwise we'll be here all night."

Molly stood, automatically tried to do something with the wrinkles in her skirt. Hopeless. "I'm going to wash my hands."

Charlie picked up another piece of pizza. "You'd better hurry. I'm ravenous. There might not be anything left."

Zachary pulled up a chair and helped himself to a piece. "What's doing?"

"Looking for a needle in a haystack." Charlie reached for another Coke. "She thinks maybe we'll see the same face pop up in different crowds, so we're reviewing whatever tapes we have left on all the abductions or disappearances in the past year. Smart girl. It's worth a look. A lot of sickos out there. Wouldn't surprise me none if one of 'em showed up." He took a long drink, belched, and rubbed his stomach. "It's a damned good idea. I'm sorry I didn't think of it myself."

Zachary was good at listening for innuendo. "But you don't think we'll come up with anything?"

Charlie glanced at the door and satisfied himself that they were still alone. "Look, there are approximately eight hundred thousand kids who go missing each year. Think about that. *Eight hundred thousand.* It boggles the mind. Statistics say if you don't get the kid back in the first thirty hours your chances of doing so are slim-to-none. Of course, many of those kids are used as pawns by their ever-loving parents squabbling over divorces and delighting in hurtful custody battles, and maybe there you've got a shot, but here ... I don't know. Odds are, a kid's worst enemy is someone close, someone the kid trusts."

"Well, that eliminates Petey's father."

"Yeah, sure does. The guy's got my vote for asshole of the decade."

Zachary finished his first piece and started on a second. "So how far did you two get?"

"Molly's got a list of eight names, counting Petey. We've reviewed tapes on six."

"No matches?"

"Not unless it's Lloyd."

"I heard that. Shame on you, Charlie. Lloyd's only doing his job." Molly sat down, accepted a piece of pizza from Zachary.

"Yeah, you're right. Besides, Lloyd C. Cranshaw doesn't have the brains for anything more than spritzing hair spray and showing off his gorgeous dental work."

Molly laughed. "Shh. Remember where we are. The walls have ears."

"Let 'em listen. Hey, did I ever tell you about the time we went to the toy factory?" He explained to Zachary. "Every Christmas they do a piece like it, mostly for the parents to see what's hot. Well, this time we went to the factory instead of a store and they were testing a new robot, about this high," he gestured to his waist, "and we get there and the robot takes one look at Lloyd and, well, it must've been love at first sight. Those people were pressing buttons and waving remotes but nothing they did deterred that robot from following him about. It had its shiny black eyes fixed firmly on our star. We couldn't leave until Lloyd promised to take it to dinner."

Molly laughed again and Zachary silently blessed Charlie. He seemingly had an inexhaustible supply of Lloyd stories and he told them with a wonderful deadpan delivery until they were ready to get back to work.

"Petey's tapes or the Newell tapes, Molly?"

She bit her lip, all traces of laughter gone. "Let's do Petey's first, so Zachary can get the hang of what we're looking for. He's familiar with the Newell scene, and that helps."

"You got it."

It wasn't easy, watching it all over again. Molly's ravaged face, full screen, appealing for information. Shots of Cunningham Park, of the circus. Charlie froze frame after frame; they examined the faces, looked for something, anything, out of place. Finally the last tape was run. Charlie's voice came out of the darkness. "Again?"

"No. No. Not again. There's nothing. Nothing."

Zachary switched on the light. "You've done enough, Molly."

"No. It won't be enough until Petey's home." She took a deep breath. "I'm sorry. I'm on edge. I shouldn't take it out on you two."

"Hey, I'm cool, Molly–Uh-Oh. You want the Newell story now? It's the last one."

"Sure."

Charlie slipped the first tape into the machine, nodded to Zachary to cut the lights. The chill February landscape flickered to life. As they had been doing, they ran through each tape in its entirety, then went back for a closer look. Frame by frame the tragedy played out. Molly wasn't interested in shots of the plane, of crying children, of shell-shocked teachers. She wanted to concentrate on the crowd. *Somebody* had walked away with Timothy Newell; she would bet the little boy hadn't disappeared on his own.

The first tape showed nothing; the follow-up tapes yielded the same goose egg. No match from any of the other tapes with someone from the Newell tapes.

"That's it, Molly. Sorry." Charlie extracted the tape and reached to shut off the machine.

"Wait."

"You got something?" He shoved the tape back in. "Tell me where."

"Not this tape. The first one. The Brenton School. I keep on thinking I'm missing something."

Charlie obligingly inserted the proper tape. He caught Zachary's eyes just before he hit the lights. Neither one wanted to tell her it was hopeless.

The tape ran again. Lloyd checking his makeup in the CBN van's outside mirror; impatiently motioning Charlie away. A slow pan. The picture dipped, veered back up.

"Stop. What's that?"

Charlie froze the frame. "What're you looking at?"

Molly sat forward. "Not here. Go back."

Lloyd made kissy motions in the mirror. "This what you want? Hey, Molly, I was only kidding. It can't be Lloyd."

She wasn't paying attention to anything but the screen. "There. Freeze it." Her voice was breathless. Zachary moved closer, bent over for a better look.

"Done. What are we seeing?" Charlie glanced at Zachary again.

Molly grabbed Zachary's hand. "Tell me."

"I see a car. Well, the back of a car, to be precise."

Charlie scratched his head. "A nice new shiny Caddy. Must've cost a bundle."

"Yes." A high, excited voice.

Zachary looked at her worriedly; she was getting more wired by the moment. "It's not the only car there."

"No, it's not, but it's the only one with mud smeared over its license plate. A nice new shiny Cadillac with mud smeared all over its license plate. Why?"

Charlie shrugged. "The day was awful. The roads were shit."

He looked to Zachary for confirmation, but Zachary was squinting at the screen. "Run the tape forward a bit." Again they watched as Charlie panned, then the picture dipped, came up again, slid past the Cadillac. "Stop. There, right after you slipped." Zachary tapped the screen with a finger. "You must have knocked into the Caddy. The mud's slipped from part of the plate."

Molly delved into her tote, came up with her tape recorder. She recorded the particulars, never taking her eyes from the screen. She'd give it to Glen. It wasn't much, but it was the only thing she had.

Thirty-One

"I shouldn't give you the name." Glen took another bite of bagel, cinnamon raisin, his second. "These are good. Where'd you get them?" Carefully he sucked cream cheese off his thumb.

"You'll have to ask my neighbor, Denise. She brought them over earlier." Molly was content to wait. Glen was going to give it to her, otherwise he would have phoned. He was stretching the rules; and if he had to assuage his conscience, then so be it.

"It might not even be the right guy. We only had the partial."

Molly pushed the plate of bagels closer to him. "Try a sesame. It's my favorite." He could have every bagel on the damn plate if it would help. "It's a man, then?"

"Nah. This'll do it. Gotta watch my waistline." Glen lifted his cup, sighed, and put it down without drinking. "It's a man. Registered to a Harry Kemp, domiciled in Manhattan."

Molly took a deep breath, slowly let it out. She had to concentrate to keep her hands from trembling. *Manhattan.* What was he doing in Cedarhurst?

Glen easily anticipated the question. "He's got a business, Encore, Inc., in Queens. Could have been going about his business, stopped to gawk. It isn't every day a plane takes a nosedive into a bunch of kids. We've got no call to investigate him, Molly."

But he had. He had gone so far as to find out about his business.

"My advice, you and Pamela forget about it."

"Pamela?"

"Yeah, Pamela."

Molly read him loud and clear. "Okay."

"Good." His eyes fell on the chart. "One other thing. We've identified the child's body. I wanted you to hear it from me before it's all over the news. He was Michael Barclay. The ME put a name to him the other day, but we didn't give it out until we notified the family."

Molly went to the chart, lightly brushed her fingers over the name. Michael Robert Barclay. Age five. Missing from the backyard of his home in Sheepshead Bay, Brooklyn, when his mother stepped inside to go to the bathroom. Found in a plastic garbage bag stuffed inside a suitcase buried in a shallow grave off the Saw Mill River Parkway. With every iota of her being she prayed his fate would not be Petey's.

". . . The President is set to meet with his economic advisers at the White House later today. Closer to home, police officials have identified the remains of the child discovered in the shallow grave beside the Saw Mill River Parkway. In sports, the Yankees are home tonight against the Boston Red Sox, while the Mets—"

Swearing, Pamela got out of her car and hurried inside. She was sweating, her clothes were sticking to her, and it wasn't eleven yet. And she had come up with another giant zero. A blast of cold air hit her, making her drying sweat feel icy. Heaven after the oven outside.

"Pamela?" Ellen came through the door to the house carrying a glass. "I thought it was you."

"Is that for me?"

"It's iced tea. If you wait a moment I'll make you an iced coffee."

"Give it here. My tongue's hanging out."

Ellen watched while she gulped thirstily, smiled when she made a face. "I told you it was tea."

"I hate tea. Tea is for when you're sick." She rotated the glass, sloshing the liquid. "Any messages?" Ellen reached for a stack of pink slips, deftly removed the glass before handing them over. Pamela rapidly shuffled through them. Her eyebrows went up. "Good. Good. I knew he'd come through."

"Molly's message?"

"Yes. I needed something new."

"You checked out the Drummonds? The adoption was on the up-and-up?"

"I didn't say that. I think their lawyer's into feathering his nest the fast way. Either that, or the Drummonds are dirty. Something smells bad, but my money's on the lawyer. His name came up the other night. The Brooklyn support group."

"Black-market babies?"

"Probably. Who do we know who wants a baby?"

Ellen didn't even blink. "My nephew just got married. My sister's middle boy. The accountant. You know, Howard—the one who graduated from Binghamton last year."

"Yeah? Congratulations. He's no good. I need somebody past it, somebody who looks desperate, whose biological clock has stopped ticking."

"I'll make some calls."

"I want a married couple. This turkey'll probably check them out before he cozies up. And I want them—"

"I know. As soon as possible."

"This afternoon. I want them to get an appointment tomorrow with Lawrence Burkhardt." She handed Ellen a slip of paper. "This is his address. I need to know for sure we can cross him off the list as far as Petey's concerned."

"Right. Oh. Did you hear they identified the remains of that poor child?"

"It's all over the news."

"You don't think the same . . . ?"

Pamela sighed. "Try not to think." She looked at Molly's message again. "Encore, Inc. I wonder what it is."

"They replace lost items. You know, if you have a set of china or crystal or something and you break a piece, they track down the pattern and replace it."

"Nice work."

"My sister's husband inadvertently threw out two of her good silver pieces. The pattern was old and she had to use a professional to get them replaced. I thought the name was familiar, so I gave Ruthie a call."

"And?"

"She used Encore, Inc. No problem."

"As I said, good work. I'm going to take a quick shower, then I think I'll run by Kemp's house. See what I can dig up. Did Molly say where she'll be?"

"She's still in court."

"If she calls again, tell her I'll get in touch as soon as I've got something. And Ellen? After you set up the meet with the lawyer, I want you to start the usual background checks on Encore."

"I'm already on it. I figured you'd want it." She hesitated. "Uh, Pamela? Do you think this could be it?"

"Who knows? All I do know is it's better than what I've got. The support groups have yielded only lawyer Burkhardt and a really off-the-wall rumor about reincarnated kids." She shrugged. "I'd *love* this Kemp guy to be the one, but ... we'll see."

The trail was old and cold. Just thinking about it put her in a lousy mood.

Her mood was not sweetened by the ride into the city, nor was it helped when she couldn't find a meter and had to garage her car. The rate chart provided a mild shock. "Seven-fifty for the first half hour?"

The attendant, busily feeding a ticket into the time clock, gave her and her much-used Chevy a disdainful look. "Plus eighteen-and-a-quarter-per-cent tax if you ain't a resident of Manhattan."

"I ain't."

The attendant's look said he believed it. To add insult to injury, he produced a line drawing of a car and walked around the Chevy, meticulously circling every dent and scrape on it on its corresponding place on the drawing. He presented it to her with a smirk. "Sign."

Pamela scribbled her signature, then stomped out onto the street. It wasn't bad enough she had to deal with crooks and murderers and kidnappers, now she had to deal with snobs, and this one right out of the South Bronx, she'd bet her last pair of pantyhose.

If anything, it was even hotter in Manhattan than it had been in Queens. The tall buildings trapped the heat;

the cement sidewalks absorbed it, radiated it, cooking her from the soles of her feet upward. Dressed in a linen suit, she felt suffocated before she reached the corner. But the suit was part of the image she needed, so she pushed her discomfort to the back of her mind.

Harry Kemp's co-op was on Fifth Avenue, facing Central Park. Pamela crossed Fifth and settled herself on one of the wooden benches lining the park's stone wall, where she had a good view of the front of Harry's building. It wasn't unpleasant, the full-leaved trees shaded her, so she sat for the better part of a half hour, watching the activity across the street. When the doorman began to look at his watch every few minutes, she knew it was time to make her move.

She had a million approaches, an angle for every situation, but number one on the list always served her best: money. Offer money and stand back—sometimes *jump* back—and watch them talk. The doorman—just call me Kahlil, ma'am—was no exception. After watching him operate, nothing would surprise her. He probably had a bank account in Switzerland.

Kahlil didn't want coffee; he always took a little walk on his break. Probably running numbers, was Pamela's uncharitable thought. They walked up Fifth, found a bench a couple of blocks away. She asked about the building. He relaxed, probably thought she wanted to buy. If she sold her soul she wouldn't be able to afford an apartment there. Not in this lifetime.

Kahlil had seen the color of her money; he set out to snare a potential big tipper. The building was rife with celebrities. He mentioned an actor nominated for an Oscar three times. Pamela wasn't impressed; he hadn't won. Kahlil rushed on: a Nixon Cabinet Secretary; the hottest sculptor this side of MOMA; a rising star with the Met; a lead dancer with the Joffrey; and a certain Russian who had been the most sought-after guest conductor worldwide.

She had thought the Russian gentleman deceased. Not as of noon, Kahlil assured her. He had taken his limo to the Four Seasons for lunch, as he did every other day. On the off days he dined at La Côte Basque. Pamela allowed herself to be impressed.

Kahlil was in a rush to get back. The shoppers were probably expected soon. Pamela estimated he got a dollar a shopping bag, curbside to elevator. She fiddled with the clasp of her purse. "One other thing . . . Harry Kemp."

"Harry's a big tipper."

Figured. She showed him a fifty. With the twenty she'd already given him, it wasn't bad for a coffee break. Six minutes later she knew everything Kahlil knew about Harry Kemp. Unspoken but coming through loud and clear was that Kahlil didn't like him. His money was okay, but that was as far as it went. When she tried to find out why, she hit a wall. Some things just were.

Miraculously, Pamela found a coffee shop on Madison that had a telephone book. She looked up the name Kahlil had given her, then went back out into the heat and hailed a cab. Cheaper than ransoming her car. She had the cabbie stop three buildings down and walked back to the address, a few steps below the co-op in magnificence. Quite a few. No doorman. She rang bells, got lucky on the second try. A syrupy sweet voice said, "Yes?"; Pamela was afraid she'd get a cavity just by listening. Sweet Voice buzzed her in with the flimsy excuse of a forgotten key; a victim in the making.

Betty Latrobe, apartment 3B, wasn't in. Pamela took a seat on the worn stone steps of the emergency staircase where she had a good view of Betty's apartment. Two hours later the small elevator that had given Pamela a touch of claustrophobia wheezed to a stop on the third floor and a tall, statuesque woman stepped out. Bingo. Kahlil had a good eye. Pamela moved to intercept her. The woman never blinked. Cool. But then, Pamela didn't imagine she posed much of a threat. Betty was six feet to her five-four.

"Jillian Raven?" *That* got a reaction, but the girl was good. She covered it up almost immediately. Pamela hurried to explain what she wanted.

"Harry? You want to know about Harry?"

"I'll pay."

Jillian laughed. She took out her keys. "Come on in. I'll tell you anything you want to know about Harry. On the house."

Sweat beaded Harry's forehead, ran down his temples, soaked into his collar. The warehouse was a goddamn oven; impossible during the day, even worse at night when the huge overhead doors were locked shut. He should have said the hell with it, grabbed an ice-cold brew, maybe picked up a broad for a little party time. Instead he'd waited until everyone had left, needing to be alone. But no matter what he did, he couldn't make the figures come out right. Damn that old bitch Clarice, dying and leaving him holding that fucking hunk of glass. Fifty thousand. Every time he thought about it he wanted to howl. There had to be someone on the face of the earth who wanted it.

He spent another hour scrolling through the business's database, looking for a name. Someone out there had to have a deep purse and atrocious taste. He just

WHERE'S MY BABY?

had to be patient. The business had to produce, more important, had to have the appearance of producing.

You'll never amount to anything, Harry, never be any good, Harry, never—

"Shut the fuck up."

What did she know? He was good. Didn't his other enterprise prove it? There was the answer; he'd have to pull another job. Sweat poured from his armpits, further soaking his shirt. The media blitz on the Deere snatch was just starting to taper off. He'd have to be careful, snatch a kid from someplace else. Accessing his personal file, he studied the lists. Two possibles. He tried the first. Ten rings. No answer. Tough luck for them. Quickly he tried the second, counted the rings. Eight. Nine. He'd give it ten, to be fair, but he was sweating so much the fucking phone was slipping from his hand. A sign? Ten rings . . .

"Hello?" Out of breath. She'd run to answer.

Suddenly Harry froze. Was it too soon? He'd known the Deere snatch was a mistake, taking a kid from someone in the media, but the skinny broad had been willing to pay double. Only a fool would turn down a sweet deal like that. And Harry Kemp was no fool.

You're no good, Harry, no good no good no goooood . . .

"Hello . . . ?"

Harry pulled himself together, started talking. When he was through, he unlocked the drawer where he kept his floppy tapes and carefully backed up his personal files. No reason not to go for that beer now. Maybe he'd give Jillian a call. He hadn't seen her in a while. Just thinking of her, all six feet of her, made him hot. He dropped the floppy into the drawer, forgetting to lock it.

Thirty-Two

"I was so sure. When I saw that car with the mud on its license plate I knew. I just *knew*. The Caddy's owner had something to do with Timmy Newell's disappearance." Molly paced the small open area of the office, reminding Pamela of a tiger she had once seen in the Cheyenne Mountain Zoo in Colorado Springs.

Sitting with her well-worn leather executive chair tilted back at an alarming angle, Pamela moodily watched her. "He checks out." Molly stopped and glared at her. Pamela shrugged. "I'll grant you he's one of life's nastier specimens, but there's nowhere to go from here. The business is clean and so, apparently, is his personal life."

"You can say that after listening to that poor woman? He beat her, Pamela, and for what? A rash on his chest?"

Pamela locked the cassette of her conversation with Betty Latrobe/Jillian Raven into the top drawer. "So the man's a shit—an abusive shit, if you will—but that doesn't make him a kidnapper." She held up a finger. "And if he *is* a kidnapper, that doesn't necessarily make him *Petey's* kidnapper. More slugs than we like to think about are crawling around out there. Now. We have other leads we can ... damn, there's the phone."

Molly resumed pacing, her mind flying off into a million directions, but no matter where it went, she kept on coming back to one thing. Gut instinct. And hadn't it been Pamela who had counseled following gut instincts?

"Shit. I was afraid of that."

"Bad news?"

Ellen appeared with a tray of sandwiches and a pitcher of lemonade. She set it down on the desk. "The Landaus?"

"Yeah." Pamela chose half a tuna sandwich. "That was David. He and Marcy saw Burkhardt. They got real cozy real fast once Burkhardt got a peek inside David's wallet, but all he's pushing is newborns. He must have a good source."

Ellen poured lemonade, motioned to Molly. "Come. You won't have time to pick up anything before you go back to court."

"I'm fine. Burkhardt is the Drummonds' lawyer?"

Pamela shook her head. "The very same. David hinted broadly they wanted an older child, a boy around four, but Burkhardt said he no can do. David said the guy was amazed. He thought everyone wanted a newborn."

"So that lets him off the hook?"

"As far as Petey, I'm afraid so. But Mr. Burkhardt is gonna find himself in a whole lot of trouble once I make a call. I know guys on the force who just love an operator like him. They'll put him and his little operation out of business so fast the good attorney won't know what hit him."

Ellen nudged the sandwich plate closer to Molly. "You've got to eat. You're too thin."

Dutifully Molly picked up a sandwich half. Pamela eyed her. "I thought we might have something with Burkhardt, but as I was saying before, we aren't out of options. I'm going to check out some more support groups on the general theory that if we kick enough stones we might turn up something we can use. Now—"

"I want to dig deeper on Kemp." Molly leaned forward. "You're the one who told me about gut instincts, Pamela, and my gut is growling over this guy."

"We've got to stay focused. Kemp may or may not be many things, but right now we've got nothing to link him to Petey."

Slowly Molly put down the uneaten sandwich. Her eyes were wide, intent. "Focused? That's what I am, what I've been, from the instant Petey's hand left mine. Every thought I have, everything I do, even every breath I take, is focused on one thing and one thing only. I want my son. I want him back where he belongs, and there is nothing and no one who can or will sway me from that goal, and right now my gut is telling me Harry Kemp had something to do with the disappearance of Timmy Newell, and if that is true, then maybe, just maybe, he had something to do with Petey's kidnapping. I cannot and will not pass up the opportunity to find out why this is so."

Pamela looked at her long and hard. "What do you want to do?"

Molly took a deep breath. "I think we should dig deeper into his business. Maybe he did some work for the families of the kidnapped kids."

"Did you use him?"

Molly looked crestfallen. "No."

Ellen sat forward. "You know, Ruthie, my sister," she said to Molly, "was worried about using him. Not him, specifically, but such a service. Afraid they would replace the item and then come back and clean her out some night." Both Molly and Pamela were staring at her. She squirmed, looked defensive. "It's not impossible."

"No, not impossible, nor unreasonable. I've acted on flimsier theories." Pamela patted her pockets, grimaced, then went on, thinking aloud. "We need his customer database. That'd be the easiest way to cross-check the names. Okay, let me get to it. You'll be in court again this afternoon if I have to reach you?"

"Nope. I'm going to tell Kent he'll have to muddle through without me this afternoon. I'm going with you."

"The hell you say."

"The hell I am. There's no way you can stop me."

Pamela huffed a bit, but gave in without too much of a fight. When she looked at Molly she kept on seeing the tiger.

Forty-five minutes later they sat in Molly's Taurus in front of a red-brick warehouse on a seedy Maspeth street that dead-ended at one of the sections of Calvary Cemetery. Pamela's gaze swept the old buildings, the barred windows. Graffiti splotched the walls, the huge overhead doors, and even the dark-green Dumpsters, a familiar sight in industrial areas. The macadam was worn through in spots, the original cobblestones laid bare, giving the street a neglected air. "Nice neighborhood."

Molly pushed her dark glasses more firmly against her face. "I've seen worse. Ready?"

"Remember, I'm a ditzy matron rolling in green. You're only to be seen. I want you to fade into the woodwork." A wicked gleam appeared in her eyes. "No matter how dirty it is. Understood?"

"Why? I want to be able to participate."

"You're just along for the ride, and if you won't play it my way, then I'm not going in." Her look softened. "Look, you're a reporter, not a detective. It's a different technique, believe me. Besides, your face has been plastered all over the media. I don't want someone recognizing you."

That argument put her over the top. Pamela rang, then rang again, an old-fashioned doorbell located to one side of the only people-sized door. Nothing. She grabbed the doorknob, twisted, and pushed. The hollow steel door gave, revealing a narrow corridor lit by a single fluorescent bulb. Sounds of typing came from the other side of a window set in the far wall. The typing stopped when Pamela rapped smartly on the window. A female voice, somewhat muffled, called, "Who's there?" and seconds later a young woman's face appeared.

"Is this Encore, Inc.?" Pamela asked, in a voice so low even Molly, who was almost attached to her hip, had trouble hearing.

The young woman looked puzzled, and yelled, "What?" when Pamela repeated the question in an even lower voice. Tucking a strand of frizzy blond hair behind her ear, she pointed to the door. She wore worn denim and a work shirt; her mouth worked; gum cracked. "What kin I do fer ya?"

Pamela went into high gear, in a whispery voice that forced strict attention. She was a widow with a sentimental attachment to everything her dear departed had given her, and unfortunately, her favorite, her very, very favorite piece—very old, very rare, very expensive—had been destroyed by a careless maid. She took a breath.

The young woman, eyes glazed, dove right in. "My boss isn't here. You'll have to call."

Well aware Kemp was absent since Ellen had called earlier, Pamela looked aghast as she maneuvered inside the small office. Molly followed, amused and impressed by the performance. Settling herself firmly on the only available visitor's chair, Pamela announced she was interviewing. This was not the only firm that replaced fine items, and given the state of the economy, she would be surprised if they weren't interested in satisfying a potentially lucrative customer. When *she* made a decision she would call, but first . . .

What about confidentiality, security, provenance, warranty, references? Angela pleaded ignorance on all matters. In that case, Pamela said, she'd be on her way. Getting up, she lurched, bumped against the desk, knocking several items to the floor. Angela hurried around the desk. Pamela waved her away. "No, no, it's my own fault. Let me." She bent down, momentarily blocking Angela's view. "So clumsy. Here," she held up a pen holder, a pen, and lastly, a day-by-day appointment calendar.

Angela accepted Pamela's profuse apologies, looking like she wished the Enterprise would transport her unwelcome visitors to another galaxy. At her ditziest, Pamela suddenly decided she wanted a tour. Angela was steamrollered.

The only other office was empty and tempting. It had a clear view of the huge warehouse area beyond, filled with row upon row of pallets piled with boxes and crates. Molly glanced at Pamela, quickly looked away. When they were far down a row, she murmured in an embarrassed voice that she needed the rest room. To her delight, Angela pointed her back toward the office area. Pamela deftly steered Angela toward the far side of the building, where men were working.

Molly waited until Pamela and Angela were strolling down an aisle where the pallets were piled high with crates. Heart pounding, she slipped inside Harry Kemp's office. It was his; she had no doubt. A plaque sat on the desk:

THE BUCK STOPS HERE.

Someone had pasted a hand-lettered sign on the bottom:

I HOPE SO.

Cute. The room had a small desk crowded with a telephone, a computer, three boxes of floppies nestled next to it like little ducklings; three chairs, one of them broken; a scarred credenza groaning under the weight of ledgers; a dot-matrix printer; a copy machine; a fax machine; and several metal file cabinets—unfortunately with the drawers locked.

A careful type, Harry Kemp. Quickly she tried the desk drawers, breathed a sigh of relief to find them unlocked. The top drawer was crammed with paper clips, boxes of staples, rubber stamps, stamp pads, a bottle of Tylenol, packets of sugar, rolls of stamps in different denominations, and other uninteresting items. The file drawer held manila folders. A cursory examination showed shipping manifests and other documentation. The side drawers were stuffed with stationery, order pads, and more supplies, mostly boxes of floppy disks and ribbons for the printer. The bottom drawer was more interesting. Next to a crushed box of Q-tips, half empty, and a pair of shoe laces still in the package was a small rolltop file cabinet, the kind used for floppies.

Why keep it in a drawer? Molly's hand hovered, hesitated, then quickly rolled back the top. The first floppy was labeled BACKUP 01—DIFFERENTIAL. The second, labeled BACKUP 01—FULL. Eight others, all the way to BACKUP 09—FULL. This time she didn't hesitate. She put all ten disks into her shoulder bag.

"That took real balls. I'm proud of you."

Molly swung into the stream of westbound traffic on the LIE. "I've never done anything like it."

Pamela laughed. "You sure picked a good time to start."

"Angela will know who took them."

"All she'll remember is a ditzy broad, and dollars to donuts, she'll conveniently forget we were ever there."

Molly passed a limousine and maneuvered back into the middle lane. "Was there anything on the appointment calendar?"

"Yes and no. I only got a quick peek. Mr. Kemp had no appointments in the middle of February."

Timmy Newell. Molly's fingers tightened on the wheel. "What about June?"

"Sorry. I didn't have time. But we've made a beginning, and we have the floppies."

Pamela took one look at Ellen's face when they walked into the office and snapped, "You can stop fussing. I told you we'd be all right."

"I'm not fussing, as you call it. I know you're perfectly capable of taking care of yourself. Haven't you told me so time and again?"

Pamela glanced at her watch. "So what are you still doing here? It's past your quitting time."

Ellen turned to Molly, and seeing alarm immediately spring into her eyes, said hastily, "Zachary called. His little girl broke her leg."

"Oh, no. I'd better call him right away."

"You won't reach him. He called about thirty minutes ago and said he was almost halfway to New Hampshire. He said to tell you he'll call."

"Did he say how bad it is?"

"He didn't sound overly alarmed." Ellen smiled gently. "He sounds like a sensible man."

"He is." High praise from Pamela. She glanced significantly at Molly's shoulder bag. "Come on. We've got work to do." Ellen said good-night and Pamela immediately sat down at the computer, Molly hovering anxiously at her side. "Are you computer literate?"

"No." One of the items on the chart—the original organization chart—was to buy a computer for Petey. Intellectually curious, he deserved a head start on the tough world of kindergarten, and she meant to give him every advantage she could. That's what a mother was for.

But what kind of mother let her child be stolen from her arms?

"Molly? You okay?"

Molly saw the concern in Pamela's eyes and couldn't help the words from tumbling out, hard and bitter and tasting like ashes in her mouth. "Maybe I don't deserve to get Petey back. I didn't take very good care of him, did I? I let some . . . some *creep* just walk up and take him away. Maybe he's better off where he is. Maybe—"

"That's enough." Pamela slapped her pockets. "Shit!

Why I ever agreed to that stupid wager I'll never know." She gentled her voice. "Look. You're just reacting. Settle down. Go sit somewhere, you're making me nervous."

The sustaining adrenaline had fled. Molly felt like a rag doll, wished she could find a nice comfortable burrow somewhere safe where she could crash. But there was no place on earth like that for her until she had Petey back. Idly she watched Pamela insert one of the disks, type a couple of strokes, then peer intently at the screen. In the next instant she twisted to face Molly, a huge grin on her face. Molly sat up, all tiredness forgotten. "What?"

"A bit of luck. Harry Kemp uses the same backup program I do."

"So we can read his disks?"

"You betcha." Pamela jumped up and began searching through a cabinet. "Just as soon as I find the manual. This is a restore procedure, and I've never attempted one. I don't want to screw up now. Now, where . . . ? Aha!" Her grin flashed again, transforming her face, giving her an appealing, somewhat elfin quality. Quickly she scanned the manual, nodded; her fingers went flying over the keys.

Molly moved her chair closer so she had a good view of the screen. After a few minutes, Pamela let out a deep sigh and sat back. "Here we go." Lines of type began scrolling up the screen. "This will take some time. Why don't you see what you can find in the kitchen? I have a feeling this is going to be a long night."

Molly wasn't the least bit hungry but she reasoned Pamela needed her strength. She found the refrigerator well stocked, unlike her own these days, and put together a light meal of cold chicken, tomatoes, potato salad, and fruit for dessert. She arranged the dishes on a tray and poked her head into the office. "Iced tea okay?"

Pamela didn't even bother to turn. "Do I look sick?"

Molly laughed. "What, then?"

"Anything else, I'm a human garbage can."

Molly grabbed two cans of Coke and hurried back, setting the tray on the desk. Pamela had just shoved in another floppy. "How're you doing?"

"Almost done." She glanced at the tray. "That looks good. What's for dessert?"

"The fruit."

"Butter pecan ice cream would be better."

"I didn't see any."

"It's in a white paper bag in the back of the freezer. I have to hide it, Ellen thinks I have to watch my cholesterol." The computer beeped. She swiveled, expertly removed one floppy, replaced it with the next. "Not long now. Mr. Harry Kemp is about to spill his guts."

By the time Molly had finished with their few dishes in the kitchen, Pamela was scrolling through Harry Kemp's files, so immersed Molly didn't disturb her, not even to ask if she still wanted the ice cream. When the phone shrilled they both jumped. Pamela waved her hand. "Get it, would you? It's probably Zachary."

It was and he sounded tired and down. Lauren had a compound fracture requiring surgery.

"How is she taking it?"

Molly could almost hear his shrug. "Kids are resilient. Besides, they've got her sedated."

"Sounds to me like you could use something."

"Nah, I'll be okay. As soon as she can travel, I'm bringing her home." A pause, then his voice came, deep and husky down the line. "What about you? Why are you at Pamela's so late?"

Whether out of a superstitious fear she'd jinx it or something equally primitive, she didn't want to say anything. Not yet. So she said they were working on something, and left it at that. Zachary was either sensitive to her mood, or so preoccupied by his own troubles that he didn't pursue it.

A short while later Pamela sat up straight, peered intently at the screen, and let out a low whistle. "Well, hel-lo."

Molly was instantly at her side. "You've found something?"

"I've accessed his customer database. I want to try a comparison of my database of missing children with it, but it's a humongous job and Ellen is the best one to do it. Right now, we can work with his personal files. He had passwords blocking access, but like most people, he chose an easy one. Boss. Big surprise. But, the fact he thought he had to have them protected is interesting. I'm beginning to agree with your gut instinct; Harry Kemp bears investigating." She held up a cautionary hand. "We can't afford mistakes. To start, make a list of the names on your chart while I see if I can print some of these files." She tapped several keys; the printer whirred to life.

Molly jotted down the names; she could do it in her sleep.

Tabitha Gerard
Suzanne Lind
Wilson Whitman
Timothy Newell
Amy Derleth

Mary Ann Szell
Michael Robert Barclay
Peter Deere

She handed it to Pamela, who immediately picked up a pencil and made a second column. "These are their approximate ages, aren't they?"

Tabitha Gerard	6
Suzanne Lind	4
Wilson Whitman	5
Timothy Newell	6
Amy Derleth	5½
Mary Ann Szell	3
Michael Robert Barclay	5
Peter Deere	4½

"Yes. What have you got?" Molly took the papers Pamela handed her, quickly scanned the first.

J/V W	JW—h/f	Tom/6
H/E A	JS—w/m	Susan/4
W/B G	MS—w/m	Jenny/7
D/I H	DC—w/m	Karen/6
E/C R	AR—h/m	Billy/8
G/S K	IB—w/gm	Jennifer/2
J/M N	MD—w/m	Robert/7
C/J J	FG—w/gm	Rachel/4
B/E G	TG—h/f	Michael/5
P/R T	MC—w/gm	Matthew/4
S/D B	RD—w/gm	Angie/2

She frowned, turned to the second page. "Another list?"

A	15.
W	20.
R	20.
J	20.
H	40.

"I don't understand. What am I looking at? The only name match from my list with this is . . . oh, my God . . . no . . ."

Alarmed, Pamela snatched the pages from her hands. "What do you see? Where's the match?"

Molly stabbed a finger near the bottom of Harry Kemp's first list. "There. Michael. Michael slash five." Michael Robert Barclay. Age, five. Found dead in a suitcase beside the Saw Mill River Parkway. She couldn't say it out loud; it was too obscene.

They stared at each other; then, grim-faced, Pamela went back to the computer. "I'm going to see what else I can find. Call Charlie Lee. I want a copy of CBN's Brenton tapes and I want them as of yesterday. First thing tomorrow morning I'm going to Glen."

Thirty-Three

Pamela was on the phone to Molly before nine the next morning. "Did you get the tape?" she barked, without so much as a greeting. Voice hoarse and scratchy; she sounded as if she hadn't gotten much sleep.

Molly's heart started to beat a bit faster. "Yes."

"Good. Stay put. I'm going to call Rowley to come out. Okay?"

Both Molly's heart rate and her respiration increased. "You've found something else?"

Pamela sighed. "Not really. I just think we've got enough to give the police. Since time is of the essence, the more manpower, the better. Rowley's task force and the feds have got it."

Glen and his partner, Sidney Salem, arrived on Pamela's heels. They took seats at the kitchen table; Molly dispensed mugs of coffee. Somehow the homeyness of the kitchen seemed more fitting than the living room this early in the day. Although the temperature inside the house was comfortable, sweat dotted Glen's forehead. He swiped at it with a paper napkin, then wrapped his hands around his mug, his eyes fixed on the items Pamela had put on the table. "What ya got?"

Pamela rubbed the back of her neck. "I'm not sure. Let me fill you in, then you take a look. We've got two tapes, the video from CBN, which you already know about, and an audio I taped with a woman named Betty Latrobe, professional name Jillian Raven. Listen, then we'll get to the other stuff."

"Nice guy, this Kemp," Glen said, when it ended.

Sidney Salem's sad beagle eyes studied his coffee. "Likes to beat up on the ladies, but does that translate to kidnapping?"

Pamela shrugged. "He does a lot of traveling. There's time unaccounted for. He could be up to anything."

Molly leaned forward, unable to keep still. "He wasn't here in the middle of February, the same time Timmy Newell disappeared."

Detective Salem looked interested. "How do you know?"

"I got a look at his secretary's appointment calendar," Pamela said. "February had a chunk of blank pages."

"It's not much, Pamela," Glen said. "All you've really got is means for February." He cleared his throat. "Ah, what about June?"

"His secretary was breathing down my neck. But . . ." She handed several pages to him. "There are these."

He held them so Sidney could see. "What am I looking at?"

"A printout of a few of Harry Kemp's personal files." Glen raised his eyebrows but she ignored the implicit question. "I'd say at the very least they're interesting."

"Is it some kind of code? Do we have to go one up or two down in the alphabet to find the key?"

Pamela's voice suddenly became abrasive. "Do what you have to do, Glen. All I," she looked at Molly, "all we know is Petey is still missing and we will do anything, look anywhere, for a clue."

Abashed, Glen appealed to Molly. "I didn't mean—"

"I know."

Sidney let out a low whistle. He tapped an entry.

Glen's eyes went from the paper to Molly's chart. He went over, studied the entries under "Michael Robert Barclay." With his back to them, he threw out a question. "Where'd you get the files?"

Molly opened her mouth, but Pamela was quicker. "It's not important. They're genuine, believe me."

A tense stillness suddenly engulfed them. Then Glen turned, smiled at Molly and lifted his shoulders slightly. "I guess it's not important. For now. You've piqued my interest." He nodded to his partner, who gathered the exhibits. "You'll be hearing from us."

Molly arrived at court fifteen minutes late to find an empty room. Her first thought was *The Twilight Zone,* but her second was more practical. Illness, the bailiff said when she tracked him down. One of the defendants was in the prison hospital. Probably his lawyer was trying to scare up some witnesses, was his cynical opinion.

Whatever. Molly called Kent and reported the adjournment. "Okay," he said, "that's news, too. Don't worry about it, cookie. Go home and get some rest, you sound like you could use it."

Molly preferred the old Kent. Definitely.

Her Taurus was air-conditioned heaven after the brutality of the streets. Not yet noon and the air was heavy and thick; you needed strong lungs to extract the molecules of oxygen. Two cars were doing battle over her parking space, a plum; she had fed the meter for five

WHERE'S MY BABY?

hours. She hesitated before leaving the lot. Where to go? Who to see? What to do? Just like a teen, playing hooky and finding it was no fun to do it alone. If she hadn't banished self-pity she would have loved to indulge.

Suddenly she knew exactly where she wanted to go. She didn't call until she was almost there. In the neighborhood, for real.

Susan Newell opened the door, sad-eyed, wan-looking, and obviously pregnant. Score one for Charlie Lee. "Come in, won't you?" Politeness under adversity. One way to cope. Molly understood; coping was something she was trying to master. The house was dim and cool. Susan led her to the den, chose a leather armchair, indicated Molly should find her own seat. "Are you here as a reporter, Ms. Deere, or are you here as Petey's mother?"

The kitten had claws. Molly supposed she deserved it, but it hurt nevertheless. She had thought them sisters in a fortunately exclusive sorority. "I'm not sure why I'm here. I'm not sure of anything anymore."

Brutal honesty. Susan took her time examining it, searching Molly's face as if she could pierce her flesh and read her mind. Perhaps she found an answer, perhaps not. She finally relaxed enough to nod. "Yes. I know exactly what you mean." Her hand crept to her stomach, cradling the new life.

Jealousy stabbed Molly. Irrational. Overwhelming. Then sanity flushed it out and she felt shame. No child could replace another. But still, she couldn't bring herself to offer congratulations.

"I thought of you, when they found that little boy's body." Susan looked momentarily surprised she had said anything so revealing.

"Yes. I thought of you also."

Susan curled her hands into white-knuckled fists. "I was happy . . . *happy* it wasn't Timmy, although I knew he was somebody's little boy, that some other mother would have to grieve. Does that make me an awful person?"

"It makes you human." Molly sighed. "We're all grieving, aren't we?"

"I guess." Susan shifted to a more comfortable position. "Although you're the only other woman I know whose child was kidnapped. It makes a difference. I mean, you can lose your child in a hundred different ways, but having someone *take* him . . . well, it makes it worse."

"You've been to a support group." It wasn't really a question.

Susan made a face. "We're in therapy, my husband and I, and the doctor thought, well, he strongly encouraged us to join a group. We went a few times, but it wasn't for me, and Tim, Sr., when he heard about that woman . . ." A ghost of a smile passed fleetingly across her face.

Intrigued, Molly pursued it. "What did he hear?"

"It was so stupid I had to stop Tim, Sr., from saying something rude. He has very strong opinions, and he doesn't suffer fools lightly, especially when it's such an emotional matter . . ."

Molly, remembering her own experience with the support group, took a wild stab. "Did it have anything to do with reincarnation?"

Bull's-eye.

Susan looked amazed, then suspicious. Molly held up her hand. "I'm not here for an interview. Please, you have to believe me. You're not going to tune in and hear a word of this. I had a similar experience. I heard something about reincarnation at a support group."

Somewhat mollified, Susan still hadn't embraced the idea of Molly's innocence. "What did you think?"

Molly shrugged. "I assume it's supposed to make you feel better, the idea your child is living again."

"I guess," Susan said, "but the only thing that will do that for me is to have my Timmy back home."

Amen. Molly thought about how similar she and Susan were, despite the obvious differences. She also thought about how different they were, how Susan seemed content to sit and wait, while she ... was doing what? Was she any closer to finding Petey? Or was she running around chasing her own shadow, setting up straw men to satisfy her need to be doing something?

All the way home Molly had that nagging feeling again, the one that made her feel she knew something but didn't know what it was she knew. She needed to think. Perhaps it would come to her if she stopped pushing so hard.

Harry waited until he heard the outer door close behind the two detectives before he rushed into the bathroom. He splashed cold water on his face and over his neck. It trickled down both the front and back of his shirt, making the wet cotton cling to his sweaty skin. His chest itched like hell. That damned rash he couldn't get rid of. He wanted to rip off the shirt. He wanted to howl. He wanted to punish something, someone.

He thought of Jillian, knew he didn't have enough money to have her ever again. She had made it very clear the other night. So what? There were plenty of Jillian Ravens in the world. Plenty of bimbo bitches who would do anything once you waved enough green beneath their greedy noses.

Money could buy anything.

The thought gave him a moment's ease, but then his mind segued to the last half hour and he broke out in a drenching sweat. What the hell were the police doing sniffing around? Asking about his business, his trips. Where had he been in February? In March? In June?

How the hell should he be expected to remember? He traveled so much one place was the same as the next. Sometimes it was hot as hell and sometimes it was snowing.

They had reminded him legitimate businessmen kept records. He had bristled at "legitimate." What the hell did they think he was up to? They had glanced into the warehouse, seen the crates and boxes piled on the pallets. They hadn't yelled search warrant, hadn't asked for a little look-see. If it was stolen goods or drugs they were after, wouldn't they have come prepared?

Stolen goods was a natural, given the nature of his business. He had considered it, then rejected the idea. Too obvious. Now drugs . . . Jesus. They couldn't suspect him of drugs. Not him. Drugs were dirty. Not that he hadn't thought about it. But he wasn't disposed to share, and nobody ran a drug empire alone.

No. He had rejected the obvious. Nobody could say Harry Kemp was predictable. He had figured out a scam no one in their wildest dreams would think of, would even suspect. And even if they did, even if someone pointed a finger at him, there was no proof. None.

Someone rapped on the door. "Hey, you all right?"

He finger-combed his wet hair, jerked the door open. Angela's frankly curious eyes studied him. "What, you got no work?" She held up her hands, backed away.

Nosy bitch. Probably wanted a blow-by-blow. She should live so long. He didn't get cozy with the help.

He felt better. Much better. Whatever those detectives suspected, they had no proof. Nothing. A big goose egg. All he had were a few files that would mean shit to anyone else. Only he could decipher them.

Better to get rid of them. Play it safe.

It took less than thirty seconds to erase them from the hard disk. There. He was safe. Nothing and no one to point a finger to Harry Kemp. Wait! His backup disks. Better erase them, too. He opened the bottom drawer, feeling a vague sense of alarm to find it unlocked. Quickly, he peeled back the roll top, looked into the file cabinet. No disks. Nothing. Bile rose in his throat.

You'll never amount to anything, Harry, never be any good, Harry, mark my words, Harry, Harry, Harrrrrrrrry . . .

He barely made it to the bathroom, emerging sometime later to find himself alone. Big and shadowy, the warehouse was suddenly full of menace. Spooked, he grabbed his jacket and flung it over his shoulder. The street outside was empty, too. Except for a plain-vanilla sedan with a man sitting behind the wheel. Waiting for him? A tail? Harry told himself not to be paranoid, but when he pulled away in his Cadillac and the car pulled in right behind him, he ran out of rationalizations and gave way to terror.

Zachary had left a message on Molly's machine. Everything was okay; they were coming home. Lauren wanted to show off her cast. One more night alone; she hadn't realized how much she had come to depend upon his strength, his calm, no-nonsense approach to everything.

322   *Elizabeth Ergas*

A quick check of the refrigerator gave a choice of tuna or peanut butter. Only a matter of minutes to make a small tuna and tomato salad and a glass of iced tea. She forced herself to eat without gulping the food. The lists would still be there when she finished, as would the nagging feeling she had had all day, now stronger than ever. When she was through, she rinsed her dishes and settled at the kitchen table.

She was sure, *sure,* the lists held some answers. The first step was to break the original list into several smaller ones, each with one or more elements in common. But no matter how she studied them, they still had no meaning. Feeling chilled, she adjusted the air conditioner's setting and made a cup of coffee in the microwave. It was dark outside now; the sun had slipped beneath the horizon without her noticing. After closing the curtains, she picked up the list with masculine names in the third column.

J/V W	JW—h/f	Tom/6
E/C R	AR—h/m	Billy/8
J/M N	MD—w/m	Robert/7
B/E G	TG—h/f	Michael/5
P/R T	MC—w/gm	Matthew/4

Then she studied the list with feminine names.

H/E A	JS—w/m	Susan/4
W/B G	MS—w/m	Jenny/7
D/I H	DC—w/m	Karen/6
G/S K	IB—w/gm	Jennifer/2
C/J J	FG—w/gm	Rachel/4
S/D B	RD—w/gm	Angie/2

WHERE'S MY BABY? 323

It looked more promising. All the w/m and w/gm listings in the middle column were aligned. She went back to the first list, tried a new order.

J/V W	JW—h/f	Tom/6
B/E G	TG—h/f	Michael/5
E/C R	AR—h/m	Billy/8
J/M N	MD—w/m	Robert/7
P/R T	MC—w/gm	Matthew/4

Another possibility occurred. Quickly she filled in a new sheet, studied the results.

B/E G	TG—h/f	Michael/5
J/V W	JW—h/f	Tom/6
E/C R	AR—h/m	Billy/8

The numbers in the third column were now in ascending order. Which suggested yet another alignment. As the columns formed in the new list, she became excited.

S/D B	RD—w/gm	Angie/2
G/S K	IB—w/gm	Jennifer/2
C/J J	FG—w/gm	Rachel/4
P/R T	MC—w/gm	Matthew/4
H/E A	JS—w/m	Susan/4
B/E G	TG—h/f	Michael/5
D/I H	DC—w/m	Karen/6
J/V W	JW—h/f	Tom/6
W/B G	MS—w/m	Jenny/7
J/M N	MD—w/m	Robert/7
E/C R	AR—h/m	Billy/8

The key had to be the second column. If she could only figure out what w/gm, w/m, h/f, h/m stood for. Was the "h" for Harry or was that too easy? Probably. Maybe she should alphabetize the first column and . . . with a cry she swiped her arm across the table, scattered the papers. Who was she fooling? She could make lists all night, indeed until the cows came home, as her mother was so fond of saying, and it wouldn't mean a thing.

Leaving the mess, she turned off the lights, went upstairs, and fell into bed. Sleep was instantaneous and deep. Sometime later she awoke with a start, disoriented to time and place, a dream fast fading, with an urgency to capture it overriding everything else. Eyes closed, she drifted, reached, grasped a wisp of something. Gone. Her head ached, her left arm was numb from pillowing her head, and when she turned on the bedside lamp, she discovered she was sprawled on top of the covers, fully dressed.

The clock read 3 AM. She should roll over and go back to sleep. Impossible at this hour to think clearly, although she could think about those coded lists from now until she was eighty-eight or a hundred and eight and she wouldn't get any closer to deciphering them without the key.

Why would a businessman need coded files?

Taxes. Was he keeping a second set of books? Possible, but not probable. They would have to look normal. Normal. Hadn't Susan Newell said something about that? No, they had been talking about their sons, about how nothing and no one could replace them.

Replace.

Harry Kemp ran a replacement business. Lose it, break it, destroy it, give it away—no matter, he can replace it. Harry Kemp could replace anything and everything, except children. No one could do that. Just like Susan Newell, Molly knew were she to conceive and give birth again, the new child couldn't possibly replace Petey. No child could. Susan Newell had said having her Timmy home was the only thing that would make her happy.

Amen.

God, she missed Petey so. She would do anything, *anything,* to get him back. Seeing Susan had been a mistake. It had stirred up things she'd rather not think about, like the support group, about how some people were so distraught they believed . . .

Reincarnation.

She and Susan had talked about that, too.

Replacement.

A chill invaded her. She jumped up, rubbed her arms, looked wildly about, wanted to run outside and yell and shout and scream . . . Pamela. She had to tell Pamela.

"It's goddamn three in the morning. Whoever you are, this better be good," Pamela growled.

It was good, all right. Molly knew it was. Trying to keep her emotions in check, she talked about rumors and replacement and reincarnation as if the whole thing wasn't bizarre. She didn't think it was.

Neither did Pamela.

Thirty-Four

"Let me get this straight. You think Kemp is replacing dead kids? He kidnaps a kid and sells it to people who have lost a child, right?"

"Right." Molly, dressed in T-shirt and jeans, her shower-damp hair pulled back into an untidy ponytail, shook her head so vigorously the wet ends whipped around to plaster against her cheek. Impatiently she scraped them off. "I think he sells these people on the idea their child has been reincarnated. Don't ask me how. I don't have a clue. But I think he somehow convinces them they'll get their own child back."

Pamela yawned and rubbed her eyes. She was wearing a hastily donned old pair of sweatpants and a faded T-shirt sporting a smiling Mickey Mouse. "I can just see Rowley's face when we lay this on him."

Molly liked the way she said "we." "Should we call him?"

Pamela checked her watch. "It's too early. Let him sleep. I guarantee you he'll be more receptive after he's showered and had his coffee. Besides, we really don't have anything to give him yet. Nothing besides speculation."

"Bizarre speculation, you mean."

"I'd call it creative." Pamela yawned again. "Coffee?" She set up the automatic brewer, then took the stool next to Molly at the counter separating the kitchen from the eat-in breakfast nook that had sold her on the house. "I spent more years than I care to remember on the force. I used to think I'd seen it all, but I hadn't seen nothing, as the saying goes." Idly she tapped her nails against the counter. "Once you get past the part about reincarnation, what you've got is a straight scam. There's nothing unusual about that."

Put that way, Molly agreed with her. She accepted a mug of dark, aromatic coffee, said no to sugar and milk. Wrapping her hands around it, she stared down, afraid to voice her deepest fear.

Pamela had come to know her moods. "What?" Molly shook her head, not yet ready to share. Pamela didn't push. "I told you I keep up with the support groups, at least as much as I can." She took a sip of coffee, grimaced, added a generous helping of sugar and stirred vigorously. "I've heard that rumor, too. I always discounted it. The people in the groups are grieving. And moreover, diverse cultures believe in reincarnation, in many different forms." She shrugged. "Who's to judge? Whatever helps, I say. Anyway, I didn't give it another thought. I wish now I had. The problem is how to find these people. If we could just find one couple, one customer of Kemp's, we could make our case. Do you remember the name of the couple who dropped out of the Roslyn group?"

"No, I'm sorry, I don't. I can give Tess McLoughlin a call. The meeting was at her home."

"Good idea." Pamela checked her watch again. "We'll give it a little more time. Meanwhile, let's have a look at those lists again. You know, I study them until I'm cross-eyed, thinking I've got a pattern, but all I come up with are new lists and more questions. It's damned frustrating." She slapped her hip, remembered she didn't have pockets, and wiggled her eyebrows. "Got a butt?"

"Remember the bet?"

"Spoilsport. C'mon. Bring your coffee. I've got the lists in the office. As soon as the sun peeks over the horizon, I'll put in some calls. I want names of people who've dropped out of support groups, let's say within the past year. Maybe, just maybe, we'll get lucky."

Within seconds Molly was staring at the familiar list. "Lucky with what?"

"Look." Pamela poked a finger at the middle column. "Every time this h slash appears, the letter before it is the same as the last letter in the first column. Read the first entry across."

J/V W   JW—h/f   Tom/6

So obvious, once pointed out. Molly had pored over that list and never noticed it. Of course, she had concentrated on the last column, the one that didn't have Petey's name. She clamped down hard on the queasiness that threatened every time she thought about it. Quickly she scanned down the columns.

E/C R   AR—h/m   Billy/8
B/E G   TG-h/f   Michael/5

"You're right, they are the same. Initials, do you think?"

"If we're lucky."

WHERE'S MY BABY?

"You keep saying that, using that word. What does luck have to do with it? Luck would have been me breaking my leg and never taking Petey to the damn circus."

If Pamela was surprised by the outburst, she didn't show it. "Tell me what's on your mind."

"No."

"Tell me. It won't put a hex on it."

Clever Pamela. Molly couldn't resist any longer. Keeping it bottled inside was like having a quart of lye churning in her stomach. "Petey." Always Petey. As long as she took breath it would be Petey. "This is supposed to be about Petey, isn't it?"

"Of course it is, Molly. I haven't forgotten for a single second."

Molly's face screwed up and she began to cry. She pushed the list toward Pamela. "Look. Look at the third column. He's not there. My baby's not there."

"You're pulling my leg." Glen Rowley swiveled away from Pamela to contemplate Ellen, who was fixedly staring at the quiescent fax machine, as if will alone could get it to produce. "Tell me she's pulling my leg. Dead kids being reincarnated and you're not laughing?"

Pamela was about to tell him to put a sock in it and listen, just listen, when Sidney Salem spoke up. "She didn't say they were reincarnated. She said the marks were made to think they were. Somehow."

"How?"

Pamela took a deep breath. So he was thinking, he just had to sound off. She shrugged.

"Great."

The phone kept her from making an ill-advised retort. Ellen answered, put the caller on hold. "Tess McLoughlin, returning Molly's call?" She squinted at her watch. "Molly should be home by now, should I give her the number?"

"No, I'll take it." The others tried not to listen, but the room was small. They also couldn't miss Pamela's satisfied smile.

"Got something?" Glen asked.

"You bet. The names of the couple who dropped out of the Roslyn group and ... it seems the wife's mother—her *dead* mother—picked up a telephone and told her their kid had been reincarnated."

Something sparked in Sidney's dark eyes. "No shit. That's all I'd need, Gracie's mother calling for a little chat. She was a real—"

"Witch, and my advice is not to worry. Your mother-in-law is dead. D-E-A-D." Glen pushed a wave of hair out of his eyes. "Didn't you stick a pin in her?"

"And held up a mirror." Sidney nodded solemnly. "You think we should check out the swamis? See who'd be likely to think up a scam like this?"

Pamela slapped her pockets, muttered a low-voiced curse. "You thinking Kemp could have a partner?"

Glen shrugged. "Anything's possible." He got up. "We'll get on it. By the way, it's time for you to give on the source of those lists. If we're going to get anywhere, we're going to need the whole enchilada." Pamela nodded to Ellen, who reached into a cabinet, retrieved Harry Kemp's backup disks and handed them to Glen. "Just fell into your hand, I suppose?"

Pamela smiled. "Some things never change. I still love it when you suppose."

WHERE'S MY BABY?

* * *

Harry had spent a lousy night and so far the day hadn't been much better. His stomach was queasy, his head hurt, and he was sweating like a pig, none of which did much to sweeten his temper, never the best. At least once an hour he opened the bottom drawer and looked at the empty file cabinet, as if by some miracle the disks would reappear. After this futile exercise he would stroll through the warehouse to the open loading bays and peer at the street. Very casual. He fooled no one, not the men or Carl Morgan or Angela, who had retired to her office in huffy silence after he'd yelled when his lunch was delivered without mustard on the corned beef. The sandwich ended up in the garbage, not for any lack of a condiment, but because Harry had lost his appetite.

The man sitting in the sedan parked across the street had something—no, he had everything—to do with it. He had cop written all over him, as had the guy last night and the one who had followed him from his home this morning. If the brazenness of the surveillance was meant to intimidate, it was certainly succeeding.

So he felt no surprise when the two detectives loomed behind Angela in the doorway. None at all. What he felt was a sick resignation, almost a feeling of inevitability. Polite, they wanted to chat, their place this time. Harry accompanied them without any outward show of emotion, even managing a cool nod for Angela and the instruction to let Mrs. Mosby know he had located the Ming Dynasty gilt-bronze figure of Kuan Yin she wanted. Wanted. The woman was positively salivating for it, had hinted she didn't care where or how he acquired it. But he was a legitimate businessman. Everything aboveboard. If the mention of this rare coup impressed the detectives, they gave no sign, merely waited with their patented politeness while he spoke with Angela. Which gave Harry heart. He *was* a legitimate businessman. Absolutely no proof otherwise.

The man who had been on stakeout stood next to the detectives' car, smoking a cigarillo. He gave Harry a mean-looking grin. Harry wanted to rearrange his fillings, but in his guise of innocent businessman, had to content himself with another of the stiff little nods he seemed to be perfecting. They put him in the rear; the white detective got in beside him, the black detective got behind the wheel. They were silent; more intimidation, he supposed. Well, it wasn't going to work. He wasn't going to *let* it work, even if he was up shit's creek without a paddle.

You'll never be any good, Harry, mark my words, Harry, you'll come to a bad end, Harry, Harry, Harrrrrrrrrry . . .

For the first time in many years he didn't try to block it out. It wasn't a friendly voice, but at least it was familiar.

When Kent got a whiff of a home-alone case from rescue workers on the scene at a two-alarm fire in Astoria, he pulled Molly from the seemingly never-ending carjacking trial and told her to hustle on over. Within twenty minutes of her arrival, firemen had confined the blaze to the upper stories of the six-floor building. The three children were said to be on the fifth floor. Neighbors reported not seeing the parents in several days. Kent put her on the air live and then came back on the line after her report.

"Any word from anyone?"

He sounded almost as nervous as she felt. "Not yet. Pamela's sitting by her fax waiting for something. She won't tell me what."

"What about the police?"

"We haven't heard from Glen since he took the disks."

"Okay. Hang in there, cookie."

As if she had a choice.

Which was exactly what she said to Charlie Lee a little while later when they were standing behind the police press barricade, waiting for the outcome of a second rescue attempt. The first had been turned back when the ceiling over the staircase had collapsed. The firemen were now trying to effect a rescue from the roof.

Charlie's face was shiny with sweat and his T-shirt more wet than dry. "You do what you gotta do, Molly–Uh-Oh. You know that."

Boy, did she ever, but the need to have the nightmare over, to have Petey back where he belonged and their lives return to normal, was growing by the second. The other possibility, the dark thought Petey might be forever lost to her, was something she didn't want to consider, yet it wouldn't go away. So she repressed it, each and every time it popped up. But right now she felt so jumpy she could hardly stand to be in her own skin, and it was because of Harry Kemp. "It's Kemp, Charlie, I know it is. I feel it in my bones."

"You gotta give the police time to do their thing. If he's the one they'll nail him."

For a second, Molly's frustration escaped her control. "I don't care if they nail him. All I care about is getting Petey back."

The sympathy in his eyes would have undone her had

not her beeper gone off. She jumped, pulled it from her tote, stared at the readout.

"Kent?" She shook her head, hardly daring to hope. Charlie looked around. "I don't see your car."

"It's at a meter on Steinway."

"Too far." He took her elbow, escorted her to the CBN van, and told the occupants to get out. Rachel Godwin-VanHorn opened her mouth, caught sight of Charlie's expression, and left with the others. He handed the phone to Molly and turned to leave. She caught his arm.

"Please. Stay. I need a friend." Her fingers felt like limp noodles, but she managed to get the number. As if from far away she heard Glen's voice, coming past the rushing of blood through her ears. She pressed a hand to her heart, trying to slow its frantic beat.

"We've taken Kemp into custody. I wanted you to be the first to know."

"He's the one who kidnapped Petey?"

"We're questioning him, but so far it's no go. A real cool customer. Denies doing any wrong. He maintains we're blowing smoke, says we have no evidence, nothing but allegations."

"What about the CBN tape? The disks?"

She could almost hear Glen shrug. "We're working on it."

He hesitated, and Molly pounced. "What? Tell me." Beside her, Charlie shifted his weight. "It's him. You think it's him, don't you?"

"It's just a feeling, Molly."

She took a deep breath. "Thank you."

Glen's voice took on a cautionary note. "He's right when he says we've got nothing concrete. Not yet, but we're just beginning. He's an onion, and we'll peel him layer by layer if we have to. Hold it a sec." Someone spoke to him, then he came back. "Okay, here's the other reason I'm calling. We won't be able to keep this quiet for long, so since you did the legwork, you get the break. The in-custody-for-questioning routine. Remember, Molly, not a word more, even if Kent threatens to pour honey over you and stake you out on an anthill."

As if she'd do anything to jeopardize finding Petey. "That wasn't necessary."

Glen had the grace to sound abashed. "Yeah, sorry. Habit, I guess."

She looked at Charlie, eyes glimmering with new-found hope. "It's him, Charlie, I know it's him."

"Sounds like." He touched her shoulder. "You okay?"

"Compared to what?"

He laughed and then glowered as the door burst open and Rachel Godwin-VanHorn glared at them, said, "Move your ass, Lee. The firemen are bringing out the three kids now."

"Alive?" Charlie asked.

Rachel shrugged her slim shoulders. "I didn't ask. You've got five seconds to get us rolling."

Molly stared after her. "Lovely person."

"Yeah. I never thought I'd say it, but I can't wait for Lloyd to get back."

Ellen heard WAND's three-note call and turned up the radio's volume. "Pamela, listen, I think this may be it."

"This just in to the WAND news desk. WAND reporter Molly Deere has learned from a reliable source the special task force investigating recent disappearances of several area children has taken a man into custody for

questioning. Four-and-a-half-year-old Petey Deere, Molly's son, was kidnapped from a circus in Cunningham Park last June. There are no details at this time, but stay tuned to 990. We will keep you informed of all the latest developments. Now, we are going to Molly, who is live—"

The fax machine came to life. Pamela pounced, hovered until the papers came out. She studied them, then shrieked, "Oklahoma!"

"You got something?"

Pamela's hand was shaking. "I got something and the something I got is a match." She slapped the paper to her chest, then held it out. Tears shone in her eyes. "I *knew* we were on the right track. Look, Ellen, the fifth name. Howard and Elaine Andrews. H slash E space A. Initials. Just like we thought. And look here," her voice rose in excitement, "look at Kemp's second list. The first line is A and then 15. What do you want to bet our boy Kemp sold them a child for fifteen thousand?"

"What do we do now?"

Pamela was already on the phone. The conversation was brief. "That was Cynthia Sharp, the psychologist who organized the support group in Tulsa. I asked her to find out why the Andrewses left the group. If we're right, it's because they got a child from Kemp."

"Is it Petey?"

Pamela shook her head. "The third column next to their entry says Susan slash 4."

"But . . ." Ellen looked stricken. "But if . . . Pamela, Petey's not on the list."

"I know."

"Does Molly . . ." She couldn't finish the thought.

"She knows. She's making herself sick over it."

Ellen made a little flipping gesture with her hand. "Then how ... I mean, what ..."

"Kemp is the best lead we've come up with, but without hard evidence the police won't be able to hold him for long. If we can put him with one of the names on the list we'll have a lever. He might ultimately need to plea bargain. You don't get something for nothing in this system." Ellen still looked doubtful. "Besides, who said this list is complete?" She said it as much for herself as for the older woman.

Ellen's concern deepened. Pamela wasn't fooling her. "What can we do?"

"We wait. We wait for Cynthia to call back and we wait for answers to all the other queries I've sent out."

Ellen wearily rubbed the back of her neck. "We do so much waiting you'd think we'd be good at it by now."

Pamela caught herself before she slapped her empty pockets. Progress, of a sort. She gave Ellen half a smile. "Not in this lifetime, I'm afraid."

Thirty-Five

With two young girls dead and their three-year-old brother fighting for his life in the burn unit of Elmhurst General, the police vigorously pursued the on-site investigation into the whereabouts of the three victims' parents. It didn't take long; an uncle of the children arrived, took one look at the body bags being loaded into an ambulance, and started screaming invectives at his absentee sister and her live-in boyfriend, who either was or was not the father of one of the children. The man was so hysterical it was difficult to understand him. A neighbor, made homeless by the fire, said she thought the missing couple was in Atlantic City. "It happens every once in a while. They get the urge, they go. The older girl, she's maybe ten, eleven, now, they leave her in charge."

Molly interviewed neighbors, relatives, and witnesses, got statements from the police, called in the story to Kent, while a rage of monumental proportions built inside her. Novia Smith and Curtis Matthews didn't deserve to be parents, so flagrantly abrogating their responsibilities.

"Chill out," Kent said when she offered the opinion

WHERE'S MY BABY? 339

the two, who had been located at the craps table, should be prosecuted for murder. "You're taking this personally. Go home, Molly, you've had enough for one day."

Great advice, but home was no haven. She called Zachary, and to her delight, reached him. "I was just about to call you," he said. "We were wondering if you can come over. Lauren can't wait to show you her cast."

For the first time in days, Molly smiled. "I'm on my way."

The Midtown Tunnel was probably a smarter move, but she took the Queensborough Bridge into Manhattan, then circled around Lexington and Fifty-ninth until she found an illegal space in front of Bloomingdale's on Third. Without a qualm she stuck her press ID in the windshield and went up to the toy department. Her beeper went off just as she finished paying for the most expensive doll in the store.

Pamela.

Luck was with her; the DOT hadn't towed her car. "It's Molly." A lousy connection, but it would have to do.

"I'm pretty sure I've connected Kemp to a couple in the Tulsa area. Howard and Elaine Andrews. The Andrewses have acquired another child. A little girl."

Not Petey. Intense, crushing disappointment.

"Molly? Listen. This is good. We need to get evidence. The police can't hold Kemp for long without it. The listing in the third column of the Andrews' entry was Susan slash four. I've faxed a photo of Suzanne Lind to my contact. She's going to have the police take a look."

Pamela sounded so up. Molly struggled with herself, managed to congratulate her.

"We're only beginning, Molly. I'll call when I know more."

Black despair descended. Petey wasn't on the list. She was no closer to finding him. She wanted to go home, roll into a ball, and cry herself into a stupor. But then her gaze went to the gaily wrapped gift and she knew she wasn't that selfish. At least not yet.

Zachary must have been watching, for she barely reached his front door before he had it open and pulled her into his arms. "How are you?"

"Hot, tired, depressed, frustrated—"

He kissed her, then looked into her eyes. "You've come to the right man. God, I've missed you." He kissed her again, hard, then reluctantly released her. "I heard the news. I assume it's Kemp in custody?"

Molly blinked. Zachary had been gone only a few days, but so much had happened. She held up the gift. "First things first. Where's Lauren?"

The little girl was overjoyed to see Molly. Unlike her father, who looked like he had been through a harrowing experience, she appeared as sunny as ever. The big cast on her leg didn't seem to bother her overmuch. She immediately insisted Molly sign it, which she did, drawing little flowers around her name. Then she produced the gift, and when the doll emerged from the wrapping, had the satisfaction of seeing Lauren's eyes light up. They left her busily trying to decide on a name.

A tray with lemonade and cookies sat on Zachary's desk. Molly drained half her glass in a single gulp. "Lauren looks good. What did the doctor say?"

Zachary laughed. "He said to try and keep her from

breaking the other leg before this one's healed. She's determined to go to day camp."

"Is that wise?"

"She's fine." He took Molly's hand, led her to the couch. "Now. Fill me in."

Molly's reportorial skills allowed her to tell the gist of the story in the shortest possible time. Zachary looked a bit dazed when she finished. "He was selling kids? Who would pay—what? Fifteen? Twenty thousand?—for a child when there are so many ways to adopt older children?"

"He had a scam."

"It would have to be a helluva good one."

"Oh, it was. We think these couples lost a child. Kemp convinced them the child was reincarnated. We've heard a really bizarre rumor about dead relatives calling. . . . What is it?"

Zachary's big body jerked back as if he had been struck; he appeared upset. "Nothing. Go on."

"That's it. It's so frustrating. One minute I think we're so close, we're going to find Petey, and the next. . . . The police only became interested in Harry Kemp when they saw the name Michael on the list. They thought . . ."

Zachary took her hands and gently squeezed. "If this is true then Kemp is a greedy bastard with a scam. He wouldn't hurt what people are willing to pay so much for."

"I know. I keep telling myself that over and over, and besides, Petey isn't on the list. Harry Kemp may well be a kidnapper and a seller of children, but it also may be he had nothing to do with Petey." Without warning, tears streamed down her cheeks.

Zachary held her close and let her cry. When she was

through he handed her a tissue and told her to blow her nose. Then he asked her to explain what the lists meant.

While he studied the lists, she walked to the window and stood looking out at the vest-pocket garden oasis of green-leafed trees and bushes interspersed with bright pools of flowers. She was wondering who tended them when something prompted her to turn. Zachary was staring at one of the lists. She had crossed the room before she even realized she had moved. Laying a tentative hand on his arm, she regarded him anxiously. His face was drained of color, and when he lifted his eyes, stark anguish churned in their depths.

"Molly . . ." He took a deep breath, let it out. "Molly, I . . ." Whatever it was, it appeared to be tearing him apart. He pushed to his feet; the papers fell to the floor. Mechanically she bent, gathered them.

Zachary fought a fierce inner battle, mercifully short. On one side was his professional ethics, his pledge to protect his patients, and on the other side was Molly, and his feelings for her. In the end it was no contest. Molly's eyes brimmed with questions and something else, a growing awareness, a hope. "I think I know what one of those entries means."

She held out the lists. Her hand trembled. "Show me. Which one?"

His finger moved across the line.

D/I H   DC—w/m   Karen/6

"Something and Irene Hall. I'll have to look up his name, but I'm sure it starts with D. They lost a child named Karen. Irene never recovered from her death. She, ah, went into past-life regression therapy looking for her."

"Karen was six years old?"

"No, she was older. I think she died six years ago."

"Six years ago!" Dizzy from rising excitement, she took a deep breath, forced herself to calm. "Karen slash six. Zachary, that means the entry for Michael—Michael slash five—isn't his age. It means," she checked the list, "B and E G lost a boy named Michael five years ago."

"Then the third column isn't a listing of missing children, it's children who died and—"

"It doesn't matter that Petey's not on the list!" She threw herself into Zachary's arms. "I've got to call Pamela. We've been looking at this all wrong."

Pamela answered before the first ring had died. "Oh, Molly, I was just going to call you. I'm afraid I have bad—make that disappointing—news. I finally heard from the Tulsa PD. The Suzanne Lind lead is a bust. The Andrewses little girl is no older than three. There's no way it could be Suzanne. I'm sorry, Molly, I thought we had something going, but—"

"Pamela, listen. We do, I'm sure of it. We've just been going at it from the wrong angle. I'm at Zachary's and I showed him Kemp's lists, and he recognized . . ."

Zachary slipped from the room and stood with his back against the closed door, rubbing his hand in circles over his chest, trying to erase the hollow feeling. Petey's misplaced file. Irene's failure to keep her appointment in June. June. Just about the time Petey was kidnapped. He'd have to check the date to be sure, but he knew, he *knew*. Had Irene used him to get to Petey? An absurd thought. Irene had come to him first. She couldn't possibly have known Petey would be a patient.

Feeling haunted, he peeked in on Lauren. Watching a video, she had the new doll tucked securely against her side. She saw him and smiled, the smile that always filled him with joy. His face shifted to answer it.

Irene Hall always wore a smile after she had been regressed and thought she'd seen Karen. Her blond angel. If she would go to the length of buying a kidnapped child she would want one who looked like Karen, wouldn't she?

"Daddy?"

Lauren had long hair the color of ripe wheat. She was his angel. Had Irene been after his daughter? Had something gone wrong?

"Daddy!"

The note of alarm got through. "What, pussycat?"

"You looked funny."

He went over, kissed her on the forehead, gently tickled her ribs. "So why aren't you laughing?" The tickling worked; Lauren forgot her momentary fear in childish giggles. He gave her another kiss, made sure she didn't need anything, and went back to Molly. The instant he saw her he knew what he had to do. If he had been used as a pawn, she had to know. As concisely as he could, he laid bare his thoughts and fears.

Molly had no interest in placing blame. She thought a moment. "She'd want another girl, another blond angel, wouldn't she?"

That's what he had told himself. Irene had been obsessed with Karen, with who she had been, what she had been. But then . . . the one piece he had been holding back, even from himself, could be contained no longer and he told Molly about Irene's last session, when she had been the leper Thomas and Karen had been his mother.

The implications weren't lost on Molly. Suddenly she

had a death grip on his arm; her fingernails dug into his skin. "Where is she? I want to see her. Now."

"She failed to keep her last appointment. She may not be there."

"I'll find her." She took her hand from his arm, deliberately stepped back. "Look, if there's some kind of code that prohibits you from doing this, then pretend I was never here."

If there had been a line, Zachary didn't hesitate in stepping over it. "She lives in Connecticut. Let me get her file."

Thirty-Six

When Douglas found two strangers on his doorstep he wasn't all that surprised. When they identified themselves a sick feeling of inevitability came over him. When they said they wanted to speak with Irene he invited them inside. He led them into the living room and headed straight for the bar. They declined the offer of a drink; he needed one.

"My wife isn't here." He held up his hand to forestall questions. "I don't know where she is." They exchanged glances. Douglas knew it wouldn't end there. "I haven't seen her since June."

Something wild and savage kindled deep in the woman's eyes. "My son was kidnapped in June."

Douglas recoiled; Scotch spilled over his hand. He dabbed at the wetness with his handkerchief. "I know. I recognized your name." Silence, save for the sound the ice cubes made when he nervously jiggled them.

"Do you also recognize my name?"

Douglas drained the glass and carefully set it down on one of Irene's prized mahogany end tables. "Yes, Dr. Slater, I do. After Irene . . . left, Nancy, my sister-in-law, told me my wife had been seeing you. Some nonsense about reincarnation."

"Irene didn't think so. In fact, that's why we're here."

"It's all nonsense. When you die, you're dead. Dead and gone. There's no coming back. The dead don't make phone calls." Oh, God, he needed another drink.

Molly fairly bristled with tension. "Who called and told your wife Karen was reincarnated? Was it her mother?" From the look on Douglas's face, she was right on target.

"I identified the body. Delia was dead." He poured a hefty drink, took a deep swallow. "I even went back to see the ME. No mistake. Delia's dead."

"Delia was Irene's mother?" Douglas nodded. "W slash m. Wife's mother. You'd better sit down. We've got something to tell you."

"I don't believe it." By this time Douglas had worked a third of the way through the bottle of Scotch and showed no inclination to stop. "Irene'd never kidnap a kid, she doesn't have it in her."

"She paid someone to do it for her, and from this list it looks like she paid him double his fee." When Douglas stubbornly maintained his denial, Molly lost her fragile hold on patience. "I'm sorry, but it really doesn't matter what you believe. Forty thousand dollars isn't petty cash. The police will look into your wife's affairs. They'll—"

"No police. I've got a private investigator searching for her. Surely he—"

"I've already called them." Douglas lurched to his feet, stared in shock. Trembling with emotion, Molly jumped up to face him. "Did you think I would pass up the chance, any chance, to find my son?"

"Irene walked out on me. That's all it is. We were going over a rough patch. All marriages have them. Surely you understand? She thought I was, er, cheating on her." His expression said he had been. "She's angry. Her mother's death pushed her over the edge. She'll settle down and come back when she thinks I've been punished enough. Besides, if she had no intention of returning, she wouldn't have called."

"From where?" Zachary's voice was harsh, demanding.

"I wish I knew. I'm telling you, Irene is off somewhere sulking. When she gets over it she'll return. I know what I'm talking about. Let me show you."

Molly looked at Zachary. He nodded, followed close behind as Douglas went upstairs, opened the closets in the master room. "See? She left all her clothes. She's coming back."

Zachary eyed the glass in Douglas's hand. "Is she drinking again?"

Molly sucked in a breath; he hadn't told her Irene had a problem with alcohol. Douglas's answer was written all over his face. Her stomach lurched. "How bad is her problem? Is she an alcoholic?"

"She only started drinking after Karen . . . after Karen died. We saw she got help. Dr. Powell had the problem pretty much licked, and then . . . and then her mother was killed and made that goddamn phone call saying Karen had returned . . ." He stared at a picture of a smiling Irene prominently displayed on the dresser. "I want to show you something else."

They followed him down a short hall. Sweat dotted his forehead; his skin had taken on an unhealthy, chalky hue. With a visible effort he threw open a door and switched on a light. "Karen's room."

A shrine. Molly's heart contracted. She felt Irene's pain as surely as she felt her own.

Douglas was careful not to step over the threshold. "Karen was a beautiful child." His voice hitched; he turned it into a cough. "She'd be eighteen now. I sometimes wonder. . . . But that's behind us. She's gone. Irene couldn't forgive me for not being able to. . . . What's the use? We all grieve in different ways, don't we, Dr. Slater?"

Molly's quiet voice broke the suddenly charged atmosphere. "You think your wife took my son, don't you, Mr. Hall?"

"No! That's why I brought you here. To see this. She knows Karen is dead. Drowned six years ago in that goddamn camp I insisted she go to. My fault."

Drowned. Karen Hall had drowned. Water. The link. Rational or irrational, Irene Hall had put Karen's drowning together with Petey's fear of water and . . .

"She must have gotten to Petey's file." Zachary's eyes begged forgiveness of Molly.

"Oh no! No . . ." Drawn inside, Douglas stood next to the bed, anguished blue eyes staring at it.

"What is it? What's wrong?" Molly cried.

"Mr. Bear-Face," Douglas quavered. "Mr. Bear-Face is gone."

Molly was so wired Zachary wanted her to spend the night at his house. He wanted to be with her when she came down; he feared the fall would be precipitous. They argued for much of the drive home; then, abruptly, she fell asleep. With the burning light in her eyes shielded, she looked exhausted.

As well she must be. Her life had been turned into a living hell, a never-ending nightmare, and possibly—no probably—it was his fault. His goddamn fault. Giving Irene the opportunity, however innocently, to go through his files. He hit the steering wheel, cursed viciously under his breath.

If Irene did, indeed, have Petey.

Things certainly seemed to point that way. But things could be deceiving. Zachary thought about the story of the elephant and the six blind men.

Molly opened her eyes when they were on the FDR Drive. She yawned, stretched and sat up straight. "Where are we?"

"Almost home." She didn't say anything, leaving him with the impression he had won the argument. He should have known better. When they turned into his block Molly told him to drop her at her car before he garaged his. "If you're worried about Lauren, don't. I have a guest room."

"Um."

He was afraid um meant no, and he was right. Molly kissed him, a good-bye kiss, car keys in hand. "Call when you get home. I want to know you're safe. I'll be out in the morning, if it's okay?"

Molly sensed his need, said it was fine. Traffic was light this late at night. She made the trip driving on automatic, her mind so busy she had to work to keep her thoughts from flying off in all directions. Her focus was Petey. Getting Petey back. After that . . . but those thoughts were a luxury she couldn't yet afford.

True to her word she called Zachary as soon as she got home. She could sense the newfound guilt evident in his voice. She wanted to tell him it wasn't his fault, but she couldn't absolve herself from guilt, and so didn't even attempt to help him. Getting Petey back would be a first step for them both.

Tiredly she rubbed her eyes as she called Pamela. "Is it too late? Your message said to call no matter the time."

"Who can sleep?"

"You've got something." Her breathing quickened. "Irene Hall?"

Pamela snorted. "I'm good, but not that good. You only called a couple of hours ago. Anything new?"

"It's her, I feel it. She told her husband she now has everything she wants. He thought it was their separation. Zachary, well, he says she's obsessed with Karen. Having her back would give her everything she thought she wanted."

Pamela was quick to pick up on the hint of unsureness. "He's the doctor, isn't he? He should know."

"He's feeling guilt. He thinks he provided the opportunity for her to find out about Petey's fear of water, and that she just grabbed the ball and ran."

"But he does think it possible Irene paid Kemp to get her child back?"

"Yes." Excitement erased fatigue. "She took Karen's teddy bear when she left. The discovery shook her husband. I think it made him a believer."

"Good. I've got something, too. Another match on Kemp's list. I'm flying out in a couple of hours to take a look." Silence. "Molly? Did you fall asleep?"

"No. I'm here. Pamela, I don't want you to leave. I've got a gut feeling Irene Hall has Petey. We've got to find her. She's unstable. She's drinking."

"I'm on it. Glen's on it, too, and so's the FBI. We'll find her, Molly."

"I need you, Pamela."

The older woman sighed. "We've got to get hard evidence to hold Kemp. If I can come up with it, we can hold it over his head. He may be our quickest route to Irene Hall. And besides, the child just might be Petey."

That got a reaction. "Should I come with you?"

"No, Molly, I'm just going to take a look. Stay by a phone. You'll be the first to know. Either way."

Thirty-Seven

Fallon, Nevada

Pamela had no trouble finding Fallon. The man at the car rental agency at Cannon International Airport, halfway between Reno and Sparks, had given her a map, marked the route, and told her no one could get lost. Not even a little lady from Noo York. Big joke. As far as she could see, there wasn't more than one major road, most of it running through a landscape that looked like the moon.

Getting to Fallon wasn't the problem, but finding the Robinson place was another matter. Asking for directions was out; she didn't want to raise any curiosity. So she drove in the general direction marked on the map, stopping to read the names on fences and mailboxes. The hour was still early; few vehicles passed, most of them pickup trucks. She was reading the names on a cluster of boxes when an orange-and-black minivan drove by. Pamela squinted after it, called herself every kind of moron, and followed it, a camera with a zoom lens in her lap and an open portfolio of photos on the passenger seat.

The school bus stopped a quarter of a mile down the

two-lane road. Two little girls, a woman, and a dog waited. Pamela obediently braked when the bus flashed its warning lights. Two boys, about eight and twelve, waited at the next stop. Pamela wasn't worried. If she didn't hit pay dirt this way, she would follow the bus to the school.

Two more stops. Nothing. Then a long stretch of road, past fields with neat rows of growing things. A city girl, Pamela couldn't guess what they were, but hoped they were cantaloupes. The bus slowed, flashed a warning. Ahead a woman and small boy hurried down a side road. She picked up the camera, brought the boy's face up close. So excited her finger shook, she took as many pictures as she could before the boy climbed into the van. It drove off but Pamela didn't follow. She had what she had come for.

Timmy Newell.

Molly closed her eyes, fought against a swamping jealousy. Even without reason she had hoped . . .

"Molly? I know you're disappointed, but this gives us what we needed."

Disappointed? Devastated, more like. "What happens now? Will the police go and get Timmy?"

"No. He was taken across state lines, so the FBI is handling it. They'll move slowly; they can't afford to alert Kemp's customers. They want to locate the other children first, if they can."

Molly took a deep breath. "Then Irene Hall has Petey, which scares me to death. In her last call she was drunk early in the day. She's unhappy, most likely because Petey isn't what or who she thought he was. She might . . ."

"Might what, Molly?"

She had thought of a thousand terrible things during the night, all of them too awful to express. "I can't . . . oh, God, she might hurt him. She might . . ."

"The FBI is using all its resources to find her. I'll be home in a couple of hours. Hang in there."

What else could she do? The question haunted her. She took a shower, made coffee, spoke to Zachary, who said he was coming out, and called Kent. She wouldn't be working until they found Irene Hall.

Kent's antennae immediately went up. "Spill it, cookie, you know you can trust me."

She did know it; he had proved it. He whistled when she finished, was silent a moment, then said, "You know . . ." He whistled again, a low sound that intensified Molly's fear. "If she bought the reincarnation bit . . ." Kent's voice sharpened. "She bought it, all right, she's got Petey . . . but Petey's not Karen, not a little blond girl with blue eyes. Not in this life."

There. It was out in the open. Trust Kent to be the one to say it. Molly made a strangled sound. Her worst fear, the final nightmare, aired in the light of day. "Karen died at a summer camp in Maine."

"Call Rowley. If the FBI isn't already on it, he's the one to get them moving."

Molly was in a hurry now. They both knew she wasn't going to leave it to them.

"Oh, and cookie? Give me a call. I can't wait to break this story. Being virtuous isn't my style."

Much to her dismay, Glen didn't dismiss her fear. "We've got agents combing the area. If she's there, they'll find her. The local sheriff was alerted last night. He promised to put his men into the field at once." Glen sounded as urgent as she felt. "I'll call. I promise."

It wasn't good enough. Molly flew upstairs, grabbed a change of underwear and a toothbrush, and stuffed them into her tote. She remembered Zachary when she was backing her Taurus out of the driveway. She hit the horn until Denise poked her head out of a window. "Watch for Zachary, will you? Tell him I'll call when I can."

Denise nodded, yelled, "Where're you going?"

"Maine." Some primal instinct told her Petey needed her. It also told her she was running out of time.

Rangeley, Maine

Mitchell Nash, sheriff of the Rangeley Lakes Region, had been expecting Molly for some time when she walked into his office. "Molly Deere? I've got messages for you." He pushed several pink slips toward her. "Sit. We're still looking for your boy. No sign of him or the woman, but this is a big area to cover."

Molly sank into a chair, more tired than she could remember ever being. She had taken two planes and spent hours on twisting, bumpy roads. The imperative within her was like a ticking bomb, reminding her of time running out. "Have you checked the camp? Karen Hall drowned in the lake there."

A lean man with thinning auburn hair, the Sheriff's bushy russet brows shielded shrewd light brown eyes set in a face composed of sharp angles, and he exuded confidence. "That would be Camp Manitook, out on Mooselookmeguntic Lake. We went out there, but there's nothing. The place is boarded up. The camp failed a couple of years back—bad economy—and the drowning didn't help. Parents shied away."

"That's the place she'd go. I'm sure of it." She leaned forward, strain showing in the tautness of her posture. "Did they tell you she thinks Karen is reincarnated? That she's Petey?"

Mitchell Nash thought of his own two children and knew there was nothing of comfort he could say. "Every person under my command is in on this, Mrs. Deere, plus the FBI and the park rangers, who know every inch of the forests. We're searching rental properties, hotels, motels, and campgrounds, and I've got a man in the county courthouse checking deeds, looking for recent home purchases. Every canoer and backpacker who comes through is questioned. We're covering grocery stores, outfitters, gas stations, restaurants, and every nook and cranny in this corner of Maine. If Irene Hall is in the Rangeley area, we'll find her."

Molly stood clutching the pink slips so tightly they crumpled. The sheriff came around the desk. He spoke in a softer tone, showing compassion. "Tell my secretary where you're staying."

"You don't think she's here, do you?"

Mitchell Nash let his silence answer.

Another kind of silence permeated Camp Manitook. It spoke of abandonment, of failure, of decay. The deteriorating wooden buildings were sad, empty of the ringing shouts, the laughter of days past. Molly stared sorrowfully at the flagpole; white paint peeling, rusty winches, empty of rope, turning squeakily in the wind. She closed her eyes and a circle of children, young faces innocent, raised the flag as sweet bugle notes soared into the clear air. Ghost voices whispered, laughed, a part of the place forever.

But yesterday was gone. The real world waited at the shore of the lake. Mooselookmeguntic. An Abnaki Indian name. A moose's feeding place.

No moose foraged there today. Molly walked to the lake's edge where gentle waves lapped over earth embedded with small, smooth rocks and licked the roots of ancient trees crowding the shore. She stood looking out over the gray-green water. The sound of it, rippling an endless loop, melded with the voice of the wind, soughing through the firs. The sun had set and dusk was fast erasing the detail of day, replacing it with the murky shadows of early night.

Molly opened her heart and her soul and listened, listened to the music of the lake. Surprising, its gentle rhythms, its song of beauty; but most surprising of all, in this place of violent death, the feeling of peace eternal.

Alone. She knew it as surely as if she had searched every inch, every crevice, of rock and woods and shore. The water glimmered now more gray than green. She had come so far, had been so sure . . .

"Peteeeeeeeeeeeeeeeeeeey!"

The primal cry erupted from the deep well of her despair. It skimmed across the water, a shock wave of anguish. A flock of loons took to the air, eerie voices crying a ghostly reply.

Molly turned and fled.

Her motel room was rustic, decorated to be quaint; it smelled of disinfectant overlaying mildew. Lucky to get it, she was told, with all the excitement of FBI field agents, not to mention it being the height of the summer season. Molly had no complaints. It had a bed. Covered in old-fashioned white chenille.

After she opened the window, the wind brought the smell of pine. She wanted nothing more than to take a quick shower and fall into bed, but she had people to call. Out of habit she switched on the television, turned to CBN. A weekly round-table discussion on the economy. She turned off the sound.

Zachary must have been sitting by the phone. "Molly! I've been trying to reach you for hours. Are you all right? Why didn't you wait for me? I would have gone with you. You shouldn't be alone."

"It's all right. I'm fine. How's Lauren?"

"She's fine, but you don't sound so great. More like exhausted, strung-out, down—"

"All that and more. It doesn't matter."

"He's not there?"

"Not a trace." Wearily she rubbed the small of her back. "The sheriff seems to know what he's doing."

"Yeah. I spoke to him a couple of times."

"He doesn't think Irene is here."

Zachary's sigh traveled the line. "I don't, either. I don't think it would even occur to her to go there."

"But Karen died here, Zachary. I went to the camp. I stood on the shore of the lake."

"She isn't there, Molly. Irene believes she's in Petey now. A new life. A new Karen, if you will. The place Karen died would be the last place she would go."

"But she's distraught, not thinking clearly. And with liquor clouding her brain . . ." Molly's eyes were grainy from tiredness; she rubbed them with her knuckles. "I'm not thinking clearly, either. I'll come home tomorrow."

"Get some sleep."

Excellent advice. But first, Pamela. She had left two messages with Mitchell Nash. She was angry. Molly had no business going off the way she had. If she wanted Maine checked out, then she should have told her to do it. She was the private investigator, in case Molly hadn't noticed.

So tired and so down, Molly was close to tears. "I had a gut feeling. I had to come."

Pamela, bless her, didn't argue further. She simply said she understood.

Molly took a quick shower, wrapped herself in a towel, brushed her teeth. The woman in the mirror was a stranger; a washed-out, anemic-looking person with empty eyes. She hated the sight of her, so she quickly shut the light and closed the door, hoping to lock her within.

The room was getting cold. She lowered the window, went to turn off the television, and froze with shock. A full-face picture filled the screen. Words appeared beneath it, neatly centered.

IN CUSTODY ON CHARGES OF SERIAL KIDNAPPING

Harry Kemp! She didn't need the sound to know she'd been betrayed. In seconds she punched out a familiar number, waited impatiently, rage seething as she studied the monster's face. The well-known voice triggered outrage. "I knew you'd be there!"

"I didn't leak it." Kent sounded as upset as she felt. "Some yahoo stringer for one of the wire services sniffed it out. I wouldn't jeopardize Petey's safety for a story. You should know that."

She did. She told him so. She also told him she understood he couldn't let it go, not now.

Sleep came because she was exhausted. And with it came the recurring nightmare, but this time, when the wave hovered over her, leeching light and air and promising death, she didn't want to escape. She wanted to walk into the smooth green-black wall of water and let eternity take her.

Thirty-Eight

He didn't have a life, not in his office and not here, in his home. Of the two, Douglas preferred the office. True, the FBI had intruded into the agency, with their "discreet" agent monitoring his phones, his fax, even, ludicrously, his E-mail. Irene knew as much about computers as dinosaurs did about space flight. Maybe less, given her difficulty in learning to use even a VCR. He had tried to tell them she wouldn't get in touch with him there, but they wouldn't listen and he didn't have much to argue with. Not when they suspected him.

Oh, they didn't come right out and say so, but he knew. Overly polite, they were systematically dissecting him and his life. His golfing buddy, Jim Brainard, who also happened to be his doctor, had called to know if it was okay to release medical data to some guy at County Medical Insurers' Group. Was it an HMO? Real subtle. Let them look. They wouldn't find anything. At least, nothing to do with what Irene had done.

Uncomfortable thoughts. After a day full of suspicion he had wanted nothing more than to come home to a stiff drink and some peace and quiet. But he was host to

WHERE'S MY BABY?

the FBI there as well, although they had set up in the dining room and for the most part stayed out of sight.

Not so Nancy. She and Andrew had been waiting when he got home, an unlovely new habit. Nancy had immediately vented her outrage, starting with the two Federal agents who had shown up on her doorstep and continuing with all her grievances against Douglas. It seemed as if everything that had gone wrong in Irene's life was directly attributable to him. He took as much as he cared to and then pointed out her sister was the kidnapper, not him. That gained him an icy silence filled with palpable waves of fury.

He didn't care. A silently furious Nancy was better than a verbally abusive Nancy. After several stiff drinks he managed to doze, awakening abruptly, completely disoriented when a phone shrilled. Nancy sat in the ladder-back chair, spine rigid, signaling disapproval. So it hadn't been a dream. Too bad.

An agent came into the room, turned on the television. A man's face filled the screen; an announcer read the sensational story. It was out in the open. They all knew Irene. Now they all had the same fear.

The call came five hours after the story broke. Nancy, asleep on the couch, strain showing in the tight lines around her eyes and mouth even while she slept, sat bolt upright and blinked like an owl. Andrew turned off the television and went over to her. Douglas, who had been moodily watching his ice cubes melt, didn't know if he meant to reassure or restrain her. The agent came back, told him when to answer.

"Douglas?"

He pressed the receiver to his ear, suddenly unsure.

This was Irene, his wife, the woman who had been the mother of his child. She was insecure, unstable, deeply depressed and dependent on alcohol. But a kidnapper?

"Baby? Are you all right?"

"Douglas . . ."

"I'm here, Irene. Talk to me, baby, tell me what's wrong."

"Everything. Everything's wrong. I thought . . ." Her voice, thick with alcohol and self-pity and something new, something Douglas couldn't readily identify, broke despairingly.

"What? What did you think, Irene? You can tell me."

"I thought I would make a new beginning. I thought having Karen back would be everything—"

His head was spinning. It was true. Irene had someone else's child.

"—but it's not. She's not the same. She doesn't know me. And now everyone knows—"

"Knows what, Irene?"

"Don't pretend, Douglas. Don't pretend the way you have for six years. I saw him tonight. They'll want her back and I can't allow it. She's mine. She just doesn't *know* it yet, but she will. We'll go back to where it started. I'll show her our happy place and then . . ." Her voice slurred, became more difficult to understand. "After, we'll be together again. A new beginning. My blond angel will be mine again."

"Irene! Please, baby, I don't understand." But he was very much afraid he did.

"Yes you do. You know very well, Douglas. I'm sure you saw him tonight. You know what I did. I thought I was getting Karen, but he's not the same. He cries for his mommy. I'm his mommy, but he can't see, he can't . . ."

Douglas finally identified the new element in Irene's voice: sorrow.

"Give me the phone, I want to talk to her."

Douglas strong-armed Nancy away. "Baby, listen to me. It's all right. Tell me where you are and I'll come. We'll make it all right. Tell me where you are, baby. Where are you? Irene. Irene?" He stared at Nancy. "She hung up." He was shaken and frightened and he didn't care who knew it. Even Nancy backed away from the look in his eyes.

The agent left the room, returned several minutes later. "They got a fix on her. A phone booth outside Orlando."

Douglas knew the answer, but he asked anyway. "Irene?"

The man shook his head. "We know the area now. We can put more men into the field. We'll find her."

Douglas picked up the phone. Nancy stared at him, eyes bleak. "What are you doing?"

He took a deep breath. "The decent thing."

It was pitch black and cold and her first thought was that she was dead. Drowned. Swallowed by the huge green-black wave that was the doorway to hell. But hell wouldn't have a pleasant piney scent, nor would it be cold, nor would bells ring, nor . . . bells? Molly sat bolt upright and groped for the light or the phone, whichever came to hand first. "Hello?"

"Molly. It's Zachary. Wake up, sweetheart."

Zachary. In the middle of the night. It couldn't be good news.

It wasn't, but then, it wasn't as bad as it could have been. She kept telling herself that, over and over again.

Either that or give in to the wave, which seemed to hover over her still, even though she was very much awake.

Thirty-Nine

Fear accompanied Molly as she drove the lonely Maine roads in the middle of the night. No one to check her imagination. When the fear became too overwhelming she forced herself to remember the joys. Like treasured snapshots they played across her mind. The first time she had seen him, red-faced and squalling, long skinny body topped by a head full of fuzzy black hair. She had been frightened then, too, abandoned by her husband, alone with a precious new life dependent on her for survival. The fear had never really gone, but over the years it had dissipated. She could manage. During the flight from Bangor to Boston, sitting stiff with dread amid bored and yawning businesspeople, she stared inward, seeing Petey in his bath, Petey playing in the snow, Petey staring with wide-eyed wonder at a butterfly, Petey with food speckling his T-shirt. So many pictures; from the moment of his conception he had been her shining jewel.

On the ground in Boston she called Pamela. No Irene; not even a trace. She felt it as a crippling body blow. "It's been hours. What are they doing?"

"They're looking." She didn't tell Molly they might

not be inclined to share information. Not at this stage. It had been Douglas Hall who had called Zachary after he couldn't reach Molly.

"Where? Florida's a big place." Irene could have headed north, could be to the Carolinas by now. Or maybe west. Or south. The fear was back, full blast, eating at her strength, her ability to think straight. She couldn't dismiss the thought that Irene Hall had given them a clue.

"They're all over, Molly. There's Disney World and—"

"Disney World? Do they think she's on a vacation?"

Pamela struggled past her own fear. "She called from Orlando. It's logical. Who would notice a particular woman and child there?" Silence stretched so long it became unbearable. "Molly? Come to New York. It's best to wait here." Another silence during which Pamela could almost feel Molly's pain. Then Molly said she'd be on the next shuttle to La Guardia. Pamela felt as though she'd won an epic battle; she didn't want Molly to be alone.

Zachary's six-foot-plus frame stood out in the crowded terminal. Made breathless by a combination of excitement and fright, Molly literally threw herself at him. "Anything new?"

"Pamela's on the phone with Rowley now." He took her arm. "I told her we'd wait in the restaurant over there."

Molly tugged free. "No. I need to get to Florida right away." Irrational compulsion. *Where* in Florida?

"Pamela will pick up our tickets when we get a destination. You're not going alone. Not this time. Come on. We have time."

"Petey doesn't have time." She could see the words

WHERE'S MY BABY?

hit him with the force of hurled stones. She could also see the compassion in his eyes. She didn't want it. "Do you have a copy of the tape of Irene's call? Something you said last night keeps playing through my head."

He had her arm again. "I've got a transcript."

Zachary was bigger and stronger. "Good enough." He handed her several sheets of paper as soon as they were seated. A waitress approached, coffeepot at the ready. The thought of food made Molly ill. Zachary didn't press her, although she looked like she hadn't eaten in days. While the waitress poured he ordered bagels and cream cheese and told her to bring a couple of muffins.

Molly read through the transcript quickly, then a second time, more slowly. She shoved the papers aside and wrapped her hands around the steaming mug; she looked like she was hanging on for dear life. "Irene Hall is going to kill herself and Petey so they will be reincarnated into a new life together, right?"

"It appears that way. Yes."

Molly nodded, grateful not to have to argue. "The question then becomes where—and how—she intends to do it." She took a quick gulp of coffee, winced when the hot liquid seared her throat. "I think she's told us part of it. The where part, which is more important right now." She quickly found the place. "There."

We'll go back to where it started. I'll show her our happy place and then . . . after, we'll be together again.

Zachary glanced up as Pamela slid into the booth beside Molly. "Douglas doesn't know what place she means. They vacationed often in Florida, at different sites, both with and without Karen. He . . ." Molly was smiling. It looked ghastly. "What?"

"*I* know where it is." She twisted toward Pamela. "Can you get in touch with Douglas?"

* * *

Earth to earth; ashes to ashes; dust to dust. Try as she might, Molly couldn't stop thinking about death. *In the midst of life we are in death.* She shuddered, felt Zachary take her hand. Life and death, two points on infinity's loop. Had Irene's unstable mind come full circle? Had she taken Petey back to where she had conceived Karen? The connection was obscure, but if she was right . . . if she was right then life would be filled once again with unlimited promise, with that intangible tang of hope. But if she was wrong . . .

Molly was first off the plane, Zachary right behind her. Key West's heat rolled up the gangplank in waves; the pavement was dazzling, too bright for naked eyes. She pushed her sunglasses into place, tried not to pant as her lungs fought for oxygen. Two men were running toward the plane; a third followed more slowly.

Douglas.

Her heart started a tattoo. She couldn't wait. She yelled to them, all her suppressed hope making her voice squeaky and breathless. "Have you found them?"

The answer was yes and no. The two men introduced themselves, showed identification, and quickly ushered them toward a waiting helicopter. Molly didn't hear a word they said, not past the point where they told her Irene had rented a boat.

Water.

She should have known. Karen had drowned in it; Petey was afraid of it. Irene's unstable mind had made a connection.

The two agents didn't come with them. The ride was noisy and mercifully short. Again two men met them when they landed, on a small patch of ground behind a

WHERE'S MY BABY? 371

marina. Molly didn't wait for introductions; she only cared about one thing. "Have you found them?"

The shorter one, who had a chin dimple to rival Kirk Douglas's, apparently got the short straw, for after a baleful look at his partner, he admitted they hadn't found Irene's boat yet. Miles of open ocean, coastline dotted with coves, bays, hidden harbors, islands; all had to be searched. Molly rudely interrupted. Douglas held the key. Had he and Irene come to Key West hoping to make a baby? Specifically, had they made love in a special place, on a hidden beach?

Douglas turned a dull red, but Molly was relentless. She demanded charts and maps. The two agents hustled them into the marina's office. Molly shoved a chart under Douglas's nose. "Think. Did you rent a boat for a day, a week? Think. Where would you have gone? Think. For the love of God, *think!*"

Douglas slowly placed a finger on the chart. "We stopped here for a couple of days. I . . . we . . ."

The taller man jotted down the coordinates and disappeared into another room. "Jasper'll radio the location. We have Coast Guard boats in the area."

"I'm going," Molly said. "I need a boat. Petey's afraid of water. He needs me."

"She's quite right. Irene doesn't need to be more upset than she already is. Seeing her husband, or maybe even me, might help to—er, avoid a precipitation of unpleasantness."

Molly threw Zachary a grateful glance. He, at least, understood.

"Look, we'll send in a Coast Guard cutter. They'll board and seize before she knows what's happening."

"And what if she panics, acts at the mere sight of them? Are you willing to bet the life of the little boy?"

He wasn't. He, too, disappeared into the other room. Molly watched a big clock against the far wall tick off forty-two seconds before he came back. "Jasper called them off. She won't see anything official."

"Good." Molly had one more battle to win. "I'm going."

"Yes, ma'am. We'll take you." Dimpled Chin had ceded all points.

Molly had to admit that once he committed, he wasted no time. They went out the back door and ran down a long pier. A deep-sea fishing boat–for-hire was tied up near the end. Jasper came pounding down the dock behind them; he and Zachary saw to the lines. One glimpse of the bridge, bristling with instruments, told Molly it was no ordinary marlin or tuna boat.

"Should be thirty, forty minutes," Jasper said. "Don't worry, Fenton's a terrific pilot. He knows every reef and shoal in the Florida straits, and he won't get lost." So his name was Fenton; it had a more reassuring sound than Dimpled Chin.

Douglas went immediately to the port rail and gazed out to sea. Any sympathy Molly might have felt was buried beneath her fear. Zachary climbed up to the bridge. Drained, she took one of the seats facing the stern. After a few minutes Zachary came to stand behind her. She could feel the tension radiating from him, knew on an instinctive level he had learned something new. Something bad.

Swiveling, she grasped his hands. "Whatever it is, I need to know." He drew her up, slowly ran his hands up and down her arms. Instantly the dragon of despair uncoiled deep in her gut. "You're scaring me, Zachary. Have they found Irene? That's it, isn't it? They've found her . . . Petey . . . he's hurt—"

WHERE'S MY BABY?

"No. No, Molly. Petey isn't hurt."

"Then tell me. It couldn't be worse than what I'm imagining."

"They've sighted her boat. She's docked in a small cove . . ."

"And?"

"A report just came over the radio. Someone took a few sticks of dynamite from a construction site a few miles from the marina."

Worse than her wildest imaginings. "Does Irene know what to do with dynamite?" she yelled to Douglas. His face crumpled. He looked as bad as she felt. Almost. "Where?"

"Her father was a contractor. He often used it."

Jasper stood behind them. "I'll radio the info."

Sea, sky, the rush of wind. Time slipping away. Jasper came back, his face sober. "We're almost there."

And then they were there. A picture-postcard cove, lush vegetation overhanging a dazzling shell-strewn white-sand beach, gently rolling lace-capped waves lapping the shore. A gleaming white boat rode at anchor, the last touch in what could be a fantasy travel poster. Island Paradise. Dream-Vacation Getaway. Tropical Splendor.

But this wasn't a fantasy; it was all too real. Fenton throttled down, easing them into the cove. The water was shallow, green with an occasional purplish tinge. Jasper kept checking his watch; his walkie-talkie erupted every few seconds with a burst of sound. The engine sputtered, coughed, as Fenton slowly maneuvered them close to the other boat. No one was up top; Molly wondered if Irene had taken Petey ashore. Her eyes raked the shoreline, tried to penetrate the mangrove thicket. Were they in there, or had they gone inland where tall trees—palm trees, gumbo limbos, pines—crowded together in dense profusion? Dark shapes on the shore slipped into the sea. The sea and sky dazzled her eyes, making it impossible to separate shadow from substance.

Fenton cut the engine. The sounds of paradise swelled. Insects whirred, birds communicated, wavelets slapped against the hull. Without the wind of their passage the air was hot with a soft breeze; the smells of salt and rotting subtropical vegetation competed for predominance.

Jasper cupped his hands. "Ahoy! Ahoy the *Sea Urchin!* We have engine trouble and our radio's down. Permission to come aboard to use yours." His walkie-talkie sputtered; he turned it off. "Ahoy the *Sea Urchin!* Permission to board."

Molly whispered in Jasper's ear. "Maybe she's not there?"

"She's there." He sounded very sure.

Fenton came swinging down from the fly bridge, using the rails more than the steps. He checked his watch. "Thirty seconds." Jasper nodded agreement; Fenton went back to the bridge.

Molly touched Jasper's arm. "I want to go."

He shook his head. "Better stay here. It's safer." Belatedly realizing what he had said, he threw her a sop. "It won't take long."

Molly didn't argue; she would simply go. Out of the corner of her eye she saw Zachary moving closer. She braced; no one was going to stop her. No one.

Suddenly Jasper jumped over the railing and vaulted onto the *Sea Urchin*'s deck. At the same time Fenton started the engine and swung them away, opening a chasm of water between the two boats. In disbelief

Molly looked down at the widening gulf, saw through clear water brightly colored fish playing hide-and-seek in a coral reef.

Douglas's shout brought her attention back. A woman had come on deck: Irene Hall. Molly recognized her from her photo, but she hadn't been prepared for her thinness, her almost ethereal look.

Molly fought for breath past a lump on an elevator ride from her stomach to her throat. Where was Petey? Were they too late? No. No. No, no, no, no, *nooooooooooooo.* Then Zachary clutched her shoulder and she looked past his pointing finger to where Irene pulled a small body out from behind her. Petey! Petey, her baby, alive and well. Alive and well and whole, *thank you, God.*

Jasper walked toward Irene, calm voice explaining their "plight."

"Get off the boat!" Irene's yell startled a white heron into flight. Petey cringed; Irene hauled him up against her.

Molly's arms ached to hold him; her need to soothe his fear was so overwhelming she started to sway.

Jasper advanced on Irene, talking continuously. Two shapes arose from the depths of the water; men climbed aboard the *Sea Urchin,* rocking it beneath their weight.

"Get off! Get off!" Irene's shrill cry pierced the air. She backed up, Petey held hard. "It's set to blow!"

"Peteeeeeeeeeeeeeeeey!" The little boy's head turned toward the familiar call. "Petey! It's Mommy!"

"Mommy! My mommy!" He struggled, arms flailing, feet kicking, and then he broke free and went running to the rail. "Mommy. Mommmmmy!"

Molly kicked off her sandals and jumped overboard. The warm water immediately tugged at her sodden clothing, hampering movement. She didn't have a plan; she only knew she had to get to her son. It wasn't far, but it seemed like the width of the English Channel.

Irene disappeared below deck. Jasper followed, quickly reappeared, dragging her. He flung her toward one of the men, shouted there was no time.

Molly tread water, held up her arms. "Come to Mommy. Jump, Petey. Now!" If she lived to be a hundred, she would never forget that moment. Her Petey, so afraid of water, climbed onto the gunwale and launched himself into the sea. He sank like a rock, but Molly was already underwater, reaching for him, pulling him into her arms. Then she felt a pair of strong arms come around them both, felt strong thighs flex and push, and in seconds they broke the surface. Zachary, dark hair slicked back, gray eyes glinting, water streaming down his face, gave her a big grin and a quick, hard kiss.

The *Sea Urchin*'s engine roared, the boat turned toward the shore. A man threw Irene overboard, dived in after her. Jasper and the other man burst from below, made running dives into the sea.

Someone tried to take Petey from Molly's arms. She clutched him tighter. Zachary gently pried him away, handed him up, then boosted Molly aboard. She immediately reached for Petey. Fenton gave Zachary a hand, then ran for the bridge. The engine roared to life, and as soon as the others were aboard, Fenton executed a tight turn and made a run for the open sea.

Just in time. A deafening sound rent the air. In the next instant the day turned red as the *Sea Urchin* exploded into a fireball that rose like a pillar high into the sky.

Boats magically appeared from where they had hove to out of sight. Men boarded, held low-voiced conversa-

WHERE'S MY BABY?

tions. Irene, stonily silent, was wrapped in a blanket and transferred to another boat. Douglas went with her.

Molly was oblivious to everything; she had her son in her arms again. Then Petey squirmed around, smiled angelically at the big man who had quietly come to stand beside them. "Zach'ry! Zach'ry! Did you see me? Did you see me? I swimmed!"

Forty

The resilience of youth. The phrase kept running through Molly's head. Petey was a bit subdued and had a tendency to slip his thumb into his mouth, a long-corrected habit, but otherwise he seemed okay. Puffed with his accomplishment, he told the doctor at the hospital the police rushed them to how he had "swimmed" in the ocean. After he informed him, "No needles."

Zachary observed him carefully, finally told Molly to chill out; Petey was in better shape than she was. Without doubt. Her youth was gone and her resiliency seemed to be at its lowest ebb. But she had never been happier. It was as if Petey had been born to her a second time. She constantly had to fight the urge to check his sturdy little body, the way mothers count a newborn's fingers and toes.

The local police, the FBI, and even the Coast Guard wanted "a few questions answered." Molly stonewalled them, one and all. They had Irene Hall. They had Harry Kemp. They could question Petey at a later date—not now. She and her son were together again. Her main fear now was that Petey wouldn't forgive her for what had happened.

WHERE'S MY BABY?

Zachary, as seemed more and more usual, read her mind. He suggested they both get help. Post Traumatic Stress Syndrome was very real. Dressed in borrowed scrubs while their clothes were dried, they had a conversation while standing in a busy hospital corridor. Molly's adrenaline rush was subsiding. Suddenly shy, she avoided Zachary's gaze. "Couldn't you help us"

Zachary cupped her chin, tilted her face until she was forced to meet his eyes. They blazed with silver light. "A doctor shouldn't treat those he cares for." His thumb brushed her bottom lip. "And I care for you and Petey. I care deeply, Molly. I just didn't want to say anything, not while you were under such pressure." His lips met hers in a short, possessive kiss.

They took a late-afternoon flight home. Molly wanted Petey to be in familiar surroundings as soon as possible. They had a short wait and the only seats they could find had the little television sets attached. Petey wanted to watch, and because she was being indulgent, Molly fed money into the slot. Lloyd C. Cranshaw's perfectly made-up face filled the small screen. "... We switch now live to Topeka, Kansas, for CBN's exclusive interview with the mother of the alleged serial kidnapper, Harry Kemp." Petey reached for the dial; Molly stayed his hand. The picture zeroed in on an elderly lady. The reporter barely got a question out before Mrs. Kemp started talking. "I knew this would happen. I told him many times, I did, I said, 'Mark my words, Harry, you'll never be any good, never amount to anything.' I used to tell him, I did. I used to say 'Someday the whole world will know what a failure you are, Harry.' " She sniffed righteously. "I was right. See what he's done? I said, 'Mark my words, Harry—' "

Molly changed the channel, much to Petey's delight.

She turned her head so only Zachary could hear. "Mommy dearest, in the flesh."

Zachary sighed. "It's not surprising. It fits right in his personality profile. He likes to abuse women, which generally means some trauma early in life."

"Ergo, the mother?"

"Most likely. Kemp was into abuse in a big way. Jillian Raven's a good example. I'll wager she's not the first he's used his fists on." Zachary took Molly's hand. "Preying on grieving women like Irene is a form of abuse. And so is the heartache he caused you and all the other women whose children he stole. It's all abuse."

Jasper and Fenton walked into the terminal just as they were about to board. Dressed in slacks and sport shirts, they looked far different from the two "fishermen."

"We just wanted to be sure the three of you got off all right." Jasper made it sound like they were a family. "We also wanted to warn you. The story's going to break soon. The press will probably be waiting when you land in New York."

Molly stared at him in horror. The loudspeakers announced final call for their flight. Wildly she looked around. She needed a phone and she needed it *now*.

Jasper looked concerned. "I didn't mean to alarm—"

"It's not that. I'm a reporter. I've got to call my boss. I'll be right back." She handed Petey to Zachary. She wasn't taking any chances.

Zachary automatically accepted the child. "It's too late. He'll understand."

She opened her eyes wide. "Kent?"

Shifting Petey's weight, Zachary took Molly's arm. "You're right. You'll call him from the plane. Let's go."

As they moved toward the gate Fenton produced a

bedraggled-looking bear. He tucked it under Petey's arm. "We found it in Ir—ah, in the car." He took Molly's hand and held it in a warm, tight grip. "You're one hell of a brave woman. You have a nice life now, you hear?"

Molly's hope of quickly getting Petey back to a normal life was next to impossible. The press didn't leave them alone. The story was just too big. Some nights when she turned on the news it seemed as if they had interviewed everyone she had ever known. Her mother, in retirement in Arizona, gave a creditable performance, hair colored, washed, and set for the occasion. Her ex-husband Roy was another matter. He still threatened a custody fight and fired his first salvo over a national network.

"Fuck him and the horse he rode in on." Molly laughed, a true sound Pamela hadn't heard before. She slapped her pockets vainly and grinned. "How did you ever marry that asshole?"

"That asshole gave me Petey."

"Yeah, I know what you mean. Brandon, the righteous little jerk, made it all worthwhile for me."

"Righteous? Jerk?"

"He won't let me have one—I say one—celebratory cigarette. He says a bet's a bet."

Molly poured vodka into Pamela's lemonade. "So you'll have a celebratory drink. Different poison. If they weren't so bad for you, I'd buy you all the cigarettes you want. I can't thank you enough—"

"You've already thanked me." Pamela's voice was gruff. Her eyes, when they rested on Petey, busy building a lopsided city of the future with materials from his Erector set, turned suspiciously misty.

"You only said I couldn't thank you until Petey was back safe and sound. You never put a limit on the number of times I could do it."

Pamela snorted. "By the way, Glen wants to come out. I told him I'd ask you. Take my advice, Molly. The feds won't give up until they have a complete report. Petey is part of it. Let Glen talk to him. They know each other. But make it conditional. Tell Glen he's representing the whole ball of wax."

Two days later, on a sultry Sunday afternoon, Zachary brought Lauren to the house for a barbecue. Zachary reigned over the grill, a pile of hot dogs and hamburger patties at his elbow, an apron around his middle and a silly white chef's hat falling over one ear. He wielded his spatula like a conductor's baton.

Molly's heart was full. Times like this were what she had prayed for.

Petey was thrilled with Lauren's cast, now covered with signatures and drawings. He wanted to know if her leg hurt, if she had cried, if there had been a lot of blood, if she had seen the bones all sticking out.

"That's enough, young man." Molly gently stroked Lauren's shining blond hair, noticing her complexion had become a bit greenish.

"I wanna sign it." Petey's lower lip was thrust out. He pointed to one of the few spots left. "Right here."

"You can't write." Lauren was fast recovering.

"Can." Petey looked mutinous.

Molly decided to intervene before all-out warfare erupted. "I'll help. Get a crayon, Petey, and while you're at it, bring out some of your toys. I'm sure Lauren would like to play with something."

She started to rise, to go with him, for she still didn't trust him out of her sight, not even in their own home. Zachary waved her back. "I'll go. You girls can talk about us while we're gone." He gave them an exaggerated wink.

Lauren was answering Molly's question about day camp when the kitchen door banged open and Petey exploded outside. Molly bit her lip. Petey had brought his baseball and bat, his dinosaur robot, his two favorite racing cars—the red one and the blue one—all piled in his arms. He came running across the backyard, predictably tripping before he got halfway across. Toys spilled. Molly couldn't help it. Her smile turned to a laugh, but the laugh faded when Lauren abruptly started to struggle to her feet.

"Lauren . . ." Zachary started toward his daughter, stopped when he saw her expression. It was . . . joy. Absolute, pure joy.

Lauren was on her feet now, lurching toward Petey, who had managed to retain his grip on one item. A brown teddy bear. Molly had meant to see that that particular item was returned to Douglas Hall, but had apparently forgotten it.

Lauren's slender arms enfolded the bear. She hugged it, hard, then gently rubbed her cheek against its worn fur. "Mr. Bear-Face. Mr. Bear-Face."

Shocked, Molly's eyes flew to Zachary. His eyes were narrowed, fixed on his daughter. Then they swung to Molly. For long moments they stared at each other, silently made a decision. Some things were better left alone.